PENGUIN B

SIX CLEVER GIRLS
• Who Became •
FAMOUS WOMEN

Fiona Farrell was born in Oamaru. She has worked
as an editor, teacher and writer in Canada, France
and New Zealand and now lives with her partner
on Banks Peninsula. Fiona's poetry and short stories
have been widely published, and a number of plays
performed. She is the author of a collection of
poetry, *Cutting Out*, and a collection of short stories,
The Rock Garden. Her novel *The Skinny Louie Book*,
published by Penguin in 1992, won the fiction
section of the New Zealand Book Awards in 1993.
Fiona has also received an Arts Council Scholarship
in Letters, in 1991, and in 1995 she was the
Katherine Mansfield Memorial Fellow
in Menton, France.

SIX CLEVER GIRLS
● Who Became ●
FAMOUS WOMEN

A NOVEL

Fiona Farrell

Illustrations by Anna Crichton

PENGUIN BOOKS

PENGUIN BOOKS

Penguin Books (NZ) Ltd, cnr Rosedale and Airborne Roads, Albany,
Auckland 1310, New Zealand
Penguin Books Ltd, 27 Wrights Lane, London W8 5TZ, England
Penguin USA, 375 Hudson Street, New York, NY 10014, United States
Penguin Books Australia Ltd, 487 Maroondah Highway, Ringwood, Australia 3134
Penguin Books Canada Ltd, 10 Alcorn Avenue, Toronto, Ontario, Canada M4V 3B2

Penguin Books Ltd, Registered Offices: Harmondsworth, Middlesex, England

First published by Penguin Books (NZ) Ltd, 1996
3   5   7   9   10   8   6   4
Copyright © Fiona Farrell, 1996

Editorial services by Michael Gifkins and Associates
Designed by Richard King
Typeset by Egan-Reid Ltd, Auckland
Printed in Hong Kong

The assistance of Creative New Zealand towards the publication
of this book is gratefully acknowledged by the publisher.

For Susannah
For Ursula
With love

A GOOD DAY

IT WAS CAROLINE'S IDEA.

She was the one who passed the note to the other five while Butch had her back turned to them, scraping Latin roots onto the blackboard.

'Centum. One hundred.'

Scree. Squawk. As if the board itself were composed of dense cranial matter into which the words must be driven, letter by letter. Scratch. Squeal.

Then blip. One little ball of rolled-up paper landed on Raeleen's desk, one to Heather and another to Greer, making her jump. (She'd been drawing a star.) Butch swung round, long neck wattled like a turkey's snaking from her Peter Pan collar. Form 2A froze.

A thirty-second stand-to.

Then, 'Centum' said Butch. 'Copy, please, and add as many words as you can think of which include the root. Do we understand, Greer?'

Greer said we did.

'An example, please, Heather?'

'Century, Miss Butcher,' said Heather, palming the little ball of paper up her shirt sleeve just in case Butch checked.

'Bene,' said Butch. 'Optime.'

She turned back to the board and blip, blip, paper balls hit Kathy and Margie. Caroline threw like a boy, with a flick of the wrist, accurate to the inch.

Greer added a spiral to the star and a puff of smoke and some flowers in an elaborate web tangling the margins of the page and out among the Latin roots. With her left hand, down under the desk, she unfolded Caroline's paper ball. 'Behind toilets lunchtime,' in Caroline's plump lettering. Then, with

9

a flourish and a row of exclamation marks like a picket fence: 'P.P.!!!!!!!'

Greer looked over her shoulder and nodded yes. Then back to her exercise book. Centum: one hundred. The web needed more detail to balance properly at the top. She added a spider, a teapot with flowers steaming out of the spout and a fish with butterfly wings. She dotted the wings all over.

Margie Miller, up the front where Butch could keep an eye on her, nodded yes to Caroline and copied from the board, wondering if Butch had ever done it. You were supposed to be able to tell from the way people walked and Butch sure walked funny, sweeping through the halls in her Batman cape, feet turned out at ten to two on three-inch stilettos, but maybe that was bunions, not sex. ('Our Butch has got bunions, a nose like a pickled onion dee dum dee dee . . .')

She was rumoured to have a fiancé killed in the war. A pilot. But like all the girls, Margie had watched her carefully during the Anzac Day assembly and she was not convinced. 'Lord of our far-flung battle line,' carolled the girls while Greer Bott (who had done Grade Three Trinity and Royal) hunted about for sharps and accidentals on the school piano. Margie had mouthed the words and observed Butch narrowly.

Would she cry? Would all that stuff about the slopes of Gallipoli and age-not-wearying-nor-the-years-condemning-them squeeze a pensive tear from those pebble eyes? ('. . . dee dum like a squished tomato and eyes like green peas . . .')

Not a drop.

Miss Butcher sat up there on the stage through 'God Defend', all three verses, legs splayed so the front two rows could see up her skirt, her composure complete. So, was it true? Miss Gibbs always cried and had to leave the stage because of her brother. But not Butch. Did she ever have a fiancé? And if she did, did they do it? When? How often? Did she ever cry out in ecstasy? Did she ever tear her clothes off and writhe in his arms?

Margie doubted it. She suspected privately that Butch was like her old walkie-talkie doll at home, with a navel and properly moulded buttocks and nothing between but blank pink plastic.

Raeleen and Kathy were playing Hangman up the back and it was a toughie. The little man already had his gibbet, his rope and his head. Five more guesses and it was all over, – a – at – – –. They nodded yes to Caroline, they'd see her there. Heather winked too: OK. Then got on with it.

She would never admit it to a soul, but she liked Latin roots. She liked the idea that words were made out of bits and pieces of other words and that they came from all over the world. Century, she wrote. And centenary. Centipede.

Or should it be centepede? Three e's? Or four?

There couldn't be many words with four e's.

So Caroline had her gang. She looked over at Helen Brassington to see if she had noticed. She had picked Greer Bott partly because her desk was right in front of Helen's so she was bound to see the note. Helen appeared to be concentrating on her writing, but Caroline suspected it was an act. No one could be that absorbed by Latin roots. She watched closely and Helen looked up. Just for a second. But long enough to confirm it.

Hate. Fury. Disdain.

Ahh, thought Caroline. That's better. Now I've got to you. Now you can feel what it's like to be left out. It was open war between them now and they could move onto the next stage of hostilities. Building alliances. Devising strategy. They had fired the first shots.

But Butch was walking between the desks, up and down the trenches with the ruler swagger-stick tucked in her gown sleeve. Any misdemeanour and the ruler slammed down on the desk, the talon fingers drummed on the skull. She was by Greer's desk now and tearing out a page webbed with flowers and butterflies.

'Flibberty-gibbet,' she hissed, wattles flushing crimson with rage. 'Scatterbrain.'

Greer trembled, Butch looming at her shoulder, and fumbled with her pen. Caroline got her head down. If Butch suspected sympathy she turned on you too and anyway Greer was a twit to be so careless, a twit to doodle so obviously, a twit to cry when she was caught fair and square. Centum, wrote Caroline hurriedly. Century. Centenary. She looked over at Heather's desk because Heather was good at this sort of stuff, but Heather had her arm crooked round her work. Umm . . . thought Caroline, digging a hole in the kauri square on her ruler. Recent, she wrote. Then decent. And innocent.

At lunchtime they occupied the bench behind the toilet out of view of the staffroom. Caroline got there first to bag it and sprawled eating the salted peanuts she had bought on the way to school with her lunch money. A few yards away through the wire fence, Helen Brassington was shooting goals on the basketball court with Jan Te Awa: close in, side on, front on, under the net. She was better at shooting than Jan and was being encouraging. 'Oh, good shot,' she said whenever Jan got one through the hoop, or 'Nearly!' when she missed by miles. Caroline had read once in a *Reader's Digest* about the power of mental suggestion so she practised, now, on Helen. She emptied her mind of all distraction. Miss, she thought. Miss.

Helen kept on shooting. One hand, clean through the net.

Heather arrived. And Kathy, who stretched out on the hot concrete to eat her lunch, dealing with the orange first: two round eyes, a nose and a row of jagged teeth, carving with her best nail, the only one she'd been able to grow so far. Kathy nibbled when she was bored. She nibbled when she was reading. She nibbled when she was worried. It didn't leave a lot of growing time. But somehow she had managed to spare her right index finger and it was now a fine crescent tip, perfect and pink. Good for carving.

'Where's Margie?' she said. 'And Greer? I saw you throwing them notes too.' Caroline said Greer was probably bawling in the loo and Kathy said wasn't Butch an old bag and god, it's hot, I'll tan my legs.

She put aside the orange and fumbled under prickly grey serge for her suspenders. Heather looked inside the toilet door. 'Greer?' she called. 'Are you there?'

No answer.

But one door was firmly shut and she could hear the sniffs. She went into the next cubicle and stood on the seat to look over the partition, and there was Greer lifting her face towards her on the other side, damp and pink.

'Come on,' said Heather. 'Blow your nose. We're all waiting.'

'Bu-bu-bu,' said Greer. 'I look aw-ful.'

Sob.

'No, you don't,' said Heather. (She did. She always looked awful when she had been crying. Her glasses misted over, her face gone soft and boneless with grief like a saggy balloon.)

'And I ha-haven't got a hanky,' said Greer.

'Use loo paper,' said Heather. 'Now, come on. Open the door.'

Greer blew her nose on a stiff sheet of Jeyes. Then she opened the door. 'Everyone was laughing,' she said.

'No they weren't,' said Heather. 'They were just glad it wasn't them.'

Margie Miller was standing by the basins back-combing her hair.

'I don't know why you bother,' said Heather. 'You'll only have to flatten it all out when the bell goes.'

Margie combed furiously, dragging her hair into an erect matted tangle. 'So?' she said, tugging and wincing.

'So, it's a waste of time,' said Heather. 'And it splits the ends.'

'So?' said Margie, and she sleeked a layer of smooth hair over the top with the tail of her comb. Her pale mouse face looked out from the mirror, satisfyingly dwarfed by a ginger helmet. No. Not ginger: strawberry blonde. A model on the cover of last week's *Post* who was every bit as ginger-haired as Margie, had been described on the inside as Linda, 38-24-36, a model from Dubbo, and a strawberry blonde. It was a definite improvement on ginger or red or carrot-top. It sounded like milk shakes or ice cream, delectable and desirable. Margie fixed a couple of strawberry blonde kiss curls with crisscrossed hairclips on her cheeks, then sucked in to check the effect. Beside her Greer Bott was snuffling and splashing cold water on her face to conceal the crying. Margie patted her hair approvingly. She wished she had time to do a flip-up round the bottom. But it was half-past already and she was hungry. 'Come on,' she said.

Greer put on her glasses, the thick lenses magnifying damp lashes and pink-rimmed eyes, and they went out into the sunshine.

It was hot for September. They sat on the bench, stockings rolled to their ankles. Kathy made a row of orange-peel teeth and turned to Greer who sniffed still into her Jeyes tissue.

'Gel,' she said, lisping and spitting round white pith, 'Gel, you have been at my gin again. This Is Simply Not Good Enough.'

Greer smiled dimly, and rolled the tissue to a damp cigar. Then Caroline offered her the last of the peanuts, so she licked up salt and brown wings and minded less about Butch and the tender patch on her shoulder where the talons had left their mark.

Out on the court Jan Te Awa tried a shot from right under the goal. And missed. 'Good try,' said Helen brightly, but Jan was getting fed up, you could tell.

'You're so brown, Kathy,' said Heather. 'It's sickening.'

Kathy lay back, long elegant legs tanned already, all the way up to where they disappeared into a grey bundle of tunic and a grubby white cotton triangle. She grunted. She was so careless. Never looked in the toilet mirror, her clothes always dishevelled and she spent most of her lunch money on lollies. At present, the passion was Buzz Bars. Last month it was Crunchies. Yet, against all the odds, she was beautiful. Clear skin, wide brown eyes, even teeth, thick curling black hair and when she moved she was graceful, effortless. She reminded you of a cheetah.

Loose-limbed, easy.

Heather surveyed her own firm white thighs and freckled knees. She ate the nourishing banana she had bought at the dairy in unwilling preference to a Cherry Ripe, knowing though as she bit that her teeth, those brand new adult teeth she has had only five years, were punctured already and shiny with amalgam. It was just not fair.

Raeleen lay on her stomach on the concrete, organising an obstacle course for a row of ants that dot-dot-dotted from a hole on the toilet wall to the rubbish bin. She felt moody and restless. She placed a stone and an apple-core in their way: a stone mountain and an apple-core range. Let's see which ones will decide to go over, round, or under, which will decide to go back.

'Right,' said Caroline twisting her peanut bag in a knot and chucking it in the bin.

It was time.

She dragged the book from her tunic front and found the page. The book was showing signs of wear, the covers gone, and several loose pages fluttered to the ground. The girls looked over their shoulders then drew in closer.

'Certain ones, yes,' said Norman. 'But not all. For instance, all women have erotic areas around their breasts and also around their bodily orifices.'

'Orifices?'

'Openings.'

'Like what?'

Norman half turned on his side and ran the tip of his little finger around the opening in Allison's ear. Immediately her skin . . .

'Mmm,' thought Heather. 'Orifice.' Drawing the sound of it out between her teeth. Savouring the mouthful of it. More succulent than penis, or vagina, or penetration.

Kathy split her orange in five segments then handed them around. She liked fiddling with her food, gave it to others, ate carelessly, indifferently.

The pieces were so juicy you had to lean over so the dribble wouldn't stain your shirt collar.

Allison whirled towards him and slapped him. 'Don't you dare call me a liar,' she shouted.

He grasped her two wrists and forced her down on the blanket . . .

Caroline read and the girls leaned back, hands sticky, mouths sweet and tingling. Jan Te Awa had tired of missing goals and was trading rabbit punches with a couple of kids from 2B who went on the same bus. Helen was on her own, bouncing the ball and running, pretending to surprise herself with fast shots over the shoulder. What a twit. Caroline could feel her looking over at the group behind the toilet and she talked more quietly so the girls had to lean in closer.

The cars, shiny, sophisticated, American, drove off from the lake towards Peyton Place with their crews of satiated teenagers and Raeleen said, 'Yuk, I'm never going to let any boy do that to me and that's for sure.'

She had her period this morning, the second one. She'd been prepared for the first, had read all about it in the Health Department pamphlet her mum had left in her hanky drawer on her eleventh birthday, but somehow she had missed the bit that said you went on having periods, month after month, year after year, practically until you were dead. She had thought you had one and that was it: you were grown up, you could have babies. Five days bleeding, and you could get on with the important things like swimming or training for the Junior Nationals. The book had not made it clear that it was describing a lifetime sentence to sore stomachs, headaches, bulky sticky pads between your legs and the reek of raw meat which you had to hope did not hang around you as it did round Yvonne Donaldson, so that everyone knew you'd Got It.

While Caroline was reading, Raeleen was planning how to get off PE. She was hopeless at telling fibs. To do it properly she would have to manufacture a real headache. She'd have to work on that vague pressure behind the eyes till it was convincing and then she would be able to look trim Miss Cathcart in her white shorts straight in the eye and plead for the sick bay and the grey army blanket up to the chin and the hotty and the distant sound of the other kids fooling around on the tennis courts. That way, no one would see the bulk of her pad through her red regulation rompers, nor would she have to change in front of other people.

Once upon a time, years ago, in that distant kid-life before the blood, she'd stripped casually in the changing shed or at the beach with only a towel for cover and she hadn't cared a bit, racing to be first in. Now, she dawdled to last, waiting till everyone else had dragged on their togs and run squealing and shoving from the sheds, which smelled of sweat and wet feet, to the cool rectangle of water in the pool.

Once they'd gone, she could change, pulling her togs on under her tunic, twisting and tugging so that no unexpected intruder could see this dreadful body which sprouted and bulged against her will, growing breasts which swelled and swelled so that it seemed they would never stop and she would end up like Tits Tisdall at the town library who you could see coming round the shelves bosom-first. Raeleen's brother and his friends made a game of waiting in the Reference Section just for that. 'Man! That's gotta be a size forty-three over-shoulder-boulder-holder!' they said. 'What a pair of boobs!'

Raeleen hated it. What a fat stupid ugly word: boobs. What stupid swellings.

What ugly pricklings of black hair, pressing their way

through her nice smooth brown skin. And how ugly it was, that blood oozing secretly from her. No one would ever see her naked or touch her or put his finger in her orifices. Ever.

'Don't be dumb,' said Caroline. 'If everyone felt like that the human race would die out.'

Caroline was always so sure of things, so uncomplicated. She was the leader of Tui Patrol, Captain of Featherston House and winner of the Junior Speech Competition two years running. (Her topic this year: School Uniforms. Necessity or Nuisance?) But on this point Raeleen was equally certain.

'Not me,' she said. 'You can have my share of the babies if you want to save the human race.'

A column of ants skittered up and over apple core ridge so she poked a deep valley in their dusty path and spat on it to muddy it up. The ants paused at the swamp. Raeleen slumped back against the bench.

She was furious with her body, furious with her stupid aching head and her stupid cramping stomach and most of all with her stupid leaden legs. She used to like her legs: the way they could pump her round the track faster than anyone else in the Juniors, girls or boys. When she was running she never felt unsure. She could see herself before they were even on their marks, passing the others effortlessly, way out in front, breaking the tape. When she was running she could hear nothing but her own breath and her heart beating steadily and far away on the outer limits of awareness, the shouts of the other kids: 'Go Raeleen! Go Raeleen!'

And now look at her: aching and dumpy and all she wants is that bed with the army blanket and a hotty and the worst thing is that this is how she is going to feel for ever and ever. And all for some stupid puking peeing baby. She hated babies. Her cousin Laura had said: 'Here, Raeleen, would you like to have a hold of Richard for a moment?' Thrusting at her a cold damp bundle smelling of sick with a splotchy pug-dog face fringed with thin black hair. Laura was in town for Plunket and a bit of shopping and Mum had made macaroni cheese for lunch and they were having it properly in the dining room at the table.

Raeleen held the bundle stiffly, breathing through her mouth so she wouldn't gag.

'OK,' said Laura. 'All set.'

Raeleen looked up and there was Laura sitting right there at the table with her blouse open and a white breast like a blue-vein cheese jutting out. And the tip wasn't a pink spot like the points on her own thimble breasts but a huge purple prune from which liquid dripped onto the tablecloth.

'Don't want to give him up eh?' said Laura. 'But I'm afraid you'll have to because I'm bursting and he'll be hungry. Sister Byers always books in far too many and we have to wait for ages. He was so good. Not a peep out of him. I'll give him a feed and then you can cuddle him again, OK?'

Raeleen handed Richard over fast. He had left a damp patch on her skirt and the sour smell of him clung to her hands. But Laura smiled as she took him, a foolish adoring smile, and, not seeming to notice that he was wet, tucked him against the blue cheese breast where he sucked, slurping loudly while Laura calmly forked up macaroni cheese with her free hand.

Thank goodness Dad wasn't there. Or Graham. Raeleen was hot and prickling with disgust and embarrassment. She was sitting right opposite so she kept her head down and pleated the hem of the tablecloth into a concertina frill.

Slup. Slup. Slup.

'That macaroni must be cold,' said Mum. 'I could pop it in the oven if you like and you could have it later.'

'Oh, don't bother,' said Laura. 'I'm ravenous these days. Eating for two I suppose.'

Mum's voice was stiff. She didn't approve of this sort of thing but Laura was a real Porteous. Loud, vulgar, uninhibited, like her father, Raeleen's Uncle Mort, who drank his tea out of a saucer and said, 'Steady the buffs!' when he belched at the table.

Mum liked to do things properly. She would, of course, being sort of royal: descended from an early settler and a Maori princess down on Stewart Island which accounted for Raeleen's dark colouring. Mum believed there was a time and place for everything.

She caught Raeleen's eye. 'Go and show Sharon the chickens,' she said. 'She might like an egg to take home for her tea.'

Raeleen did not like Sharon who was five and whiny. ('Having a bit of trouble adjusting to the new brother,' said Mum. 'And she's always been spoilt.') But she leapt up, grateful for release.

Sharon had eaten a spoonful of macaroni cheese, said yuk and gone out to the kitchen where she was pouring jelly crystals into the fish bowl.

'Come on,' said Raeleen. 'Come and see if Banty has laid you a nice egg.'

Sharon did not answer. A thin trickle of raspberry pink sugar rained down on the guppies and settled in a glutinous mass round the pond weed and the little china house and the plastic mermaid.

'You'll kill the fish,' said Raeleen.

'No I won't,' said Sharon. 'They like it. They're eating it. It's their pudding.'

'You can take an egg home for your tea,' said Raeleen.

'I don't like eggs,' said Sharon poking at the jelly with a spoon. Pieces broke free and floated like small rubber rafts to the surface.

From the other room Raeleen could hear Laura's loud call-the-cows-across-the-hills voice: 'Whoops! Got to watch him, he's a spitter just like Sharon. They eat so fast they can't keep it all down. Though Sharon was worse. When she threw up it just went everywhere. She could toss for two or three feet.'

'Raeleen used to bolt her bottle too,' said Mum in her patient I-understand-completely voice.

'Sorry about the cloth,' said Laura.

'It doesn't matter,' said Mum. 'Raeleen? Raeleen? Could you bring a squeegee please?'

Raeleen grabbed Sharon's hand so that Sharon said, 'Ow you're hurting,' and swept the milk money from the shelf. 'Back in a minute,' she called. 'Shut up, Sharon. We'll go round to the shop and buy you an iceblock.'

As they passed the dining room window she waved. Laura sat there, both breasts exposed and the baby slung across her shoulder, its eyes crossed and a streak of white spittle oozing from its mouth.

'No way,' said Raeleen sitting in the sun by the toilets. 'Not me. You can have dozens of kids if you like but I'm not going to have a single one.'

Her legs ached. She took a handful of small stones and dropped an avalanche on the ants. Stupid things. Marching along without thinking, one behind the other, because that's their nature. That's what ants do.

But she felt sorry for them too, struggling through the rocks and boulders, so she broke a scrap of Belgian sausage into microscopic pieces, just big enough for each insect to carry comfortably.

'Please,' murmured Rodney against her skin. 'Please. Please.' She did not stop him. Her tight red shorts slipped off as easily as if they had been several sizes too large . . .'

Kathy nibbled at the perfect nail. Just the edge where it was rough. She was not really listening to Caroline at all (but what a bitch Betty is, poor Rodney . . .). She was wondering if she should let her mother know that it was Parents' Day on Thursday. If she didn't take the notice home would her mother find out from someone else – Margie's mum for instance, over a packet of Pall Mall filter and half a dozen eggs at Miller's dairy? And if she did find out, would she guess that Kathy hadn't told her deliberately?

'Parents' Day?' Her mother's face puzzled, forlorn,

registering the hurt of another blow, another slap. 'But Kasia has said nothing about that.'

Except of course that her mother would not say 'nothing' but 'nossing' like some cartoon character, like silly Minette in 'Tess of the Towers' in the *Girls' Crystal. Mon dieu! Zees ees not – ow you say? – le creeket, n'est-çe pas?*

A comic Frog. 'But Kasia has said nossing about zees.'

And Margie's mum who is ordinary, like all the other mothers, who doesn't fuss or weep, would say matter-of-factly, 'Oh well, I expect she forgot. You know what kids are like.' She'd shrug it off as of no account. But Kathy's mum would take her cigarettes and her eggs and come home grieving to the house which is a little shabbier but otherwise like all the other houses on the street – if you ignored the fig tree by the back door.

'Bloody stupid,' said her father, year after year. 'It's far too cold here. It'll never fruit. It's just taking up space. You could put parsley there, or mint, so you wouldn't get wet feet trekking all the way down to the vege patch whenever you want a sprig.'

He was right, too. Kathy noticed after that that all the other houses had parsley or mint by their back steps or maybe a few freesias or a flowering currant. But never, never a fig tree with its fists of green fruit and its big biblical leaves. Another joke.

Visitors always commented on it. 'A fig tree? My goodness, I've never seen one before. I didn't realise they could be grown this far south. What's the fruit like? Anything like a dried fig?'

And you had to say well, actually, you didn't know because the fruit never ripened. Just set like so many door knobs, hard and impossibly bitter.

But the damage had been done. The visitors were on the alert. They knew they were somewhere foreign. Exotic. They were on the lookout for other symptoms of strangeness: funny mannerisms, funny cooking smells, snails and frogs. Joke food.

And then your mother arrives and it's confirmed beyond doubt.

'Allo,' she says, and sometimes she forgets and shakes hands or kisses – both cheeks too, not one – and she's too enthusiastic, too emotional, and her hair is dyed blonde when mothers never colour their hair, but let it fade or grey as it will, not seeming either to notice or worry. And she calls you 'Kasia' which is your real name, not 'Kathy' which is ordinary, unremarkable and the name everyone else knows you by because you insist on it.

You can see the visitors take in this strangeness and the way the living room is wrong, veiled from light even in winter with thick velvet chairs with little lace squares on their backs, instead of the functional wooden-armed settees you see in ordinary homes, and the way your mother makes coffee and it's such a fuss, with the real beans she buys each year when they go to Christchurch and which she hoards carefully, thinking they are a treat, though other people drink instant or the chicory stuff your mother says is not coffee at all. They sip their real coffee gingerly and add lots of milk to the tiny cupfuls and say, 'Delicious, but goodness it's strong isn't it?' And they nibble the nut biscuits which your mother bakes instead of scones and fruit cake and say they'd like the recipe.

All, all wrong.

Kathy could hardly bear it. It was becoming worse and worse. She tried now not to bring friends home.

'But 'oo are your playmates?' says her mother, dragging a lettuce in pieces for a salad instead of chop-chopping it in shreds. 'I don't know your friends any more. This Caroline (Carr-oh-leen) – you could ask her for tea, no?'

'I don't have playmates any more,' says Kathy. 'That's kids' stuff.'

How could she explain that asking Caroline for tea, bright-eyed satirical Caroline, would be hopeless, when her mother has tipped the ripped-up lettuce into a bowl and is making a dressing from oil and vinegar, knocking at the sides of a cup with a fork tap tap tap and saying as she always does, 'Estragon. Or basil. How is it possible to live without them? How is it possible to make a green salad or tomatoes or a vinaigrette? This country!'

'They do things differently here,' says Kathy, as she always does. 'They use that condensed milk stuff. From a tin.'

Her mother is astonished. Milk? On a salad? Is this how Mrs Miller makes a salad? Yes, says Kathy, and her mother says that is so curious. She will ask Mrs Miller for the recipe next time she is in the shop. An appalling thought.

'Don't,' says Kathy. 'No, don't. It doesn't matter. And oil and vinegar is much nicer. Truly.'

Her mother rubs a bowl with garlic (more joke food) and says thoughtfully that she supposes it might be quite nice, thick and creamy like a *vraie mayonnaise*. She'll try it. She'll ask Mrs Miller tomorrow. And Kathy says, 'Stop fussing, stop fussing, oil and vinegar is fine, stop making such a fuss about a damn salad, a damn damn blasted salad.'

'Don't speak like zat please,' says her mother. Pourquoi est-tu fâchée ? Why are you of a bad mood Kasia?' And Kasia/Kathy yells, 'I'm not fâchée! And it's *in* a bad mood, *in* not *of*. You always get that wrong!'

Then her mother says, thin-lipped, 'And you are so clever always. Me, I am the imbécile. Imbécile to come here. Imbécile to believe. Si seulement j'avais été plus raisonnable . . .'

Which means that she wishes she had never married Dad. That she wishes she had never believed the nonsense he told her back in Alexandria, the fable of a country which became lovelier, more civilised, more peaceful as it was further away so that he was quite honestly able to tell this young French woman with her tailored suit and ash-blonde hair and her exquisite lips, that back home there was a spacious house waiting with plenty of room for kids, a huge garden, up on the hill with a view of the harbour and only a few blocks from the shops. And in the summer, there was a little place in the country peaceful and remote, where he could fish and she could lie back and relax . . .

Around them on the Midan the traffic had eddied and a dense press of bodies edged the café tables in a confusion of sound borne on a soft wind, desert-dry, bone-dry. The young woman had sipped her Pernod and visualised the distant scene: a big white house like the ones on Ma'amoura but built high on a hill to catch the sea breeze. A garden with trees – cherries and figs – and a vine-clad arbour where they could eat on summer evenings. A short walk to the shops where the cook would be able to buy provisions each morning. A sea-front with cafés on the boulevard where she could meet with the other young wives for coffee at eleven.

The vision danced beyond the horizon, tantalising, delightful. Quite unlike the present reality of the third-floor apartment with three girls, father and mother, confined in exile in Egypt, dizzy still and disoriented after the flight from Cracow, to Paris, to Marseilles, to Alexandria.

The white house shimmered like a migraine caught behind the eye and she watched it as she watched this young soldier, Harry, in his trim uniform, his eyes bright and dancing because he is talking about home.

She wishes now she had never listened. She wishes she had not been convinced of the mirage, nor married, abandoning all that was familiar and safe, to win it. Her sisters furious, saying fool, fool, idiot, and she angry refusing to write, ever, to admit defeat. Her mother dying and her father too, when they were far too young, but flight and loss had aged them, left heart and lungs vulnerable. And she had not been there to help or soothe. Another failure. Another defeat. She shuts it all away except in these sudden moments when her daughter turns on her, young and angry and says, 'And you wish you had never had me.'

But, 'Ah non, non, non,' says her mother and the salad bowl falls into the sink. 'Never. I could never wish that, never.' And she's crying now and holding her daughter close, muttering the baby talk with which she has comforted nightmares and fever dreams. *Ma petite fille. Mon trésor. Calme-toi.* And Kathy too is in tears.

Hopeless.

Kathy brought no one home. Not even on her birthday. This year she planned a picture party at the Regent with her name flashed up at interval on the screen: Happy Birthday Kathy Scott! Then ice creams at the Apollo instead of the agony of an all-wrong birthday tea with a funny cake and no cheerios or fairy bread.

The edge of the perfect nail tore unevenly and Kathy nibbled across, trying not to bite too close to the quick. She would not tell her mother about Parents' Day. That way, she would avoid that dreadful moment when she is sitting, one of those submissive heads bowed over books and exercises and Butch being sweet up the front saying, 'Good afternoon, Parents. Welcome to Form 2A. The girls (gels) are completing a mathematics exercise. Do feel free to walk about and take a closer look at their work.'

When Kathy looks up there's her mother dressed up as she always is for school occasions in a net frill of a hat (doesn't she realise that no one wears silly little hats like that?), her too-blonde hair curling in a halo, her fur around her shoulders, her gloves on, smiling and winking. ('And why don't you wear a plain coat?' she asks her mother. 'It's silly. Fur's too hot anyway.' But her mother says her jacket is vison – very expensive, the best quality, given to her in Paris by her Uncle Claude as a twentieth birthday present and of the best quality, and the coats here are so badly cut, so dull.)

She will smile and wink, then she will walk towards Kathy, but pausing on the way to look at the other girls' work and Kathy will hear her approaching.

'Oh, zees is lovely. So neat. So compleecated. You are very clev-air, no?'

And the kids squirming, not answering, heads down and pink at the praise. 'Not really,' they mutter, anticipating the

teasing they're in for afterwards: 'So clevairrr, eh? So
. . .' And no matter how much she explains, her moth[
not understand, just says, 'Oh, they are so shy, these
Zealand children. But everybody likes a little praise, no?'

Then, she is there. Beside Kathy's desk. Her perfume on
the air sweet and strong. Another thing the kids always notice.
'Gee, your mother smells nice.' Or, earlier, when there were
boys in the class back in primary school, 'Pooh! What a pong!'

Kathy has tried to deal with that too. Last Christmas she
bought her mother plain eau-de-Cologne. Mrs Miller had a
bottle on her dressing table, unopened, in a blue carton with
For Mother scrawled on the front in gold italic.

'Oh, how delicious, Kasia!' her mother had said. She took
deep appreciative sniffs, she dabbed a little behind her ears.
The scent was pale and faintly antiseptic, like violets.

She placed the bottle stage-centre on the tallboy, but
she never wears it. She chooses instead the Chanel, purchased
each year like the real coffee on the trip to Christchurch.
One exquisite fragile bottle so expensive that Dad always
says, 'Bloody hell, Rene, a family of four could live on the
price of that,' though he hands over the money because it is
her birthday treat, her choice.

The Chanel is borne back home and buried among her
scarves in the top drawer because the light might weaken it
and each morning, even when they are up at Hakataramea
with Dad fishing and miles from anywhere, she puts a little,
delicately, on each wrist after she has brushed her hair and
pursed her mouth for the lipstick and then, finally, she is
dressed.

The scent permeates her clothing, her cupboard, her
bedroom.

And here she is in vison, frilled hat and Chanel leaning
over Kathy's desk and Kathy must at last raise her head and
acknowledge her. This is my mother. The whole class will
know it now.

This is my foreign, peculiar, embarrassing mother.

A Good Day

The perfect nail was a goner: down to the quick like all the others but Kathy has decided: she will lose the newsletter, drop it in the gutter on the way home and act innocent confusion if Mrs Miller spills the beans. (Parents' Day? Didn't I give you the notice? Gosh, sorry.) She will be spared humiliation.

Kathy pulled up her stockings and wondered if there would be time to go down to the shop for a Buzz Bar before the bell went.

'May I look at you then?'

She had clenched her fists but she did not close her eyes or turn away from him. 'Yes,' she said.

'You are truly beautiful,' he said. 'You have the long aristocratic legs and the exquisite breasts of a statue.'

She let out her long-held breath with a sigh that made her quiver, and her heart beat hard under her breasts. He placed his lips against the pulsating spot while he pressed gently at her abdomen with his hands. He continued to kiss and stroke her while her whole body trembled under his lips and hands . . .

'God it's hot,' thinks Heather Crombie, sprawled at the other end of the bench. Her brain was turning to jelly, a pink mush in the round bowl of her skull where orifice centipede centimetre abdomen bubbled thickly. Pulsated thickly. She hated the heat but sitting out in the sun was a necessary annual torment if she was ever to achieve a tan. It wasn't fair. Kathy and Raeleen and Caroline turned brown at the very beginning of summer without effort and without pain while she had to endure the slow transition from dead white to a sort of pale beige, like milky coffee sprinkled with brown sugar freckles.

She had tried everything: oils and lotions, a tanning cream which turned her instantly carrot yellow and made her feel sick, a foil-lined box she made from a tea chest which the *Australian Post* said was Bronzing the Busty Beauties at Bondi. She had lain in the chest for fifteen minutes like a kind of baked potato before emerging sunburnt under her chin, behind her ears and along her eyelids.

Heather Crombie was designed for cold weather.

She liked winter. She liked rain and hail and riding to school with her hat flipped back straining at its elastic, her cheeks scraped by an ice wind so that she arrived bright-eyed and glowing. She liked her clothing to cover her completely, which drew attention to her blue-grey eyes (Caroline had told her they were her best feature), rather than the pallid nothing of her skin.

'I don't know what you're so worried about,' her mother used to say. 'You've got beautiful skin, like Grandma Findlay. She used to spend hours rubbing lemon and oatmeal and olive oil onto her face and hands to keep them pale. And she always wore a wide-brimmed hat and long sleeves out of doors. She looked lovely, right into old age.'

'But I'm not Grandma Findlay,' Heather wailed. 'And that was in the olden days when the fashions were different and right now everyone is brown.' Brown like Kathy and Raeleen and Caroline. Brown like the girls in *Seventeen* who wore off-the-shoulder white broderie blouses and Bermuda shorts and went off to college, bronzed and glossy, with complete sets of matching luggage. All freshmen and sophomores, all astonishing white teeth and optimism.

Heather had locked herself in the bathroom and examined her body minutely, from the front, from the side and with a lot of twisting and straining from the rear.

Round face, when the ideal, according to *Seventeen*, was the triangle. Shoulders, white and bony. Rabbit teeth, with a gap at the front and several fillings. Plucked-hen skin.

Outie. (Mum said the nurse hadn't cut the cord properly but never mind: lots of people had them. Heather had checked surreptitiously in the changing room at the baths and they didn't: most people had neat tucked-away innies.)

Fat bum.

Fat short legs. (Mum said they were 'sturdy'. She said

Heather had always been 'such a sturdy little girl' as though it were a compliment when everyone knew that what was needed were long legs, long slim legs, like Kathy's.)

No one would ever ask Heather Crombie to model the Preppy Look for the Girl on the Go!

No one was ever likely to tell her that she had aristocratic legs and the exquisite breasts of a statue.

Orifice. Centenary. Sophomore. Her brain had melted. No longer even a pink mush but a clear liquid like the jellyfish she and Shona used to catch at Friendly Bay and keep in buckets to melt under the sun. In the winter she was not like this. When the temperature dropped she was quick and chatty and clever and people laughed at her jokes. 'Gee, Heather,' they said. 'You're such a dag!'

In the sun, however, she was stupid. She was addled. She could blurt out anything, clever or silly, sense or nonsense, truth or lie.

Beside her on the bench lay her lunch. Two sandwiches oozing butter and melted mutton fat. A chocolate wheaten run to a brown stain on the paper bag and tepid orange cordial in a bottle.

She was hopeless at lunches. Raeleen's lunch sat beside her own, scarcely touched and neatly contained in a proper plastic box with little compartments holding a club sandwich, a boiled egg with salt in a little twist of paper and a spoon, a slice of chocolate cake with thick creamy icing and an apple. But then, Raeleen's mother made her lunches.

Heather sat in the sun feeling heatstruck and queasy and wondered if Shona would have eaten her mutton sandwich or if it would have been chucked in the shrubbery behind the bike sheds where everyone at South Primary customarily abandoned unwanted lunches. She wondered too if she should move. At the other end of the bench by the toilet wall there was a black slab of shade where she could sit if she wanted, with her head out of the sun while her legs continued processing in the full glare. It would be lovely. It would be sensible. She'd have a headache if she sat where she was much longer, but it was too hot to move, too hot to make the decision.

She took a tentative bite from the sandwich and it glued itself instantly to the roof of her mouth. She simply could not swallow though she was hungry. Breakfast had been inedible: tea without milk because she had forgotten to put out the bottles, slimy eggs. She had looked up the recipe book for instructions, but nowhere among the recipes for Eggs Florentine, Coddled Eggs, Devilled Eggs and Spanish Omelette had there been an explanation of how to produce a plain boiled egg, just the way Mum did them, with the white set but the yolk still a little runny so that you could make soldiers with thin fingers of buttered toast.

Two minutes she had finally decided, and watched anxiously as they jostled about in the enamel saucepan, cracked and trailing white mucus. She'd made toast but in the rush to drain the eggs the bread had caught at the edges. She scraped off the burn and poured the tea which had leaves like dead ants adrift on the surface and Dad had said she was a 'fine wee cook' and gone off to work.

Shona wouldn't eat the toast and the last of the bread had gone for the lunches, so Heather drew a Humpty on her egg and Shona sliced off his cap. 'Yuk,' she said as white dribbled to the plate. 'Can I have a Weet-Bix?'

'There's no milk,' said Heather then, as Shona seemed about to cry, 'but you can have one with butter and honey instead, OK?'

Shona said OK and after she'd eaten, Heather walked with her to the gate of South Primary. She stood and watched as her sister skipped away amongst the other kids, skinny in her shiny shoes and new tartan frock because she had insisted and Mum wasn't there to say no, it wasn't suitable for school. Her hair was tangled. 'Ow,' she had said, as Heather tried to brush it out before doing the plaits. 'You're tugging.' Heather gave up the effort to disentangle rubber bands and ribbon and fine fair hair and left it in a mess. She simply couldn't face tears again.

Last night she had woken with a jump. She lay there for a moment wondering if it was morning already, but the light shining into their bedroom was too pallid to be the sun and the town was so quiet that she could hear the waves down on the foreshore by the railway station washing in and out. A steady breathing.

Across the room from the soft hump that was Shona under her kitten eiderdown came the sound of muffled weeping. Through the wall, Dad snored rhythmically. A long rasping breath. Hold. Shudder. Out. He'd gone to sleep again with the light on. She'd sort him out later.

Shona was upside down under the eiderdown.

'What's the matter?' said Heather crawling down into the black burrow of bedding beside her sister. 'Shhh. Don't cry.' Shona was still half asleep.

'Rabbits,' she said, slurred and snuffily. 'The big black rabbit ate Tiggy and it grew and grew and I tried to run away but it ha-ha-had sharp teeth and I couldn't find the door to get inside and . . .'

There was a damp patch on Shona's nightie and the boiled cabbage smell of pee. She clung to Heather in the dark and Heather cuddled her, stroking her hair the way Mum used to and saying, 'Shhh, shhh, it's only a dream,' then drawing her gently round so her head was on the pillow.

Shona's arm was tight round Heather's neck.

'I want Mummy,' she said and Heather said well, she'd probably be up next week to visit, only seven more sleeps, she said she'd come again soon, but Shona said, 'I want her now.' And there was nothing Heather could do but hug her and sing 'Mammy's little baby loves shortenin' shortenin'' till her sister quietened and lay still, breathing evenly.

When Shona was asleep, Heather padded on cold feet through to her father's room. He was snoring, sitting upright against a pile of pillows in the middle of the double bed, the light on, *Best Bets* open in his hands, whisky in a glass and a cigarette burned to the stub in a charcoal ridge on the bedside table. The acrid smell of burned wood hung in the room.

Heather put the stub in the paua shell ashtray she'd bought him last Christmas and took his glasses from his nose where they'd slid to a lopsided tilt. He stirred a little, said, 'Tha' you Chrissie?', his accent broad Scots as it always was when he was half asleep, or drunk, or angry.

'It's Heather,' said Heather. 'You've left the light on again.'

'Oh,' said her father, settling into the pillows. 'Mussa dropped off.'

Heather leaned over and tugged the light cord.

'Night night,' she said.

'Nigh',' said Dad's voice from the darkness. 'You're a goo girl, Heather. A goo wee girl and thass a fact.'

Heather gave him a kiss and his cheek was fine prickles, like a gooseberry, and his skin smelled of tobacco and foundry smoke and whisky, that warm Dad-smell. Then back on the cold linoleum to Shona who rolled over and said, 'Sleep with me Heather.' So Heather did, to drive away the bad rabbits, though sleeping with Shona was like sharing a bed with a bundle of sticks, all sharp points and angles.

Wide awake with Shona's elbow pressing at her spine, Heather tried to retrieve sleep. She looked out into the dark and did Step One: Pronto the Palomino. She grasped his powerful flanks between her knees, and together they galloped up the paddock through deep emerald grass. Usually the gallop ended with the fence. She'd feel Pronto gather himself to leap beneath her and the surge as they lifted, up and over in a single fluid movement, so that she fell gently into the grass on the other side where she slept until morning.

Step One usually worked, but it was not enough tonight, not with Shona moving restlessly on the narrow sagging bed, so Heather proceeded to Step Two, in which she was at once floating up, away from the house, higher and higher, and yet able to turn and look back at the girl who was herself, who had shrunk to a microscopic dot in a tiny house on a small island on an insignificant planet which was only a speck in a limitless universe.

In this vast expanse, what happened to Heather Crombie was of absolutely no consequence whatsoever. And from Step Two it was a short leap to Step Three where what happened to Heather Crombie could be far outweighed by dozens of worse fates.

Heather had worked hard at Step Three. She had collected examples from magazines and books: stories of kids in the *Woman's Weekly* who had bravely survived the loss of arms or legs or the girl in the iron lung in Auckland. Joan of Arc in the *Heroines of History* pictures on the wall at school, with the flames licking at her feet, or Edith Cavell being shot by the firing squad for helping wounded men. Or Katy breaking her back in *What Katy Did*. Or Anne Frank.

That's it: think about Anne Frank. By comparison with what had happened to Anne Frank, Heather Crombie had suffered nothing. All that had happened to Heather Crombie was that her mother had left. Walked out one afternoon while they were at school so that they came home to a couple of cake tins on the kitchen table filled with afghans, which were Heather's favourite, and coconut squares, which were Shona's. There was a basket full of folded washing by the back door and a paper package of mince oozing blood in the sink. 'Cook this for tea,' said the note pinned to the wall. 'Add one onion chopped and 2 carrots (in safe). Will phone tonight.'

She'd gone. There had been a row the night before but nothing out of the ordinary. Dad had yelled because Mum had gone to the Farmers' sale and bought them a dress each. Beautiful tartan dresses with white collars and black velvet bow ties.

'Very smart,' said the saleslady as she whisked in and out of the fitting room, her eyebrows two interrogative arches stencilled to her forehead.

Shona had stood there smiling up at her goofily and

making no attempt to hide her holey singlet and then Mum had pointed out that the dresses had a tiny fault in the seam stitching and were they by any chance factory seconds? The arches lifted an eighth of an inch and the red lips unzipped long enough to say that Madam would understand that these were after all sale stock and priced accordingly and Mum, meek, flushed, said yes, of course she understood that, while Shona twirled to make the stiff petticoat stand out. Could she take them on apro, said Mum. 'I'm afraid it is cash only, Madam, for sale specials,' said the red lips.

Mum hesitated. Heather slowly unzipped the dress. It fitted her perfectly, and it didn't matter that Shona's was almost the same, only red instead of green. Never had her waist looked so slender, her legs so perfectly formed. The dress smelled of newness and starch, the colour made her hair a deep chestnut instead of ordinary brown and her eyes were quite definitely blue – almost azure. She dragged it over her head rustling, not caring either if the saleslady saw her grey singlet or the thimble bumps which were her developing breasts. It didn't matter.

New dresses didn't matter.

But Mum was suddenly reckless. She was saying they would take them, they needed something nice for special, it wouldn't take a minute to mend the seams, and they were walking out of the shop swinging the bag with Farmers printed on the side and Mum saying that what they needed now were some decent shoes and new white socks – better still, some nylons for Heather. She was growing up. So they stopped at Hosiery on the way out for a pair of Woodsmoke Sheers and a Fayreform Easy to hold them up. And in Butlers' window they found a pair of black patent strap shoes for Shona and some white slip-ons with a tiny Louis heel for Heather which were on sale too and only half price.

Heather stood at the X-ray looking down at her feet bones furled comfortably and correctly like pale fans inside her first pair of high heels and felt pure joy. On Sunday when she went to church she would be new all over. They walked home and on the way they stopped for lemonade spiders at the Apollo to celebrate properly.

That night there was a row. They lay in bed listening. Dad was saying he'd had a gutsful of Mum running round town putting him into debt and making him look a bloody fool and he'd put an ad in the paper, saying he wasn't responsible, that'd put a bloody end to it. Mum, low and bitter, was saying it wasn't her that had them in debt, it was him and those damn horses and she was sick of living on nothing, she'd had a career before she married him and she could earn more than him even now, if he'd let her, she could still manage eighty-five words a minute and they'd been sorry to see her go at Lane Lattimer, Mr Lane had even come down to tell her so personally and he'd said there would always be a place for her if she wanted to come back.

'But you've got kids,' said Dad. 'And it was you that bloody wanted them, remember? Now you've got them you can bloody well look after them.'

'Oh, I'll look after them all right,' said Mum. 'On ten pounds a week. You expect me to manage on ten pounds a week? Rent and food and clothing and no chance of putting a down-payment on a house and I'm not moving to one of those State boxes and now Heather wants to do piano. And you always take your share for the pub and the races.'

Dad said he needed a drink after a week of her going on and on and stuck down at the foundry shovelling shit. He was entitled to a bit of relaxation.

And Mum said, in that quiet dead voice, that that was the problem, wasn't it? He was entitled, he earned the money, he was head of the house and she was just the skivvy and Dad said not much bloody cop as the skivvy either, the place was a tip.

Silence.

Shona was lying on her back with her eyes shut and her hands over her ears which she still thought made her invisible.

'My pigeon house I open wide,' she sang, 'and set my pigeons free . . .'

Then Mum said, so quietly that Heather could hardly hear it, 'I warn you: I shall leave you. I shall walk out that door and not come back.'

And Dad said, 'Fine. Try it. See how long you last.'

'I could go back to work,' said Mum. 'I'm a trained secretary. I've got a career, remember.'

'Oh yes?' said Dad. 'A trained secretary fourteen years ago. You wouldn't last five minutes in a modern office. I'd give you a week before you came snivelling back.'

Silence.

'You have no respect for me, do you?' said Mum. 'You don't believe I could cope. All right: you like bets. I'll make a bet. I'll go back to work and I bet that in a few months I could clear the debts and save enough for the down-payment for a house. Ten quid.'

Dad thumped the table. They could hear the blow of it.

'For the last time, you're not going back to work,' he said. 'Making me look more of a bloody fool in this town than ever.' His chair crashed to the kitchen floor.

'I'm off,' he said.

'Let me guess,' said Mum. 'Down to the Tas?'

'Maybe,' said Dad. 'Somewhere where I don't have to listen to a useless bloody woman yabbering on about bets and her fucking ex-career.'

The door slammed.

The house went stony quiet.

Next morning everything was as usual. Weet-Bix and milk on the table and pixie cosies on their eggs which were lightly boiled with fingers of buttered toast. Their blouses were ironed and hung on the chair so they wouldn't crease, their lunches wrapped in greaseproof on the bench, then the kiss. 'Bye Heather. Bye Shona. Be careful crossing the road.'

Mum left that afternoon. She caught the 2 o'clock to Dunedin where she was going to try and get a job back at

Lane Lattimer. No one in town need know but she would pay all the bills and save enough for the down-payment on a house, and when she had she'd be back and not a moment before.

She rang to tell them this that evening. Dad gripped the receiver so tightly his knuckles went white. 'What the hell do you think you're playing at?' he said. 'Have you gone off your head or something?' Their mother's voice was a distant rattle, their father's pure Glasgow, spitting and furious.

Shona was crying. 'Here,' said Dad. 'Here are your kids. Maybe they'll be able to talk some sense into you.'

Shona cradled the receiver and said nothing. Heather said, 'Hullo?' when it was her turn and this stranger said through beep beep beep and the rattle of coins in the slot that it wasn't forever, she'd be back as soon as she had a bit put aside in the Post Office and there were chops for tomorrow's tea in the fridge and Heather was a big girl now, she'd manage.

Beep beep beep went the phone. 'I'll have to go now,' said the stranger who had a curious high, excited voice. 'I'm out of coins. Look after . . .' The phone went dead. They were on their own.

A week later Mum was back, sitting on the step patting Tiggy and smoking a cigarette when they came home from school. Shona dropped her satchel and climbed onto her lap. Heather hung back by the corner of the verandah, not trusting herself to speak immediately. She picked a periwinkle from the vines tangling the trellis.

The radio was playing in the kitchen. *Ta-ammy*, it sang. *Ta-aamy. Tammy's in love.* Mum stroked Shona's hair and rocked her to and fro and Shona snuggled in like a puppy, sucking her thumb.

Heather peeled away blue petals one by one, exposing the golden crown of the fairy toothbrush.

'How's school?' said Mum.

'Fine,' said Heather. 'How's Lane Lattimer?'

Mum said not too good. No luck at Lane Lattimer. Her

speeds had gone down without regular practice and at Lane Lattimer they were all using dictaphones now and electric typewriters and a different filing system and the young girls were just so efficient. Plus they looked good. No one wanted an older woman in the boardroom if they had a choice. But she had a job at the Public Trust, just filing and typing but it paid well, and a cheap room up York Place.

Shona tugged at Mum's ear. 'It's swimming sports tomorrow,' she said. 'I'm in the egg and spoon.'

'I hope you win,' said Mum.

'Parents can come,' said Shona.

'Oh, I'm sorry,' said Mum. 'I've got to get back tonight. I'm only here today because I got a lift up with one of the girls who had to go to a funeral. And I wanted to see how you were getting on. I miss you.'

'What about Dad?' said Heather. 'Are you going to see him?'

Her mother did not answer, undid Shona's hair and began to replait it, strand after strand.

'Not yet,' she said.

'So you're just popping in. Then you're running away again?' said Heather.

'I've just put the tea on,' said Mum. 'There's a steak and kidney pie that should come out at six and some baked potatoes. Oh – and there's some mushrooms. Real ones. Pirate ones. We found them in a paddock near Hampden on the way up.' She flipped Shona's plaits over her shoulders.

'There you are, princess,' she said.

Shona twisted on her lap and hung on tight.

'Don't, Shona,' said Mum. 'I've got to get ready. I'm getting picked up in a minute. You'll make me late.'

Heather pushed past her and thumped inside, past the table set for tea and the basket of clean washing. She shut the bathroom door and turned the key.

Tap tap tap.

'Heather?' said her mother. 'Heather. I'm sorry. I really

am. I'd just had enough. Do you understand? We were getting nowhere, we were going down. I want a house, I want nice things for you and Shona and I've waited and waited but we were never going to have them. And it's not forever, just till we're right again. You're coping aren't you?'

Heather sat on the toilet seat thinking about Gladys Aylward and the orphans in China. About Amy Johnson flying into the sea. It could be worse.

Her mother knocked again. 'Heather?' she said. 'Come on. Please. I'll be up as often as I can. Next week perhaps? I'll come on the bus. Would that be nice?'

Then there was Mary Queen of Scots, thought Heather, picking bits of chenille from the seat cover. She was kept prisoner for years and years then had her head cut off by her own cousin. There was a picture of her on the wall above her desk at school, walking to the scaffold as a Heroine of History with her little dog under her skirts.

Shona was crying. 'Heather?' said Mum. 'Please, Heather. Come out and look after Shona. I can't leave her on her own like this. I can't leave her crying.' A car drew up outside and tooted.

There was the girl in the *Weekly* who had her face burned. 'Heather?' said her mother. Pleading, desperate. Tootooot went the car. Shona was crying now, a hiccuppy wail through the door.

'I have to go,' said her mother. 'I have to go. Stay here, Shona. Please. Be a good girl, Heather will come out and take care of you.'

Tootooot.

Then the sound of feet, running, a door opening and slamming shut, a car revving and she was gone. Heather opened the bathroom door. Shona was curled in a tight ball on the floor, crying. Heather sat by her stroking her back and Tiggy settled on her lap and they sat there in the hall until five o'clock and the thump of Dad's bike on the wash-house wall.

'You're not to tell Dad Mum visited, OK?' said Heather. Shona sat up, blew her nose and nodded. Then they went out to the kitchen where Heather dished up the tea while Dad had his wash. But first she took the newspaper parcel full of mushrooms and dumped them over the back fence into the Ranginuis' vege garden.

She loved mushrooms and the gathering of them, walking with their mother over the paddocks behind their house, scanning for the white caps buttoning gully or spur, and not bothered about the signs saying Trespassers Will Be Prosecuted, which was like in the Lord's Prayer, because Mum said land belonged to everyone, it had been made over billions of years under the sea and no matter what the farmers thought they were temporary, just tenants like themselves, so they were entitled as long as they did no harm and closed the gates.

They called it 'pirate food': mushrooms, and blackberries, plums and apples from the side of the road, and mussels and seaweed like limp wet lettuce from the rocks at the beach, and walnuts if the tree hung across the pavement. Pirate food was free and it was the best, but tonight Heather flung it away, into the very middle of the Ranginuis' blackcurrant patch, and went inside to spoon up steak and kidney for the others.

Dad said she was a dab wee cook and no mistake and he was just going to pop down to the Tas for a yarn and he'd be back before they went to bed. Shona picked out all the kidney and fed the bits to Tiggy, which wasn't allowed because it taught Tiggy bad habits, and Heather made fork patterns on mashed potato. She couldn't eat a bite. The smell of mushrooms clung to her hands like damp. Like a heavy cold. Like tears.

Nobody knew, of course. She couldn't tell a soul, not even Raeleen who was probably her best friend this year. You talked endlessly, about boys or school or other girls, but never about home. Once her best friend in Standard Three,

Jennifer Young, told her that the little round marks on the back of her left hand were cigarette burns.

'Yuk,' said Heather. 'Didn't that hurt?' And Jennifer said yeah, a bit but she didn't care because Mack thought he was the boss around the place because he was Mum's favourite but she wasn't going to get him his cup of tea ever, not even if he burnt her all over.

'Cigarette burns would sting, wouldn't they?' she said to Mum one Saturday morning while Mum was putting rollers in her hair, the little ones which turned the front under.

'I should think so,' said Mum, her mouth tight round a plastic pin. 'Why?'

'Oh, nothing,' said Heather 'Just something Jennifer said.'

Mum poked the pin through the tight auburn sausage roll. 'Ow,' she said. 'I wish I could afford a proper perm.'

Pause.

'Heather,' she said, 'you don't talk about us do you, to your friends?'

'Course not,' said Heather. She poked her little finger into a roller and watched it go numb at the tip.

'Because home is private,' said Mum. 'No one else is interested. You know that, don't you?'

Heather tapped her finger on the dressing table. It was completely dead. She couldn't feel a thing.

'Course,' she said. She would never talk about home. How could you talk about it? About the endless bitter rows over a meal too late to the table, over mates who stayed till two a.m. drinking homebrew out in the shed, over new shoes, or the house which they would never be able to afford. Over money. ('I don't have to account for every bloody penny to you . . .' 'Just throwing good money after bad and there's no such thing as a sure bet so grow up for God's sake . . .' 'Nagging bitch . . .' 'I had a career before I married you, I was the best secretary they had and Mr Lane came down himself to tell me . . .' 'Plenty of women manage on half what I give you a week . . .' 'You give me? Father Christmas himself . . .'

'I'm entitled to a bit of relaxation . . .' And on and on and on.)

Not about the nights when Dad sprawled on the sofa, morose, saying so much for the land of bloody opportunity, eh? When he hopped the boat back in 1946 he'd planned to have his own engineering business by the time he was thirty – but blokes like him never got the chances, eh? Stacked against you from the word go. Once the bosses got it in for you and you were down on your back you never got up again. You didn't know what you had till you lost it and he'd been happy back then, in the Royal Navy and seeing a bit of the world, free as a bloody bird.

Or happy, singing and telling them about the time he'd landed in Dunedin and met their mother one night walking down Princes Street and he'd thought she was a real doll and he'd bet Munro a quid she'd go out with him and sure she did, but not before he'd spent five quid on flowers and chocolate. She never came cheap, he said, did Chrissie.

'Love me tender, love me sweet,' he sang, reaching out to pull Mum toward the sofa, his eyes soft and pink at the thought of her in her high heels and tight little perm, the best secretary they'd had in years at Lane Lattimer on the Exchange.

'Never let me go . . .'

He had a good voice. When he was in the Royal Navy he used to do Frank Sinatra songs at concerts and everyone said he could have been mistaken for Ol' Blue Eyes himself. Now he preferred Elvis, and when he sang, you'd think it was the King.

And Mum laughed and said, 'Now come on Dave, you'll feel better for a good sleep,' and usually he agreed, and settled quietly enough under the tartan rug on the sofa, his mouth hanging open like a kid's and snoring so that they giggled but quietly, careful not to waken him because if he wakened he could as easily be angry, roaring, hitting out. 'Lady Muck, don't come playing Lady Muck with me.'

Shona sat up in bed with her eyes shut and her hands over her ears.

My pigeon house I open wide and set my pigeons free . . .

'No,' said Heather with her finger inside the roller so numb it could belong to someone else entirely. 'I don't talk about home.'

Because of the no-speaking rule, Heather had perfected the art of evasion. Yesterday she explained to Butch that her mother was visiting her sister in Timaru so would be unable to come to Parents' Day. And when Kathy rang to invite her to her birthday on Saturday week, she play-acted, said, 'Hang on while I ask Mum,' cradling the phone in one hand and calling, 'Hey Mum, is it OK if I go to Kathy's birthday?' to an empty kitchen.

The fridge whirred in the corner. The cat opened one yellow eye and yawned.

'Yes, I can come,' she said to Kathy. 'See you.'

Technically it was lying, which was also wrong, but Heather was caught between two sets of injunctions.

'You goddam sonofabitch,' roared Lucas, beside himself. *'You goddam whorin' little slut . . .'*

Heather's head throbbed and her eyes dazzled from lack of sleep. Steps One, Two and Three had all failed her last night. Pronto was a kid's dream, Anne Frank was long ago and in another country. Lying on the saggy wirewove, one arm round Shona who fidgeted and muttered in restless, rabbit-ridden sleep, she had devised Step Four. She had told herself a story. Not a daytime story, a story written in an old exercise book with girl detectives or love, but a night story, about how she herself becomes ill. Terribly ill. With polio like that girl in the iron lung. She had lain sleepless in the dark, feeling the weight of the machine gather round her, the restraint of that huge metal cylinder with its tubes and dials and its mirror for reading. Her legs, heavy and paralysed, prickled nevertheless with panic at the confinement.

No. On second thoughts, not the iron lung. Not polio.

TB, like Katherine Mansfield, who was delicately pretty and wrote the story about the little lamp which Butch said was a masterpiece. She died young but famous.

Or maybe she has had an accident? A non-disfiguring accident? Or maybe she has tried to kill herself? In despair she has drunk all the disinfectant in the blue bottle in the wash-house cupboard, with its skull-and-cross bones label and its *Instructions for Emergency Care*.

Anyway, she's sick and lying in bed. A white hospital bed. Her eyes are closed, her hair no longer brown but golden against her bloodless pallor. At the foot of the bed stand her father and Shona and suddenly, her mother is there too! Dad has had to ring her, of course, and she has rushed immediately to her daughter's side! She kneels by the bed stroking Heather's hand. 'Oh, my darling,' she murmurs, her eyes welling with tears. 'Oh my poor baby!' 'There, there, Chrissie,' says her father putting his arm around Mum's quivering shoulders. 'No point blaming yourself now. What's done is done. She was a beautiful girl and deeply sensitive. More sensitive than we were cognisant (from the Latin root *cogitare*, to think) of.' Her mother is overcome with emotion.

But suddenly Heather's eyelids flicker. She makes a miraculous recovery. In a matter of minutes to the astonishment of the medical establishment she is sitting up on the bed and her family gather round her. They talk and laugh and eat all the grapes and chocolates and they vow never, never to quarrel or part again. When Heather's strong enough, they say, we'll go on holiday, we'll go to Caroline Bay. Or London. Or to a tropical island.

The Ranginuis' rooster had crowed and dawn was colouring the edges of the bedroom blind when Heather fell at last into a brief skimming sleep from which she woke at seven with the tiny knot of pain behind her eyes which had threatened all day to unravel and tangle her skull. The sun made it worse. She needed to move. She needed to keep her wits about her and think things through properly and logically.

This was important because no one else seemed to be thinking at all. Shona said nothing except in dreams and she was too little, anyway. Her father came home each night, ate his tea, and went off to the Tas or out to the shed to work on the model of the *Hood*, which he had been making ever since she could remember, not stumbling down the hall to bed until late, while seventy-five miles away Mum lay in a strange bed after filing and typing all day to pay off the debts.

It was a mess. Heather Crombie licked melted chocolate from her fingers and tried to find something solid and sensible, but it was all a horrible mucky mess.

Lucas grabbed Selena and when she wrenched away from his grasp he was left holding the entire front of the girl's blouse. Selena backed away from him, her breasts naked and heaving in the light of the room's unshaded electric bulb, her shoulders still covered ridiculously by the sleeves of the faded cotton blouse . . .

Margie Miller licked the kiss curl in place on her cheek. Now that her ear lobes had stopped being red and puffy from her attempt to pierce them with a safety pin, she could wear her hair in a kind of beehive again instead of all brushed flat the way good kids wore theirs, confined by an Alice band or pretty bow. The clips tugged and her scalp tingled still from the fierce back-combing. But it would be worth it.

Butch would go do-lally, drumming her fingers on Margie's desk and telling her to leave the room immediately and tidy her hair because she won't have her in the class looking like that. Margie knew better than to look truculent. She favoured innocent astonishment and the subtle pleasure of watching the wattles flare.

'Yes, Miss Butcher,' she would say. 'Sorry, Miss Butcher.'

Nice as pie. And you leave the room for the toilets, which ponged a bit but where you could settle for a quiet smoke amongst the soothing trickle of leaking cisterns. Ten minutes to disentangle her hair. Ten minutes less of that little drip Toto and his *père* and *mère* at the *plage*.

After school she could do it all over again: tease and tangle till her hair was an inflated puff, on which her hat could perch precariously but only as far as the corner of Spenser Street where she'd stuff it in her case, hitch up her uniform, take off her gloves and bike the rest of the way home free. And this time it would be her mother who said, 'Margie, you look terrible. What have you done to your hair, for goodness sake?' Looking up from the *Weekly* crossword with a cigarette in one hand burning down to her fingers and a stubby pencil in the other and noticing vaguely that her youngest has changed in the last year. No longer that sweet skinny little kid but a rebel, a widgie, someone who is definitely Heading for Trouble.

A rebel. Like Selena. But no one was ever going to push her into a corner and rip her shirt off. Margie Miller lay in the sun and wondered vaguely why Selena didn't just boot Lucas in the nuts. Boys hated that. It didn't matter if they were stronger just so long as you moved fast. She had tried it on Pete when he was being a pain, calling her Maggotbrain over and over one Sunday afternoon. One kick and he'd fallen to the lounge carpet instantly and her mother had run in, said she must never do that again, it was dangerous.

Pete still called her Maggotbrain, but he kept a wary distance.

Margie-the-rebel lay in the sun and wished, eyeing Heather Crombie's chocolate-stained fingers, that she hadn't used quite all her lunch money on the packet of Albanys in her bag. The rep had left them at the shop last night and she'd been arranging them on the display stand which had a picture of Edmund Hillary saying he chose Albanys for his expeditions because he wanted Nothing But The Best!

She'd pinched a pack but had to pay for it with her lunch money because Mum was always so careful with the till, and she'd tried one out this morning in the toilets when she had been sent out to get rid of the nail polish. It hadn't in fact been that nice. It left a cold cavernous space at the back of her throat and made her feel a bit sick, but at least she had done it: brought a packet of smokes to school and smoked one. Half a one. The other half fizzed and spattered in the toilet bowl, releasing tiny shreds of tobacco, and she left it there, floating, so the other kids would know, while she chipped away at hardened layers of Passion Red.

Now she was hungry. Heather had a sandwich she wasn't eating, but it looked horrible: thick slabs of bread and greasy mutton. She'd die rather than eat that. Margie leaned back in the sun smelling Menthol in her hair. She was definitely getting the knack of it, even the lighting-up which was the tricky part. She practised for fifteen minutes last night in the bathroom, watching herself in the mirror closely, appraising the curve of the fingers, elegant and easy, miming match strike and the draw, eyes half shut seductively, the pause with pursed lips, the exhale, slow and sexy.

Pete had hammered at the door. 'Come on, Maggot. What are you doing in there? Have you died or something?'

He was in a fuss because he wanted to be in the shop when Janice Bates (Jail Bait) came in for a pie and some fags as she did most nights. Big deal. Neil had told him that Janice was the town bike and hung around with Mervyn Hinkley and the heavies down at the Apollo but Pete had said shut up, he could look after himself and mind your own fucking business and they had scuffled on the lounge floor and broken the standard lamp. All over Janice Bates. Janice Bates with her straw hair and her matador pants and tight white cardy, teetupping into the dairy on tiny red stilettos, or in leather glued to Mervyn Hinkley's broad black back as he gunned the Harley along Shakespeare Street on a Friday night.

Margie had sat in a booth at the Apollo and studied her closely. Janice leaned against the jukebox playing 'Love Letters in the Sand' over and over. She had a stupid giggle and a silly baby face but she could really smoke. Her technique was faultless. She tapped a cigarette carelessly from the packet, tucked it between her full red lips and leaned forward for a light. She inhaled, looking up at Mervyn through narrowed eyes, her breasts brushing the sleeve of his jacket. She held the cigarette casually between red-tipped fingers, cool and assured, and exhaled across one shoulder. Boy, could she smoke.

Margie had looked in the bathroom mirror and tried a left-hand draw but her fingers were too stiff, too amateur.

'Mags,' Pete called. 'Look, just hand out the aftershave and the pimple stuff, will you?'

It would look better, she had decided, if her fingernails were crimson.

Pete's voice shrilled between octaves as it was still prone to do when he was angry or excited. 'Maggot, come on.' Then, turning nasty, 'If you're piercing your ears again I'll tell Mum. And I'll tell her about the ciggies.'

He had seen them, the sneaky bugger. He had been messing about in her room. It was time to give in. She put the cigarettes back in the pack (she'd try again tomorrow). 'All yours,' she said, opening the door. 'Keep your hair on. Janice Bates wouldn't notice a pathetic little drip like you if you stripped naked and danced on the counter.' Pete slammed the door.

'Hey Caroline,' said Kathy. 'Red alert. Gibbsy.' Miss Gibbs was circling the basketball court. Caroline shut *Peyton Place* and tucked it down her tunic front. Margie Miller mightn't mind if she got into trouble this year, but Caroline did. Not the way Greer minded, bursting into tears the minute Butch lost her temper. (Dumb. People like Butch got meaner if you cried.) No. Caroline minded because she wanted a pony and if she got top in class again this year, her mother had promised her one. If she got offside with Butch that would ruin her chances because Butch played favourites and Caroline was working hard at becoming a favourite. The trick was to do it without making the other kids think you were sucking up.

A Good Day

Caroline intended to be first in 2A, voted Most Popular Girl and mounted on her own pony by Christmas. Pinned by her bed was The Plan:

Aim 1 (in red capitals). Do homework 1 hour per night.

Aim 2 Help Mum (messages, dishes, ect. Mon-Sat. Tidy room Sun.)

Aim 3 Be kind to friends.

She had been working on it, by day helpful, industrious and kind (except to Helen Brassington but she deserved it), and at night enlisting divine assistance. Caroline had been sent to Sunday school when she was five. To St Martins, where her parents had been married and the children had one by one been christened with godparents and a silver spoon and the Carstairs christening gown with its myriad of tiny Victorian tucks and frills. She liked Sunday school. She liked wearing her best frock and white sockettes. She liked the little stickers for attendance which earned a prize at the end of the year. She liked the songs and the stories and the nativity play where she usually got to play the Angel because she was tall and did elocution.

She said her prayers carefully every night. At present her prayers are for success and popularity. Please, let me be popular. And help me to get good marks in the French test.

She didn't mention the pony, of course, because it might seem like a direct request and long experience had shown that such prayers were unlikely to be answered. Caroline had a strong suspicion in fact that enquiries after a pony, a new bike, a tennis racquet and other material goods might be offensive to God. Accordingly, she filed her most deeply felt entreaties at the very end of the nightly series, after a. The Lord's Prayer, b. blessings on the family, c. forgiveness for sins committed during that day and d. thanks for blessings received (an invitation to a birthday party, 18/20 for her Queen Elizabeth I project, a clear day with Butch).

Tucked away inconspicuously in this fashion, her requests, she hoped, might be acceptable. Just as it was wise to ask her father for money for the pictures immediately after dinner when he had had a whisky and was feeling mellow and a little careless. It was all a matter of timing and presentation.

That was how you won. That was how she got first last year and was able to walk up onto the stage among the towering arrangements of carnations and roses her mother as President of the PTA had helped organise. She had shaken hands with the Mayoress and received her prize. It looked nice, bound in blue leather with the school crest stamped in gold on the cover: *Six Clever Girls Who Became Famous Women*.

The book was a bit of a dud. She had flicked through it that night and it was boring: Joan of Arc in that uncomfortable-looking armour riding to Reims. Elizabeth I enjoying herself while poor Mary Stuart was stuck in prison. Elizabeth Fry being nice to some prisoners and Sarah Siddons being dramatic and someone called Margaret Wilson tied to a stake and drowning and Mary Kingsley walking off into the jungle in a stupid-looking hat.

Being famous never seemed to have much to recommend it. Apart from Elizabeth I, if you were famous you ended up being burnt or dying of radiation like Marie Curie or of TB like Grace Darling and Katherine Mansfield and all the Brontës, or getting shot like Edith Cavell or spending your whole life with sick, ugly or dangerous people.

She put the six clever girls on the shelf with the cover front-on to show the school crest, and took out the *Girls' Crystal* she had borrowed from Margie and stuffed under the mattress: 'Tess of Dovedale Farm', 'Sandra Burgess Girl Detective', and 'The Third Form at Bellingham Towers'.

In a way it did not matter really that the prize book was boring. The main thing was to have been first, to have walked across the stage in front of pupils, parents and friends-of-the-school while her list of achievements was read aloud – First Mathematics, First Social Studies, First French, Second

English – and the pupils, parents and friends clapped. That was what mattered.

And now there was an additional incentive: the pony. He was going to be grey or maybe chestnut with two white socks. He was going to be 14.2hh. He was going to be at least part-Arab. He was going to be a good jumper. He was going to be called Aladdin. Caroline anticipated success. There was a tin of saddle soap in a box under her bed, which she had bought with her birthday money, alongside the collection of old copies of *Horse and Pony*, two *Pony Annual*s and a velvet cap and a bridle which her cousin Elizabeth had given her last year when she sold Regent. 'You have them,' she said. 'I don't have time any more for riding now I'm studying for exams.'

'Hmmm,' said Caroline's mother. 'Studying boys more like it. Last year it was all horses, horses, horses. Now it's all boys, boys, boys. It must be such a worry having a daughter like that. What a good thing you're sensible, Caroline. I'll never lose a moment's sleep over you.'

She certainly wouldn't. At least, not this year. Not now that Caroline is following the plan. Not now she is organised.

Caroline is good at organising. At Brownies she had been leader of Pixie Patrol, who week after week won Best Decorated Corner and a bag of pineapple chunks from Brown Owl, and the secret had been organisation: a roster of Pixies brought flowers each Tuesday evening – chrysanthemums, daisies and when Margie Miller was briefly a Brownie, glorious bouquets of daffodils and roses which she had nicked from the cemetery across the road on her way to the St Martin's Hall.

Caroline liked order. She liked knowing where she stood. She liked knowing who got 62 in maths and who got 58. She liked competitions where people got first if they were the best, and second if they were next best and so on right down to the hopeless ones who didn't know how to plan a proper speech on the set topic, who couldn't write neatly about 'A

Day in the Life of a Penny', who couldn't run or swim or do a clear round fast enough.

She liked her room with its pink candlewick bedspread drawn up and tucked under the pillow and her bookshelf where the books were arranged alphabetically with a large-book section underneath for encyclopaedias. Ideally she would have liked to replace the ballerina wallpaper for which she had pleaded only three years ago with something more sophisticated but her father said decorators cost good money and he couldn't tolerate faddishness so Caroline, being an adaptable child and knowing when argument was fruitless, covered every frill and flounce as best she could with pictures cut from *Horse and Pony* and was contented enough.

She couldn't understand how Margie could live in the clutter that was her bedroom in the house behind the dairy, where the bed was never made and littered with wrinkled clothes, and comics, and Minnie scratched and shredded bits of paper in her mouse-house on the windowsill.

'Don't you want to be able to find things?' she said to Margie one afternoon when she had come round to the dairy to read.

Her father did not approve of comics. At Margie's house they ate their tea with comics, newspapers and magazines spread amongst the plates: *Donald Duck, Pix, Truth, Jughead, Popular Mechanics, True Romance* and *Girls' Crystal* spattered with toast crumbs or gravy or tomato sauce and Margie's mother doing the crosswords and her brothers arguing over planed heads and the Weber carburettor and her father listening to the cricket while the shop bell jangled incessantly and they took turns to answer.

At Caroline's house, dinners were quiet affairs. Caroline's father did not like a lot of noise and chatter at the dinner table, not after a day of listening to Mrs Ngatai's lungs. ('Cough, please. And again. And again.') Or George Smolenski's ulcer or that Paisley chappie fixing him with his one good eye and bleating that his back was bad again, Doc, real bad, playing him gyp and a few weeks off work should about fix it. No. When Caroline's father ate he wanted peace and quiet, not six children yabbering.

If the family were dining alone he simply insisted on silence, a muted litany of, 'Pass the salt please,' and, 'More dessert anyone?' When the children had guests to a meal he conducted light-hearted little quizzes. 'Who is the grand old lady of Threadneedle Street?' 'What is the square root of 36?' 'What is a drachma?' On Sundays at dinner he read aloud. Dickens for choice. The death of Little Paul, Miss Havisham going up in flames, and at Christmas, Marley shaking his chains, while the children forked up their roast beef, Yorkshire pudding and potatoes.

Caroline liked it so, but she did regret the comics. The only solution was to read them on the quiet at Miller's dairy, which she did on the pretext of visiting Margie. She read, concealed by the magazine stand in the shop, or sitting on Margie's unmade bed while Margie smoked a cigarette with the window wide open and the chest of drawers jammed against the door in case of intruders. Not only was the bed usually unmade; Caroline had noticed also with some unease stained socks and a bra held together with a safety pin, and knickers, grey and crumpled. She felt itchy all over with the muddle.

'Don't you want to be able to find your clothes and your homework easily?' she said.

Margie tried to blow a smoke ring, choked and shrugged. 'Nah,' she said.

She was equally uncomfortable at Caroline's house, sitting bolt upright in her chair at the dining table, scarcely able to breathe in the unnatural hush while Caroline and her brothers and sisters expertly handled their knives and forks, piling the food on the prongs in neat stacks. Her own family used the forks as scoops so they could turn pages with their free hands. Caroline's mother sat down one end, blonde and elegant, fresh from golf or tennis, one of her Constance Spry flower arrangements haloing her immaculate head. At the other, Caroline's father fired questions from behind a bristling moustache. 'Who burned the cakes?' 'What is a Penny Black?'

Poor Caroline, thinks Margie. It must be awful to have to be so still and starchy all the time.

Poor Margie, thinks Caroline, drawing a blanket over the knickers which have (ughhh) blood stains and knotted elastic at the waist. It must be awful to be so poor and so disorganised.

It was a wonder they liked each other at all.

Helen Brassington had stopped playing shots. She was sitting over by the music room in the middle of a group of kids from 2B, probably handing round chocolate.

'What a nong,' said Caroline.

'Who?' said Kathy sleepily.

'Helen Brassington,' said Caroline. 'Helen Brassière.'

'She's all right,' said Kathy. (She thought everyone was all right, even Yvonne Donaldson who picked her nose and stuck the goop along the edge of the desk. Kathy was simply too lazy to dislike anyone. It could be very annoying.)

'Anyway,' she was saying, 'I thought you were friends. What happened?'

'Oh nothing,' said Caroline. She had blundered. An aspirant Most Popular Girl would be unwise to admit to dislike, even when there was ample reason for hatred. (Remember Aim 3. Remember the nightly invocation.) And truly, nothing had happened. They had not had a fight, tearing at one another in the cloakroom the way some girls did, eyes blinded with scarlet rage. They had not argued. They had simply changed. One week, Helen was the same person who had happily played Mary Queen of Scots to Caroline's Queen Elizabeth, servant girl to her Cleopatra, baby to her mother, injured patient to her nurse. Who held the nails while Caroline hammered when they built the house in the mulberry. Who took second go on the swing.

'Caroline's little shadow,' Mum called her.

But overnight the shadow had shifted shape and suddenly, alarmingly, looked at her sullen and side-on and invited everybody but her to her twelfth birthday party. Everybody from the old Incredible Six Club which Caroline had organised back at primary school for the express purpose of Having Adventures.

The Club had survived for five months until Margie fell off the cliffs at Bushy Beach and broke her arm. The members were getting bored anyway, the general absence of smugglers, underground caverns and ruined castles putting a severe limit on their activities. But the Six remained a distinct group from then on nevertheless, always picking one another first for rounders, always sitting together at lunchtime, or for skipping.

All in together girls. Never mind the weather girls. The rope swinging heavily over and over in Double Dutch.

Always going to one another's birthday parties.

Caroline had biked past Helen's house on the afternoon of the party and heard the record player ('We're all goin' on a – summer holiday!') and the rhythmic pick puck pock from the ping pong table in the garage and she had realised that this was war. There was no point in waiting for Helen to return to her old familiar self. She had disappeared for ever and clearly intended to take the rest of the Incredible Six with her.

On Monday it was confirmed beyond doubt. Margie Miller nudged Kathy Scott and asked Caroline, giggling, if it was true she was going to get a pony if she got first in class and Most Popular Girl?

Betrayal. Helen had told them all, joking about Caroline's ambitions while they were playing Truth and Dare at the party. Caroline laughed, of course, pretending carelessness, said, 'Nah, who cares about all that stuff?'

Across the basketball court Helen seemed to have run out of chocolate. The group around her was breaking up. Mr Brassington owned the Victoria Confectionery Company but

Helen would find that access to unlimited reserves of chocolate would not be enough.

An eye for an eye. Betrayal for betrayal.

'We haven't had a row,' said Caroline, *Peyton Place* a firm breastplate in her tunic top and the group about her, waiting. 'Helen can get pretty moody at times but it's not really her fault. I suppose it's pretty tough for her being illegitimate and everything.'

The group turned toward her at once, curious, alert.

'Is she?' said Heather.

'Oh yes,' said Caroline. Careless. 'Didn't you know? She doesn't know who her real father is. Her mother had her when she was still at school and married Mr Brassington three years later.'

'I didn't know that,' said Margie.

'I thought everyone did,' said Caroline. 'I mean, it's sort of obvious isn't it, because she's so fair and the rest of the family are so dark?'

Caroline leaned back in the sun thinking of Helen choking with tears as she told her, crying because she had just found out and it had changed everything. They had swapped secret for secret. And now, she tipped the confidence out of the bag for everyone to poke at.

She folded her arms securely across her other weapon: the book which fell into her hands quite by chance only two nights ago, tucked in amongst the gardening books and old medical texts at the bottom of the bookshelf behind the sofa, SIZZLING BEST SELLER in scarlet capitals on the cover. Caroline knew all about *Peyton Place*. Margie had brought a copy to school weeks ago, pinched from one of her brothers. They'd been down in the cloakroom rehearsing their scene from *Romeo and Juliet*. ('Divide into groups, gels, and read the scene aloud. That is the only way to fully appreciate the beauty and rhythm of Shakespeare's verse.')

Caroline's group got the tomb scene. The cloakroom was a concrete dungeon surrounded by wooden lockers. Thick pipes ran across the ceiling and along the walls, creaking and purring and clanking. Kathy stretched out on a wooden form centre stage with her coat spread over her because even on the warmest day the cloakroom was glacial.

Heather Crombie, stabbed through ('Oh I am slain') with a ruler, had been dragged ('Hey, take it easy') across the floor by Raeleen Smiler and now lay in the Capulets' vault by the boiler-room door.

'I'll bury thee in a triumphant grave,' said Raeleen. '(Just relax Heather, I know how to do this, they taught us how to lift bodies at St John's.) A grave oh no! A lanthorn slaughtered youth . . . What's a lanthorn?'

Heather was saying, Hurry up it's freezing down here, and why did Shakespeare's people always take so long to die, and Caroline as director was saying, 'Just skip to the end, Raeleen,' when they became aware that Helen Brassington and Margie Miller, who as Balthazar and the page had been able to sit over by the heater, were not paying attention. They were huddled instead over a book and Margie was saying, 'Ughhh, that's disgusting.'

Juliet sat up, Paris rolled over and Romeo abandoned the feasting presence full of light for Selena's tarpaper shack and the vile Lucas Cross and *'Yep, you're getting to be quite a gal, honey . . .'* and Selena backing away from him, her thirteen-year-old breasts naked and heavy in the light of the room's single unshaded bulb.

Selena's screams had just ripped the stillness with a sound like tearing fabric when there was a sudden chilly silence in the cloakroom.

'And what precisely is going on here?' asked Miss Iris Butcher, MA Otago, the wattles pink, the talon fingers twitching. 'Caroline? Aren't you supposed to be in charge? And may we see what it is that is so very much more interesting than one of the supreme achievements of English literature?'

Margie took the blame and it was her parents who were

called in for the interview. Margie said adults were hypocrites, because they had read it themselves and twelve was tons old enough to read any book you liked: you paid full price at the pictures and on the bus and anyway what about Juliet? She was fourteen when she slept with Romeo and her mother, Mrs Capulet, was twelve when she had Juliet so what was the diff?

The worst part was that Butch confiscated the book, tore it to pieces in front of the class and dropped the tiny shreds into the rubbish bin and no one knew what happened to Selena. Did she get pregnant? Did she get killed? It was impossible to find out.

Then four weeks later, Caroline was hiding round the back of the sofa to escape the dishes when she found all the answers miraculously tucked in between *Roses for Pleasure* and *Gray's Anatomy*.

The perfect weapon: she could take it to school. (But carefully. She'd be more discreet than Margie.) She could gather the group around her to read – except this time she'd leave out Helen. That would be her punishment: exclusion from the charmed circle who knew what had happened to the beautiful doomed Selena with her gypsyish beauty and her corrupted and abused thirteen-year-old body.

Caroline sat in the sun feeling the solid weight of the book against her chest like armour plating. Through the spangles of light which had gathered in her lashes after reading from the white pages she could see Helen glance across at the six of them behind the toilet block and she experienced a comfortable rush of pleasure. Even if she got caught (which she wouldn't. Gibbsy had wandered off already towards the sports pavilion where the kids went to smoke); even if Butch found the book and she received the whole treatment including the parent interview, it would be worth it for the bleak bafflement of that glance. Greer Bott was a bit weird and not half as much fun as Helen, but she made a sixth. Her presence underlined the shift of allegiance and what's more she sat in front of Helen so every note, every whispered exchange between members of the group would be intercepted.

Greer would do for now.

Greer herself, sitting at the other end of the row as the new member, was experiencing a different jumble of emotions. One part was unease. Caroline's voice was warm honey, dripping sin and sex into her receptive ear and she knew full well that that was how temptation always presented itself. She had her fingers crossed in her lap to ward it off but with the knowledge that this was kids' stuff, and that the proper response would have been to move away, firmly out of range.

Later . . .

Caroline's voice was soft, enticing. She had done elocution, she was always good at reading aloud, she could read with expression.

Later after they had smoked and talked, he turned to her again. 'It is never as it should be for a woman, the first time,' he said. 'This one will be for you . . .'

Warm, sweet, sticky honey. She ought to move but moving might be too obvious, might mean she would never be asked again. And that was another shameful part of the jumble: pride. Greer was flattered to have been invited. Today at least she was not one of the drips sitting by the music room to eat lunch, like Yvonne Donaldson, reading a book and pretending not to care if she had friends or not. When the note had skittered onto her desk this morning she had assumed it was intended for Helen, but Caroline had shaken her head emphatically and pointed, 'You, You.'

Greer was astounded. Caroline chose her friends from the clever and the confident and the pretty. Ever since primary school she'd watched them gather in their little group for bead swaps or knucklebones or choosing each other for Over Under and Rounders while she, plump and slow, waited in the dwindling line, hoping for nothing more than to be chosen before Yvonne Donaldson who had asthma and couldn't run for toffee so any team with her in was almost bound to lose.

This year, Caroline had seemed a lot nicer. She'd even smiled and asked if she could look at Greer's Life Cycle of the Bee which had a cross-section of a hive and a picture of a bee on a pink flower which she had copied from a magazine.

'Gosh,' said Caroline. 'Did you do all the lettering freehand?'

'Yes,' said Greer. She'd made all the letters out of inter-twining flowers using different coloured pencils, and it did look miles better than the square box letters off the tracing sheet.

'You're really good at art,' Caroline had said. 'Do you mind if I copy?'

Greer said no even though she did a little bit. Art was her only good thing, the only thing for which she was likely to receive a decent mark, whereas Caroline got good marks in everything. But never mind: at least Caroline wasn't being snobby and horrible, at least she was no longer calling her 'Goggle-eyes' or 'Queer' as she had done for years, on and off, right through primary.

Now Caroline had beckoned and Greer had followed. Caroline had offered temptation and Greer had fallen. She had let herself be flattered and through pride, she was being drawn further into thrilling sin: Selena stripped to the waist; Allison doing it, twice in one evening, with Brad; Rodney Harrington tearing the halter top from Betty's willing body. There was also the tingling possibility of being discovered down there behind the toilet block, the risk of detention or suspension or expulsion and the certainty of the Parent Interview. Greer Bott has never done anything so dangerous in her life.

The feelings jumbled and at their base, deep down, there was a kind of stirring as though someone had poked a stick down into sludge the way Auntie Dolly had to from time to time when the drain by the back door blocked.

'Quite a gal, honey,' says Lucas. 'Quite a gal.'
A sick bubble rises in her throat. Pop.

Years and years ago there was a little girl, a bit like Greer, but not quite Greer. She is sitting up in bed waiting for Paul to come and read her a story. It's *Milly Molly Mandy* which is the little girl's favourite. She likes the map at the front and the picture of the family – Muvver, Farver, Grandma and Grandpa, Uncle and Aunty – lined up with the little girl in the middle in her striped dress.

Paul comes into the bedroom in his special suit because he has to go across the road to welcome the eight o'clocks at the Odeon, standing at the top of the stairs sleek and shiny like Clark Gable and saying, 'Good evening, Sir. Good evening, Madam,' and tearing the tickets into exact halves. 'To the right Madam.' 'To the left.'

Paul sits on her bed and they pull the eiderdown up round their knees then he puts his hand on her tickly place and she puts her hand on his and he reads her the story of the Village Fair and Flower Show and when he's finished he gives her a Big Bear Hug squeezing and squeezing so she can hardly breathe, and then she licky lick licks his diddle till the sticky stuff comes, and then it's all right again. Paul gives a little moan and his eyes roll back and when they're shiny blue once more he wipes up every drop with the pointy hanky from his suit pocket. Then he gives her a kiss, says night night sleep tight mind the bugs don't bite and Greer sits up in bed walking her fingers down the lane to Little Friend Susan's house till Mum comes in from the five o'clocks with a chocolate rough or some jubes from the Nibble Nook.

Then Greer can go to sleep with the bedside light left on with its little animals running one behind the other into the Ark and the window slightly opened so she can watch the spider who knits a web each night in one corner. She watches the moths blunder into the frail threads and the spider running out to them on his long black legs to wrap them into parcels for later. Sometimes she lets him. And sometimes she stops him, reaching out to let the moths go free.

They had read all of *Milly Molly Mandy* that winter, before the afternoon when the SnoFreez machine was installed and Mum made her the very first cone. Cream oozed from the nozzle and Greer said, 'Oooh, that's funny, it's just like Paul's sticky stuff,' and her mother's hand went very still. SnoFreez spiralled from the cone to the floor.

'Oh,' said her mother. 'Oh no.'

Greer looked up and her mother's eyes were blue and frightened. 'You don't let anyone touch you,' she said. 'Not down there, do you?'

It was very quiet in the foyer, the empty quiet that hung over the theatre half an hour before the doors opened. Greer had arranged the *Movie Magazine*s in a fan on the counter. This week's star was Rock Hudson.

'No,' she said, five and three-quarters and not quite sure what was wrong but knowing it was something dreadful.

Her mother grabbed a cloth. 'Oh God,' she said. 'What a mess. What a terrible mess.' She wiped and wiped at the cream but it was no good. The mark had stained the carpet, damp and slick and no amount of scrubbing would move it.

The next night Greer said to Paul that she had a sore tummy and didn't want a story, but Paul said what a silly girl, she must have eaten too many lollies and he'd take a look, give her a Big Bear Hug and make it better. She shut her eyes tight and felt the eiderdown tugged back and his hand stroking soft on her then pressing hard between her legs and suddenly Mum was there, home early, and saying so quietly it could have been a dream, 'And what exactly do you think you're doing?'

It was not like this, not like *Peyton Place*. There was no screaming fight, no body in the pig pen, just a kind of creeping chill and a series of unconnected pictures like the shorts for the main feature.

A long journey, without Paul. She dozed with her head on her mother's lap watching the telegraph wires outside the train window smoothly tangling then disentangling as they raced by.

A room with two clocks ticking out of time and a cat like a soft white cushion whose name was Mr Fluff and a harmonium with red velvet pedals and a bed on the sofa and a picture of Jesus above the mantelpiece. Jesus looked just like Alan Ladd. He was sitting in the Botanical Gardens talking to some children.

A woman hugged her close to her spotted pinafore and said what a corker wee kiddie she was and no mistake and wasn't it a blessing the way God made sure the wild flowers were as bonny as the garden rose? The woman smelled of peppermints.

Slowly the pictures fitted together till Greer was Greer Bott who lived with her mother who was called Evie and the woman who was called Auntie Dolly and who had taken Greer's mum into care back in 1932 because it was the Depression and Greer's grandmother had got TB and couldn't cope. Greer Bott lived with Evie and Auntie Dolly at the Casa Rosa Guest House on Milton Street, Home Cooked Breakfast a Speciality. Greer had a father like other children, but he was somewhere in Australia. Handsome as all-get-out: the spitting image of Tyrone Power, and another of Evie's mistakes. Evie had terrible luck with the men.

It was a safe world, safe, though somewhat blurred till she reached Standard One when the teacher discovered that she could not read the board from a distance of more than three feet and suddenly she had pink plastic-rimmed glasses and the world switched to sharp focus. Four eyes, said the other kids. Goggle eyes.

Greer did not mind. It was amazing what you could see through glasses: you could see individual leaves on trees and clouds and the names on street signs. You could see kids when they were on the other side of the classroom or far across the playground. And if you tired of definition, you could take the glasses off and the world reverted to watery imprecision.

She was Greer Bott who was going to be a missionary when she grew up. Ideally she would have liked to be a nun but the Baptists did not have nuns. She had experimented nevertheless, tying a towel firmly round her head so that only her face showed. In *Movie Magazine* it said that this was the true test of timeless beauty which Audrey Hepburn had passed with flying colours in her demanding role as the young novice in *The Nun's Story*. Greer thought maybe the towel made her face look thinner and emphasised her cheekbones, but it couldn't be helped: she could work for the Lord but she'd have to opt for ordinary clothes.

The ambition had had its beginnings soon after the train journey when Evie and Dolly had helped button Greer into her best coat and they had walked along Milton Street to Takaro Park where a circus tent had grown overnight on the soccer field. Inside, there were rows of seats and a choir in white robes behind banks of chrysanthemums singing 'Nearer My God to Thee'. An electric organ throbbing. 'Nearer to Thee.' Then Burton Hutton of the Healing Fire Crusade spoke from a spotlit podium. He sounded like Gary Cooper, good and honest, and his face was handsome. More handsome even than Alan Ladd, but he had been wicked most of his life. He told them how he had been raised with care and love but had lost his way as a young man, following every temptation, falling into alcoholism, lasciviousness and crime. 'Are you also troubled in your heart?' he said, beyond the chrysanthemums in a ring of light, and looking Evie straight in the eye. 'Are you weary of sin?'

Greer sat in the darkness, listening to the crowd as it muttered about her. *Hallelujah. Yes, Lord.* Someone was crying, big heaving breaths. She reached for Evie's hand. Evie's hand gripped hers convulsively. Greer looked up and it was Evie who was crying. Her mouth had fallen open like a pink flap and her cheeks shone with tears and she was sobbing out loud so that everyone could hear, 'Yes. Oh yes. Oh Lord. Oh yes.'

Greer hung on, appalled, till it was time to make a commitment, right here, right now, to burn with the Lord's fire when Evie said, 'Look after her for a moment, will you, Dolly?' and Dolly smiled and nodded. *Thank you, God. Thank you, Jesus.*

When Evie returned from the front she was smiling and Mum once more. She had in her hand the special Healing Fire Bible, a heavy book bound in white vinyl with a signed photo of Burton Hutton in the front.

Evie had been released into New Life.

'Now,' she said to Greer and Dolly in the mornings as they waited in the kitchen for Mr Chambers to finish his porridge. 'Let's see what the Book has for us today.' She took the Bible from the shelf above the sink and let it flop open on the table beside Mr Chambers's sausages and Mr Coombs's rack of toast. She dabbed at the page with one finger, eyes shut.

'Hmmmm,' she said. '"And in every province and in every city wheresoever the king's commandment and his decrees came, the Jews had joy and gladness, a feast and a good day." That sounds nice. I'll make lemon meringue for pudding.'

'And I shall do the cupboards,' said Dolly.

'When I'm calling you-ooh-ooh, oohoohoohoo,' carolled Mr Coombs from the dining room.

Dolly looked round the slide. 'They're ready,' she said. 'Here you are, Greer. You can take Mr Chambers his sausages and ask Mr Coombs if he wants honey or marmalade this morning.'

Mr Coombs travelled in lady's shoes and that wasn't easy with his build, by hokey it wasn't. Mr Chambers represented the Toy and Novelty Co. Once when Greer went into the dining room he was sitting at the table with a bloody bandage and an arrow through his head. Another time he complained because there was a fly in his fried egg and Dolly was mortified until he picked it out with his fingers and it was only plastic after all. He was a real dag.

Greer held the plate in a teatowel so as not to burn her fingers.

'My word,' said Mr Chambers. 'That looks good. But what have we here?' He reached up and took sixpence from Greer's ear.

'A tip for the maid,' he said. 'Like in all the best hotels.' He laughed, round and jelly-pink like Oliver Hardy.

'See?' said her mother when she brought the coin, still warm from being inside her head, back to the kitchen. 'A good day. What did I tell you? The Book's never wrong.'

The Book in the morning and Gentle Jesus meek and mild at night guaranteeing that he would take her soul to heaven if she should die before she woke. A dreadful thought, that: that death could sneak up on you like Grandmother's Footsteps, on tiny chicken-feet, while your eyes were shut. She lay awake for hours fearing it, had to sleep always with the bedside lamp left on and the curtains drawn tightly round the sunroom windows. And the relief of waking, the sun up and Dolly humming hymns as she gave the roses outside Greer's window their early morning drink. The relief to be still alive!

During the day Greer's safety from peril passed into the care of guardian angels. You could not see them either but there was a picture of a little girl hand in hand with one above the dressing table in Dolly's room. Greer's angels were tall and blonde and looked a bit like Randall Scott.

Dolly did her bit too, feeding her up because she was peaky: plain wholesome food and Clement's Tonic by the spoonful, the window jammed open an inch from the top at night, rain or no, and prayer, constant prayer.

Dolly prayed as the spirit prompted, wherever, whenever. She prayed in the garden as she picked off dead heads. She prayed in the dining room, down on her knees on the lino among the tables with their cruet sets of tomato and Worcestershire sauce – though not of course when there were guests present. Prayer was a discreet matter. (Remember the

Pharisees.) She would pause momentarily half way up the Milton Street steps on her way back from the shops. She'd rest the string bag full of groceries on the hand rail and if you looked up her eyes would be shut, her lips moving. Just for a few seconds while Dolly had a wee word with the Lord.

'Lord, we crave thy blessing. We beseech thee for thy help in time of trouble and that thy plan for us will be made plain. Amen.'

Using the special God words: beseech, crave, thee and thy.

She did not always know why she was suddenly prompted to prayer. Greer found it embarrassing to begin with but she became used to it and simply sat and waited, perched on the steps eating the little box of raisins Dolly had bought her for being a good helper.

'Now, I wonder what that was all about?' said Dolly, gathering up the shopping.

When they got home, sooner or later, it would be explained. Once it was Dora Jones down the road at the Braemar who had had a giddy spell. It was interesting that the Lord had chosen Dolly to be his instrument since under normal circumstances Dora might have been considered competition. The Braemar had a better view of the harbour and was popular with the holidaymakers – though Mr Chambers had told Dolly in the strictest confidence and between you, me and the bedpost that while the Braemar was clean enough, there was no comparison when it came to the breakfast: just two little strips of bacon and an egg and never fried bread and a tomato like at the Casa Rosa and he knew for a fact which table his boots would be under!

Still, Dolly had prayed for Dora and she came right again in a day or two, no harm done. Just as Bert Dombrowski the milkman recovered after slipping with a crate on the Milton steps while making deliveries one frosty morning and Tai Te Moana who brought the coal survived that terrible accident when his truck struck a train out on Highway One and he was pinned under the tray for over an hour.

Dolly's prayers always had a purpose.

Dolly prayed for Greer and Evie too and under her regime they flourished, both growing pink and plump. Plumper, Greer had begun to feel, than was strictly desirable.

Greer went to school on weekdays and helped with the shopping and the meals and the cleaning at the Casa Rosa. On Sundays she went to Sunday school and then walked to the Gardens with Evie and Dolly, to play on the swings and feed the ducks when she was little and now, to admire the flowers and have an ice cream at the Tea House.

Evie cooked and cleaned and went to church and prayer group where she repented the indiscretions of her youth and offered herself up, cleansed and pure, to the Lord, her one remaining weakness a fondness for Hollywood.

Dolly did not really approve. She said those movie stars did not set a good example but Evie said some of them did: they had benefits for all sorts of charities and Doris Day for example had donated thousands of dollars to cancer research and anyway, you couldn't call going to the pictures wicked could you? It wasn't like pride or covetousness, was it? And surely the Lord wanted his children to be joyful? Saturday night at the movies, a choc dip and a seat in the front row of the balcony made her joyful and surely there could be no harm in it? She never went to horrors or murders, only the good ones, musicals, historicals and such.

Dolly patted her arm, seeing her so intent, and said she was probably right and she, Dolly, was old-fashioned. The young ones had the right to a bit of fun. Evie was back home, that was the main thing, safe and sound praise God, with the little one who had been named after Greer Garson in *Goodbye Mr Chips* which was one of Evie's favourite films. 'Now, Greer,' said Dolly, 'play us a tune.' And Greer, who was having lessons from Mrs Chadwick up on Keats Street, sat at the harmonium beneath the picture of Jesus and played Dolly's favourites: 'Love Divine All Loves Excelling', 'Onward Christian Soldiers', 'Abide With Me Fast Falls The Eventide'. She pumped furiously at the red velvet pedals and tugged out all the stops – the ten-foot diapason, the tympanum and the celeste – and Dolly pulled the kitchen slide open so they could hear while they did the dishes.

'Onward Christian soldiers, marching as to war . . .'

Greer felt good when she played the harmonium: pure and good right through. Sitting in the sun behind the Girls' High toilet block she was less certain. God had her every thought and action, however secret, under direct scrutiny. He could detect pride and corruption. Greer removed her glasses. That way, she felt slightly less visible. She arranged a compromise: she would stay and listen since leaving would give offence and that would be wrong. A sort of unkindness. And in compensation, she would a. go without pudding (and it was lemon meringue pie tonight which was her favourite) and she would b. ride all the way up Spenser Street on the way home without stopping and she would c. voluntarily give Mum a hand with the guests' toilet. Mr Coombs was getting a bit shaky and missed occasionally. ('Poor old thing,' said Evie, wringing out the mop. 'It's so much easier for us women to stay clean.')

Surely that would be penance enough?

Then Caroline squealed. A sudden shriek. She tumbled from the bench.

She was writhing on the ground, struggling with the neck of her blouse.

'She's having a fit,' thought Greer. Like the woman possessed by demons. A pig would squeeze from her body and run across the basketball court to the sea at Friendly Bay and drown. God had seen her after all and decided to cast down his wrath upon them. She glanced up uneasily at the sky above the gym roof. But Margie was laughing.

'Now give us your cheese scone, Caroline,' she was saying. 'Go on.'

Caroline screamed. 'Get it off! Get it off.' Clawing at her school tie, at her collar.

'Scone first,' said Margie.

'In my bag,' yelled Caroline. 'Now GET IT OFF!'

Margie put her hand on Caroline's twitching shoulder. 'Hold still, dumbie,' she said. 'All this fuss over a teeny weeny insect.'

She pulled a weta from the neck of Caroline's blouse. A huge weta. Two inches long at least. It swam between her fingers on empty air, its skinny legs waving frantically. Margie held it a second then flipped it at Raeleen. 'Ughhh,' squealed Raeleen. 'Ughhh.' And flicked it from her skirt onto Heather who batted it squealing at Kathy who shook her head so it fell to the ground by Greer's foot.

Ughhh, yuk, say the girls. *Ughhh, gross. Don't let it near me*.

Greer looked down at the insect where it lay on its back pedalling furiously and she squealed too since all the others were, though she wasn't really bothered at all. She didn't mind insects. She liked watching them busy about their hunting and flying at her bedroom window each night.

The weta had round, protuberant eyes. She wondered what it was seeing as it lay there: probably a whole ring of girls in thousands of tiny pieces, like a kaleidoscope, like the bee's eye she had drawn for her Life Cycle poster.

'Ughhh,' she squealed though, not to be left out.

'Don't squash it,' said Margie. 'It's too good to waste. I know what: I'll put it in Butch's bag. Serve her right.' She leaned over and picked the insect up.

Oooh Margie, say the girls. *Oooh, she'll freak, she'll kill you. You'd never dare*.

'Go on,' said Raeleen. 'Go on. I bet you an iceblock you'd never dare.'

'You're on,' said Margie.

Margie liked slugs. And spiders. And worms. And murders and accidents and diseases. When Caroline went to Margie's house it was to read comics. When Margie went to Caroline's house she looked out the medical textbooks stored on the shelf behind the sofa in the lounge. Tucked in behind the Sanderson print she examined photographs of throats blackened by diphtheria, the characteristic swellings of von Recklinghausen's disease, illustrations of rashes and congenital abnormalities. At the dairy she read the *Picture Posts* and *Truths* and selected the most disgusting stories to tell on Monday mornings.

'Hey, did you know there was this woman who murdered her husband then left his body locked in the house for two weeks while she went away on holiday and they found him because of the flies covering the window? Fact.'

'Hey, did you know that in Africa they sew up the women's bums so they have this tiny hole to pee through? Fact.'

Ughhh, said the girls. *Yuk. That's disgusting.*

Margie sits back, satisfied.

'Do you know,' she said now, putting the weta into Raeleen's lunchbox with some grass and a couple of slaters for company, 'that insects are the only thing that would survive an atomic bomb? And afterwards they get huge on the radiation so if there's a war there'll be these enormous wetas, like twenty feet high. Amazing, eh?'

Caroline shuddered in spite of herself. She honestly truly hated insects. When she squealed it was not play-acting. Spiders in the bath, slaters on tree trunks, night beetles and moths blundering round a room at night, mosquitoes in tents hovering overhead with their high-pitched whine – they all drove her frantic. She lay in bed with the blankets drawn round her head because she had read somewhere that moths were attracted to pale surfaces thinking they were the face of the moon. She never lay on the grass because Margie had told her once about the kid who lay on the ground and an earwig crawled in his ear and chewed its way through his brain laying eggs on the way so that he had these awful headaches and a couple of weeks later all these baby earwigs crawled out from under his eyelids. Fact.

Caroline had a horror of their plastic-coated skittering multitudes.

Margie had always laughed at her for it, refusing to believe it was serious.

'Go on,' she'd say, proffering beetle or spider. 'Touch it, sookie. Honestly, it won't bite. In Australia they have these spiders that can kill you in five minutes. They live under toilet seats so you always have to check before you sit down. But here there's only katipos and you only get those at the beach and you can tell them because they've got a skull mark on their backs – a tiny red skull. And this isn't a katipo so go on: hold it.'

Caroline tried, but she couldn't. She honestly couldn't. It was her weak spot. And Margie knew it.

The others were giggling now, urging Margie to find some spiders, a few beetles, another weta to add to the zoo destined for Butch's handbag. A moment ago, Caroline had them round her listening as she dealt out the good bits from *Peyton Place*. Now, no one will meet her eye.

What an idiot she must have looked, lying on the ground screaming. And worst of all, Helen Brassington had noticed. Caroline could hear her clearly across the basketball court and she was laughing. She, like Margie, knew the fear. She had seen Caroline weep rather than dislodge a cobweb in the playhouse in the mulberry.

Caroline stood up quickly and straightened her collar.

'That's pathetic,' she said to Margie, who was deflecting a row of ants from the toilet wall into Raeleen's lunchbox. 'Butch won't notice or even care. It's kids' stuff, putting creepie crawlies into people's bags.'

'It worked on you,' said Raeleen, who was getting fed up with Caroline. She always wanted to be the boss, always had to be in charge. 'You were really scared,' she said. 'Hey, Margie, have some more ants.' She dropped an apple core coated with black dots in with the weta.

'So?' said Caroline. 'Everyone's frightened of something.'

'Not me,' said Raeleen.

'Speeches,' said Caroline. 'You're scared stiff of doing speeches. Last time you shook so hard you dropped your notes. And no one could see what you were so frightened of. It was only us you were talking to, not assembly or anything and you talk to us every day without your knees knocking.'

Raeleen said nothing in reply. It didn't pay to tangle with Caroline when she was in a mood. And she was right, of course, about the speeches. Raeleen was terrified of speaking in front of the class, had hated it ever since primary school and, 'Good-morning-boys-and-girls, today-I-am-going-to-tell-you-about-my-pet.' She had stood then with her head bowed, looking at the floor, while children whom she knew but who had suddenly become completely alien squirmed and giggled and whispered, 'Look. She's shivering.' And eventually Miss McKinnon took pity and sighed and said, 'Very well, Raeleen. You may sit down. But do try a little harder next time.' And Richard Addison leapt up instead and did his talk on dinosaurs where he wrote all the names, spelt correctly, on the board.

When Butch announced a two-minute speech please gels, on the subject of school uniforms, equal marks for content and presentation, Raeleen had been paralysed with terror. For days beforehand she had been unable to sleep, her stomach had ached and on speech morning she had tried to get off school, tried to fabricate a cold. But Dad had felt her forehead, said, 'Come on Rainbow. Up and over. You'll feel better once you've given it a go.'

She didn't. She had dropped her notes, burst into tears and run from the room. One mark for content and a half mark for presentation. The lowest by far in the whole class. Even Caroline had not asked her what mark she got.

The insect hunters had gone quiet. Caroline was snappish and no one felt like being the next to be bitten. Margie peered into the lunchbox.

'I think I'll call the weta Meryl,' she said. 'Because it's got popped-out eyes like Meryl Leadbetter's. See?'

Meryl Leadbetter had a goitre, a thick puffy neck and eyes like marbles which bulged spectacularly and seemed in imminent danger of falling from their sockets entirely. She worked at Forget-Me-Not Florists, driving about town in a pink Standard to deliver bouquets and wreaths.

'That's what you get,' said Mrs Miller and Mrs Carstairs and Mrs Smiley and the other mothers when their children poked listlessly at their cod-in-wallpaper-paste. 'That's what you get if you don't eat fish.'

'I'll call it Meryl and it can be my pet,' said Margie. 'Do you know there was this woman in New York who kept a snake for a pet, a boa constrictor, and one night it got out and crawled down the pipes eating rats and stuff and it got out of a heating vent in this apartment and swallowed a baby? Fact.'

Ughhh, said the girls.

Margie was showing off. How stupid Caroline's fear seemed, how trivial. She pressed the point home.

'It's a pity there aren't snakes in New Zealand,' she said. 'Else I could have one for a pet. It'd be cleaner than a mouse and I could feed it squashed hedgehogs off the road, eh?'

Yuk, said the girls. *Stop it, Margie. Don't, Margie.*

'Do you know boa constrictors don't even chew?' she said. 'They just stretch their jaws wider and wider and sort of suck. That's how the family in New York found their baby. It was just a baby-shaped lump in the snake's neck.'

We've just had our lunch, said the girls. *Shut up, Margie.*

Caroline could stand it no longer.

'Huh,' she said. 'That's nothing. There was this other baby in America that got put in the oven by the babysitter.'

The girls looked up, interested.

'These people hired a new babysitter from an agency to look after their baby while they were at the pictures and when they got home they found it in the oven with some potatoes and onions.'

Eeeeh, said the girls, thrilled. *That's terrible, that's awful.*
Caroline smiled.

'It's true,' she said. 'My father told me.'

He didn't. But he was a doctor. He would know about things like that. It sounded more authentic.

Margie prodded at Meryl. Horror was her speciality, not Caroline's. Meryl waggled her feelers.

'She's so sweet,' said Margie. 'I don't know what you're so scared of Caroline. She's really cute.' She lifted Meryl out.

'Go on,' she said. 'Touch her.'

Caroline ignored her.

'The babysitter had the carving knife out on the table and a plate and everything,' she said. Hopefully. But Margie was not to be deflected. She waved Meryl slowly back and forth in front of Caroline's face.

'You ought to touch it,' she said. 'It's the only way to get over being frightened.'

Caroline drew back. 'I don't have to,' she said. 'I don't have to if I don't want to.'

'It's like riding,' said Margie. 'You know: how you have to get straight back on if you fall off? You have to just go ahead and do whatever it is you're frightened of. Hey, someone, grab her hand.'

She was serious. Caroline tried to pull away, but Raeleen (who will never forgive her, ever, for the speech) had her in a firm and slightly sticky grip and then Margie was sitting on top of her with the weta wriggling in her hand. Caroline squirmed beneath her soundlessly.

'Get her legs, Kathy,' said Margie. 'Now calm down Caroline. There's nothing to be scared of. I read about this in a magazine. It's a sort of therapy where they tie people down and give them electric shocks while they show them pictures of naked women and stuff except we won't be able to do the shocks . . .'

'Get off!' yelled Caroline and, 'Stop it!' said Heather. 'Let her up. It's not funny any more.'

'Bitch! Cow!' sobbed Caroline, the weta an inch from her face, its goitre eyes huge, its legs bristling. She kicked with all her strength, twisting and shoving so that Kathy fell back saying, 'Owww,' and Margie's skinny body bashed against the bench painfully and Raeleen tumbled forward cracking her head on Caroline's.

'Let me up,' hissed Caroline and jumped to her feet.

'Are you all right?' said Greer. 'Here. I'll give your head a rub.'

'Leave me alone, Queer,' said Caroline, shrugging her aside, so pink, so fat and stupid. Greer retreated, her goggle eyes damp and silly and hurt.

'Yuk,' said Margie. Meryl had squashed in her hand to yellow custard though its back legs still waved aimlessly. 'Now look what you've done, Caroline.'

Caroline was breathing hard. 'That wasn't funny,' she said.

Margie wiped her hand on a hank of grass. 'Yes it was,' she said. 'And it's true about the therapy. It's silly to be scared of something so teensy.'

'OK,' said Caroline. 'OK: I'll touch one of your stupid wetas. I'll touch a whole boxful if you like. I'll even let you put them down my collar. Just so long as you do something you're scared of too. OK?'

Margie snapped the lunchbox shut. 'All right,' she said. Cool. Unworried.

Caroline was spitting mean.

'The cliff,' she said. 'I dare you to climb the cliff again. You froze last time because you were scared and that's why you slipped. You couldn't look up like we told you and you fell. So: dare you to have another go.'

Silence.

No one ever talked about the accident, but they all, with the exception of Greer, remembered it. The Incredible Six lined up along the cliff edge at Bushy Beach looking back down at Margie's face pinched and white, her fingers fumbling for a sweaty grip on the crumbling orange rock and twenty feet beneath her the thin ribbon of sand, the rocks and the dumping surf. 'Just put your hand to the right,' Caroline had called leaning over as far as she could from the safe place at the top. 'Go on. It's easy.'

And Margie whispering, 'I can't, I can't,' before the sickening slide backwards down the cliff face.

They had thought at first that she was dead, she had lain so still.

'Everyone has to do what they're most scared of,' said Caroline. 'So: climb the cliff again and then I'll touch your stupid insects.'

In the silence the group realise suddenly that the basket-ball court has emptied. The bell must have rung.

'OK?' said Caroline. It was an ultimatum.

'Sure,' said Margie under the bold strawberry-blonde helmet. 'I'll do it tonight. After tea.'

'This weekend,' said Caroline.

'No,' said Margie. 'I've got to work in the shop. Tonight. After tea.'

'In front of witnesses,' said Caroline.

'If you like,' said Margie.

Caroline turned to the others. 'You've all got to come,' she said. 'You can tell your parents you're coming to my place to do homework or something. Quarter to seven at the Shelley Street corner. OK?'

OK, said the others. *Yeah*, OK.

It was all organised.

Greer caught up with Margie at the top of Spenser Street after school that afternoon. Margie was leaning on a garden fence waiting for the Waikerikeri bus and the boy who looked exactly like James Dean who sat in the back seat, glowering and sullen, as the bus farted and wheezed up the hill. He always looked at her and his gaze was hard, straight and knowing. She had asked Jan Te Awa who went on the same bus what his name was, in a casual kind of way as they waited for the drink fountain one lunchtime. Jan said Darryl Hinkley and yuk, he's a sleaze. He got this girl out at Waikerikeri pregnant when he was only fourteen. Darryl Hinkley. Brother of Mervyn, who hung out with Jail Bates on Friday nights at the Apollo.

Margie looked up at those cold eyes each afternoon, that slick black brush of hair, that white face pocked with acne and her stomach clenched.

She waited for him now at the corner with her hat off and her hair back-combed so stiffly it was immobile in the wind, and tore the wrapping from her ice-block. Usually she was able to stand talking to Heather who lived just round the corner in Tennyson Street but Heather had thought she was being mean to Caroline this afternoon and anyway she had to go into town, she said: to the library, though it was really to buy bread and animal biscuits. They probably weren't very good for you; they certainly didn't appear on the Principal Food Groups poster at the dental clinic but at least Shona could be counted on to eat a giraffe with pink icing for her lunch and that was better than nothing.

So Margie stood alone at the corner and hoped it wouldn't look obvious. It was much easier with a companion. That way you could chat and laugh and look up, taken by surprise, as the bus rattled past. This way, Darryl would be sure to guess she had been waiting.

She peeled back sticky ice-block paper and dropped it on the footpath. ('Litter, Margie. Tsk tsk!') Raeleen had bought the ice-block for her at the school dairy and it was bright blue, a new flavour. It tasted somewhere between jelly-baby and sick. She was not sure if she liked it or not. In the distance, down by the railway crossing, she could see the Waikerikeri bus, gunning smoke and preparing for the assault on the Spenser Street hill. And ahead of it, biking the whole way up with scarlet legs and straining face, was Greer Bott.

'Hey, Greer,' said Margie. 'You trying to get fit?'

Greer looked up. Sweat made her glasses misty. 'Sort of,'

she said and, grateful for the excuse, got off. (Will that do, God? I was almost at the top. Will that do?)

The bus was climbing now, grinding in low gear.

'Hey,' said Margie, licking Tropic Blue dribbles from her wrist, 'did you see Butch's face this afternoon? Wasn't it a dag?' She laughed. (Caroline had told her once that she was lucky: she had such even teeth and no fillings, and her smile was her best feature.) 'When she put her hand in the bag I nearly died.'

Greer laughed too, though to be strictly truthful the insects had been something of a flop. Margie had put them in Butch's bag while she was sharpening a pencil, just dropped them in the open flap, and Butch found them half an hour before the bell. She had put her hand in and drawn out her hanky which had a spider and a black beetle clinging to it. But she had simply flipped them both into the trees outside the window and carried right on giving them history notes. It was just the same stuff they did every year, the New Zealand stuff about Hone Heke and Waitangi.

Sniff, went Butch. *Sniff, sniff*. The wattle tree by the window made her nose run each spring, but she was able to blow her nose and talk at the same time. The class watched fascinated.

Kororareka. Hobson. Samuel Marsden.

A brief pause while she examined the contents of the hanky narrowly.

1840. Edward Gibbon Wakefield. Friendly tribes.

The hanky was returned, beetle-free, spiderless, to the bag.

'Margaret Miller,' said Butch. 'Please repeat what I have just said.'

The insects were unfortunately a flop. But, 'Oh,' said Greer as the Waikerikeri bus roared past, 'she just freaked!' She laughed co-operatively but Margie was not really listening. She was tossing up between laughter (her best feature) and cool disdain. The Waikerikeri bus coughed diesel and turned on the Main South Road and Margie glanced up, cool, disinterested, at the back window.

He wasn't there!

James Dean wasn't there!

Greer was saying something about Margie having a lot of guts to do it, she'd never dare, not in a million years, and Margie was scanning faces. All that back-combing for nothing. And suddenly, there he was. A pale face leaning over from the far corner. Darryl Hinkley looked down from a mass of grey and black uniforms and gave her one cool unsmiling wink. He lifted his hand for the most understated of waves. He had noticed her.

Margie was not quite sure how to proceed from here, but she was definitely on her way. One rebel had noted another.

'The beach,' Greer was saying. 'You're not going to do it, are you?' Pink and sweaty and concerned. She hadn't been there when Margie fell but she had signed Margie's plaster cast along with the rest of Standard Four at South Primary and she had heard all about it. Everybody had heard about it.

'I've got to,' said Margie. 'Do you want a bite of my ice-block? It's melting.'

'Thanks,' said Greer, sopping up Tropic Blue with her soft tongue.

'And anyway, it'll be worth it just to see Caroline squeal tomorrow,' said Margie. Right now, she could climb several cliffs, quarries hundreds of feet high, soar up them like a gull in flight.

'Aren't you scared?' said Greer, and Margie fell to earth, remembered the moment when she tipped her head back and looked up as everyone said she must, and the clouds seemed to be rolling over the cliff edge where her friends' faces were a worried rim of white and she became dizzy. Lost her balance. Fell.

Her neck prickled.

'Nah,' she said. But it would be nice, she decided suddenly, to have Greer Bott there. Pink, plump, dependable Greer. A sort of collie-dog, guard-dog, person. 'Are you going to come?' She asked it casually, twisting a kiss curl into a circle on one cheek. 'I don't know,' said Greer. 'I don't think I'd be allowed.'

'Fib,' said Margie. 'Say you've got to work on a project over at my place. I'll back you up if anyone checks.'

The bus was a distant red speck out along the main road. Margie stuffed her hat, a flat panama sandwich, onto the carrier and scooted her bike.

'I'll meet you there,' she said. 'Quarter to seven. I've got to go and fold papers now. Keep the ice-block if you like. I think it tastes like puke.'

She biked off up Tennyson Street and Greer turned towards the Casa Rosa, sweat running down her back, Tropic Blue rivulets on her arm and temptation raging in her soul. How would she ever get out of the house at 6.30? How could she avoid telling an out-and-out lie? Her second major sin of the day loomed and she hadn't even finished paying for the first. She felt faintly sick and it was only partly because of the ice-block.

As it turned out, getting away from the Casa Rosa was easy because Dolly's prayer group was having a pot luck tea so she bustled out at six carrying a bacon-and-egg pie, leaving Evie who was coming down with a migraine. There was only Mr Chambers booked in tonight and his tummy was playing up so Evie had made him just poached egg for his tea and a little toast while her vision split into dancing speckles then the triangular cross-sections which tell her she's in for a beauty.

She had been expecting it all day. She often had migraines on days like these when the weather changed in late afternoon and the clouds piled up like purple cushions on the hills to the northwest, driven in by a sharp wind and heavy with thunder. And the Book had said this morning, 'And they shall look unto the earth and behold trouble and darkness, dimness and anguish and they shall be driven into darkness.' So it wasn't unexpected and she had been able to get the tea organised and the washing in and folded and as the triangles dissolved into complete black-out she was able to walk away from a tidy kitchen, but carefully, as if treading on broken glass, to the cool gloom of her room for a lie-down.

'Don't worry,' said Greer. 'I'll dish up.' She gave Mr Chambers his egg. He picked at it without enthusiasm. He stirred some bicarb into a glassful of water. 'Job like mine,' he said, as the water fizzed, 'it's high pressure. All go go go.' He swallowed, pushed back his chair, belched once, seriously with his hand on his heart, then went through to the guests' lounge to listen to *Pick-a-Box*. Greer could hear Jack Redfern – 'Lie down on the balloon! Yes, that's it. Lie down!' and the static of broadcast laughter as she washed up and put out the teapot and a couple of gingernuts for Mr Chambers' supper. She did her homework rapidly at the kitchen table: ten words containing anti-, against, two maths problems (Andrew is planting cabbages. He has a garden plot measuring 12 foot by 12 foot . . .).

'So what'll it be?' boomed Jack Redfern from the lounge. 'What should she do, Ashburton?'

Greer wrestled with temptation. Down the hall her mother was a still muffled figure on the bed.

'Would you like a cold facecloth?' said Greer.

'Mmmm,' said her mother from the deep well of spinning darkness.

Greer smoothed the cloth against her mother's forehead, trying to channel the power. She'd done it a few times, the first time on the day Mr Fluff got snuffles. She had petted him and the minute her hand touched his fur he had perked up and Dolly had said she had the gift of healing. 'What a blessing!' she said. 'After all the pain of her birth!' She knelt on the carpet and hugged Greer close. 'So you've been put on earth to make people well,' she said. 'Praise God.'

Greer had had some success since with Evie's migraines,

but tonight she was distracted, corrupted, an empty vessel. She hadn't biked quite to the top of Spenser Street. There had been no lemon meringue to renounce, and she could think only of Margie Miller waiting for her at the corner. Her hands remained numb. There was no sensation of the spirit moving within her.

'So, from Ashburton, it's good night, New Zealand,' said Jack Redfern from the lounge. Evie stirred.

'Don't worry,' she said. 'This will pass. Have you done your homework?' Greer took a deep breath. 'Yes,' she said, but (with fingers firmly crossed in her lap) she had to go round to see Margie Miller to get some stuff for her history project and was that all right? She'd be back before dark. Needles pierced Evie's temples. 'Mmmmmm,' she said.

Just to be on the safe side, Greer took her bag. She'd ask Margie for some old magazines to cut up for a collage to cover her new social studies book and that way she would not have told an out-and-out lie. Maybe God would let her away with that too.

Margie was waiting at the corner and Caroline and Kathy and Raeleen were at Shelley Street and Heather caught up with them half way down Chatterton Road. She had her sister on the carrier of her bike. 'Sorry,' she said. 'Mum and Dad have gone to bowls and I couldn't leave Shona on her own.' Shona sucked her thumb and twisted a strand of hair round one finger. They had left Dad's dinner in the oven on low because he had not come home, and Heather had told Shona they were going out. They weren't to tell Dad afterwards where they had been, just that they'd gone to Caroline's for a projeck. Shona said it over for practice sitting on the carrier behind her sister's safe and solid back. A projeck. To Caroline's for a projeck.

Raeleen had on her track pants and looked uneasily over her shoulder whenever cars passed. 'Dad thinks I'm at training,' she said. 'But I've told Rowley I've pulled a muscle. If I'm caught I'm in deep trouble.'

Kathy said, 'Me too, if my mother checks,' and Caroline said if anyone tried to ring her house they wouldn't be able to get through because it was evening surgery and her sister Penny would be making the most of the opportunity to use the phone to talk to her boyfriend while Dad was busy and Mum was on reception. 'So don't worry. Anyway, they won't check.'

They had better not. Or that was the end of the pony, even if she were first in class and Most Popular Girl. Caroline biked down Chatterton Road wondering how she had let herself get into this situation. It was ridiculous. All afternoon she had been regretting it, wishing she could back out, but it would be hopeless. She would look silly if she said now, 'Look, let's stop. Let's go back to my place and we can all have vanilla milkshakes and forget the cliff.'

Impossible. She had to go through with the climb now and risk the pony and all because of Margie Miller. Yet again. She could hear her mother's voice: 'Whenever you are around that girl, Caroline, there is nothing but trouble. She is a bad influence.'

When they were little, there had been the Poop Tree. That was Margie's idea. She had started it. Caroline had been quite happy pretending that the low swoopy branch on the mulberry was a horse, a horse with wings, a flying horse. Then, one afternoon, Margie had sat on it with her pants down and yelled 'Bombs away!' dropping a small brown poop with a satisfying *splat!* onto the long grass below and the game had started. The rude risky game which came to an end the day Margie lost her balance and fell backwards and they couldn't clean her up with the hose, not properly, and Caroline's mother had said Caroline was to stay away from that child, she was not a nice little girl.

Her mother much preferred Helen Brassington who never suggested making witch's potions out of mud and Arpège and pee and feeding it in spoonfuls to Hugh who was only four, telling him it would help him to swim so he jumped into the deep end of the pool and nearly drowned. Who didn't suggest stealing the ribbons off the wreaths on a grave in the cemetery. Or teach Hugh to sing *bugger bugger bum*. Or steal money from the plate in church instead of putting it in, just to see if God would notice. And here Caroline was again: biking down a dangerously deserted gravel road with a thunderstorm imminent, to a beach where everyone knew couples came to do it late at night, through a pine plantation where everyone knew funny men lurked.

She was risking a soaking, rape, possibly murder and definitely a severe telling off and she would never never have the pony she had wished for for years and all because of Margie Miller. Her bike skidded in the potholed gravel at the end of Chatterton Road and, 'Damn!' said Caroline. 'Damn damn. Bugger bugger bum.'

Behind them, over the mountains, there was the flash of wildfire and a distant rumbling.

The road wound through the pines which muffled all sound, then out and down a series of zigzags to the beach, which was backed by African thorn and high cliffs, scarlet in the intense light of sunset filtered through purple cloud. They dumped their bikes where grass faded to sand. Margie looked Caroline full in the eye for the first time that evening.

'OK?' she said.

'OK,' said Caroline. Cool. Unruffled.

But what if Margie falls?

Margie took off her jacket and slung it over the handlebars of her Raleigh. She walked to the base of the cliff. The witnesses trailed behind.

'This is so dumb,' said Heather. 'If she kills herself you'll be to blame, Caroline.'

Caroline said accidents never happened twice in the same place, that's what her mother said. And anyway, Margie would probably chicken out, she wasn't as tough as she liked everyone to think she was.

'Want to bet?' said Heather.

Margie was ahead, scrambling now over the boulders which littered the foot of the cliff. She was not seeing rock or smashed shell or clay but concentrating all her attention on the box on the dressing table at home which currently contained the wetas, four beetles, some slugs and a handful of slaters. Caroline Carstairs was going to have the lot down her back tomorrow. She wished now that she had insisted on eating as part of the deal: *nobody likes me, everybody hates me, I'm going down the garden to eat worms . . .*

Hand over hand, searching for a grip on the rock face.

Up close the rock was webbed with ice plant roots, pink flowers and plump leaves which crushed to green slime under her fingers. She looked at the rock, at the flowers, she did not look down.

. . . long thin slimy ones, short fat fuzzy ones, ooey gooey ooey gooey worms . . .

'Please God,' prayed Greer, 'don't let her fall. Preserve her in thy hands.' ('Preserve' was good. 'Thy' was good. It was important to use the right words.) 'Keep her safe, we beseech thee.'

Margie was six feet up now and working her way along a diagonal crevice, feet prodding at the face for a toehold.

'See?' said Heather. 'I told you she wouldn't back out.'

Margie crept up. Ten feet. Twelve feet. At her back the sea was loud, dashing and dumping onto steeply shelving sand. The rock of the cliffs was deep red and chocolate brown. It was quite interesting, actually. They'd done a field trip here in Standard Four when they were doing volcanoes. They'd stood at the top of the Cape, deep among the pines, and Mr Myles had pointed out the hollow which had once been a seething mass of molten rock. It was gentle now and lined with yellow pine needles. They'd walked along the beach, safe with their notebooks in their satchels and a picnic lunch, and Mr Myles had pointed out the lava dyke at the far end, where the beach turned into Chatterton Road and the pillow lava where the rocks had hit the sea and bubbled, like toffee he said. Exactly like toffee, setting solid.

Margie made herself think about that. Up close, the rock was pitted and jagged with a million billion minute explosive craters. She pressed her fingers into a crack and pulled herself onto a shelf. In her arms tiny ropes had begun to jump and twitch. She paused, her arms spread wide, her face pressed against rock still warm from its day in the spring sun. She could hear the sea, and her heart thumping, and her breath, an uneven heavy gasping. She balanced on her toes and for just a second, she looked up. A cloud like a heavy cushion hung above the cliff, above her head.

'Margie,' called someone. 'Margie. Are you all right?' Her voice was tiny like a bird's cry. Far, far away. Far, far below.

The cushion moved above her and Margie felt panic, terror in a great prickling rush covering her body. She clung. She shut her eyes. She willed her breath to steady.

'Dear God,' thought Greer fifteen feet below on the sand, 'dear dear God, please don't let her fall, and I'll clean up next time Mr Fluff has an accident.'

Mr Fluff was getting old. Like Mr Coombs. Greer usually pretended not to notice Mr Fluff's furtive puddles behind the sofa, the black sausage curled under the occasional table, leaving them to Dolly who bent stiffly from arthritic hips and said he was a naughty boy, he was indeed, as she scrubbed at the carpet.

'I'll clean up, just don't let anything awful happen. Please,' prayed Greer, uneasily aware, however, that her prayers were suspect, that she hadn't biked quite to the top, there had been no pudding to forego, and she had compounded the debt by telling her mother a kind of lie.

'Margie?' called Heather.

'I don't like heights either,' said Raeleen. She knew just how this felt. She remembered the first time her brother had dared her to dive from the top board and she had frozen too, in her new togs, in front of all the people at the Queen Elizabeth Pool. She remembered her brother and his friends chanting. *Jump! Jump!* And all those faces turned up toward her, a pale dotted rim to that tiny patch of blue miles below where she daren't bellyflop or she would wind herself.

'Margie?' called Heather. 'Come down. Come on. It doesn't matter.'

Silence.

'She's going to fall again,' said Kathy. 'This is exactly what happened last time. She's going to slip.'

Margie was a white patch on the cliff face.

'Oh shit,' said Caroline. 'Oh shit.' And somewhere a pony 14.2hh and part-Arab, kicked up its heels and beat a swift retreat.

Wildfire flashed close by. And suddenly Caroline was running, scrambling up over the boulders, climbing fast, and Raeleen was behind her.

'Come on,' she said. And Kathy followed. Heather said, 'Stay here, Shona, sit on the sand till I get back. Find some nice shells.' And then they were all climbing, knowing their own ways up from all the times before, the handholds and footholds, the places where you had to lean or stretch, because it was really quite easy once you knew how. Greer followed so as not to be left out. Maybe the cliff would make up for not biking the full distance.

Margie was sweating, her eyes tight shut and her body pressed against the rock. 'Not far to go now,' said Caroline as she came alongside. She reached over and took Margie's cold right hand. 'Here, hang onto this and shift your weight.' She curved Margie's fingers round a knob on the rock and they gripped like a bird's claw.

'And put your foot here,' said Raeleen, who was on the ledge beneath. Margie moaned but she lifted her foot and found the hold.

Thunder rolled overhead.

'I hope it's not going to rain,' said Caroline in the bright conversational tone she normally reserved for grown-ups. 'Not with only six feet to go.' She guided Margie's hand to a crevice.

'Did you know,' she said, 'that you can tell how far off the rain is by counting the seconds between the lightning and the boom? (Put your hand a little to the right. That's it.) You count a second to every mile.'

Flash went the lightning. One elephant. Two elephants. Three elephants. Four. Boom went the thunder.

Heather looked back midway and Shona had stayed on the beach. Her face turned up to her like a daisy.

Greer thought, *this rock is exactly like hokey pokey, it looks like the middle of a Crunchie bar.* She was puffing and wishing she was fit and she'd scraped her fingers and they stung.

Kathy climbed and thought Dramatic Clifftop Rescue. Girls Come to Aid of Panic-stricken Friend. It would make a good movie.

Margie moved slowly, hand over hand, another few inches.

'That one was four miles away,' said Caroline. 'I hope you've got a coat because we'll get soaked going home.' A branch brushed her head. They were almost at the part where the cliff shelved less steeply, and in the dry clay, spiny plants grew, gorse and thistles. Raeleen guided Margie's foot to a ledge and they dragged themselves over the last few feet, on hands and knees, crawling now, grabbing at roots, small avalanches of clay and loose stones tumbling beneath their hands. Then they were there. Up on the thin grass at the top where sheep tracks wound away into the plantation and the wind tugged at them fretfully carrying droplets of rain and the sound of it blended with sheep bleat and blood beat *kerthump kerthump*. They lay on their backs beneath purple clouds piled up like an eiderdown. They were shaking all over.

The others arrived – Kathy, then Heather, then Greer, heads down, scrabbling up and away from the edge. Margie was shaking, and Caroline reached out a soothing hand. But Margie was not shaking with fear. She was giggling.

'Whoooo!' she said. 'Whoo-hooo! And now,' she said standing, 'I'm going down the fast way.' She turned, ran down the slippery clay to the very edge, spread her arms. And jumped.

Someone screamed. Greer thought it might have been her. This was it: the final judgement. God had indeed been keeping count. Sex, pride, weakness, a near-lie, broken vows – all in one day. She had climbed the cliff with the others as a kind of part-payment, but it seemed that that had not been enough. God would settle for nothing less than blood.

'Come on, sookies.' A voice like a bird's cry drifted up from the beach. 'If you're all so smart, jump. The sand's quite soft. Just push out so you miss the rocks.' Margie was alive.

The Incredible Six got to their feet, reluctant, uncertain.

'Go on,' said the distant voice. 'I dare you.'

They hesitated. Once there would have been no question. A dare was a dare. You walked through the drainage pipe by the main road where the eels were, you crouched beside the Main Trunk line while the 3.04 roared past only inches away, you took handfuls of aniseed balls from Woolworths' lolly counter, just for a dare. It would have been unthinkable to refuse.

But they were no longer the Incredible Six. They were second formers. Almost grown up and dares were for kids who didn't know that bones can break and eels can bite.

'Cowardy cowardy custards,' called Margie. 'Scaredy cats.'

Caroline stood by the edge thinking that her mother was right and that Margie was a very bad influence indeed, she'd probably kill herself. But here goes. A leap out into the empty air, legs bicycling her away from the boulders.

Once Caroline had gone, Raeleen followed. ('If I twist my ankle now that's it for the training and Rowley will kill me.')

Then Kathy, because she'd always fitted in, always done what the others did.

Heather was thinking if she was killed at least Mum would have to come home and last night's sick-bed story might have been a premonition.

Greer went last. She took off her glasses and stood at the edge looking out into the dazzle as the huge disk of the sun slipped between clouds and down into the shiny slot of the horizon. She spread her arms as the light turned her every pore to liquid gold and cast herself out, trusting to be held. The whoosh of air was sudden and the thud of landing sickening.

The Six, Incredible once more, lay in a row at the base of the cliff, hands and knees scraped and bloody but alive, and now the thunder had become one elephant overhead and then rain drove in from the hills and they ran squealing for their bikes and climbed back up Chatterton Road while raindrops dimpled the dust.

The darkness of the plantation and the funny men held no terror now, they were unmoved by the risks of detection and punishment. They rode back into town free-wheeling from the top of the hill, Caroline balanced precariously with both legs swung over the saddle saying, 'Look at me! Hey. Look at me! I'm riding sidesaddle!' And Shona hung on tight and said, 'Take me through the puddles, Heather, do all the bumps!' And Raeleen went cross-country, riding on the verges till Keats Street where they all parted, racing the full force of the rain to their separate destinations.

Greer came in the back door to find Mr Chambers having a drink of milk from the fridge.

'Ah,' he said. 'Here's the maid. And where have you been, Miss? Out with the boyfriend, eh?'

The cheek of it, when he had been pinching the milk and drinking it straight from the bottle too. Greer's glasses were all steamed up. She took them off and wiped them on the teatowel.

'Here you are,' said Mr Chambers. 'Would Madam care to try these instead?' He took a pair of glasses from his pocket and fitted them on her nose, his hand brushing her cheek. Greer looked around the kitchen. Through the glasses everything was repeated over and over. There was a pattern of twelve milk bottles and twelve light bulbs and twelve sets of curtains with their patterns of cucumbers and coffee pots.

'Fly's Eyes,' said Mr Chambers. 'They're a new line.' He wiped his mouth and put the bottle back on the shelf. 'Now,' he said, 'I'll be off first thing so what say we give the maid her tip now, eh?' Twelve white hands touched her mouth. 'Is it here?' he said. 'Or here?' The hands touched her right breast. Slid over to the left, kneading her the way Mr Fluff kneaded at a cushion.

Mr Chambers's skin was mashed-potato white. His mouths were wet and pink. 'Do you know,' said Greer, 'that you look like a slug?' Mr Chambers stepped back. 'Just a little game,' he said. 'No harm done, eh? And look.' He took a shilling from clean air. 'Here it is.' The coin gleamed in a thicket of plump white fingers.

'No thanks,' said Greer. She took off the glasses. She was tired. She wanted to go to bed. 'It's probably all covered in slug goo.'

She shut the kitchen door and walked down the hall. Dolly's light was not on. She was probably still at her tea, but the door to her mother's room was ajar. Rain drummed on the roof. Evie stirred on the bed.

'Is that you, Greer?' she said, and her voice was clear once more, not slurred with pain. 'I must have dropped off. Oh – the headache's gone. It's all over. You've done it again, girl.' So it was all right after all. Greer had been restored, a crystal vessel once more, fit to the Lord's purpose.

'Have you managed? Have you done your homework?' said Evie. 'And what about Mr Chambers's supper?'

Down the hall Greer could hear the flushing of the toilet and then the click of Mr Chambers's bedroom door. She gave her mum a kiss. 'Don't worry,' she said. 'I've managed fine. And I've taken care of Mr Chambers.'

'Good,' said her mum.

'Would you like a tune?' said Greer. 'Before you go to sleep?'

'Mmmm,' said Evie. 'That would be nice.'

Greer went through to the harmonium in the lounge. She pulled out all the stops and played 'Abide With Me' once through with no mistakes, then she went to bed where she slept deeply, the rain outside gurgling down the pipes and the sweet scent of wet leaves and smoky tarmac flooding through the open window. For the first time in her life she slept without the light on. The spider spun its web in total darkness, the animals followed one another trusting that they would find their way into the Ark.

Heather had further to go and Shona was heavy. They got soaked. Dad was not home. Heather found dry pyjamas for Shona and dried her hair fluffy with a towel. Then she wrote a long letter to their mother. 'School is alright. Margie Miller put a wetta in Miss Butcher's bag today. It was a laugh. We are fine but I think you should come home. Shona is missing you dreadfully.'

Dad came in at nine and sat on the sofa tugging off his shoes and singing, 'Are you lonesome tonight . . .' He ate his tea: the chops dried to cardboard crescents on a plate in the oven, the potatoes creviced and the peas a pile of green pellets. Then he fell asleep and Heather covered him with the rug and went to bed to finish her letter.

'Dad is lonesome,' she wrote. 'He talks about the sunny days you had together when you were young. I made chops for tea tonight. They were horrible. Love Heather.'

Raeleen had to pretend to limp in case Rowley had asked, so Dad rubbed her calf muscle and said she had to be careful not to overdo it at this stage, when she was just beginning to train seriously, and then they sat together on the sofa and listened to *Verdict*, Dad with his arm easy around her and the good smell of him: cigarette smoke, lanolin from the wool at the store, sweat and the faint sweet overlay of the aftershave she had bought him for Christmas last year. They ate a whole bag of licorice allsorts and since Mum was out at bridge he stretched his stiff leg out on the coffee table and they let the dog in. Tuss sat by the heater, his head on the sofa arm and his tongue lolling with the joy of having his ears tickled.

Raeleen thought that tomorrow, when she underwent the miraculous cure which completely restored the calf muscle, she would take Tuss with her for a long run right up the Awamoa road past the cemetery and back down Shelley Street.

'Time for bed, Rainbow,' said Dad, and gave her the last fairy mushroom. She remembered, just in time, to limp as she went to her room. Mum came in later when she got back from bridge and said, 'Dad says you pulled a muscle tonight.'

'Mmmm,' said Raeleen, pretending to be half asleep.

'So you didn't run?' said Mum, picking up her shirt and hanging it properly on the back of the chair.

Raeleen took a deep breath. 'No,' she said. (Here it comes: the confession. She is going to have to admit to the fibs, to the bike ride, to the cliff, when they had promised faithfully, after Margie's accident, never to go near the cliffs again.)

But her mother was not asking uncomfortable questions. She was in fact tucking in Raeleen's blankets properly then sitting on the end of the bed and patting her hand and saying, 'Don't worry darling, periods are awful I know, such a mess and so uncomfortable but everybody has them you know.' (Everybody? So Miss Butcher got a period? Miss Cathcart in her trim white shorts demonstrating the correct way to vault over the horse got a period? The Queen got a period? It was an overwhelming thought: all that blood, all those pads . . .)

Mum was saying that when she was young she had avoided swimming and tennis, which she loved, just because of the embarrassment. She did understand, truly she did, though women in her family were reasonably lucky in these things. They didn't grow a lot of body hair or sweat much. Not like the Porteous women who had a terrible time of it: poor Laura sweated so much she had to wear guards under her arms and she didn't shave or wax though she should, especially the top lip. It was most unattractive. And as for periods, well, Laura had told her she bled heavily, especially since the babies. 'So we're lucky really,' said Mum.

Raeleen lay under her tidy blankets feeling this new body of hers which was bleeding, but not heavily, just the merest stain, which was not too hairy and not too prone to sweat, and thought, well, it could be worse I suppose. I could have been a Porteous.

Then Mum took out a blue box. 'I got these for you this afternoon,' she said. 'Mrs Carstairs tells me that all the girls wear them nowadays.'

'Mum!' said Raeleen. 'You didn't tell Caroline's mother, did you?'

'Just a little chat when I was at the surgery for Graham's ears,' said Mum. 'She says these tampon things are quite safe, they don't rupture anything and they're much nicer and more hygienic.'

Her mother has stood casually in an office discussing periods. It was appalling.

'Was anyone else there?'

'Of course not,' said Mum. 'It's a free sample box and there's a leaflet that tells you what to do. Sleep well, darling.'

Kiss. Kiss.

When she had gone Raeleen opened the box. It was filled with white cigars. The leaflet had a picture of a pretty girl in a polka-dot bathing suit waving and saying 'Freedom!', and a diagram of bags and tubes which was her womb and vagina with one of the cigars Correctly Inserted.

Raeleen took out one of the tampons. It was enormous. How would it ever fit in the hole? Surely there couldn't be room. But then she thought of PE and pads and wearing polka-dot togs and, well, maybe . . . She could still do a length of the pool faster than Graham, overarm and breaststroke. And she could still do ten skipping stones on flat water to his eight, she could rollerskate faster, and could go straight down Keats Street and into the drive without chickening out the way he did. He could outrun her now at the sprint, but she'd work on the distance. Maybe it wouldn't be so bad.

She did not have to have babies. Lots of people did not have babies: Elizabeth I, the Virgin Queen. Joan of Arc. She lay in bed thinking about Joan of Arc, who was a Heroine of History on the wall at school. Joan was small with an urchin cut like her own, and she rode at the head of a band of tough-looking soldiers, carrying a flag. Joan must have bled too, must have had to wear a pad – though she was lucky because pads wouldn't show under armour.

Joan would have bled. And Elizabeth I. And Valerie Soper who'd competed at Rome and had her photo in the *Weekly News*.

Every woman bled.

She put the tampons in her bedside drawer. She'd try them out tomorrow when she went out for her run.

Kathy came home to find her Aunty Vera and Uncle Stan had come around to play Scrabble. She could hear the talk, the click of pieces, the radio tuned to the Scottish Country Dance session because Stan never missed that. He played with the pipe band which marched down Shakespeare Street on a Friday night, red rubber cheeks inflated, eyes popping, stepping it out to 'The Scottish Soldier' and the land-of-the-high-endeavour to their stand outside Woolworths.

She tried to slip in unnoticed but it was impossible.

'Kasia?' her mother called. 'Is that you?'

So she had to go through, say hi, her head round the living room door.

'Oh Kasia,' said her mother. 'Your hair. You are a drowned cat.' She flustered, found a towel, tried to rub Kathy's hair, saying chills, the liver, *la pneumonie*, while Kathy fended her off saying please, she was as strong as a horse, really, a bit of rain wouldn't kill her. Please. And Vera arranged her letters on the wooden rack and pretended to take no notice.

Finally Kathy said, 'Oh give it here,' and took the towel roughly, wrapping it round her head and Mum said she would make her a hot drink. Stan looked up then and said he could go for a cup of tea if she was boiling the billy and Vera said oh, she almost forgot the cake. She had brought a cake, Napoleon cake, because that was always Pop's favourite. Her eyes filled with tears and suddenly everyone remembered that it was September 22. The anniversary of Grandad Scott's death in 1954. He had collapsed at a Lodge meeting and was carried home by the brothers in full regalia. Vera could still remember him as if it were yesterday, lying on the kitchen table in his beautiful embroidered apron and looking so peaceful.

'Tea,' said Mum. 'Of course.'

Vera wiped her damp fish eyes and put the hanky up her sleeve. 'I'll give you a hand, Rene,' she said, pushing aside her letter rack.

'Oh no,' said Kathy's mother. 'Please. I shall be only a moment. Please. Don't get up.'

Vera was insistent. 'The boys will enjoy a bit of a yarn on their own while we're out of the room,' she said. 'And no looking at my letters, mind.'

'No,' said Kathy's mother firmly. 'Kasia will help me. And my kitchen is so small, there is no room for three. Don't disturb. Please.'

So Vera settled back on the sofa and wondered what to do with five O's and Kathy went with her mother where the minute the door was shut there was the usual whispered explosion: 'Always she wants to poke in my cupboards and say tsk tsk poor Harry married to this dirty foreign person! Vera is a fat cow. And cake! Cake before bed. No one will sleep afterwards.' She handed Kathy a knife and Kathy cut the cake, cream and jam spurting under the blade as she drew it down carefully through sponge and pastry. Her mother filled the kettle. Stan shoved up the slide with a bang.

'Not trying to get in your way, girls,' he said, 'but the boss wants to know if it's normal tea, because that herb stuff doesn't agree with her.' Kathy's mother held up the packet.

'Choysa,' she said.

'That's the ticket,' said Stan. 'That'll hit the spot nicely.'

Bang goes the slide. Bang goes the teapot. 'These people,' hissed Kathy's mother. 'They are from a joke.' She hated Scrabble evenings.

'I think they play it to torture me. I can speak English but the spelling! It is absurd!'

Vera always pursed her lips when Rene said such things: 'Through. Throw. Though. How can anyone make sense of this?'

'I've heard,' says Vera, 'that English is spoken by more people than any other language. It's the international tongue. You can go anywhere in the world and find someone who understands you.'

Kathy's mother says that Cantonese would be spoken by more people surely? And Vera says maybe. But only in China.

Tonight, when Kathy handed round the supper, Vera sipped tentatively, mistrustfully, from her cup, her little finger bolt upright.

'Ah,' she said, satisfied. 'The cup that cheers. There's nothing so refreshing as good old Choysa.'

'You're right there,' said Stan. 'Two sugars please. Guess I'm just not sweet enough, eh?'

Kathy's father looked across apologetically at his wife and took a large slice of cake.

'Chip off the old block,' said Vera. 'Pop always had a sweet tooth.' She lifted her teacup. 'Well, here's to his memory. He was a fine man, a good father and a loving grandad.'

'Mmmm,' said the others, without much conviction.

'I put the notice in the *Examiner*,' said Vera. 'Popped over from the office at lunchtime. I kept it simple: "You lived on earth till seventy-four, but you're in our hearts forevermore." And I signed it from all of us. It's nice, isn't it? The girl at Classifieds said she liked it better than those long flowery verses.'

'Very nice,' murmured the others.

'I mean, he wasn't much of a one for floweriness,' said Vera. And Kathy thought, that's an understatement if I ever heard one. She remembered Grandad Scott too: a mean gingery rind of a man in his dark suit carrying his suitcase and off to Lodge. They met rarely (he couldn't stand Kathy's mother) and when they did, he always picked Kathy up ignoring her protests and rubbed his face hard against hers. It hurt, because his chin was permanently coated with grating stubble.

'Hullo there, young'un,' he used to say. Scrape scrape, holding her arms in a skinny grip from which she could not escape. Dad said he had been a terror when they were kids and kept them all in order with a leather shaving strop with metal studs which hung on a nail in the bathroom. Six of the best and one to grow on. He believed in hard work, church on Sunday and a bowel motion every morning. This was the secret to long life and success. That, and blackstrap molasses. A large spoonful before breakfast. Kathy's mum he found odd: one of those dagos, wops, wogs and chinks who had the misfortune to be descended from the lesser tribes who had not had the good fortune to inhabit the British Isles and in particular, County Derry.

No, thought Kathy. Grandad Scott was not one for flowery verses.

Vera and Stan left at ten. 'Got to get my beauty sleep,' said Stan, and Vera said they had better be heading off or someone would be a sleepyhead at school in the morning. She disapproved of the way Kathy was allowed to stay up in adult company, commented often that someone was looking a bit peaky and was she getting enough sleep? So at ten on the dot Vera gathered up her knitting, found her cardy and her bag and the 'Q' which had fallen under the chair and at last they were going down the path and waving hooray and they'd be back soon to let Harry and Rene take their revenge, though of course it was a bit of a fluke getting XYLOPHONE on a triple word score: you couldn't expect a bonanza like that every time.

'Good night,' said Kathy's mother. And as soon as they'd gone, 'Thank God.' Dad took the dog out for a run round the block and Kathy, who wasn't in the least bit sleepy, helped clear away the cups. As she washed the dishes she looked at her mother with her blonde hair and manicured nails and thought, for the first time, how hard it must be for her, being reminded all the time that she was foreign.

On impulse she said, 'Oh by the way,' scraping cream from the cake plate, 'there's a Parents' Day on Thursday and we're doing a scene from *Romeo and Juliet* and I'm Juliet.' Her mother plodding from sink to cupboard putting away plates lit up suddenly, the way she could, and said, 'Oh Kasia! Juliet! You are an actress like Aunt Sophie!'

Aunt Sophie. Her mother's favourite aunt who had been an actress in Paris before the war. There was a photo of her in the album: dark hair sleeked to a curve round a perfect face, her beautiful neck rising from a froth of tulle and feather. 'À ma petite Irène. Sophie.'

'Juliet!' said her mother. 'So we must braid your hair and I have a white silk nightdress that will be perfect for her. So innocent, so young . . .' Kathy had to say quickly, no, no, they were just doing it in their uniforms, they were just reading aloud, don't fuss. 'Please don't fuss.' And her mother said, 'But the hair? Would it not make you feel the part?' Kathy said, No. No one else will be dressing up and I wish I hadn't told you if you're going to fuss like this.' And she went to bed.

But in bed she thought: an actress. She remembered lying on the bench in the basement and the chill she had felt there: what if I really were dead? What if this weren't Raeleen Smiley coming to meet me but my young lover? Maybe her mother was right and she was like Tante Sophie. Maybe she had inherited her talent? She bit into the thought, lying there in the dark, and tasted nothing but sweetness.

Margie climbed in through her bedroom window. The shop had been shut but Mum was still clearing the till and Dad was mopping the floor. She had watched them through the shop window moving about like actors on a screen between wads of cottonwool snow and Santa mouthing a bubble saying, 'Join Our Christmas Club NOW!' Round the back by the back door Neil and Gordon were working on their car. She could hear it revving. Moths blundered about in swirling blue smoke and porch light above the old Chevvy, the pile of greasy parts, and her brothers who bent over the engine, absorbed.

Margie was cold and wet and her knees were scraped from the landing on the beach. She was shaking, too, now it was all over and no one was there to see. What a stupid thing to have done – but what a buzz, eh! She caught sight of herself in the living room window, dirty and dishevelled. She did not feel like answering any questions. She waited till the Chevvy was roaring at full throttle and made a run for it. Her bike against the wall behind the rhododendrons, up on the saddle and a precarious balancing act as she pushed up the sash. You had to be careful with her bedroom window because the cord was broken and it could slip down like a guillotine, but she pushed and twisted and scrambled and finally she was in, tumbling with Minnie onto the floor.

'Ah ha!' said Pete. He lay on her bed. He was smoking one of her cigarettes. 'And where exactly have you been, Maggot? And what's it worth not to tell?'

He was cocky tonight. Not only had Janice Bates come into the shop like Marilyn Monroe on skinny little white sandals which tipped her forward somehow so her breasts seemed bigger, her behind more rounded than ordinary girls, she had also smiled at him. Said, 'Give us twenty, Sugar,' in a particularly meaningful way and winked as she left the shop to climb onto the back of Hinkley's Harley. It had been a good night.

So Margie learns an invaluable lesson: you may win a

battle but that's never the end of hostilities. And never underestimate the deviousness of the opposition. She had plenty of time to ponder this as she did Pete's paper round for the next week and folded 342 extra copies of the *Examiner*.

Caroline got home free. The house was quiet. Her father and mother sat each night in the lounge after surgery. Her mother embroidered, complicated designs of Assisi work or Hardanger, while her father attended to his stamps. He had one of the finest collections of 1898 pictorials in the country. At this time the house was to maintain a civilised silence and they were on no account to be disturbed.

Her brothers and sisters were each in their rooms supposedly doing their homework, but she could hear the faint crackling from Hugh's room which meant he was fiddling with his crystal set as usual, trying to get Russia, China, anything other than the Voice of America. Penny was curled behind the landing curtain having a whispered conversation on the phone. Only Marcus was studying and that was because he was swotting frantically for School Cert after mucking around all year painting his stupid daubs and thinking he was going to be a famous artist and not a doctor after all as everyone expected.

He'd never be famous, thought Caroline as she sneaked up the stairs, remembering to avoid the third step which always creaked horribly. Marcus was too disorganised. The bathroom was empty so she locked the door and poured herself a bath, a deep one using all the hot, and adding half the bottle of bath salts Helen Brassington had given her for her last birthday. She sank into rose-coloured steam and thought: poor Helen. Poor old left-out Helen.

Caroline had won.

She had not been caught. She had avoided disaster. Better: she had been able to behave like a heroine, racing up the cliff to rescue Margie and demonstrating a generous concern for the enemy, like Edith Cavell on the wall at school, chin up in front of a row of thick-set German officers and saying that stuff about God and patriotism and not bearing hatred or bitterness toward anyone. She had led the Incredible Six on another adventure, an adventure from which Helen had been excluded. And *Peyton Place* was tucked under her mattress ready for another day.

There was the slight problem of the insects and she knew Margie too well to expect a generous reprieve. The collection of wriggling life to be placed down her back tomorrow would be as horrible and varied as Margie could devise. But fair enough. Caroline was still ahead and she would bear it bravely.

Standing as I do before God and Eternity . . .

She lifts one arm and smooths a glove of rosy foam from wrist to elbow. She arranges a bubble-bath bikini on her smooth little breasts, which are not too big like Greer Bott's and not too small like Raeleen Smiley's.

Caroline is just right.

She has come within a breath of disaster but skidded around its edges. The Plan is still fully operational.

It has been a good day.

KATHY

*'Sarah Siddons as Lady Macbeth was the toast
of the London stage.'*

KATE, WHO ONCE, A LONG TIME AGO, WAS KATHY, curls in the big leather chair and says: 'The problem is, Howard, that . . .'

'You see, I think the problem is . . .'

She curls her legs more tightly beneath her. She drags a tissue from the box placed discreetly within arm's reach on the little coffee table with the glass cube and the single pink rose. Howard leans forward expectantly, fingers poised in a speculative arch.

'The problem is,' says Kate, 'that . . .'

Her throat is tight. Her eyes fill with tears.

Howard says nothing. He waits in the pale room. The curtain billows like a sail on the first warm breeze this spring and the cherry blossom outside the window flutters pink tulle. Cars pass by, a distant hum on Bealey Ave.

'The problem is,' says Kate . . .

Pause.

Sniff, she says.

Sniff, sniff.

The words have clotted in her throat. She wipes her eyes with the tissue and then for exactly fifty-eight minutes at more than a dollar a minute she cries.

Sniff.

It's not what she wants to do. It's not what she wants to say.

107

What she wants to say is that the problem is the script. That's what actors always say, isn't it?

Kate wants to say she's no good at improv and she's always worked to a script.

When she comes to see you, Howard, for example. She walks in the door, she sits in the big comfortable chair and she knows how it should go: she's in something by Neil Simon. She's the neurotic big-city woman fitting in a session with her therapist and shopping at Bloomingdales – only for her it's the Merivale Mall – and lunch. Except that this is one of those nightmares where she finds herself out on stage, playing to a full house, rows of critics poised to strike, and she's forgotten the script entirely.

'I don't recognise any of the cues, Howard,' she wants to say. 'I'm not even sure if this is the right theatre.

'I mean, real people don't do this kind of thing, do they?'

They might if they live in New York or Hollywood, but not if they live in Huntingdene. Real people from Huntingdene drive into town, but it's to do the shopping or to see the children at their schools, to watch them play cricket or hockey, then take them out perhaps for afternoon tea.

Then a real person might have dinner with friends or go to a concert or a film or a play if there's something decent on at the Court before the drive home. That smooth glide back along those Mid-Canterbury roads in the moonlight with Cleo or Ottmar or Tuck and Patti on the stereo because driving at night always changes the script to something cool and urbane.

And when the real person gets home, she parks the car in the garage and walks through her glistening garden all peonies, wisteria and night-scented stock and if it's Friday there's the acerbic scent of new-mown grass because Eddie comes to do the lawns on Fridays, and then she opens the door and it's *Blithe Spirit* or *An Inspector Calls*: solid, pre-war, totara-Tudor with tulips spilling scarlet petals from a Chinese bowl at the foot of the stairs and Geoffrey in his office doing his accounts or more rarely, sitting by the fire in the living room reading about cycling across Africa or trekking in Nepal because some day when he can take a bit of time out from bull sales and meat schedules and lambing percentages he plans a trip. He will sail round the islands or walk from inn to inn in the Swiss Alps. Something unpressured and free.

In the meantime of course, you can't just leave a farm to run itself.

Geoffrey is the eldest son. He has children of his own. He takes Oakleigh very seriously. You have to improve on five generations. You have to protect the past. You have to prepare for the future.

Anyway, he looks up as this person comes in and smiles, pleased she is home safe, and says, 'Hullo Kate, have a nice day?'

Kate flops into a chair and says, 'Lovely thanks, but Andrew's going to need a whole new uniform, the trousers are way past his ankles and his shirts are tight across the shoulders already. Honestly it's like that Incredible Thingummy they used to watch on television, God knows what they're feeding them but it must be steroid-enhanced or something. And Juliet's got into the A hockey team and they're planning a sports trip to Australia next term so she's thrilled about that and . . .'

Geoffrey keeps one finger on Eric Newby or one eye on the computer screen and smiles again, crinkling up the way he does and saying, 'Great, great,' though all the time there is one part of him plodding off into the distance in the footsteps of Hannibal or estimating: 'Fifty hectares into trees at five hectares a year for ten years and do I stick with radiata or should I try lucitanica? And some blackwoods in the gully perhaps for the children to harvest . . .?'

So Kate kicks off her shoes and goes out to make some coffee then sits by the fire scratching Monty's labrador belly with her stockinged feet till he stretches ecstatically and whimpers in half-sleep.

And there you have it: Coward without the cut and thrust. Priestley minus the plot.

And after a bit, Kate or maybe Geoffrey says, 'Well, it's been a long day: time for bed, darling,' and they go upstairs past the tulips to their bedroom which is primrose yellow and Sanderson chintz where they open the window an inch or two on the wisteria and the roses and they sleep in scented tranquillity till morning.

In the morning the scene changes to the kitchen, the one room to be remodelled since Geoffrey's mother and father moved into something a little more manageable in town and Oakleigh passed to the next generation. They have added Pearl Lustre and rimu trim and a microwave and a conservatory window framing garden and lawn and the protective ring of oaks and elms, planted by some earlier Fullerton, and all flushing green after another round of spring in the antipodes. Beyond them there are glimpses of paddocks which become rougher as they recede, fading from rye grass and fescue to tussock and matagouri and on upward to the pale rim of mountains.

And here is Kate, sweet and bright as Nora in her doll's house pouring coffee into the blue bowls she has bought from Thyme Cottage, the craft gallery her friend Polly has opened in what used to be the Huntingdene butchery before people started to buy in bulk at the city supermarkets. The bowls are a new line, produced by a potter who has moved into what used to be the Huntingdene cheese factory. Polly likes to feature local artists, providing they're good quality. It's important to support the district and it is something a little different for the tourists who pass through Huntingdene borne aloft on clouds of diesel on their way to Mt Cook and Milford and Queenstown.

Kate cradles her coffee bowl and thinks they're a beautiful colour, they should sell well. She stands at the rimu-trimmed bench looking out at it all and plans her day: sometimes she helps out at Thyme Cottage. Sometimes, she helps Geoffrey, though not with great skill or enthusiasm.

'I'll never make scones,' she had warned him at the beginning.

'It doesn't matter,' said Geoffrey. 'I can't stand scones anyway.'

'I won't gut things or muck out or wallow about in gumboots,' she had said. 'I hate blood and mud and I hate breaking my nails.'

'It doesn't matter,' said Geoffrey.

Nothing mattered. He wanted her.

Sometimes she goes out to the garden, not too confidently because Eddie had said years ago that she was not to touch a thing without consulting him first after he had discovered her carefully transplanting oxalis to a bed outside the living room window.

'But they're so pretty,' she had said. 'They'll make a lovely border.'

'Is that right?' said Eddie. 'Bloody weed more like. You'll have it all over my garden in no time.'

Kate registered the 'my'.

'Sorry,' she had said. The interloper, the novice, the townie.

Eddie relented slightly.

'Roses need heading,' he had said and handed her a pair of secateurs. She had received her instructions.

Geoffrey said Eddie was a rude old bugger but he had worked at Oakleigh since before the war and he was a good gardener so they put up with him. So Kate limited her gardening to snipping and picking, a gentle drift taking sprays of roses to arrange in the Chinese bowl, while Eddie muttered to himself shovelling heaps of manure onto his herbaceous border or mowing his lawn just so, in long even swathes.

Kate stands by the window and plans her day. She'll head the roses or read or go over her lines for her part with the Huntingdene Players, who are renovating what used to be the Methodist church back before declining congregations at all the local churches forced their amalgamation. They'll be doing *Table Manners* for their opening production. And if that goes well they might have a go at *The Importance of Being Earnest* or *Glide Time*. Something light, but not too light. Something they can really get their teeth into.

Then Geoffrey comes in, rumpled in his old jersey and cords, his hair damp still from the shower and she pours him a coffee in the other blue bowl and he laughs and says, 'Look Mum, no handles.' And Kate says it's a new line – they're for café latte. Polly saw them at a place in Wellington. Geoffrey says they hold a lot and that's the main thing and he looks out too at the weeping elm which took a beating in last winter's gales and he must get around to felling it properly and he looks beyond it to the hills and the mountains and says it looks like the southerly's passed and not before time with 1,400 lambs to get in for tailing and could she pick up a bag of dog biscuits if she's going into Huntingdene?

Together they slip into the dialogue for that new day.

That's what real people do. At least, I think it is what real people do. I'm not sure any longer.

I've lost the script.

That's why I have been coming in to see you, Howard, for the past two months. Geoffrey suggested it the day he found me in the spare room cupboard. He mentioned it discreetly to his sister who is a doctor in Wellington and Sarah talked to a friend of hers who is a doctor in Christchurch and he suggested you.

No one else knows. Not even Polly.

For two months each Friday I've sat in your suspiciously comfy chair with my legs tucked up which is probably significant.

A child's pose.

And I have cried. My eyes have watered, my nose has run, I have sniffed and spluttered, tearing tissues from the floral box.

Through the blur I have looked up from time to time at

the book titles above your head. *Sex in Human Loving. Making Contact. Child and Parent. Love is Letting Go of Fear.*

In here, behind the pale drift of curtain sheers, sound is muted and watery and on the shelf beside the books your tiny fish flicker in their tank like luminous purple exclamation marks. At one minute before the hour you will lean forward and you will say, 'There's a lot of pain there, Kate.' And you will hand me a pen to write the cheque and I will feel that I've failed again. Once more, I've been lost for words. My eyes are pink, my mascara smudged, I've not said what I meant to say, I've wasted $60 on tears.

And I shall have to tidy up before I meet the children. They dislike any sign of emotion. They watch me narrowly when I arrive, alert for signs of eccentricity. Andrew's friend Potter, who is already in the first eleven though he is only a third former, thinks I am good-looking for a mum, evidently. That helps. But I should not wear skirts that are too tight or too short. Not the black one for example, which I bought a few months ago on an impulse, recognising a slightly longer version of the mini I had when I was twenty and off in the Kombi with Joe and Monica and Todd.

Andrew thought it was OK, and I had good legs but not for school, Mum. 'So what should I wear to come to the school?' I said. And Andrew said just ordinary stuff, you know. Like Potter's mother. He pointed out Potter's mother to me at Sports Day. She was blonde and short and wearing a bland linen suit the colour and approximate cut of a wool sack. 'You're kidding,' I said to Andrew. 'She looks like an old ewe.' And Andrew said yes, but no one was looking at her, which seemed to be the whole point.

I went to Ballantynes and bought a gathered skirt and a loose jacket in neutral tonings. It makes me feel about eighty but my children approve.

I learned early too not to hug or kiss them in public, not my Juliet who is fifteen and taller than me and who has become a hockey rep called Jules. Not my Andrew who not so long ago refused to leave my knee to join the other children at playgroup. Now, he wriggles and says, 'Don't Mum,' if I so much as pat his arm, or try to flick back the cowlick which always falls in his eyes.

They hate it when I cry. And even when I laugh. Juliet said I laughed much too loudly at *Bugsy Malone*: she said she could hear me all the way back out in the wings and it wasn't even that funny. It had been a pretty hopeless production, actually. I said she had been wonderful as Tootsie and she shrugged: she didn't intend to do any more plays. She'd only done this one for sixth form assessment. 'Yeah,' said Andrew. 'And because Matthew Telfer was Scarface.' Juliet said shut up what would he know about it and Andrew said it was obvious and Matthew's brother was in his class and he was a dweeb so Matthew probably was too.

They hate it when I laugh or cry or sing in the car or dance to Simon and Garfunkel in the living room at Oakleigh or hug them too closely or wear my black skirt. They would hate it if they knew I came to see you, Howard. They wouldn't understand about the script.

There has always been a script, even at the most intimate and personal moments. I'd be walking through the garden to the swing with Andrew and I would catch myself thinking: Here is Kate Fullerton as The Mother.

And I'd see myself as if from one side, my hair thick and silky in its plain bob (cut at Paul Raymond's in the city, not at Krystal's Hair Salon in Huntingdene, though I know I should support local business. I do my best, but I draw the line at Krystal).

Kate-the-Mother wears a woollen skirt and an angora sweater handknitted by one of the local women whom Polly is gradually persuading to abandon homespun and sheep motifs for Kaffe Fassett and muted heather tonings. The sweaters are a success with the tourists. The fine wool irritates Kate's skin so she wears a cotton blouse under it with the collar turned up and she is all blues and browns and greens.

It's like a camouflage. She fades into this landscape.

Andrew runs ahead pink-cheeked after a good night's sleep and Kornies for breakfast.

So here they are, the Good Mother and the Beautiful Son walking round the corner of this lovely house to the swing which Geoffrey's father had slung over the branch of the weeping elm when Geoffrey was a child, where Geoffrey's children can in their turn squeal and kick their legs and say, 'Higher, Mummy. Make it go higher, higher . . .'

I knew how this part went. I'd studied it. I'd worked on back-story and sub-text for years. Kate-the-Mother was partly my friend Caroline's mum. I remembered her from childhood: cool, elegant, calmly confident. She wore a little make-up. She wore plain clothes. Her house was full of prints and books and flowers and everything was slightly worn. But Caroline's house and Caroline's mum were unmistakably classy. My home with its velvet armchairs and brocade wallpaper and my mother with her dyed hair and Chanel were not.

I watched the other mothers in Huntingdene. I learned from them how to talk about the crises of parenthood with just a suspicion of wry amusement before passing on smoothly to how to send off for the Familia catalogue which was where I had found those little overalls of Andrew's. So colourful and practical and just that little bit different.

I learned how to join in the gossip as our children played, taking an interest in who had recently moved here, who had separated and left, but discreetly, never contributing details of my own. Geoffrey's mother had been most emphatic on that point.

'You must remember, my dear,' she said, as she had showed me how to operate the stove – a towering great thing like a stud bull which occupied an entire wall of the old kitchen – 'that Huntingdene is not like the city. It's a small place and everyone knows everyone else. You will be noticed, as Geoffrey's wife. I found it difficult myself to begin with but you'll become used to it.' She pulled a lever that could have started the *Titanic*. 'And this,' she said, 'must be turned to High for baking.'

I added it all to the character study and made a mental note to order a microwave.

That was Kate-the-Mother. She's been my most recent role, but there have been others. There has always been a script.

Kathy-the-Average-Schoolgirl.

Kaz-the-Young-Actress.

Kate-the-Wife-and-Mother.

Other people don't seem to need a script. They never fluff their lines.

My mother, for example. She always knew her part even when no one else about her understood it. I see her so clearly, Howard, walking along Shakespeare Street in her vison through drifts of women in car coats and cardies.

I see her arguing with shopkeepers, not out of anger but out of habit, insisting on selecting each piece of fruit for herself, refusing this fish fillet in favour of that while the customers who understand that you take what you are given without fuss look on. And I see my mother's exit: 'Zank you. Good afternoon.' So formal.

'Not at all, Madam,' says Mr Miller with that kind of smile, that sly New Zealand smile which means rebuke. I tried to avoid Miller's dairy, walking on three blocks to the Four Square on Byron Road for the milk and the sliced Vienna where my mother never shopped and I was, I hoped, anonymous.

It was silly. A ridiculous and extreme embarrassment. My Auntie Vera would probably have said I was plain spoilt and sulky and my Uncle Stan would have said all I needed was a clip around the ear. And maybe they would have been right.

I simply refused to acknowledge my mother in any way. I refused to learn French, for example. I understood it. Of course I understood it. (*Ma petite fille, mon trésor*, the warm milk of a mother tongue, comforting bumps and bruises and nightmare . . .)

At high school we were taught French by a dour Englishwoman called Miss Braithwaite who, in a nasal drawl, flat as the marshes around Jarrow where she had been raised, droned, J'aime, tu aimes, future and past, masculine and feminine. I was probably the only person in the class who knew how it should sound: the explosive ratatat of Parisian French which my mother said was of course the best, as she mimicked the patois of the Marseillaises amongst whom she had lived for some years before her family crossed the sea into Egypt.

'Alorrr-uhh,' she would say, tying on her apron, 'on va fairr-euh un-euh bouillabaiss-euh, hein, t'sais, un-euh bonn-euh soup-euh aux poissons.' She unwrapped one of Mr Gregoriadis's cod fillets and sniffed suspiciously.

'Assez bonn-euh,' she said. 'Donnez-moi les oignons, Kasia . . .'

I knew as no one else in 3A could know, that Miss Braithwaite's version of Frongsay was a curious approximation. Miss Braithwaite knew it too. She had been recruited in Britain to teach maths but the French teacher who had arrived with her had succumbed to the attentions of the manager of the ANZ bank within three months of arrival and transferred with him to the Blenheim branch so Miss Braithwaite had taken over and got on with the job as best she could.

To begin with, she used to ask me to read aloud from the textbook.

'Qui est là? C'est Toto. Voici Toto. Toto est derrière la porte . . .'

'Now listen carefully,' she would say to the other girls in 3A. 'Listen to Kathy's pronunciation. That is the correct form of the uvular "r".'

I learned fast. Flattened each vowel to a diphthong, placed

117

the 'r' firmly at the tip of the tongue, and assiduously imitated Miss Braithwaite until I had it right: a northern-English-New-Zealand-French accent indistinguishable from all the rest.

I came twentieth at the end of the year and Miss Braithwaite was disappointed. 'A disappointing result,' she scrawled in green ink on my report. 'More effort required.' I had made my point.

Being foreign and speaking French was bad. But it wasn't the worst. One Wednesday night in 1961 my mother said, 'Come Kasia. We are going to the cinema.'

I said, 'What's on?'

And she said, 'Something true. Something you should know.'

I liked the pictures. I liked Tammy singing about being in love, and Gidget, and the *Carry On*'s. But not true films. Not documentaries. We had documentaries at school: Health Department films about periods and contraception where we giggled from embarrassment in the darkened hall, or nature films about agricultural recovery on the Volcanic Plateau. I did not want to waste a night at the pictures on something true.

But my mother said she needed someone to go with her, the film was about the war and it was necessary that I should know about it.

'Know what?' I said. 'We've done the war. We do it every Anzac Day. I know about Gallipoli and all that stuff.'

I went with her in the end, though I held out for jaffas and an ice-cream from the Nibble Nook as one of the conditions. So we sat, mid-week with a school day tomorrow in the near-empty Regent, I stuck a jaffa on top of my ice cream, and the music started.

It was OK to begin with: just the usual funny Hitler routine we could all do, fingers under our noses, stamping up and down stiff-legged and saying *Achtung!* and *Gott in Himmel!* Like in the war comics.

Then suddenly it wasn't OK anymore. There were trains.

Grey cattle wagons and skin-and-bone people in striped pyjamas, and tiny white-faced children and a freezing works chimney which belched human smoke, and heaps of sticks which turned out not to be sticks at all but arms and legs, and my mother was holding so tight to my hand that her nails tore my skin and I sat there with my ice-cream a lump of gristle in my throat and a jaffa melting to chocolate smear in my hand and the movie went on getting worse and worse so that I knew I was going to be sick but I couldn't move, not till the last flickering shot of a swastika going down in flames while the credits rolled and the lights came up around us and I was able, at last, to run away. I pushed past the usherette in the doorway and vomited into the gutter out on Chapman Street, chocdip and jaffa spattering sourly onto autumn leaves which looked like shreds of flayed skin.

My mother came out and put her arm around me.

We walked home.

At the corner of Keats Street she said, 'So you see, we were the lucky ones. My father frightened easily. He fled from Cracow in 1918, Paris in 1939, Marseille in 1940. He was a school teacher. He knew about history. My cousins, my aunts and uncles, they were the optimists. So, they were not so lucky.'

She put her hand on my arm.

'And you must never forget, Kasia,' she said. 'Because it could happen again.'

'Not here,' I said. 'Not in New Zealand.' I shrugged her hand away. I was angry, angrier than I had ever been in my life before. Angrier than I have ever been since. I was angry at her for taking me. I was angry at being caught off-guard. I was angry at those appalling lines of grey people shuffling for bowls of grey soup. I walked fast with my head down and my hands in my pockets.

'You've never liked it here,' I said. 'You've never tried to learn how to do things properly here and it's a good place. It's not like Germany at all.'

My mother didn't reply and I was too close to tears to say anything further. We walked the rest of the way home in separate silences.

But I couldn't help noticing after that that Caroline Carstairs said her father was being 'ikey mo' when he refused her the 7/6 she had told him was needed for a textbook. It wasn't completely a lie. We were doing reproduction in science with reference to dogfish, frogs and rabbits and the book was sort of related: *The Confidential Guide for the Modern Couple* which could be dispatched in a plain brown wrapper from a PO box in Timaru. It was advertised in *Truth* so it was a proper book, a kind of biology text.

'What's "ikey mo"?' I said. 'What's it mean?'

'Oh, you know,' said Caroline clicking her bubblegum discontentedly. 'Stingy. Mean. Sort of Jewish.'

In Form Four Miss Cunningham asked me to play Shylock. Caroline was to be Portia because she did elocution but Shylock was the best part, the part Laurence Olivier would choose, said Miss Cunningham, and she draped her academic gown over my shoulders and showed me how to rub my hands together and talk in a high-pitched whine.

'Tree tousand ducats, weeeeelll . . .'

The class laughed and Miss Cunningham said, 'Well done, Kathy. You've got the knack of it.'

I was puzzled. I stood there in Miss Cunningham's gown, the sleeves trailing and clinking with the small change, hanky and chalk which she always kept there and said, 'But it's not fair is it?' I was uncertain. Could Shakespeare, the Bard of Avon, be unfair?

'I mean,' I said, 'aren't the Venetians just as greedy? And Shylock loses Jessica and he really loves her, doesn't he?'

Miss Cunningham said that was an excellent point. Nowadays, she said, we perhaps saw things a little differently from in Shakespeare's time. (So he did mean it. It was very confusing.) But, she said, *The Merchant of Venice* was nevertheless a great play, incorporating one of the immortal speeches in the English language, 'The quality of mercy'. 'Caroline, could we hear those wonderful lines please?'

In assembly I muttered *OurFatherwhichartinheaven* rapidly with the rest and I went to Bible class because everyone did and it was a good place to meet boys, until I was fifteen when everyone stopped because the only boys you met at Bible class were drips, and if I was asked I said I was half-Scots, half-Polish-French and people said, 'French, eh?' because French was Pierre Cardin and Gigi, elegant and sophisticated.

It wasn't ikey-mo, funny and greedy. It wasn't pathetic, hopeless, skin-and-bone.

That was the subtext to my role as Kathy-the-Ordinary-Schoolgirl, her hat at a jaunty angle, in love with Cliff and then Paul, hating Mr Schomaker who taught geography and wanting straight hair so much that she would kneel for ages by the ironing board while Caroline pressed out the curls with a warm iron and a damp cloth.

But then I left home and Kathy no longer fitted. 'Kathy' was small town. Milkshakes and basketball on Saturday afternoons. I was at university and I was Kate.

Kate was doing a degree in psychology. It seemed as good a subject as any and she worked hard in the third term and got C's. But midway through her second year she watched a cat being turned by a lab tutor into a kind of barely animate cushion to demonstrate brain function, and she vomited into the Leith on her way home and decided she didn't like psychology.

She had had a good review for her role as the penitent whore in the Drama Society's production of *The Balcony*. K.N. in the *Times* described her as 'an attractive young actress'. It was enough. Kate skipped lectures from then on and when the Drama Society advertised auditions for *Lysistrata* she tried out. K.N. was the director. His real name was Keith and he was a lecturer in Classics: short, plump and bearded, an expert on Aristophanic comedy. He told her about the origins of drama while they were having a drink at the Cook after the auditions. It all began, he said, with fertility rites. The worship of the phallus and its power to engender life. 'What'll you have?'

Kate – sophisticated Kate – said she'd have a Pimms.

'So you could say,' he said, 'that behind all the bullshit – *A Girl in My Soup* and reviews and the well-made play and all that crap – there lies the primordial fuck. Here you are. Pimms is horsepiss, you know that, Kate? Knock that back and I'll get you a whisky sour.'

In his production he intended to return to the roots of drama, recover the horsepower that got it all going. He showed her some pictures from Greek vases: men who were short, plump and bearded. Their penises stuck out and up at improbable angles or swung about their knees.

'You see?' he said. 'Elemental stuff. Real. No crap.'

He'd really liked Kate's audition. (She'd done Juliet's death scene.) He said he thought she had real talent and could convey the essentially sensual quality he was after. He bought her a second whisky sour. A Chinese dinner. He suggested a nightcap back at his house in York Place. They went to bed.

His penis did not reach his knees, which was a relief. He popped into her and she got the main part.

She played Lysistrata naked beneath a filmy white chiton. Keith thought that was the best means of expressing the provocative sexual tension which lay at the heart of the play. And after *Lysistrata* Kate was Charlotte Corday, trembling and sleeping in another white gown when K.N. did *Marat Sade*. And then she got booted about for a season by Little Malcolm and his mates.

She was on her way.

Little Malcolm and His Struggle went to Christchurch for a student arts festival. On the second night, at a pub near the Square, K.N. was explaining the origins of drama to the woman who had played Mère Ubu for Massey's production of *Ubu Roi*. She was five foot ten with breasts that could scarcely be contained by her velvet jacket and she was very interested in Aristophanes. Kate decided to go and get something to eat.

That was when she met Joe.

Joe and Kate ate steak-and-kidney pies on a bank by the Avon and Joe said festivals like this one gave him the shits. They looked subversive but that was just on the surface. Only four per cent of the student population was actually working class and none of the plays here was really mounting a critique of society. Like in Russia they took plays out to factories and farms, but in New Zealand theatre had lost contact with its roots.

Kate said that was true and after all, the origins of theatre were in fertility rites and really elemental stuff, weren't they?

And Joe said yeah and three-quarters of the people here would be scared shitless by something genuinely elemental and he for his part had had a gutsful of plays where you needed to know the London bus timetable to make sense of the action.

'So,' said Kate-the-Student-Actress, fresh from her success as Ann and with just the faintest trace of a painfully acquired accent locatable to somewhere between Liverpool and Manchester, 'what are you going to do about it?'

Joe threw some steak-and-kidney to the ducks. 'I'm going to give the theatre back to the people,' he said.

Which is how, Howard, I became for a brief period Kaz-the-Hippy bumping in an unreliable Kombi van round the Wairarapa then down to Nelson and the Coast because Joe said it was areas like that which were the heartland.

We were a four-person company – Joe and me, Monica and Todd – and we called ourselves Venial Sins. Joe was struggling free of a Catholic upbringing. He wrote the scripts: surreal fables featuring placards, slogans, giant puppets and post-holocaust imagery, all of it intended to mythologise the land while undermining the corporate power structure which permeated the theatre as it did every aspect of our lives.

We shared the driving, arguing about the exact nature of Brecht's alienation-effect as we coaxed the van over the Rimutakas or up the Lewis. We shared hanging the lights in the bland little country halls where we played that summer, resolutely returning theatre to the people. I also played keyboards and maracas, sold tickets and coffee at the interval and acted the Incredible Needle Woman to Joe's St Vincent de Pill.

It was in Kanuka, somewhere south of Hokitika, just before my entry, while Monica who played Stella Maris the Gangsters' Moll was writhing in sensual ecstasy to a recorded blend of Zulu chant, orgasmic moaning and the theme from *Gilligan's Island*, that the first empty beer can hit the set and we realised we were in trouble.

We had indeed achieved Alienation.

The people didn't want the theatre.

I spent the next hour refunding money. Todd dropped a tab and went to watch the moonlight on the beach and I found Joe being comforted by Monica on the back seat of the van. I was sick of the Needle Woman anyway. The costume was a silver foil bikini which scratched horribly. So I said, 'Hey, stay cool, don't get up, I was going to split anyway,' and I gave them both a hug and I went home.

Joe had used most of the kitty to fill the van in Westport and it took ages to get a lift on a Sunday from Kanuka. I spent my last dollar on a packet of Snifters and they lasted all the way across Arthurs Pass and down the island and as soon as I arrived my mother made me a sandwich.

'Tsk,' she said, carving thin slices from a cold roast. 'Tsk,' as she always did. 'This meat is so dry but your father likes it so.'

I ate it in five seconds, spread thickly with horseradish. Joe and Todd and Monica had been into raw foods. Monica had travelled in India and some guru in Simla had told her the life force was extinguished by cooking. I'd just spent two months on raw carrot and sprouts, which I supplemented furtively with Buzz Bars and hamburgers. I devoured my mother's beef sandwich and cut another to eat in the bath. I needed a bath. My hair was blue and sticky still with glitter from the Needle Woman. My mother had been appalled.

'Oh Kasia!' she had said when she opened the door. 'Your hair! What have you done to your hair?'

I said not to worry, it would wash out and I'd worn my embroidered cap while I was hitching, no one had noticed.

'Oh Kasia!' she had said then. 'Hitch-hiking! It is so dangerous. There was that girl – what was her name – she was killed hitch-hiking.'

'Don't worry,' I said.

'And why shouldn't I worry?'

It was too difficult to explain that Monica had read my palm: my love-line was fractured but my life-line was solid enough. I took my sandwich and went to wash the Needle Woman away. A relief. The gel had made my scalp itch.

I was sitting on the back step by the fig tree to comb out my hair while it was still wet and vaguely manageable when my mother came to sit beside me. She had an airmail letter in her hand.

'I am glad you have come home,' she said. 'Because something extraordinary has happened.'

The paper fluttered like fine wings. She smoothed it on her knee. Her hand was trembling.

Her sister had written. Lilly had moved from Alexandria too but not until their parents had both died, their father in 1949, their mother four years later. Lilly had then, and only then, married Rudi and moved with him to Toronto where he had found a job with a clothing factory on Spadina.

Lilly continued to take her family responsibilities seriously. She wrote to her impulsive and irresponsible little sister regularly, thin blue letters emanating a kind of rebuke which left my mother irritable for hours. Accompanying the remonstrance was a mild but persistent boasting: about the house on Major Street and the new car and Rudi who was a thinker, Lilly said, like Poppa. ('A dreamer,' said my mother, rolling the paper into a ball and tossing it into the bin. 'All books and big ideas and no business sense, you'll see.')

And their son David, clever David, always first in his class.

Sitting on the step I braced myself: David was studying law now in Montreal. He would not have dropped out midway through his second year, he would never end up as the Needle Woman, he would not dye his hair or hitch-hike alone. But my mother was saying that this letter was not like the other letters. In this letter, Lilly had announced that she had found Sophie.

Tante Sophie.

Beautiful Sophie. Wife of their Uncle Claude. Sophie who belonged to Paris, the fabled city, in that fabled time before the war. Sophie was still alive.

Not only was she still alive. She was alive and living in Toronto. She had survived Buchenwald. She had met and married a Canadian soldier during the liberation. Now she was widowed and frail but she was alive, and Lilly had met her at a hairdresser's in Forest Hill.

'It is a miracle,' said my mother. 'C'est incroyable.'

The two women side by side, their hair scraped back from their foreheads, their shoulders shrouded in plastic. They look up and see one another in adjoining mirrors. Someone they had thought long dead floats to life in the glass.

And now Sophie wished to see her. It was there, in a spidery scrawl at the bottom of Lilly's letter: Je veux te voir, ma très chère Irène. She wanted to see Irène and Irène's daughter. She would pay for them to come to Canada, and 'I want to go,' said my mother. 'And I want you to come with me.'

The figs were green. Tight fists on twisted branches. I picked one and peeled back the skin. The seeds were all there inside, tiny and brown and covered in a thick sticky membrane. I had not yet been overseas and I was twenty-one and the migration had begun: everyone was temping in

London or driving a Mini to Morocco or hanging out in the Greek Islands. They sent me postcards. *Hi from Paradise!*

I wanted to fly with the flock. I wanted to drop in on Paradise. But I had planned to go alone, not with my mother on what I visualised as a kind of extended Scrabble evening with a lot of European Veras and Stans.

My mother had me by the hand. She said she was frightened of aeroplanes. My father was immersed in tying flies for the new season. He said he had had enough of overseas back in 1940 to do him a lifetime, but if we didn't mind missing summer at the crib we were welcome to go. He'd manage solo for a bit.

My mother, twenty-five summers, a quarter of a century of summers, spent flicking through magazines in a decaying shearers' van parked in a bare paddock by the Hakataramea where my father stood whistling softly and happily, casting and reeling in, casting and retrieving, managed to look minimally disconsolate. She said it would be for a month only and she would leave his dinners all prepared in the freezer. Vera said not to worry, Rene: she'd see to Harry's dinner. She and Stan would keep an eye on him and make sure he didn't get up to any mischief while she was away.

So I held my mother's hand and we lifted off from Auckland and flew north into a pink fluff of tropical cloud.

For the first half hour she gripped my fingers and refused to look out of the window, but slowly as we moved further from New Zealand she relaxed. She had a drink. A small brandy to settle the stomach. Then red wine with her meal. A Cointreau with coffee.

She began to talk to the man on her right. He was from Delaware and was on his way home after visiting his grandchildren in Devonport. He showed us photos: a couple of kids on an Optimist, squinting and freckled and over-exposed. My mother patted my knee and said she had no grandchildren yet but there was plenty of time, and the American said it was better to marry late, see the world before settling down, and my mother said oh yes, yes, or a person becomes provincial, ignorant.

They talked on through the movie and breakfast and between L.A. and Toronto there was another man on her right, just as pink, just as chatty, who manufactured light fittings. He talked about ceiling downlights and bulkheads and on to interior design and the decline of modern architecture and so to the plight of the modern city and the decline of social values. My mother contributed her nephew David-the-Lawyer and her daughter Kasia-the-Actress as proof that the decline was not universal while I cringed in the window seat and watched Nebraska Utah Iowa slip westwards chequered with snow.

As we jolted down through turbulence over a grey lake rimmed like a sleepy eye with white, my mother applied fresh lipstick and a little dab of perfume. She stepped out into Reception bright and smiling, scanned the crowd, once over, briefly.

'Lilly,' she said to a woman who was astonishingly like herself: small, blonde, and wearing a fur – not vison but some other animal as sleek and striped darker brown.

And 'Sophie,' to another woman who was older, but still finely boned, still beautiful. They wrapped their arms about one another and stood rocking gently across the barrier.

'Ma chère,' they said. 'Oh, ma chère.'

Then there was a babble of introductions and kisses and exclamation ('Oh, comme elle est belle! So like you, Irène, at the same age. So tall!'). And embraces and tears and talk and a rapid drive through four lines of glittering traffic to the apartment on Forest Hill which was jammed with men and women who all seemed to talk at once and there was coffee. ('Real coffee,' said my mother, sipping at the tiny cup. 'Ah, real coffee . . .') The sugar-dusted biscuits I remembered from childhood. And the women, like my mother, wore silk scarves to soften the neck and elegant shoes for they too understood that it was such details that mattered. ('New Zealand women,' my mother used to say, 'they think it is only a pretty dress, an expensive coat – but it is the detail that creates the effect: the shoes, the handbag, the eyebrows plucked, the nails exquisite. It is necessary to pay attention to such things.')

The women sat on velvet armchairs, each with its lace antimacassar, talking and sipping coffee from porcelain cups, their feet tap-tapping in their elegant shoes and speaking a dizzying blend of English and German and French and Polish.

They turned to me and asked me questions: Kasia, Irène's daughter, the young actress. Was I acting for the stage only or on film? What was my favourite role?

I felt awkward. 'I'm working in experimental theatre,' I said. (They were unlikely to have heard of the Needle Woman.)

They nodded their bright little heads like so many sparrows perched on a fence.

'Ah, experimental,' they said. 'That's good. It's good when you are young to take risks.'

Sophie had acted in experimental theatre too as a young woman: *Amphytrion* in 1930. Translations from the Russian – Blok, Sologub. 'It was so thrilling,' she said. 'We were young. We thought that theatre could change the world!'

'Yes,' said the women. 'You are wise to experiment now. The classical roles – Maria Stuart, Hedda Gabler, Phaedre – they can wait for later, when you have the maturity.'

I felt like a fraud. Provincial. Absurd. I excused myself. 'It's jet-lag,' I said. 'I need to stretch my legs.' My mother was talking to Sophie, hands flying. She looked up briefly with bright preoccupied eyes, said, 'Of course. Be careful,' she added, but it was purely habit. She was not worried: nothing now could go wrong.

I walked for an hour along darkened streets. Streetcars rattled by ringing their bells between bulwarks of frozen snow and the houses were still pinpointed on the night by their Christmas lights: red and green and blue. I looked from the sidewalk in at the lighted windows where people were eating or sitting, walking through the everyday theatre of their ordinary lives. I walked along the streets and looked in through the fourth wall.

That was how it was for the next two weeks. My mother talked: with Lilly, with the women and the men who visited and who all seemed to have some connection: the son of the second cousin who had settled in Manitoba, the great granddaughter of a relative by marriage. She talked with Sophie. By day they chatted over coffee, a cheerful ratatat from kitchen or living room. By night their voices hummed from Sophie's room where my mother sat by her bed. Sophie's legs and arms twitched and tingled, preventing sleep. They sat late together and read plays. At least, my mother read, taking all the ancillary roles.

Sophie recited. She knew them all by heart: Andromaque, Madelon and Elise. I could hear her through the thin apartment walls.

Songe, songe, Céphise, a cette nuit cruelle
Qui fut pour tout un peuple une nuit éternelle . . .

Sophie's voice became at such moments deep and resonant, full of force and passion.

Then it was the night before we were due to return home. I woke suddenly, the room still in darkness. By the door stood our suitcases, two dim grey rectangles in the reflected glow of the street lights outside. My mother was lying in the other bed.

She had been quiet all day, had gone out in the afternoon for a walk. I had watched her from the apartment window, seven floors down picking her way delicately through thawing snow. She was tiny and straightbacked and wearing the vison which she had brought with her. It was right here, absolutely right, in its proper element for the first time. 'Ah,' said Aunt Sophie, stroking it. 'Vison. Claude had always a good eye for fur. It was his speciality.'

I switched on the bedside lamp. My mother was lying with her face turned to the wall.

'I do not want to go,' she said. Her shoulders were shuddering. 'I do not want to go back.'

I sat by her on the bed and she turned instantly, wrapped her arms around my neck. Her skin was soft and scented faintly with Chanel. I could say nothing.

'Here I am alive, you see,' she whispered. 'There I lose my heart.'

On the table beneath the lamp stood some of Sophie's photographs, caught in a ring of light: a baby, a wedding couple, a theatrical-looking man with pipe and spectacles and an illegible dedication. There were photos everywhere in Sophie's apartment, lined up shoulder to shoulder on every shelf, jostling for elbow room on little tables and window sills. All post-war. There were no sepia prints, no military men with bristling moustaches or corseted young women. They had all gone, burned to ashes.

I looked at Sophie's photographs while I stroked my mother's hair with its brave blonde rinse. The roots were beginning to show, no longer black but tinged with grey. I thought about the crib at Haka and the pile of *Woman's Weekly*s, the silence and the tussock and briar rose, the paddock by the river.

Outside, a streetcar rattled by.

'What is it?' said Sophie, her hair tied up in a scarf for sleeping. 'Are you not well?'

My mother reached out to her. 'I want to stay,' she said.

'Naturally,' said Sophie. 'Of course you must.'

She took my mother's hand in hers and the sleeve of her robe fell back to the elbow. A thin arm, rings heavy on several fingers, the faint blue stain of a tattooed number on soft wrinkled skin.

I moved aside and Sophie took my place.

'Ma petite Irène,' she said. 'Ah, mon trésor . . .'

I flew back alone. My father snapped the silk on a Hare's Ear nymph and said what the hell was she up to? Vera had popped round with a casserole.

'Rene was always a wee bit impulsive,' she said, dishing up. 'Two potatoes or three, Harry?'

And to me in private as she stirred up some Bird's Eye custard she whispered that she personally thought Rene might be going through the change. Some women went a bit off at that time of life but in a year or two they settled down again. Probably what Rene needed was a good tonic.

So my mother stayed in Toronto and in February I abandoned psychology altogether and tried to lend some credibility to the empty boasting to Lilly's friends. I found a flat in Wellington and a job waitressing at Fiorinis and I inched slowly, line by line, toward professionalism.

I got the part of Vittoria Corombona in *The White Devil* at the Factory.

I also became the mistress of an MP.

All that Machiavellian intrigue. It's nice the way life and art intertwine, isn't it?

The MP was thirty-five, balding and built from solid four by two, but I enjoyed the secrecy. He had a wife back on the farm in Taranaki and five children and it was a conservative electorate: it would be the end of his career if the affair got into the papers, he had to rely on me to be a sensible girl and keep it quiet, but God I was gorgeous and he needed a bit of relaxation after a day listening to those clowns on the Opposition benches, by God he did. Not that his own crowd were much better at times. Fifty per cent of them were about as much use as tits on a bull.

I enjoyed it. The hours were long at Fiorinis and the pay was lousy. The MP paid for a waterbed. He brought wine and smoked salmon to the flat after midnight because it was impossible of course for us to be seen together in public.

I liked the whiff of power. Knowing what Muldoon or Kirk were up to before it broke in the dailies. The MP asked my opinion and appeared to listen as we undulated gently on the waterbed. He said it was useful to have the point of view of a young woman, it was too easy to become divorced from reality up there in the Beehive.

I felt like Lady Macbeth – only with better sleeping and washing facilities. I played it witty and sophisticated, somewhere between Stoppard and Coward.

It became boring eventually. He was promoted to Cabinet and became increasingly anxious about discovery, and he had acquired a secretary who was tailored and as well qualified as me to supply the young woman's point of view on the trade deficit. And I had a lot of work that year: in corset and bonnet as Desdemona in the Factory's production of *Othello* which was set during the Land Wars; in black Mao suit for Alvin Johnston's musical docudrama about Rewi Alley; in sunfrock and cardy for *Tuppertime*, Brian Bremner's farce about New Zealand suburbia. I worked late and slept late and really it was too much effort to be bothered with relationships. The MP and I parted amicably. He bequeathed me the waterbed.

And then I was cast as Adriana for *The Comedy of Errors*. In a scarlet bodystocking. Gino the director had seen *A Midsummer Night's Dream*. The Peter Brook version. He had also read Grotowski. We raced up ladders and along perilously narrow catwalks. Gino was tyrannical.

'Only by overcoming fear, only by completely trusting the body, can an actor be truly free to express himself,' he said. 'Our way is the *via negativa*: we must eradicate all obstacles to total creativity. Jump.'

We jumped. We ran and swung crazily from trapezes and ropes slung from the rafters in a cavernous and icy mercantile building off Lambton Quay in an attempt to achieve the ideal: total psychophysical mobilisation.

'Energy,' shouted Gino from the dim recesses of the floor twenty feet below. 'More energy!' Snapping thin directorial fingers.

We juggled and tumbled and ate fire.

On the first night, running with total commitment along

the catwalk, I tumbled and broke my leg. I lay on a pile of woodshavings groaning in the pause while the audience wondered if the fall was deliberate. Would she leap to her feet and execute a peerless double flickflack without missing an iambic pentameter?

I was in shock. My leg dead. I looked up. Geoffrey was staring down at me from the front row beside his sister Sarah who was doing her intern year at Wellington Public and had dragged her little brother along to the Factory since he couldn't spend his whole time being a bloody Aggie down at Lincoln and thinking about bloody cattle, it was time he was exposed to a bit of culture. They were sitting side by side on a wooden board muffled in coats and scarves since the Grotowskian Poor Theatre paid little heed to such niceties as heating.

Geoffrey had played a lot of rugby. He knew a broken leg when he saw one. He knelt by me stroking my hair in that strange dream time while Sarah organised the stretcher and an ambulance to A and E, soothing me the way I've seen him since soothe a sick calf.

'I'm sorry,' I said over and over. 'I'm so sorry. I've ruined the play.'

'Don't worry,' said Geoffrey. 'It was bloody awful anyway. Nobody had a clue what was going on.'

I fell in love with him on the spot. And Geoffrey fell in love with me.

'It was the way you kept reciting your lines as you fell,' he said. 'And even after you'd hit the floor. All that stuff about your harlot brow and cutting off your wedding ring. It was the only decent part of the play.'

That's how I began on my next role as Geoffrey's Wife. Lady-of-the-Manor.

There have been Fullertons at Oakleigh since 1854. They lined up along the dining room walls and looked me over when I first visited: the naval lieutenant who had fought at Trafalgar, the third son of a peer of the realm, the China missionary, the son who had been killed at Ypres, the beautiful daughter out riding with the Prince of Wales on his tour of the Dominion.

They were not absolutely sure. Trim enough, they muttered in dusty whispers, but what's the bloodline? Kate-the-Actress was not quite what they had had in mind for their Geoffrey. The other girls he had brought home had seemed so much more suitable. Boo and Teddy's daughter – what was her name? – Celia. From Cheviot. Now, she would have fitted in so nicely . . . But the Fullertons had not reckoned on the script which I played straight, no nonsense, with just a touch of humour. And they had not reckoned on Geoffrey who was, and is, in love with me.

We married despite them. Quickly and quietly. A few friends, a JP in a caftan on the lawn of the farm cottage at Taitapu where Geoffrey was living while he was at Lincoln.

His mother said, 'Oh what a pity,' when he rang to tell her. 'Everyone would have so enjoyed a wedding. You never think, do you darling?'

But Geoffrey explained that we had done it that way because it was the spirit of the thing that mattered and we didn't want a lot of fuss. His mother said he was always so serious, but of course she understood.

I wrote to my mother. She was far away, on the visit to her sister and aunt which never seemed to end. 'How lovely,' she said. 'I hope you are both very happy.' If she felt disappointment, it was muted by distance.

Such a relief. There was no wedding. No fuss. No uncomfortable blending of families.

And we've been happy, as Kate says to Howard. Truly. I love Geoffrey. I love his hopeless haircut and the way his forehead wrinkles like Monty's when he's thinking. I love watching him at work around the farm, the steady stride across the paddocks with Tess and Flo barking at his heels. I love watching him stripped to the waist, loading fenceposts or wire, the sweat catching the sun on his shoulders. I love him bundled up in a swannie on the four wheeler, or drafting sheep, or going to sleep over his travel books in the evening. I love his fantasies of irresponsible escape. I love the way he puts his arms round me as we curl to sleep in that sweet soft room at night and the rasp of calloused hands on my skin.

He is a good and steady man and I am a fortunate woman. The script has been easy to follow.

But one Thursday afternoon, two months ago, I was at the superette. Geoffrey was away at a bull sale in Hawke's Bay and I found myself standing in front of the freezer cabinet holding a porterhouse steak in one hand and thinking: is this what I like?

Geoffrey likes steak. Andrew likes steak. Juliet likes steak providing it is well done. But do I?

And do you know, I couldn't answer.

I couldn't remember.

And that was when it all began to unravel. I had forgotten who I was.

Other people seem to have no difficulty remembering. They never forget their lines. They know what they like to eat or how they like to dress. They know who they are. My mother, for example, who did not settle down again as Vera hoped but stayed on in Toronto to take care of Sophie who was not, she wrote, of good health, while I was falling off the catwalk in Wellington and marrying Geoffrey, and my father was, as he put it, seeing a bit of Mavis Goodall, the cashier at Moose's Sporting Goods down on Wyatt Street and on her own after raising a family solo for years.

Mavis was a good sort. Everyone agreed. She enjoyed Scrabble evenings though, 'I'm hopeless,' she said, giggling. 'Spelling was never my strong suit.' She loved Haka. She sewed new curtains for the crib.

'It's the peace and quiet I can't get enough of,' she said. After years of running round after her bloody kids and then running round after all the jokers at work, she could think of nothing nicer than to lie in the sun with a gin and tonic and the latest *Woman's Weekly*. She'd take as much of that as she could get.

She got ten years before my father died one afternoon landing a ten-pound brown. My mother overcame her fear of flying then and came out for the funeral, to sit uncomfortably in the front row of Gibbon Street United in her neat navy dress and a little black hat while Vera sobbed pinkly beside her.

Back at the house she said, could she help? Like a stranger, as Vera tied on an apron and heated up a few savouries.

'Oh no,' said Vera. 'Thanks, Rene, but you just put your feet up and we'll attend to everything, won't we, Mavis?'

Mavis, pale and grieving, trembled as she poured hot water into the pot and Vera said, 'You'd better give it here, Mave, or you'll burn yourself. Just go and sit with the others.'

Mavis sat awkwardly in the easy chair by the heater which still bore the print of my father's body. He had willed her the crib and the house. She twisted her hands and said she had no idea Harry would do that, truly she didn't, not when they weren't even legal and all. And anyway, she didn't want them, there'd be too many memories. Her eyes filled with tears.

'They're really yours,' she said. 'Yours and Kathy's.'

'Not at all,' said my mother briskly. 'It is all for you. I have a home with Sophie and it is to be mine always. I am very fortunate and very comfortable.'

'And I don't need anything,' I said. I had Oakleigh to care for, its rose gardens and lawns. I didn't need the bungalow on Keats Street and the van in the paddock at Haka.

Vera said if no one else minded, she'd like the mantel clock. She had never liked to mention it all these years but it was the Scott clock and supposed to go to the eldest son in each generation and that would be their Roderick since Harry had no sons. She wrapped it in a teatowel and placed it in a basket with the last of the savouries which she said, waste not, want not, she'd take home for their tea since Stan had always been partial to a sausage roll.

At the door she turned and kissed my mother.

'Well,' she said, 'Harry would have been pleased you came. And no hard feelings, eh? Goodbye, Rene. Or . . .' She paused. 'Should that be oh revoyer?'

'Goodbye, Vera,' said my mother.

After the funeral, for the first time she came to Oakleigh. We walked around the garden. Day lilies and roses in full pink and scarlet blossom. I waited for my mother to say something. I wasn't sure what: maybe, 'Why Kasia, this is beautiful.' Or, 'You have a lovely home, Kasia. A good husband. Beautiful children.'

I wanted her, I suppose, to applaud Kate.

She nipped the dead heads off a couple of roses.

'It's nice to see your home at last,' she said.

'You could have seen it sooner,' I said. 'You're free to travel.'

'Sophie needs me,' my mother said.

'You could get a nurse in,' I said. 'She can afford it.'

'She's old,' said my mother. 'And she would not like a stranger to care for her.'

'It would only be for a couple of weeks. Surely she could cope with that. And these are your grandchildren after all.'

'And I don't like to fly,' said my mother. 'You should come to visit me. You should bring the children. Sophie would like to see them.'

'I can't,' I said. 'I'm busy here.'

'Always so busy,' said my mother. 'And what do you do that is so busy?'

'The house. I help in a shop. I help on the farm.'

My mother looked dubious. 'The farm?' she said. 'So you have become a farmer now, Kasia? You always used to hate such things. And your nails: once you stopped biting you were so fussy about your nails.'

She knew, you see. She didn't believe in Kate for one minute.

'Look,' I said. 'I'm just busy. It's too complicated to explain.'

'And I too am busy,' said my mother.

Stalemate. We went indoors.

Geoffrey poured sherries and we sat in the dining room to catch the last of the afternoon sun. Under the cool gaze of the naval lieutenant and the China missionary my mother talked. She talked volubly and happily about Lilly and Rudi and clever David, who had dropped out after all which was a relief and was living with an ex-Marine and making bowie knives in New Hampshire. She talked about Sophie who was old of course: seventy-two and not always in good health but still so alive, so happy to see her friends, to talk, to listen to music. She was remarkable: after all she had suffered to be so alive!

She talked about people neither of us had heard of, with whom she played Mah Jong or with whom she had gone to this concert where Jessye Norman had sung these songs for the death of children and it was so beautiful, so stunning, oh, we were breathless, we were without words!

She talked and Geoffrey laughed or asked questions while the children brought her their models and felt-tip pictures and she said oh they were so clever, they were such clever children. They would be artists, no? And Juliet said she was going to be a farmer and Andrew said she couldn't be a farmer because she was a girl and Juliet said she could so and pushed him over and before he could gather strength to cry, my mother said, 'Do you like chocolates?'

Juliet nodded. And Andrew said he liked them too.

'Good,' said my mother. 'Because I have some presents for you.'

She opened her bag and there were gifts for all of us: a silk tie for Geoffrey. A beautiful tie: red and gold poppies from Yves Saint Laurent. Geoffrey wore ties as infrequently as he could manage and when he did it was a muted green handspun from Thyme Cottage.

He stroked the tie anyway, apparently delighted, and said, 'Great. Thank you, Irène, it's terrific.'

Perfume for me. A heady eastern blend called Czardas in an exquisite crystal phial. I had worn nothing but Arpège for years, since Geoffrey gave me a bottle on our first Christmas. I dabbed a little Czardas on my wrists.

'Ugh,' said Andrew. 'What a pong!'

'Don't be silly, Andrew,' said Geoffrey.

For the children there were toys: a talking doll called Chatty Patti and a silly make-up kit for Juliet and a muscled superhero and a little electronic game where tiny monsters were attacked by exploding asteroids.

'Hi, I'm Patty,' said the doll in a tinny mid-western accent. 'Hi, I'm Patty.'

Beep beep beep went the asteroids.

Then she handed over chocolates in a black and gold box.

'Yum,' said Juliet.

'They are Belgian chocolates,' she said. 'The best.'

Juliet was an obedient child. She hesitated, looking at us hopefully, dinner only half an hour away and two whole trays of fondants in hand.

'We don't normally let them eat sweets just before dinner,' I said. It was a prohibition passed down from Geoffrey's mother who was a believer in plain food, fresh air and regular habits. As Kate-the-Mother I had done my best to conform.

'Ach,' said my mother. 'One little chocolate. What harm can it do? And you, Kasia: you used to like chocolate.'

I did, I thought, I used to love chocolate: Buzz Bars and Moros and Winning Post at Christmas. How odd that I had forgotten.

'I'll make the salad,' I said.

My mother looked up. 'Can I help? I could prepare the bowl for you.'

'Don't worry,' I said. 'The children don't like garlic anyway. It's a very simple meal and it's nearly ready, I won't be a moment.

Hi, I'm Patti.
Beep. Beep beep.
'Another sherry, Irène?' said Geoffrey.

I shut the door on them, my mother comfortably drinking sherry with Geoffrey, my children under the table nibbling fondants. They wouldn't want any dinner, even though it was a roast and their favourite. I prodded moodily at it, a leg of lamb, surrounded by potato and pumpkin and parsnips and onions. Fat ran in clear dribbles into the pan. Good solid New Zealand food.

'Delicious,' my mother said. Without enthusiasm. She had left her salad untouched. She had said no thank you to seconds. 'You are quite a cook, Kasia, and when you were a little girl you would eat nothing!'

'Nothing?' said Andrew. 'Did you, Mummy? You must have been very skinny.'

'Oh, she was,' said my mother. 'She was so thin. She was just bones.'

'Like a skeleton?' said Andrew.

'Exactly,' said my mother. 'Exactly like a skeleton.'

'I wasn't,' I said. 'I was just ordinary. And please use your fork, Andrew, not your fingers.'

'Why do you get so irritated with her?' Geoffrey said as we lay to sleep in the primrose room. 'Your mother's really nice. You've snapped at her all afternoon.'

He had no such difficulty with his mother. They never hugged one another, never made any fuss, but when they were together they chatted in an easy, teasing manner. She asked about the farm and the garden and the district gossip, with the faintly distracted air of someone who had moved elsewhere and was really more intrigued by the lives of her current friends and bridge partners.

'Why are you so jumpy with your father?' I said. And Geoffrey said that wasn't quite the same: his father still had an interest in the farm and he was so bloody set in his ways, always going on about deer and the forestry and the Charolais.

His father had no idea of modern realities, still thought you could make a profit running only sheep.

'Like King Lear,' I said.

Geoffrey said he didn't know about that but the constant criticism drove him crazy. And I was lucky: my mother wasn't like that at all.

I lay in the dark with my children across the landing. When I went in to kiss them goodnight I found them asleep clutching their gifts. *Hi, I'm Patti*, said the doll from out of the dark.

Impossible to explain the complicated tangle of feeling: the way her gifts – extravagant and irritating – made me want to laugh and cry at the same time, the way I could feel such tenderness for her hands with their rows of rings, or her hair, still dyed blonde in defiance of all the laws of nature, while at the same time feeling such rage. Around her I felt like a snail without a shell, bare, defenceless and terrifyingly real. She knew who I was. Before her, Kathy-the-Average-Schoolgirl and Kate-the-Mother became frail insubstantial creations.

I didn't like it. I refused to visit her. She refused to visit me.

I was busy. She loathed flying.

The years slid away.

Sophie died and two years ago my mother wrote to ask me to go with her to Israel. There was a party going from her building but she wanted me too.

Geoffrey said why not? It was quiet on the farm, the children were both away at school now, you should see more of your mother. (Geoffrey, who visits his parents whenever he is in town, with firewood and fresh eggs, and receives in return, 'What's all this messing about with deer for God's sake, they're hard to handle and there's nothing to farmbred deer in my opinion, no flavour, give me a decent roast any day and all deer were good for in my time was shooting . . .')

I flew to Toronto. I went with my mother to Tel Aviv and

to Jaffa and to the Galilee, to Haifa and Tiberias and Acre. On the last day we went out to walk in Jerusalem. The streets were crowded, the heat intense and the guidebook mentioned a spring.

The noise and heat receded as we entered the tunnel. We walked into cool darkness holding candles in our cupped hands. Flame flickered on damp walls pitted with ancient pickmarks and when I turned my mother was behind me, her face lit up, her eyes bright.

The water was surprisingly deep. The tunnel was filled with its stealthy trickling and our skirts clung to our legs, sodden and heavy. We walked in silence.

Midway, my mother stopped.

'Listen,' she said. 'Such silence, yet so many people have been here.'

Our shadows leapt in candle-light together and apart on the walls. She bent and scooped water from the spring. She dabbed some on her face then she reached up and laid her hand on my forehead.

'Oh Kasia,' she said. 'Oh Kasia. Mon trésor. Ma petite fille.'

Her hand left a damp print on my skin. I put my arms around her and hugged her close. She felt so small suddenly. Smaller than me, but strong and certain, and I felt such love for her that I could scarcely bear the knowledge of it.

She died last year. A sudden death. She was knocked over by a car on Bay Street and never recovered consciousness. The funeral is a blur. I have forgotten it completely. I flew home and got on with it. I cried a good deal and people were sympathetic, but what else can you do?

Until one afternoon I was standing in the Huntingdene Superette with a porterhouse steak in one hand and I'd forgotten if I liked it. And I drove home in a panic which would not pass till I curled up in the cupboard where I had stored her things: her vison, for example. I took it from the hanger and made a nest, a warm furry nest in the darkness and lay there in the faint scent of Chanel and that's where Geoffrey found me when he got back from Hawke's Bay.

'What are you doing?' he said, rumpled and worried.

I said I was thinking.

I was thinking about my mother. I was thinking about her and Sophie, the two of them in a ring of light above the sleeping city, the one reading, the other recalling her lines right to the end.

'. . . *Seigneur, voyez l'état où vous me réduisez.*
J'ai vu mon père mort et nos murs embrasés . . .'

Their voices hum in my ears.

'*J'ai vu trancher les jours de ma famille entière*
Et mon époux sanglant trainé sur la poussière . . .'

That's why I've been coming to see you these past two months, Howard: because I have been thinking. And this morning as I drove in down Thompsons Track, the mountains on my left glistening under snow and the willows on the river banks scarlet fuses about to spring into leaf, I heard that Margie Miller has died. A climbing accident in the Himalayas. I've been thinking about that too.

I've reached a conclusion.

I think perhaps it is time to stop acting.

Because this woman blowing her nose and reaching for her bag and uncurling from your big leather chair is not Kathy.

This woman signing a cheque in payment for your attention is not Kate.

This woman walking out of your hushed room for the last time, Howard, is Kasia.

And that's what she has been trying, for the past hour, to say to you.

GREER

'*Margaret Wilson's clear young voice rang out
above the rising waters . . .*'

GREER ADDS A TOUCH OF CADMIUM RED TO THE body of a crab spider and turns the board so that the morning light falls full on the paper. Miria had said Martinville would be perfect. A couple of miles off the main road at the end of the gravel. She had drawn a map, marked the cottage with a crisscross, said Greer would easily recognise it as hers from the rose over the verandah.

'Albertine,' Miria said. 'And she'll have gone mad. She likes having the place to herself and I haven't been over for ages. I'll give you some clippers in case she needs cutting down to size.'

Miria liked roses. She knew their names and their habits, said Gloire de Dijon was a bit of a madam, fussy and inclined to ball, and Cécile Brunner was pretty enough, though leggy. She grew them round her unit where they jostled for space, tangling the unwary on their sly little barbs and reaching across the fence to trespass on Greer's side. Miria said they were the perfect flower for a woman living alone: beautiful but well armed. Nobody messed with Mme Alfred Carrière. 'If you need a bit of peace and quiet to get some work done,' Miria had said, snipping off a dead bloom, 'I've got just the place for you.'

Greer needed peace and quiet all right. A deadline on Friday and the unit in Rangitikei Close small enough when she was there alone, but crowded now that it was shared with Susan and Tom and Alice. She had come home on Wednesday night to find a web of black ink all over the spider chart for Educational Publications and FUCK OFF elaborately bombed across one corner.

Tom was asleep but Susan said they'd had a really nice day, she'd made a picnic and they'd gone down to the river and Tom and Alice had caught some tadpoles and they'd seemed to be settling down at last so maybe everything would be all right after all.

So Greer said nothing. She dumped the ruined artwork, hours of it, in the bin and went outside to hack at the flower border. Miria was deadheading her roses.

'Martinville,' said Miria. If you wanted a bit of peace and quiet, that's the place. Once it had been quite a settlement, with a store and a smithy and a church and a school for the children of the Scandies who were clearing the Ninety Mile Bush. But that had all gone now: there was just the church, which was really nice, worth a visit, but only used occasionally for country weddings, and the Jacobsens up on the hill, and the cottage.

'You can go over tomorrow first thing,' said Miria, 'and work straight through.'

But it was hard to get away first thing. It took time to pack all her materials and the art board and some food into her Honda City, then Alice, who was helping, tripped over the front step and grazed her knee and in the flurry Greer mislaid her keys and it was mid-morning before she left and midday before she arrived in the valley, winding along a gravel road between hillsides of close-cropped grass though in the gullies there were crevices of growth to mark where the bush had been. And at the crossroads there was the tip of a white wooden spire behind a black slab of macrocarpa and Miria's cottage where Albertine had indeed gone mad, hanging in theatrical swags along the line of a sagging verandah.

Greer stopped the car. Stood in the sunshine peeling her sticky shirt from her shoulders. Silence. Sheep bleat. Magpies gargling over by a woolshed. The rattle of swamp grass on the flat.

It was perfect.

Except that when she opened the cottage door, shoving hard for it was jammed and sticky with cobwebs, the whole place hummed. A steady whirr like an engine borne on the thick scent of old wood, old wallpaper and honey. In the bedroom behind the high wooden bed a dark stain spread from the scotia and when she touched it her hand came away sweet and sticky. Outside bees danced about a broken weatherboard and the ground by the waterbutt was littered with dead drones.

It took another couple of hours to go up to the Jacobsens, to phone Miria who said, 'Oh god, sorry. There's always something. Last time it was field mice in the cupboards. Ask the Jacobsens. They'll know what to do.'

The Jacobsens said Pat Paewai over at Dannevirke. He's always on the lookout for swarms, and Pat said, over distant clatter and chat, that he'd be round in the morning.

It was mid-afternoon before she was ready to work: the board placed in the kitchen window, her pens and brushes, palette and paints on the table, Forster and Forster for reference on the sill and a packet of chocomint creams within reach. She pinned up the habit sketches for the crab spider and finally, finally, she was able to make a start.

She drew the outline: the long front legs, the squat predatory body. It was warm in here in the kitchen of this humming house as the sun slid across the hillside and away, and the early spring twilight washed indigo over everything: just a single light which was the Jacobsens' warm living room a mile away to the south. She made a cup of tea, turned on the anglepoise as the light faded, settled in for the evening. And maybe it was the humming and the bees, maybe it was the unaccustomed silence, but she found herself thinking about Buntak.

Those swags of iridescent spider web slung between the

trees, heavy with moisture and so strongly woven, Don had said, that the villagers used them to trap bats and birds.

Those shining drifts of dragonflies and beetles, those petal falls of butterflies like fluttering scraps of brilliant silk, that bustle of spiders, ants and scorpions scuttling in dry leaves.

That multitudinous life. Your shoes invaded overnight so they had to be carefully emptied each morning. The wall by your bed busy with the traffic of skittering hordes attracted to the light of your lamp. The whine of attack beyond the protective drift of your mosquito net. That was what she had noticed first, on that journey upriver. The insects.

Greer had sat in the bow, Shirley behind her and Don in the rear looking pink and blotchy beside Zazawi, who steered them all steadily forward against the current while he perched, lithe and dark, on a petrol can, in baggy shorts and a torn army-green T-shirt.

The shirt might indeed have been stripped from some dead Marine, Don had said. There was evidence of the war all along this stretch of coast. The people found the remains whenever they burnt off patches for their crops: bits of fuselage, rusting motors, armaments. They made good use of it all, harvesting the war as they harvested the rest of the jungle, hammering petrol cans into cooking pots and bayonets into fishing knives.

'Swords into ploughshares,' he said, 'as the Good Book says.'

The bailer in the canoe, Greer noticed, looked suspiciously like a helmet.

Birds crisscrossed the river ahead in flocks of green and crimson, dipping and skimming from bank to bank and their songs were strange to the ear. She noted it all so that she could write about it to Evie and Dolly, with little drawings as illustrations: she'd mention the longboat and the trees and the river, and how hot it was and how she would have trailed her hand in the water but Shirley had told her the river was infested with parasitic worms which burrowed beneath the skin causing deformity, so she sat still instead, jammed against a box labelled in Shirley's neat hand MEDICAL FRAGILE. Her feet had gone to sleep but the faintest movement sent the narrow boat rocking so she tried to ignore the tingling.

Behind her Don was talking to Zazawi, flat vowels rasping against the sibilant patter of the local speech. Her feet were numb, her hair was greasy, her skin was sweating and lumpy with insect bites, but none of it mattered.

This was the vision made fact.

This was the image which had presented itself to her with such clarity only a few months before, when she had sat in the back row of the Wyatt Street Sunday School Hall to hear Don and Shirley Dearborne: *God's Purpose in Buntak. An Illustrated Talk. To be Followed by Supper.*

Here was the river. Here were the birds and insects.

'They're rather blurred, I'm afraid,' Shirley had said, flicking the remote control on the Sunday school projector. 'It's not the focus. It's the film. It deteriorates so quickly in the humidity.'

Here was a longboat. Here were some typical houses.

They looked quite attractive on the slides, but the houses were in fact very dirty, she said. The people had no idea of cleanliness as we understood it. They kept their pigs under the house and simply swept all the rubbish down through a hole in the floor for the animals to dispose of. The projector whirred and the stinking houses perched like long-legged wading birds above the golden haze of the filthy river.

And these were the children who were real little charmers, such bright-eyed kiddies, though in many cases those big brown eyes concealed cataracts and disease and those plump little tummies were as often as not the result of worms or poor dietary habits. The children clustered within the frame looking out at the audience assembled in their rows beneath a red and yellow banner reading *Jesus Loves Me!* while the Zip whistled to the boil and the Women's Fellowship Supper Committee tried as quietly as possible to organise cups and plates of asparagus rolls behind the kitchen slide.

You could see, however, said Shirley, in the alert expressions of the children the effect of mission teaching which was after only five years beginning to show results.

You'd notice that there were no slides of older people. That was not because there were no old people but because they still believed that a devil inhabited the camera and that their souls would be sucked from them with each exposure. Their word for camera was 'soul stealer'. So they hid their faces and once someone had stolen Don's Kodak and they had found it quite by chance in a clearing some miles from the village wrapped in a red cloth and weighed down by a pile of stones. Don had even been physically threatened when he tried to take a photo with a telephoto lens of an old woman.

Tsk. Tsk. Just fancy that, said the audience.

But, Shirley said, thanks to the support of churches in New Zealand and elsewhere, such superstitions were gradually being driven back, at least in the river settlements like Buntak where the children were receiving the blessing of a proper education.

Whirr click went the projector.

A slide of children sitting in a row in their school on the village square or 'awa', heads down over exercise books and HB pencils which had been bought directly with the proceeds of a Bring and Buy sale in Gore. Don called it 'the assault on Darkness' and the victory was there for all to see in the faces of the young, open and unafraid, compared with the haunted expressions of the old who were trapped in fear and still sleeping as they had done for generations in the deep night of idolatry which only the power of the Gospel could dispel.

Whirr click.

Greer sat in the back row as image succeeded image and heard in the squealing of the Zip and the buzzing of the projector a still small voice.

Follow Me, it whispered.

Follow Me.

It was not at all like Hollywood. Not like the Ten Commandments with thunder and lightning, but an absolute conviction that this was where she was intended to be.

Follow Me.

She had gone up to speak to Don after the talk, but 'Thank you,' was all she was able to say. Don had rested his asparagus roll on his saucer and taken her hand in his and said that it was always a special blessing to be able to share the work of the mission with those at home.

Greer had walked out of the hall and back home where she had made a cup of Milo and opened her Bible for guidance. The Bible had read, 'Get thee out of thy country and from thy kindred and from thy father's house into a land that I will shew thee,' which confirmed it beyond all doubt. Greer had received a Call.

The bliss of it. The absolute certainty of it.

The joy of telling Dolly and Evie and Dolly hugging her in the kitchen of the Casa Rosa as she wrapped sixpences for the Christmas pudding and saying she had always known Greer's birth had a purpose and it had just been a matter of waiting till it was revealed. And Evie kissing her, weeping, saying she'd miss her but that was to be another little cross and she'd be helped to bear it. You were never given more than you could bear.

The sense of purpose as she was training, the sudden clarity of it all, her life developing a pattern and logic it had never possessed before. At last the ecstasy of the journey toward Buntak up that coiling ochre river. And the loss of it all.

Out on the estuary of that same river, clinging to the flimsy struts of a jermahl, one of the bamboo fish traps the people erected all along this stretch of coast, where she had balanced uneasily hoping that out here, in the open, away from the encircling jungle where it was only too easy to become lost, she might be seen by some passing fisherman. She might be found and taken to safety. The jermahl had creaked and teetered beneath her weight. Behind it stretched the river caught between banks of mangrove and casuarina. Before it was the dazzle of the open sea. At its base the water licked at her feet like small dangerous tongues. River, jungle and sea all a blur because she did not have her glasses. They were back on the floor of her room, smashed and useless, back at the beginning of her flight to this dreadful, empty place.

She had hung onto the bamboo. Sunlight had tangled in her lashes like slivers of broken glass and she had felt it all disappear. The bliss. The logic. The certainty.

Faith is like a clear liquid. You can be filled with it as a crystal vessel. You can be broken and it can drain away. You can feel it seep.

The river, the sea and the jungle and somewhere to the north or south or east or west lay the village of the original vision: the river flowing by the houses on their spindly legs. There, a man teetered on a dugout, drawing in a line, the white flicker of a fish's belly on every hook. A woman pounded rice in a wooden trough, last year's baby bobbling at her shoulder to the percussive beat, next year's already a smooth swelling beneath her sarong.

Shirley had told her the villagers had a very effective abortificant, some berry or other from the forest which had to be soaked for months in running water then dried and pulverised before it could be safely used and that a thimbleful of the powder in liquid brought on the bleeding in just a few hours. Processed and marketed in the West it would make a fortune, but the women were reluctant to reveal its exact source and so far no one had been able to prise the information out of them.

They resorted to it themselves only rarely, in times of acute food shortage when flood or cyclone had destroyed the clearings where they grew their crops, as had happened back during the second year of the mission. That year, Shirley said, there were no babies.

The lean brown pigs had been slaughtered one by one and the women had hoarded their meagre stores of hill rice and walked far into the jungle to gather roots and berries. The children's bellies had swelled, but the mothers' bellies had remained unaccustomedly flat and their breasts hung like empty pockets from which the youngest suckled long past the time of weaning.

Then the bad season ended and with the crops the babies came again, the dancing and feasting for a new birth and the fathers holding their sons and daughters up to the sky while the umbilicus still pulsed then laying them to the earth which Don said they called 'the Mother of Men'.

Shirley said the Mother of Men was crawling with worms and cysts and all manner of infection and it was a miracle more of the people did not die in the first few months of life. It was such an uphill battle to try and convince them of the need for more hygienic practices, though they were gradually teaching the younger ones proper habits through the school. The women were beginning to bring their babies to the clinic in greater numbers. They sat on the step talking and laughing and flapping away the flies with graceful hands flaky at the joints with scabies or picking lice from one another's hair while they waited for Don or Shirley to perform their mysterious rituals with vial and needle.

They handed Shirley their babies and giggled as she held them to her drip-dry, polyester-blend lap.

'Hold him,' they said. 'Hold him against your belly. You catch a baby.'

They did not of course believe that pregnancy would inevitably follow such simple contact. The people of Buntak, Don said, believed that insemination occurred when a woman lay with a man who had stood out in the rain and received the seed from the sky. Shirley had drawn some good clear charts for the clinic wall which outlined the actual process and they had tried to explain it properly. The people nodded politely as Shirley described the sperm and the ovum and their coupling in the fallopian tube.

'Ah yes,' they said. 'Ah, so that is how it is.' Then they went and stood bareheaded in the rain, arms spread to receive the bounty and they lifted their children to the sky and laid them to the earth's breast.

Shirley held the babies as instructed, smiling at their mothers' good intentions.

'You have to humour them,' she said. 'They are like children but they mean well and in time they will come to understanding.'

She remained childless. God had not seen fit to bless them as yet.

Greer clung to the jermahl.

'Dear God,' she had prayed.

Dear Lord and Father.

Our Father which art.

Dear Jesus.

Gentle Jesus meek and mild.

She looked for Him and He was nowhere to be found in that endless dazzle.

Back in the village all was order whether its source was God or some more suspect local deity. A man gutted a fish, quickly, expertly, flicking the remains to the pig. A woman washed rice, her long fingers combing the pale grain. Children tumbled, arguing over whose turn it was to fetch water, their voices pitched to that universal whine. *Why is it me, it's always me, she never does anything* . . . And on the edge of the village in their square clinic on the square compound Don would be writing up the daily report and sorting supplies, tidying away the edges of the day before the orderly retreat to the evening meal and the hour by the lamp as night seeped down between the trees.

If it had been an ordinary evening Don would sit on one side of the table attending to his insect collection. Beetles, moths and butterflies netted and killed then pinned in shallow wooden trays, each carefully labelled. *Sceliphron laetum* (Sphecidae). *Exeirus lateritius* (Stizidae). Don was writing a book: *Insects of the Riri Coast.* He had shown Greer the introduction.

'The World teems with insect life in multitudinous variety. Of God we say "World without End" but we could with as much truth say of the creatures He has created "insects without end" for there are over three million species and their total numbers are beyond estimation . . .'

He was very knowledgeable. Greer had watched him take a beetle between his pale fingers. 'Fiddle beetle,' he said. 'Mormolyce. See how big the wing covers – the elytra – are? Hence the name. The Museum of Paris once paid a thousand francs for one of these.'

The fiddle beetle wriggled in his hand, its long antennae waving. *Help. Help.* Don dropped it into the killing jar: an old medicine bottle containing plaster of Paris and just a pinch of sodium cyanide. The beetle struggled for a second then was still.

It was pinned now to a tray, one of an orderly row.

While Don organised the insects of the Riri Coast, Shirley read her gardening books and planned the garden she would make once they got back to New Zealand. She planned camellias and dahlias and a liquidambar on the lawn for the autumn colour. She grew a few daisies round the clinic but it was hopeless with the pigs everywhere and the people here didn't understand the point of growing flowers.

Don and Shirley and an ordinary day. But out here on the jermahl there was no order any more, no safety, no design. There was no guardian angel or loving saviour whose express concern was Greer's safety. She was on her own. Behind her in the darkness beneath the jungle trees laced with creepers and those huge golden webs lay Fariedah, knees curled to withered breast, her arms tight around her body.

Fariedah.

With her dark bright eyes and her skin like crumpled brown paper.

Except today skin and eyes had been invisible. Her whole body had shimmered in a gleaming sheath beneath the strip of scarlet bunting which was her old sarong, neatly folded and draped across a branch as if she had removed it simply to sleep. That was what Greer had noticed first. The flash of red. And then the noise: that soft insistent buzzing beneath the ferns, the barely discernible sibilance of absorption.

Fariedah had lain quietly, her body given over without resistance to the jungle and now it consumed her, leeches and countless other tiny beings feasting greedily so that every part of her seethed with life and the sweet hyacinth stench of decay hung heavy beneath the forest canopy.

Greer had knelt beside her on the forest floor where scorpions skittered tail up amongst the leaves and snakes slid on their narrow paths and all the teeming millions whose sting or bite could produce rash or fever or suffocation and she thought about Spring Afternoons.

Spring Afternoons. And weddings. And funerals. And Dolly arranging Erlicheer, irises and daffs in coffee jars for the tea tables or chrysanthemums and lilies in towering confections for the church. When the Spring Afternoon was over, the last sponge drop eaten and the cups arranged in upturned rows on the wooden trays beneath the bench, or when the hearse had drawn away black and sleek with its trail of bereaved vehicles, or when the confetti had been swept from the steps and the wedding party was down at the Gold Room for chicken and pavlova and speeches, Dolly brought the flowers home to the Casa Rosa. She popped a Disprin in the water for long life and there they stayed till their stems had frayed and their petals had fallen and they were thrown on the compost after being disentangled from the styrofoam and wire which had transformed them from mere flowers to 'Tranquillity' or an illustration to the text: 'Consider the Lilies of the Field', the words in Dolly's best italic propped against the vase.

On the forest floor Fariedah's body gleamed and squirmed, the eyes become two shiny black sockets. Greer had knelt alongside feeling her own blood seeping through her arteries, her own breath enter and leave and knew that this was death and no amount of floral arrangement could alter it.

This was not death as it had been conducted back at Public: the discreet laying out behind closed curtains, the muted whispering so as not to disturb the other patients, the crêpe-soled entry of the undertaker. There was no comfort here, no sighing that this was blessed relief, that Fariedah had gone to a better place and was home at last. This was a swollen, brutal, consuming dead end.

She knew that this was the normal way of death here. Don had told her right at the beginning that the people of Buntak had no concept of a loving Saviour, no notion of heaven and the forgiveness of sins. The people lived out their lives in darkness, observing a faith cobbled together from a version of Islam they had learned from the traders who had visited this coast for centuries, coupled with a primitive animism which involved the worship of trees and rivers and so on.

You could hardly, Don said, call the result a religion as such. They were born, held to the sky and the earth and there were some rituals associated with daily life – little offerings to local spirits, a few festivals when they danced and slaughtered a pig and drank a kind of rice wine to universal and complete intoxication, and when they were old they returned to the earth.

'Have you noticed,' he said, 'that there are hardly any old people about, or people with severe disabilities?' It was remarkable, given the hard lives the people led, and when he had first arrived he had ascribed it to natural good health and an exceptional resistance to disease after exposure to every virus in the book. But ten years in the field had taught him some harsh facts. The people here were as susceptible as the white man to ill health in old age but their response was typical.

Instead of offering the hand of love and caring to the sick and the elderly they believed that their infirmity was punishment for offending some spirit or other and abandoned them to wander off alone into the jungle where they either healed or died. The afflicted simply curled up under a tree and let nature take its course.

The young were adopting more enlightened views and came along to the clinic for treatment, praise God – but the old clung stubbornly to their traditional ways. They occasionally accepted antibiotics from the clinic but placed as much faith in scraps of red cloth worn round the forehead to prevent the entry of the evil that was ill health.

'I suppose it's not so different to us really,' said Greer, measuring out some Myacin at the clinic bench. 'I mean, that's why we call it malaria, isn't it? We believed it was carried on bad air. And not that long ago people in the West wore red flannel against chills and carried pomanders against bubonic plague.'

She rather liked the old people's headbands. They wore them with a brightly striped sarong slung low over the hips or tied at the breast with a long cord from which feathers and pierced stones were suspended. The effect was rakish and cheerful, a bright chatter of colour against the khaki greens and browns of the jungle.

Back in Dunedin on their last furlough Shirley had bought up a job lot of cotton dresses and shorts from a warehouse in Mosgiel which she had distributed to the young people. Light pastels. Pale pink. Pale blue. Lemon.

The young people had liked them and Shirley had registered a victory for modesty and progress, but Greer, watching the old people perched like so many brilliant parakeets around the awa, thought the modern dress pallid and fussy by comparison.

She screwed the top back onto the medicine bottle.

'Or influenza,' she said. 'That just means "the influence" doesn't it? And we call it that because people used to believe that it was some kind of bad spirit at work, not a germ or a virus at all.'

Shirley sprinkled disinfectant on the dispensary table and wiped vigorously. 'Maybe,' she said. 'But this is after all the twentieth century and in this day and age no one need live in such ignorance. Praise God.'

Fariedah had been one of the old people on the awa. She was brought in one morning by Moses who helped out with the clinic garden. She was his grandmother, he said, as he carried her easily, draped across one shoulder, up the steps and laid her on the table. She had raised him as the old often did, gifted with one special child to keep them company.

She lay on the table breathing unevenly, her eyes shut, her arms hanging limply till Moses tucked them carefully under the rug with its peggy-square patches, each labelled for the parish which had made them: Parklands, Wainuiomata, Opawa.

He had found her down by the river, he said, lying face down on the path but still conscious and when he asked her what had happened she had said the black cloud had come down.

'What's that?' said Greer, and Moses looked embarrassed, said it was an old thing, something from the old people.

Don peered in Fariedah's eye as it rolled loosely in its socket.

'The black cloud,' he said. 'It's their version of the evil eye. They think an angry spirit settles on them in a cloud and that's what makes them ill. It's TIA, of course. Or a stroke. We'll have to wait and see.'

Fariedah's mouth sagged sideways. Greer remembered her from the very first day in Buntak: a little bright-eyed woman who had been squatting by the clinic wall early in the morning talking to the tall young man who was Moses while he trimmed back the bougainvillea which grew outside her window.

She was talking rapidly, too rapidly for Greer to be able to distinguish clearly any of the words she had been learning ever since the call to Buntak. She thought she may have detected 'mother', 'sister' and 'house' in the sibilant rush while Moses snipped on stolidly saying only from time to time 'Deh' which seemed to be Buntakese for 'Ah hah', and Greer had sat up in her narrow white bed and written it all down for Evie and Dolly: a long diary letter about the journey and she had drawn some little pictures of the window and her bed with its swag of net and the platoon of cockroaches which was marching determinedly across the wall and she had felt complete and overwhelming joy.

The joy of knowing she had heard the call and not failed. She had come to Buntak as directed, her life was to be spent in quiet, purposeful activity in accordance with God's plan.

Fariedah had been part of that joy. She was part of that first morning when the whole village swam in a sort of heightened reality. The houses hovered at the river's edge, a woman wove a brilliant red and yellow band, the warp wound around her foot, a man slept on one side in a slab of black shadow, slapping at flies with a thin calloused hand. The children in their pastel dresses chanted, 'Bold Eng-lish sai-lors rob-bed the Span-ish ships and car-ried home the boo-ty to lay at the feet of their Queen,' from their readers, wilted crimson copies of *Our Empire's Story* each with an inky inscription on the flyleaf: *John Robertson Williams Standard 6 Windsor School Windsor North Otago Otago South Island New Zealand The Pacific The Southern Hemisphere The World The Solar System The Universe 1938.*

Greer stroked Fariedah's hand as Don peered and tested and assembled the drip then felt for the vein in the thin arm. The dextrose level dropped slowly and suddenly Fariedah's eyes fluttered open.

She looked up at Greer, at Don, at the clinic walls, and her eyes darkened with panic. With her strong arm she reached for Moses.

'Can she go home now?' he said. 'She is frightened.'

Don said it would not be wise, not immediately. She could become very ill and that would mean she should go down river to Semonjok, to the big hospital.

Fariedah gripped Moses's hand hard. Tug. Tug tug.

'No,' said Moses. 'She wants to stay in Buntak.'

It wasn't wise, but he insisted, carrying her to her house on the river bank and Greer followed, holding the drip aloft on the narrow planking. She stayed with her for the afternoon and visited her the next day, and the next, stepping carefully on the narrow planks which tethered house to land, the medical kit heavy in her hand.

'You can't help admiring the old people,' Don said. 'They're tough. You just watch. She'll be back on her feet in a week or so.'

Moses cared for Fariedah tenderly, feeding her little patties of hill rice which she mouthed clumsily between numb lips. Greer sat by while she ate, watching the pattern of light and water on their quiet intent faces, listening to the slap and suck of water against the piles beneath the house.

Fariedah looked across at her and smiled. A funny lopsided grin, the rice white pap on her tattooed chin.

'Isn't this silly?' the smile said. 'What a lot of fuss over nothing.'

Greer smiled back.

Fariedah began to speak again, though slurred and slow, and she recovered some sensation in arm and leg. Greer and Moses helped her walk, hesitant on the uneven floor. Up and down. Each of them holding one arm. She leaned against Greer but she was so little, so slight, that there was scarcely any pressure at all. They walked slowly, up and down, through dappled river light.

Shuffle and hold. Shuffle and hold.

'You're right,' Greer said to Don one night as they completed their notes and cleared away after clinic. 'They are tough. She's making an amazing recovery.'

Don patted her hand. 'It's not just due to an iron constitution,' he said. 'It's not just because she's tough.'

His hand enclosed hers. Warm and slightly damp. There were tiny tufts of fair hair on each knuckle.

'She's scarcely receiving any medical attention,' said Greer. She could not withdraw her hand. 'So it must be largely her determination.'

'And prayer,' said Don. 'And you.' Now his other arm encircled her shoulders. 'If Fariedah becomes well perhaps it may lead the others to have faith in us and our ways.'

His breath ruffled her hair. His belly was a smooth curve against her.

'It is you that she trusts,' he said. 'You are His instrument.' His hand stroked her back.

'You have brought such light to this place,' he said. 'You are like a daughter to me.'

Over his shoulder Greer could see Shirley silhouetted against the clinic door. 'Have you seen the syringes?' Shirley said evenly, and Don, disengaging, said they were in the cupboard, he'd moved them from the open shelf for greater security, just in case.

He never embraced Greer again but from then on she felt Shirley watching her closely and there were tiny encounters: the slight nudge as Don stood by her at the bench. The way he reached around her, brushing her shoulder to pick up some pen or bottle. 'Excuse me,' he'd say and sometimes, if they were alone, he would add, 'my dear.'

Shuffle and hold. Shuffle and hold.

One morning Fariedah stopped mid-step and pointed with her good arm to a corner among the rafters. She said something which Greer could not understand but Moses reached up rapidly enough into the darkness and lifted down a carving. It was a sort of wooden bird, but with paws and a massive protruding penis, intricately carved and draped in the same red cloth the old people wound around their foreheads. A bunch of faded green feathers was pinned to its head while termite holes peppered its belly.

Moses handed it to Fariedah who cradled it awkwardly crooning, then pushed it into Greer's arms.

'She wants you to have it,' said Moses. 'The hantu. Very old.'

There could be no doubt of its age. It looked ancient. Primeval.

'I couldn't,' said Greer. 'It's yours.' Fariedah made impatient noises.

Push push. Pushpush push.

She took Greer's hand in her own tiny claw and folded it about the hantu's head. Then she pushed her gently toward the planks leading to the shore.

'Go,' the good arm gestured. 'Go.'

When Greer reached the bank she turned to look back. Fariedah was sitting on a mat in the sun and Moses was filling her tobacco pipe.

Don said Greer was a lucky girl. The villagers did not readily part with their treasures – and never to his knowledge with the hantus. Once they'd been everywhere, in houses and on special trees and hung from the prows of fishing boats. An American missionary who had worked downriver twenty years before had preached against them and demonstrated their inefficacy as spirit guards by burning a few on the awa – but after he fell and drowned in the estuary one night in only two feet of muddy water they had sneaked back into the houses.

This was a significant gift, a mark of the special place Greer was building in their lives.

Shirley touched the feathers gingerly and said what an ugly thing heathenism was when seen at close quarters and that burning was perhaps still the best solution.

Greer looked at the bird's head, the tiny peckpecking of

chisel marks and said no, not burning. It must have taken such ages to make.

Don said with stoneage tools, weeks. Months perhaps. It looked like teak and it was remarkable how intricately it had been worked. You had to hand it to them: the Buntakese were remarkable craftsmen. She was right not to consider burning, he said. Besides, the people had not forgotten the earlier destructions and it would certainly give offence. Greer always sought the ways of peace.

Shirley washed her hands at the sink.

'It's an ugly thing,' she said. 'It's evil. Keep it if you like, but not in the house, please.'

Don said would it not be better to do as Greer would no doubt suggest: accept the hantu as a gift, another blessing? And instead of burning, they could sell it. Authentic carvings like this one were scarce and a collector would pay a good price for this down in Semonjok. They could use the money to buy some new books for the school.

'What do you think, Greer?' he said.

Greer said she did not like the hantu especially. (The creature perched between them on the clinic bench, its huge penis jutting, swollen, the tip worn smooth and glossy.) But it had been given to her in friendship, she was sure of that. And you could not destroy what had been given to you in friendship could you?

Shirley tidied the bench, her mouth a tight line. 'All I know,' she said, 'is that I don't want it here. I don't want that ugly thing near me.' She twisted the top on a half-empty bottle of Myacin. The bottle snapped suddenly in her hand. Splinters of clear glass stuck in a puddle of strawberry-scented syrup.

'And look,' she said. 'Just look at that.'

Her thumb was cut. Blood dripped onto the mess. She looked across the bench at Greer.

'You have brought an evil thing into my house,' she said. 'And I want it taken away.'

'It may have had power once,' said Don. Quiet. Reasonable. 'It may have been evil once, but no longer. A mightier God has seen to that.'

Shirley ripped at a piece of Elastoplast.

'Don't you preach at me,' she said. 'Don't you tell me what has power and what hasn't. It's an ugly thing, an evil thing, and I want you to TAKE IT AWAY.' Her voice rose, her hand trembled as she tried to staunch the flow. Blood seeped through the plaster. Across the compound a couple of old people looked up from their chat.

'Calm down,' said Don. 'Calm down. You're becoming hysterical.'

'I am not hysterical,' said Shirley. 'I just don't want that horrible thing in my home. She brought it here and now I want her to take it away again.' Her voice broke on a sob.

Don patted her shoulder. 'Shhh,' he said. 'Shhh. Greer meant no harm. Shhh. We'll pray for guidance. Let the Lord decide.'

The Lord suggested selling. So Greer wrapped the hantu in a pillow slip and placed it in the suitcase under her bed where she kept her treasures: her best sketches, her drawing pens and inks, a red and yellow striped piece of Buntak weaving, bundles of cards and letters. It could stay there till the next trip downriver.

A few mornings later she woke just before dawn. The day was a pale wash at the window in its fringe of scarlet bougainvillea. From the room next door came a low moaning. Greer lay looking up at the embroidered text above her bed: *Christ is the Head of This House. The Unseen Listener to Every Conversation.* And tried not to eavesdrop.

The walls were thin and she often felt uneasy, hearing the muted conversation only a few feet away, Don's voice a warm insistent burr she could sense rather than hear, Shirley a light and rapid staccato. And the muffled moans she assumed were orgasm. At such times she got up and went out for a walk or reached for her drawing pad and tried to concentrate on sketching. A flower, a cockroach, whatever came to hand. She did not like to think about Don and Shirley's sexual life, or about anyone else's for that matter. Not even her own.

She wasn't exactly inexperienced. She had had a boyfriend, back in Waimaru, when she was training. Les was a farmer out at Patton Flat. On Fridays he came into town to do a bit of shopping and take her to the pictures. He liked action. Together they watched *The Dirty Dozen* and *The Alamo* and *The Train* and *Goldfinger*, Les's hand tightening convulsively on hers during the shootouts while with the other he scooped popcorn from the carton with a regular motion.

Scoop munch munch.

Scoop munch munch.

Les was a bit of a pig. He ordered triple cones and kingsize dairy milks and ate with a careless continuity which ignored crumbs on his tie or ice-cream on his chin. But at least his presence meant that Greer was part of the crowd. At least she had a boyfriend with whom she could sit hand in hand in the stalls at the Regent.

At least she could say, 'We're going to the pictures on Saturday.' That casual, essential, 'we'.

She licked her chocdip, ignored the rhythmic munching by her shoulder and closed her eyes during the killings.

After the pictures they stopped for pies or fish and chips at the pie cart then drove up to the lookout overlooking the city. Les switched on the radio in the ute and then ate his pie and two scoops while she ate her fish fillet, trying to make herself peel off the batter because that was the bit that was fattening though it was also the bit that tasted best. And when they had finished, Les wiped his mouth with the back of his hand and his hands with a bit of paper torn from the pie wrapping then turned to her and kissed her.

His flat wet tongue prodded at her lips. He tasted of tomato sauce.

Greer kept her mouth shut.

Les said she was a refreshing change, not like lots of modern women who rushed things, made a guy feel nervous and he liked to take his time too. But as Friday night succeeded Friday night and Greer's mouth remained closed he became more pressing.

'What's the matter?' he said. His calloused hand on her knee was hot and sweaty. They had just seen *A Fistful of Dollars*. He had moaned when Gian Maria Volonte went down in a hail of bullets.

Greer fiddled with some ear tags which were clipped to the glove box.

'I don't like it,' she said.

Les was silent for a moment. 'You mean you don't like me?' he said.

'Oh no,' said Greer. He sounded so disappointed. 'I like you.'

'So relax,' said Les. 'I mean, we're not going to sit round holding hands for ever, are we? It's not as though we're going to go all the way or anything. I don't believe in sex before marriage either. I want to be able to respect my woman. But it would do no harm to get to first base.'

He leaned toward her. His hand gripped her leg. His breathing was loud in her ear and his mouth was wet.

She pushed him away.

'Don't,' she said.

They sat in silence. Below them the town was rows of light. Beside them a darkened Austin Seven jiggled on squeaky springs.

'What's the problem?' said Les.

'Germs,' said Greer. A very little voice.

'Germs!' said Les. 'Heck! I haven't got one of those overseas diseases or whatever it is you're worried about. I can't say I haven't slept with anyone before but I've always, you know, worn an overcoat.' Silence. From inside the Austin came muffled moaning and laughter.

'I guess I should get back,' said Greer. 'It's late.'

Evie didn't exactly wait up. But she sat and watched the late movie till Greer came in.

'Right,' said Les. 'Back to Mum, eh?'

He didn't phone again. Greer saw him a couple of years later in the Freshamart. He and a curly-haired woman were pushing a trolley loaded with sugar and flour and cans of baked beans and pineapple rings and a large tub of Neapolitan down the Baked Goods aisle.

'G'day Greer,' said Les. 'This is Annette. How are you getting on these days?'

Greer said fine, still at Public, and Les said that was the ticket.

'How are things out at Patton Flat?' said Greer.

Les said beaut, and Greer noticed that Annette was wearing a sort of barbed wire entanglement of wedding and engagement rings and was, she estimated, about eight months pregnant. Then Les winked and said they'd better be hitting the trail, they had to get back for milking.

See you round.

They sauntered off toward the Fruit and Veg, Annette leaning companionably on Les's shoulder. Greer picked up some chocomint creams and a Sally Lunn and thought as she stood in the express checkout that on the whole she was glad she wasn't Annette. Annette looked as though she was developing oedema.

Occasionally one of the other nurses would organise a blind date for her for a ball or an evening dining and dancing at the Sheraton. Sometimes her partner would ring later and say he'd enjoyed meeting her and would she like to go to the pictures, but she was often tired after work and she liked her evenings to herself.

She put on her slippers, opened a packet of chocomints and watched TV, and in the mornings she listened to the others talking about this gorgeous guy they'd met at a party and the ensuing fluster of love and the end of love, engagement rings and kitchen evenings and broken hearts and petty, painful infidelities and weddings with smorgasbord receptions and bouquets and organza. And really, it all seemed too much of a bother.

Then she was twenty-eight and everyone else from her year seemed to have left to marry or travel or work in another town and she was a staffie and run off her feet and much too busy to think about all that.

'I'm a confirmed spinster,' she said to Susan who was leaving at the end of her second year for Thai silk, a reception for a hundred and a honeymoon in Fiji. Susan who believed in true love, who had met James and it had been exactly like in the movies, their eyes locking across a crowded A&E room when he came in to get his collarbone set after a car smash on the main North Road, was appalled.

'You musn't say that,' she said. 'Just you wait till they get a look at you in this dress.' Greer was to be her bridesmaid in cerise with a sweetheart neckline.

'Always a bridesmaid, never a bride,' said Greer and she was right: it was more complicated than necklines and Thai silk.

She was a confirmed spinster. She was on the shelf.

Susan sent her a card from Fiji. 'This place is wonderful! James is wonderful! Marriage is wonderful!'

But Greer preferred the shelf. The other was much too messy, much too frightening.

The moaning from Don and Shirley's room grew louder, more insistent. It was far too early to get up. Greer lit the lamp. She took her sketch pad from the suitcase under the bed and began to draw a bougainvillea bud. She tried to listen only to birdsong as it crescendoed in the forest and the sky lightened.

There was a knocking at the door.

Don hovered.

'Sorry to disturb you,' he said. 'Shirley's unwell.'

It looked like she had a perforated ulcer, something beyond their facilities at any rate and he had radioed for help. They'd be going downriver to the strip at Semonjok in twenty minutes or so. His smooth pink face was creased with worry.

But he was back to normal when he returned two nights later, Shirley recuperating down at the military hospital. It wasn't an ulcer, he said, but some kind of food poisoning. And here he was, taptapping to bring Greer an early-morning cup of tea.

Greer was sitting up to sketch a moth which had blundered onto her lamp and stood tip-toe on the shade, its wings spread, brown and orange. Her glasses were on the floor along with her Bible and writing pad and she was peering at the insect thinking how extraordinary it was, and how pretty. Such a perfect assemblage of tiny limb and muscle. Don, when he entered, was a blur beyond the mosquito netting.

'Room service, my dear,' he said.

Then abruptly he was in focus.

'Ah,' he said. 'Oxyambulyx. A nice specimen.' He leaned toward the lamp.

'Did you know,' he said, 'that the male is able to locate a receptive female from over ten miles away? The pheromones emitted by the female are an extraordinarily powerful attractant.' He plucked the moth from the shade with one deft movement.

'And if you wish to draw it or any other butterfly or moth,' he said, 'you can kill them simply by pressing here.' His fat fingers held the insect in a pincer grip. 'On either side of the thorax.'

The moth fluttered and was still. He placed it carefully on the bedside table and then his hand was advancing like some huge pale spider slowly, mesmerically beneath the mosquito net and along her wrist, her arm, then round her breast and *my dear, my dear* and he was beneath the net and above her, his mouth over her mouth and holding her tightly against his straining body, then his penis was thrusting between her legs and he reared up then fell forward groaning, *My darling, oh my darling*, into her hair.

Greer said nothing. A millipede rippled up towards the ceiling.

Don stood up and her glasses crunched beneath his foot.

'I'm sorry,' he said. 'I'm so sorry.'

The bougainvillea tapped at the wall like thin fingers.

'She gives me nothing,' he said.

The millipede slid into a crack and disappeared.

'Forgive me,' he said.

Greer looked up at the white ceiling.

When he had gone at last, she got out of bed. She went to the clinic and made up a mixture of Savlon and water and washed till her body was red and stinging. Then she took the hantu from the case and carried it across the boards to Fariedah's house. The bird lay heavy in her arms and its penis pressed uncomfortably against her side.

Two children sat on the step playing with a little black pig.

'Fariedah?' said Greer. 'Where is she?'

The children, still sleepy-eyed, shrugged.

'Gone,' they said.

'Where has she gone?' Greer said.

They shrugged again, waved vaguely towards the awa, the houses fringing the slow river, and beyond that the darkness which was jungle and mountain ridge and beyond that river valleys and more villages and more jungle away out in the ulu where the word of the Crucified Christ was yet to be heard.

'Don't know,' they said. 'Somewhere.'

The piglet squealed and teetered from the child's grasp on peg legs. Greer tucked the hantu under her arm and turned uncertainly. Across the awa she could make out the white polyester blur which was Don walking toward the clinic exactly as he did every morning. She kept her back to him and blundered away from the village and into the trees, knowing that it did not matter where she went now because she was losing her way and in this blur she found Fariedah in her shimmering silken sheath.

She had placed the hantu beside her, then vomited and lain cheek down on the earth. The Mother of Men reached out for her then, sending out tendrils which sneaked about wrist and ankle and the spores of mosses and ferns settled on her sweating skin in their billions seeking out her crevices.

Panic prickled at her back. She stood swaying and then she was blundering through a place where every tree looked like every other tree and the sun swung about crazily overhead, its regular path abandoned, and there was no clear way forward and no clear way back.

She found the sea. She waded out to the jermahl and waited hanging there in the sun and dazzle till some fishermen found her and she was saved. Except that nowhere now was safe. She was on her own.

She had to leave Buntak of course. It had been a mistake, she had said. She had believed she had been called but she had realised that she had been mistaken. She had to leave and it was best she left quickly so that the mission could set about finding a replacement as soon as possible.

She said this to Don and Shirley. Don listened without meeting her eye. He carefully spread and pinned the wings of a dragon fly (Anex: Aeschnidae) and said it was a serious decision and they must pray for guidance. Shirley, pale still in delicate recuperation, said that Greer had obviously already given the matter much thought, and it was not for them to question or intrude. She embraced her and her lips brushed Greer's cheek, light as dismissal.

It was harder to tell Evie and Dolly.

'What went wrong?' they said, concerned anxious eyes watching her as they sat at the kitchen table at the Casa Rosa. 'We've been worrying ever since the Book said, "His children are far from safety and they are crushed in the gate neither is there any to deliver them." We knew you must be in trouble and we've been praying so hard for you.'

Impossible to explain. Impossible to say, 'But prayers won't do any good. There's no one listening.'

And impossible to live with their bewilderment.

She moved north. She found the flat in Rangitikei Close, she found a job: Ward Three. Long-term medical cases.

But the deep green corridors slid about, dazzling like deep water, and when the old women in the ward lay with their bird hands clasped on the coverlets after lights out, their mouths gaping in sleep, she saw the bones beneath the skin and a shimmering on the skin and panic rose in her like a dark flood. She had lost the gift of healing.

She retreated to a quiet life. The flat in Rangitikei Close, free-lance illustration and a tabby from the pound whom she called Milly. The ground steadied a little.

Every week she received an aerogramme with a picture of daffodils by the Avon River on one side and a page of closely written detail on the other.

'Life goes on as usual here at the Casa Rosa. Dolly made some marmalade last week and it was much appreciated by the regulars. I've had a wee bit of a cold but nothing serious. Bert Dombrowski passed away on Thursday. It was not unexpected as he had been unwell for some time but he will be sadly missed . . .'

And in return each Sunday afternoon she sat down with a cup of tea and a chocomint cream and wrote a reply.

'Not a lot to report this week. I've had some work from Educational Publications: illustrations for a story about fantails, and another about kauri. Milly has had a snuffly nose but seems OK now. The dahlias look a real picture at present . . .' A banal recital of tiny events which always left her feeling vaguely depressed.

'Hope you are both well. Love, Greer.'

Then a month ago, Susan arrived. Susan, Tom and Alice.

Three uneven shadows through the bubble-glass panel on the front door.

Susan did not even say hullo, just slumped at the table, her head in her hands to hide the bruise flaring purple on her left cheek saying *sorry sorry she didn't know what to do God what should she do she was just so scared James would come after her she was so sorry to land on Greer like this but honestly she didn't know where else to go, she couldn't go to her mother's that's the first place he'd look and she couldn't take any more, normally he was so nice but suddenly there'd be a row out of nowhere over something stupid like the car keys or a dress she was wearing or because she had forgotten to buy bread and God she didn't know what to do, what should she do sorry sorry.*

The words dead flat, a pre-recorded message.

Greer made her a cup of coffee and switched on the heater in the lounge for the children and said, 'Don't worry, it's fine, stay as long as you like. You'll feel better once you've had a sleep.'

'I haven't slept in five nights,' Susan said. 'And, God, I must look such a mess. I haven't had a shower or a shampoo in ages.'

'You look fine,' said Greer.

She didn't. Her hair was lank and greasy, her skin where it was not flaring blue-green was a peculiar ashen grey.

When they were both working together back at Public, she had been so pretty, plump and pretty in her junior's cap. And then she had met James who had skidded into a corner on the Main North Road and broken his collarbone and it was love at first sight across a crowded emergency room.

He was just so gorgeous, pale skin and piercing eyes and a five o'clock shadow like some French film star that, well, she had melted and they had married and moved to Invercargill, had two children and lived in a beautiful house in Rosedale.

Each Christmas she sent a card. Candles and holly and a photo of Tom in the garden in front of the beautiful house. An embossed fir tree and a photo of Alice in her carrycot. A simple gold star on heavy white card and a photo of Susan, James and the children seated on the sofa smiling. *Season's*

Greetings, in gold italic. *Season's Greetings from the Beecham Family*.

And now here she was with her Cardin overnight bag and her two silent children and a bruise like a flower on one cheek. Usually, she said, in the same monotone, James was smarter. He hit or kicked her on the abdomen where it did not show. He was a very deliberate basher who worked her over silently and methodically once every couple of months or so in the beautiful bedroom: because of the car keys or the bread or because she had flirted at a party.

'Though I didn't,' said Susan. (Pert little Susan, chatting up the house surgeons back at Public in her blue and white stripes.) 'Truly I didn't. I was too scared even to look at anyone in case he noticed and took offence.'

He beat her and she tried not to cry out because she did not want the children to hear, but two weeks ago she had looked up and seen Tom standing in the bedroom door watching.

He said nothing then and would not speak about it later.

It was terrible. And they said children from abusive homes ended up abusing their own partners and she couldn't bear to think of her children being harmed like that so she'd waited till James was at work, packed the car and driven to a refuge and they'd been kind but Tom simply refused to come in out of the car and so she'd driven north, straight through to the ferry, too scared even to stop for a coffee.

Now she was tired, nearly collided with a truck on the Foxton straight, and she had to have a sleep. Would it be OK . . .? Would Greer mind . . .?

Greer made them baked beans and toast and the children ate silently, then she moved her art board from the spare room and she stood on one side of the sofa bed and Susan stood on the other, flipping the sheets and tucking in the corners properly from long-remembered habit.

'God I'm sorry about this,' said Susan. 'You're going to so much trouble and I'm being such a nuisance.'

'You're not being a nuisance,' said Greer. 'Now, get into bed and I'll get you some arnica for that bruise.'

She felt strong and purposeful for the first time in years. When she dabbed ointment on Susan's cheek, Susan flinched, then she drew up her nightie. Under the silk her breasts were black.

'I told you he usually goes for the abdomen,' she said.

They stayed. Susan had no money. She was scared to cash a cheque, she was scared to register for welfare, she thought she might try and find a job in Auckland but she was scared because she hadn't finished her training and she hadn't worked since she was twenty-four and she'd read that it was impossible for older women to find work, she was scared that James would have contacted the police, she was scared to let the children out of the house in case they were recognised . . .

The children sat on the sofa with the curtains pulled, watching television, flicking between channels.

'Is this the holiday?' Alice said.

'Don't be stupid,' said Tom. 'We're never going home again.'

Alice's lip trembled. 'What about my guinea-pigs?' she said. 'Who's going to feed my guinea-pigs?'

'They'll be fine,' said Susan. 'Daddy will feed them.'

'He didn't feed Tweeter,' said Tom. 'Remember? When we went to school camp? When we came home his bowl was dry and he'd chewed all his feathers.'

'Tom!' said Susan.

'Well, are we going home?' said Tom.

'No,' said Susan. 'We are not going home.'

'Told you,' said Tom. He flung down the remote and slammed off into the spare room.

Alice wept.

'He's really a very sweet kid,' Susan said, rocking her daughter to and fro, to and fro. 'He used to play with Alice for hours and try to make her laugh.'

Greer's quiet little flat had filled suddenly with people. By day, there were arguments and tears. At night, after the children were in bed, there was talk.

'It's so good to be able to talk to you,' Susan said. 'I've never been able to talk to anyone about this before.'

And Greer felt the tremor in Susan's voice and with it a curious excitement. She, Greer Bott, was special, selected from all Susan's friends – smart, exciting, interesting friends – to be her confidante. It was simple then to reach out, to put her arm around Susan's shoulders, to draw her against her own warm and ample body. They talked and talked, the heater whirring, the outer world a distant hum.

'. . . and then,' Susan said, 'then he said I was imagining things and that Lois was just a colleague and a bloody good one too, a real asset to Digitech and he even said I should apologise to her for being rude and . . .' She hiccuped to a halt.

'Oh hi, Tom,' she said.

Tom stood in the doorway, tousled in his pyjamas.

'Can't you sleep?' she said.

'Nah,' said Tom. 'Stink bed. It's all lumpy.'

He slumped onto a chair, switched on the TV. McGyver thrust his way into the room.

'Tom!' said Susan.

'What?' said Tom, eyes on the screen.

'You can't just walk in like that,' said Susan 'and switch on someone else's television.'

'It's crap anyway,' said Tom. 'Why doesn't she have a video or a computer or something?'

'Her name is Greer,' said Susan. 'Now go to bed.'

He stood up. 'Alice has peed the mattress again,' he said as he left. 'It pongs in there.'

'Oh Greer,' said Susan. 'Oh Greer, I'm sorry.'

'It doesn't matter,' said Greer. It truly didn't matter.

The bruise on Susan's cheek was fading to the faintest smudge. They talked. Susan told Greer about James, and in return Greer told Susan about Evie and Dolly and the Casa Rosa and the call, about Buntak and Don and Shirley, about Fariedah and the jermahl, and how everything dissolved in that empty dazzle.

'I used to believe there was a purpose to things. You know? We were all part of this grand design. And all at once I didn't,' she said.

She was fumbling and it was important to be accurate, to say exactly what happened. It was important that Susan understood.

'It was like being tipped over. All the faith just spilled out. And somehow I've ended up here and I truly don't know why. It all seems so pointless, such a tiny life to be leading.'

In the silence Susan lent over and kissed her. Softly, sweetly, on the mouth. She held Greer's face between her hands.

'Maybe,' she said, 'maybe it was to help us.'

Her hands were cool and smooth, her lips were like crushed silk.

Then, last Sunday, Susan made macaroni cheese for tea. Alice sat at the table feeding pieces to Milly who sat up nicely and begged. Tom prodded at his plate. 'Yuk,' he said. 'I hate macaroni cheese. Why can't we have McDonalds?'

Susan sighed and pushed her hair back.

'Because we can't afford it,' she said. 'Do you have any idea how much it costs to eat out? And you'd be hungry five minutes later.'

'Well, why don't you cook proper food?' said Tom. 'Steaks and that like you used to?'

'We don't need meat to be healthy,' said Susan.

Tom put down his fork.

'Is Greer a vege-nut or something?' he said.

'If you can't behave,' said Susan, 'go and eat your tea in your room.'

'It's not my room,' said Tom. 'And it's not our house.'

'Well it's all we've got at present,' said Susan. 'And Greer's being really kind to let us stay.'

'She's not being kind,' said Tom, and he was scarlet suddenly and yelling. 'She's not doing it because she likes us. She's doing it . . .' he said, the fork trembling in his hand. 'She's doing it because she's an ugly, fat lezzy.'

The fork slammed against the wall. Macaroni cheese splattered the floor.

'I'll have to go,' Susan said. 'This is hopeless. I'll have to find a place of my own.'

'Don't,' said Greer. The thought was appalling. 'We'll manage somehow. We'll go to counselling or something. Please don't go.'

The next day she found *Fuck Off* bombed across the Spiders of New Zealand.

Late at night, it is quiet in the cottage at Martinville. Too quiet. Greer switches on the radio above the range, an ancient cathedral model which ebbs and flows on waves of crackling static. She forces her hand to stay steady, adding a dab of cadmium here, a white highlight there.

The Nursery-web Spider spinning its white protective membrane. The Wolf Spider. The Crab or Flower Spider which binds the female with a silken web before mating.

She works all night through Alistair Cooke and selections from Gershwin and serials and BBC game shows and as the sun rises on Friday morning, there's a recorded warbler and the news through a rush of static.

Greer adds a touch of cadmium red to the body of a crab spider, a final touch of white as highlight, and she thinks she hears that Margie Miller has died in a climbing accident in the Himalayas, but before she can think about that properly, Pat arrives rattling down the gravel road in a battered red ute. He drags on gauntlets and veil, hands Greer the same and prods at the rotten board.

Behind the board, between the joists, the wall is solid honeycomb. A finely wrought structure from which honey seeps to the ground and a dark cloud of insects whirls about their heads. Pat breaks off a piece of comb and examines it.

'Cracker,' he says. 'Nothing wrong with that.' He begins to transfer comb from the wall to a bee box, humming steadily.

'They're all girls,' he says. 'And they like a bit of song.'

It's midday before he's finished and the bees are in their temporary hive in the back of the ute, the wall cavity is scraped and powdered and the weatherboard is patched. Greer makes a cup of tea and they sit on the back step in the sun to drink it. A few bees hang about by the water-butt.

'They're smart,' says Pat. 'Bringing in water to cool the brood on hot days, dancing to show where the nectar is. And do you know, when they come to a new place they set up the combs in exactly the same direction as in their old hive? They use the earth's magnetic field to set themselves straight.

'They're smart all right.'

He leaves at last, rattling back up the road with the smart ones and Greer takes a final look at the Spiders of New Zealand. They're a bit rough but they will have to do. She packs her car with the board, the pens and paints and anglepoise and then, because it is a beautiful afternoon she goes for a walk. Just a short walk, up the road past the concrete foundations which would once have been the shop and the smithy and the school, to the church. It is pretty, as Miria had said. A plain white box with a tiny spire and eight rows of unadorned wooden pews, a cobwebbed pulpit decorated with a bowl of plastic lilies, a harmonium in one corner with faded velvet pedals. The light is filtered through frosted glass, pale as water. Greer sits at the harmonium and tugs at a few stops. Ten-foot diapason. Tympanum. Celeste. She finds a chord. Another. Then, the sequence of marching feet which is 'Onward Christian Soldiers'. Then 'Abide with Me'. And 'The Lord's My Shepherd'. All Dollie's old favourites. It's amazing how much she can remember.

And when she has finished playing and she feels quite ready she pushes back the stops, shuts the door on the plain white box, walks back to her car, and begins the long drive home.

CAROLINE

*'Elizabeth danced merrily at court while her cousin
Mary Stuart languished in captivity . . .'*

BEING A REVIEW OF THE CAREER OF CAROLINE
Jane Carstairs who graduated in 1970, joined Finnerty Jansen
Rowe in the summer of 1971, moved upon marriage to
Morgan Jeffries and Stanway, was sidelined, near dead and
buried, as Braithwaite Salmond restructured and refocused
in 1988 but rose again to burst through the glass ceiling to
an office on the twelfth floor of Tremayne Prentice where
she now sits on the right hand of JT himself at the partners'
meetings on Monday mornings.

From whence she may yet come to judge the quick and
the dissolute.

1.   *Caroline Jane Carstairs is energetic and hardworking.*
On Friday morning 22 September Caroline startled one of
the cleaners on her way in.

'Oh,' said the cleaner looking up at her in the mirror.
She wore a red dress patterned with hibiscus and comfy
running shoes, her hair was drawn back in a heavy bun, her
ears covered in two bright yellow Walkman muffs. She stood
holding an aerosol can in one hand and a green handiwipe in
the other and Caroline could see herself reflected across her
left shoulder: a pale background wraith in cream linen and
navy, the two of them caught within one frame by subtle
architecturally designed overhead lighting.

'Excuse me,' said the wraith.

It was the same woman Caroline passed most mornings on the way in. Usually she was carrying a couple of shopping bags and heading with a heavy steady tread off toward the train station and the long ride home. They'd been caught once on either side of the automatic door, and mimed to one another through the glass. *Your swipe or mine?* Caroline had smiled at the mime, said, 'Good morning,' as they passed. She liked to be on reasonable terms with the staff at whatever level. Not too friendly, not too distant, but the woman had nodded, bent down to gather her bags and walked past.

There was really no point in trying to extend ordinary courtesies to some people.

Lyndsay, who also went to ShapeUp after work, had defended some cleaners who had been laid off following charges of theft. She said it was a terrible life, that typically such families had two jobs or more: the women worked cleaning offices, three hours a day after a 3 a.m. start to get into the city, and some worked night and morning, six till nine at night, four till seven in the morning. And the husband might work during the day and drive a taxi at the weekends. That way, there were no problems with childcare.

'If they've got preschoolers they get by on catnaps and a couple of hours sleep,' she said. 'And they never see each other and they earn less than nine dollars an hour. Bloody terrible, isn't it?'

'Mmm,' said Caroline. Steam rose from the spa into the glass dome above their heads.

'So much for cradle to the grave, eh?' said Lyndsay.

Lyndsay had been a member of the Socialist Society back at University. Caroline remembered her from the anti-Vietnam demonstrations, her blonde hair flying in the wind as she stood on the steps of Parliament to address the crowd.

She'd never quite lost the impulse.

Then, Caroline had rather envied her.

'Ho Ho Ho Chi Minh!' Lyndsay had cried and the crowd had joined her.

'Ho Ho Ho Chi Minh!'

Caroline had followed, carrying her placard with *Men for Mutton* printed in big letters but Lyndsay was up the front arms linked with Lenny Saunders who had been described in the *Dominion* as 'a leading student activist': all long dark hair and flashing eyes. He looked like Zapata. He looked like Fidel minus the cigar. He looked like Che Guevara minus the bullet holes.

Lyndsay was also very photogenic. When she was interviewed during Germaine Greer's visit the reporter had been confused. Why, she asked, had Lyndsay, who had been Miss Mount Maunganui back in 1966, got involved with Women's Lib?

Lyndsay said it was because she had become aware of the oppression suffered by women down through the ages under the rule of the patriarchy.

The *Dom* published the two photos side by side: on the one hand Lyndsay in togs and high heels wearing a slightly lopsided crown and being kissed by the runners-up. On the other, Lyndsay minus bra, bouffant and eyeliner.

'From Teen Queen to Bra Burner!' read the caption.

Even without the symbols of oppression, Lyndsay looked gorgeous.

She leaned back in the spa and said it was terrible, wasn't it, that people had to live like that, and Caroline said yes but presumably it was better than where they'd come from or they wouldn't be doing it. The most recent wave of immigrants always had a rough time until they got established. They arrived, got stuck in and in time they got their reward in seeing their children succeed in the new environment.

She couldn't really be bothered. The steam rose, she'd done her fifteen minutes on the exercycle and twenty laps of the pool and now she wanted to lie back and relax after a busy day. The last thing she wanted was a lecture in political correctness. Lyndsay never knew when to relax.

Lyndsay was saying but that was just the point: these

people weren't receiving any reward, their kids were ending up unemployed and hanging round the video parlours and . . .

2. *Caroline Jane Carstairs believes there is a time and place for everything.*

Caroline had reached over and pressed the jet button. Tiny inquisitive spurts of water nuzzled at her legs and shoulders and the pool seethed. Lyndsay's mouth opened and shut through the steam.

'Mmmm,' said Caroline from time to time.

'Ah ha.'

'Really.'

Lyndsay could be very boring.

Sometimes she regretted having persuaded the other partners to employ her.

3. *Caroline Jane Carstairs believes that a little courtesy never hurt anyone.*

Caroline and the oppressed office cleaner stood shoulder-to-shoulder in the women's loo.

'I'll go downstairs,' said Caroline.

But the cleaner said don't worry. She had a soft high voice, surprising for such a big woman.

'I'm finished,' she said.

She neither smiled nor took off the headphones. She gave the mirror one final wipe then gathered up her cloths and sprays at one end of the bench without meeting Caroline's eye while Caroline combed her hair and squirted a tiny whiff of Joy behind each ear.

She wanted to use the toilet but not until the cleaner was out of the room, and now that she was committed, now that she had come in at the cleaner's invitation, the cleaner seemed in no hurry to leave. With infuriating deliberateness she transferred the sprays and polishes to the little trolley, carefully she balanced the mop and the bucket, then finally she had gone. The lavatory seat was still damp and cold and Caroline remembered Lyndsay telling her about her boarding school where the toilets were outside and the prefects used to send the littlies out to warm the seats on cold nights.

It was all rather irritating.

Out in the corridor the woman was plodding towards the lift. She reminded Caroline of a cow, the way she walked, big and docile and deliberate, swaying heavily and blocking the corridor. The lift doors slid open and took them both into grey pile and polished reflective metal and they stood side by side, the cleaner looking up at the lights flashing 9, 10 11 as though there might be a surprise. As though she needed to watch. As though the lift might spring something new: a sudden dip from 9 to 3 then a return to 6.

It was not going anywhere special.

The doors slid open on the twelfth floor. Caroline stepped out.

4. *Caroline Jane Carstairs sets clear goals and objectives.*
Caroline liked this part of the morning particularly. She enjoyed waking early, getting the jump on the drowsy town, doing her yoga by the open window then showering in the clean white bathroom, blank background to her naked body which was still slim, still tanned and toned because she worked at it, had no intention of letting herself go. Evan rose late, rushed about finding briefcase and keys and had a coffee in town. She preferred the slow start, the news rattling out disaster as she had her breakfast: two thin slices of toast with just a scraping of marmalade, two coffees, one with milk, the second short and black. She liked finding her little grey 320i parked neatly in the garage and she liked the drive into the city along near-empty streets with Schubert on the stereo.

But most of all she liked the arrival: stepping out of the lift at Tremayne Prentice into the empty corridor, muted grey and newly vacuumed so that it was as if she were walking across untrodden snow, as if she were the first on the beach after the tide had receded, as if she were the first to set foot in the kingdom. Ahead of everyone. Ahead of Forbes: ahead of JT.

She liked her quiet office with its view of the harbour and the hills beyond dusted still with spring snow. She liked hanging her coat on the hook behind the door and flicking on the computer so that it beeped and hummed and readied itself while she checked her diary.

Her lists: on the one page, appointments. On the other, jobs to be done: correspondence to answer, opinions to be completed, Court documents to draft, billings to finalise. Each little list a part of the Grand List, the list which was not printed anywhere but firmly pinned to the walls of her mind: The list which was Caroline's latest Five Year Plan.

Every five years Caroline reviewed her life, professional and private. Every five years she planned future developments:

1970–75: Staff solicitor (commercial) with good firm. Fiat 850. Visit Britain/France. Improve backhand. Lose 10 pounds. LLM.

1975–80: Partner. Fiat X19. Visit Italy/Germany. Own house. Invest in art. $60,000 fees.

1980–85: Law Society Committee. $100,000 fees. Alfa T.

1985–90: Involvement in Law Reform. BMW. $160,000 fees.

1990–95: Advisory work for Government or Law Commission. Judicial appointment?

It was important to retain the overview.

Caroline liked reading her daily list then checking the mail, scrolling through and registering the skirmish and the major battle, the profit and the loss. She liked the concentration of activity it all represented, all that raw emotion, all those primal sins – greed and covetousness and anger and lust – given controlled expression, and she liked the drama of their interaction, the bluff and the invention, and the way she was part of it all.

She liked entering hours spent, liked the ranks of client numbers, active numbers 1, 2, 3 or 4, her life reduced to six-minute units of her time.

She liked placing her files on her desk close to hand and working steadily until the thud of other feet in the hall and the buzz of conversation beyond her door signalled the arrival of Marike who would sit at her desk drinking coffee and resolutely ignoring the telephone until 8.30 and not a moment more.

Marike was smart and sharp but she lacked commitment.

It wouldn't do. Caroline planned a steady assault of urgently required typing only a few minutes before five. She resolutely delayed signing documents until the last possible moment.

There are many ways to skin a secretary.

5.   *Caroline Jane Carstairs dislikes interruption.*
That was how Caroline liked to begin the day.

On Friday 22 September, however, she did not have the place to herself. The Xerox was spitting copies *pt-tit pt-tit* behind Marike's desk, and the door across the corridor opened suddenly as she was passing and Lyndsay backed out carrying a manila folder.

'God,' said Lyndsay. 'You gave me a fright.'

'Sorry,' said Caroline. 'It seems to be my morning for it. I nearly stampeded a cleaner in the ground-floor loo.'

Beyond Lyndsay's shoulder she could see a cluttered room, the desk lamp on, coffee mug on the desk, and a little clump of cigarette stubs in an ashtray.

'You won't tell on me to Marike, will you?' she said. 'I had to get this done for Mallisons in a hurry and it's a complex case and nicotine's the only vice I have time for these days.'

Caroline laughed and said her lips were sealed and went into her office. But the arrival was spoiled. She was no longer first in the pool. Then there was a quick tap at the door and in a moment her whole day was ruined.

Lyndsay stands there in her room and says it is going to become public knowledge today anyway but she just has to tell Caroline in person and in private before anyone else because she has been such a support over the years and how lucky it is that they are both here early this morning:

Lyndsay has been invited to be Counsel Assisting the Commission of Inquiry into alleged child abuse and violence at Lulworth Welfare Home.

6. *Caroline Jane Carstairs does not let emotion cloud her capacity for rational analysis.*

'Oh well done,' says Caroline. 'Oh, that's marvellous. That's terrific. They couldn't have made a better appointment. We should celebrate. Dinner at Fino's for a start. Oh, that's wonderful.'

And when Lyndsay has left she sits twirling her pen as the computer hums and the harbour shatters into billions of tiny glistening shards in an early morning wind.

Caroline sits and thinks, hard, about her career. It is urgently necessary to compile a new list, a new Five Year Plan. It is urgently necessary to review her progress thus far.

7. *Caroline Jane Carstairs made a promising start.*

Back in 1970, Caroline shared a flat with Lyndsay in Dunedin. Lyndsay had got all A's in her fourth year: A-plus in Conflict of Laws, A's in International and Company and A-minus in Commercial, points ahead of Caroline though Lyndsay had found time to be Student Vice-President and spent hours smoking small brown cigarillos and planning student action round the kitchen table in their flat in Cargill Street.

The third flatmate was a music student. She played her silver flute in the bedroom, her head bent to one side and her sweet pink mouth puckered, breathing a lilting music, while out in the kitchen Lyndsay jabbed at the air with her cigarillo and said apathy was the real enemy of the left, not right wing politicians.

'Sit on the fence and you deserve to end up an omelette. That's Humpty-law,' she said. She was quick and witty and intense and she had waist-length blonde hair.

She had three offers at the end of the year. Jansen Finnerty Rowe was the third.

Caroline was home when the secretary rang.

'Jansen Finnerty Rowe,' singsonged the voice on the end of the line. 'Is Lyndsay Davois there, please?'

'Oh I'm sorry,' said Caroline. 'She's up in Wellington at the anti-Vietnam demonstration. Could I take a message?'

She left a note but Lyndsay was tired when she got home and in the jumble of posters and bits of paper pinned to the wall by the phone the note went unnoticed.

'Oh what a shame!' said Caroline when the note was finally discovered.

'Doesn't matter,' said Lyndsay. 'I don't want to get sucked into the system and I'd rather work somewhere small helping ordinary people.'

8. *Caroline Jane Carstairs is thorough.*
That was lucky, because a day or so later Jansen Finnerty Rowe rang again and this time it was for Caroline.

So Caroline moved to Auckland, where she found a flat in Freemans Bay from which it was a pleasant walk in summer to a small office in a large building where she worked, dressed as befitted the dignity of the profession, looking out onto a concrete wall. Caroline worked hard and long, preparing detailed notes on every file, reading not just the textbooks but the cases quoted in the textbooks, following up reference and precedent. Her opinions were models of thorough analysis.

Just along the hall was Jon McNulty. He was tall and self-assured and the son of P.J. McNulty of McNulty Construction, creators of fine office blocks on valuable slabs of downtown real estate.

Caroline watched him at Finnerty's reception for the new

staff. Jon was drinking whisky and water and leaning against a bookshelf talking to one of the secretaries. The prettiest one. She laughed a lot and tossed her hair about and Jon laughed too and leaned toward her to whisper in her ear and she laughed once more showing all her teeth. Then Jon looked up and looked straight at Caroline. And the look said, 'Isn't this easy? What a fool she is and what a silly, easy game I'm playing with her.'

He was perfect.

She watched him one afternoon that next week at work in front of District Court Judge Hornblow, defending Reid Rawlings's son, Ben. District Court Judge Hornblow was small and smooth-coated with pointed terrier teeth and a snappish disposition. Ben was eighteen and cool and he had allegedly stolen a cigarette lighter, a comb and two packets of chewing gum from Singh's dairy on Newmarket Road. He said he'd simply forgotten to pay.

Reid Rawlings was the Minister of Defence.

It was a hot afternoon. District Court Judge Hornblow was impatient to be finished. Mr Singh was plump and smiled all the time from sheer nervousness. He had seen, he said, a young man loitering very suspicious in his store and when he asks him if he can look in his bag the young man is angry, but Mr Singh's nephew hears the anger and he comes into the shop and when the bag is open, the young man says sorry he forgot. But he did not forget. (Mr Singh grinned more broadly.) He thought it is just an old man here and he is stupid.

Jon was conducting the defence. Ed Finnerty had insisted. Better to have an unknown in court, since Ben seemed determined to plead not guilty and have his name in all the papers.

'If you get a well-known lawyer,' he had said to Reid, who was more than a little irritable, 'the media will be onto it straight away. The best we can hope for is as little fuss as possible.'

Caroline watched as Jon, the unknown, stood up. He said that he did not intend to cross-examine.

Ben went a little pale. Ben's mother back in the gallery leaned forward, clearly regretting the fee.

Then Jon pointed out, with all due respect, sir, that the prosecution, more particularly Mr Singh, had neglected to identify his client as the person who was loitering suspiciously in his shop and was subsequently found to have in his possession a cigarette lighter, a comb and two packets of chewing gum.

'Hmmm,' said District Court Judge Hornblow. His shirt clung to his back, his thinning hair was sleek with sweat. Mr Singh had a most annoying smile and it had been a long session.

He dismissed the case.

'Well done,' said Caroline as the crowd jostled and left the court and Jon said thanks and now he could do with a drink.

They had a drink and then dinner and then since it was a warm night they walked along the waterfront and Jon said he loved finding the gaps. He'd played halfback at school and that was what he liked: grabbing the ball and through the gap and over. He loved the game of law.

Caroline decided to fall in love with him.

9.   *Caroline Jane Carstairs focuses on the solution not the problem.*

It was not a good idea to fall in love though the wedding was tailcoats and no expense spared in Jon's school chapel. Ed Finnerty had taken her aside when the engagement was announced and explained that they'd be sorry to lose her, very sorry indeed, but it would not be possible of course for her to continue at Jansen Finnerty Rowe. They never employed married couples. It was standard policy.

Caroline had not anticipated this.

It had not occurred to her that marriage to Jon might be

anything other than advantageous. Nor did it occur to her then (though it occurs to the older Caroline, sitting in her office, twirling her pen and looking out at the early traffic scurrying into the filing-box canyon along the motorway) to ask, 'But why me? Why shouldn't Jon leave?'

Because she knew the answer without asking.

Jon was competent. Jon was embarked on a promising career. Jon was handy crew on Finnerty's yacht.

There was no point in protest. She left without a murmur for a job with Morgan Jeffrey and Stanway. Not quite so prestigious and further away out in Newmarket, on the wrong side of a snarl of motorway construction, but interesting nevertheless.

She made the most of it.

She worked long and hard. She researched every file she was asked to look at, taking her usual meticulous notes: she agreed, of course she agreed, with Stanway and the senior partners on contentious non-legal issues while occasionally arguing with flair and determination on what was unlikely to cause dissent. She admired Theresa-the-secretary's children, who smiled toothily from the plastic photo cube on her desk at reception, and in return Theresa let a few things slip: that Morgan wanted to develop the corporate/commercial arm of the firm while Stanway favoured a strictly conveyancing base; that Stanway was not in the best of health.

On Saturdays they sailed with Jon's friend Marcus or played tennis clad in snowy white and went out in the evening to dinner. Or they drove out of the city. 'To pillage,' Caroline said, when people admired one of their trophies, some amusing or valuable object found in a country second-hand shop: a jukebox, for example, which played Elvis and Chuck in a corner of the dining room alongside a table they'd picked up out beyond Maungaturoto, solid kauri under layers of ghastly green paint. They'd found the clock on the same trip: an American steeple, c.1830.

'It's a dreadful old thing,' the woman had said, drying

her hands on her pinny and apologising over and over for the mess in the front room. Caroline had glanced over the mess briefly: a Victorian grandfather chair covered in a worn quilt felted with dog hair, a wooden table amongst the rabble of plastic gladioli, radiogram-liquor cabinet, TV trays and chrome and vinyl chairs. The woman had offered them a cup of tea: tea with condensed milk, and a couple of water crackers spread with butter and placed on a rather nice piece of Clarice Cliff.

'It used to chime,' said the woman, dusting the clock with her cardy sleeve. 'But it made such a racket and set the dog off so Ernie disconnected it at the back.'

Jon gave her thirty dollars for it which she pocketed quickly beneath her apron, blushing and saying she hoped they'd find some use for it.

Caroline patted the dog, a scrappy Yorkshire terrier with a runny nose and pink eyes. 'He's lovely,' she said as the terrier rubbed his skinny body up and down lasciviously against her shoe. The woman smiled, as delighted as if she had been complimented on a child's beauty or intelligence.

'He's company in the evenings,' she said. 'We don't get a lot of visitors out here, not unless they get lost like you and need directions back to the main road.'

She threw in the plate because Caroline admired it, for another five dollars.

In the distance a tractor ground slowly up the muddy hill. 'Oh dear,' said the woman. 'He's back early and you haven't finished your teas.'

Caroline stood and picked up the clock and the plate and said they'd have to leave to find their way back to the road in the light so thank you for the tea and the conversation.

The woman opened the front door which was stiff and rimmed with draught stopper and stood on the step to wave them away. 'Drop in again now you know where we are,' she called.

There was the table, the grandfather chair, not to mention

two sheds, a barn and a row of bedrooms with clutter in every room. 'Thanks,' said Caroline. They'd certainly be back.

A muddy Ferguson chugged around the corner of the implement shed and the woman turned away instantly, her hands twisting in her pinny.

Jon switched on the stereo and they hit the highway back to the city. *Hey Mr Tambourine Man* they sang, one of the shoals of flickering winking homebound townies.

'You've got a wonderful eye,' their friends said, sipping their margaritas and eyeing the latest acquisitions, restored and polished and placed in the tiny white flat amongst the other treasures. Jon's friend Marcus was a journalist for *Living!* He featured their flat in an article titled 'Up-Town Style!'

'This light-hearted synthesis of old and new, kitsch and antique, exactly reflects the vibrant non-stop lifestyle of its young owners who thrive on life in the fast lane . . .'

The young owners appeared in *Now!* magazine in black tie and off-the-shoulder red silk with Ed Finnerty and his wife Lucia at the Law Society Ball. Ed had put his arm around her and said Morgan had told him Finnerty Jansen Rowe's loss had been Morgan Jeffrey and Stanway's gain, then he told the joke about the lawyer who wanted to hire a secretary and so he gave three women five hundred dollars and said what will you do with that and this one did that and that one did this and so, and so, in the end who did they hire? Why, the blonde with the big tits of course!

'Oh Ed!' said Lucia.

Caroline laughed too. After all, Jon was not yet a partner.

10. *Caroline Jane Carstairs knows that success requires determined effort.*

Jon's motivation was becoming a problem.

In the summer of 1975 Jon's father, P.J. McNulty of McNulty's Construction died while applying a final coat of Moss Green to the spouting of the bach at Hatfields Beach. It was a shock to them all.

Jon read at the funeral: for everything there is a season. It changed him overnight. The uptown lifestyle slowed to a series of quiet evenings at home, sprawled on the sofa watching everything from *Coronation Street* to the *Late Night Horror*. Caroline was working part time on her LLM, studying at nights at the kauri table with the TV chattering at her back.

It drove her mad.

'Why don't you go for a run?' she said. 'Have a game of squash? Go bar-hopping with Marcus?'

But Jon seemed determined on going to seed, spreading visibly because while he sprawled, he ate. He consumed Sarah Lee Cinnamon Swirls, he shovelled in popcorn and chippies. She could hear him as she studied the tables for employment in the clothing industry 1950–1970 or struggled with the Law of Bodies Corporate and Unincorporate.

Crunch. Crunch. Crunch.

He needed to relax, Jon said. The job was bloody demanding. He was tired.

The apartment once so engagingly compact now began to feel crowded, cluttered with belongings.

'We need more space,' Caroline said. 'Let's move.'

She found some nice places: a villa in Remuera, a lovely two-storey place in Parnell. But Jon was disinclined to move. Too much effort, he said. It's comfortable here.

Even more alarming were the discussions in bed. One night he rolled over, held her close and said it would be nice, wouldn't it, to have a kid. Caroline was astonished. Once long ago when they were first together she had thought about having babies. It seemed to be part of the engagement/wedding sequence.

Lyndsay had had a baby. She had married Lenny who was no longer the radical student activist but a tired young GP in Wainuiomata.

Caroline visited her once when she was down in Wellington. She had picked up a stuffed bunny for Rosa at the airport. Lyndsay was sitting on the sofa watching the soaps with her shirt unevenly buttoned over straining breasts. A baby with all the charm of a boiled prune whimpered beside her in a Moses basket amongst a pile of unironed washing.

Three-month colic, Lyndsay said. That was Lenny's diagnosis and she hoped he was right because another month of it would send her completely round the twist. Lenny had clinics and was on call and out nearly every night so he crashed when he had the chance and she was the one that got up and tried to get Rosa to sleep. She spooned instant coffee lethargically into a couple of pottery mugs.

'But it must be nice to have the days to yourself,' said Caroline. 'I mean, it must be nice to be able to read as much as you like.'

'I'm trying to read for my thesis,' said Lyndsay. 'But it takes ages to get all the material out here on Interloan and when I do get it I'm too tired to concentrate. Do you want a mallowpuff?'

On screen Deanne's blue eyes widened in horror at the knowledge that Clayton had killed Brett in cold blood. And in her little basket Rosa kicked at her blanket and her mouth pink and toothless tore a jagged hole in the afternoon. Caroline had decided then and there that she did not want a baby.

Right now she was not sure if she even wanted Jon.

One Saturday they drove out pillaging. A grey day, damp warm mist creeping out of the harbour like mildew and there was nothing to be found. Somewhere near Otahuhu they passed a garage sale and Jon pulled over.

'There's no point,' said Caroline. 'These places are always hopeless.'

And it was: the usual flotsam of old toys and saucepans and plaster of Paris figurines and some sagging deckchairs and a decanter shaped like a ship in full sail. There were clothes drooping from the ceiling and in a wheelbarrow a pile of old shoes bent to other feet and smelling dankly of other bodies.

A young woman with a baby at her hip stood lopsided in the door. Another child clung to her leg.

'A lot of stuff's gone already,' she said. 'They were here at 7 o'clock bashing on the windows. Some people have got no consideration.'

The baby grizzled and stuck its fist in its mouth and the woman jiggled it wearily. Behind her hung a full-length tapestry of Elvis, sequinned and embroidered in gold thread. The child tugged frantically at the woman's skirt.

'Come ONNN.' One hand clutched the front of his red shorts where a damp stain spread. The woman looked down.

'Oh Scott,' she said. She hit him quickly, casually. 'Not again.'

There was a pause while Scott's mouth opened and he gathered breath. 'He never tells me in time,' she said in the interval before the cry. The sudden movement had startled the baby too and the whimpering amplified.

'I'll be in the house,' said the woman. 'If you want anything.'

Her eyes flickered across their shoulders to where the Fiat was parked in the drive, taking in the number plate, and she took the cash box with her. They trailed away up the path on a diminishing wail. Caroline turned over one of a pile of plates, *50 cents each*. She thought so. Coalport. An ugly pattern but it would be worth $20 on Ponsonby Road. And the Elvis hanging would be a fine touch: witty, mocking, behind the jukebox.

The woman knelt on some faded Feltex to wrap their purchases in the bare front room.

'Moving house is an awful business, isn't it?' said Caroline.

(Keep her talking. She was suspicious, wondering why these people in their flash city car and flash city clothes were wanting her things. Was she being laughed at? Was she being ripped off? There was an outside chance she might have heard of Coalport. Keep her talking.)

'And this must be a nice place to bring up kids.'

'Yeah,' said the woman. She reached for the Coalport. For a second she lingered.

'Are you moving into town?' said Caroline.

'Oz,' said the woman. 'They've shut down the freezer and my husband says there's more opportunity in Oz.'

She wrapped the plate in a page of the *Sunday Sports*. $20. Maybe $50. She placed it with the couple of pieces of Lynndale Ware in a plastic bag.

'I don't really want to go,' she said and her tough little mouth trembled. 'I don't know anyone over there. I've lived here all my life and my sister's next door but Duane says New Zealand's fu— finished and it's better to move while we're young and once we get to the Gold Coast we'll be all right.'

Caroline took the bag and said Duane was probably right. The room smelled of wet nappies and cigarette smoke and failure. She wanted to get out onto the road, the windows on the Fiat wound down to blow away the reek of it. But what was this? Jon was saying they were interested in the decanter and how much was it? The woman looked at them sidelong and said $60. It was a good one. It had a label from Germany and they had got it as a wedding present and it was like new. And Jon was actually handing over the money and saying thanks and good luck in Australia. Caroline was speechless. It was ugly, but not wittily ugly, just cheap.

'What on earth made you do that?' she said when they got back into the car and Jon said he didn't know. He just felt sorry for her, that's all.

Jon was becoming a worry.

Another year and he had still not become a partner. Ed Finnerty took her aside at a barbecue in Devonport one evening and said that between you and me Jon wasn't living up to expectations. Lacked the instinct for the jugular which characterised the first-class lawyer.

'You've got to be a bit of a bastard,' he said.

'Like you?' said Caroline.

Ed snapped open a can of beer.

'Like me,' he said. 'Or,' as he handed it to her, lager frothing over her hand, 'like you, madam.'

Across the patio Jon was helping himself very seriously to some potato salad. His head was bowed and already thinning on top and he looked from this angle more rounded than she remembered. Softer.

11. *Caroline Jane Carstairs has from time to time bumped against the glass ceiling.*

Caroline had a discreet affair with Ed. Nice and quiet, said Ed. Steady as she goes and nobody need get upset and everybody will be happy.

Except that one weekend when she had told Jon she was working in Wellington, Ed's car clipped a culvert on the road from Pauanui and they wobbled for a hundred yards then flipped upside down into a paddock. Ed snapped his pelvis. Caroline hung upside down from her seatbelt and looked out at a startled cow and thought, 'Well, that's that.'

Her marriage wobbled then flipped upside down and ended and no one was very happy at all for a while.

Caroline tried not to fret. She concentrated on becoming a partner.

Morgan Jeffries and Stanway was an oakpanelled kind of firm. Stanway was upholstered in grey from head to toe. Jeffries was a fanatic trout fisherman and the walls were lined with his trophies, all with their mouths open gasping, and Morgan took snuff. You could hear him sneezing explosively from the front office.

'God,' said Lyndsay when she came once to visit Caroline. 'It's like *Wind in the Willows*. I keep expecting rabbits in woolly mufflers to walk down the hall. How can you stand it?'

Lyndsay had begun working at last, in a converted butcher's shop in Wainuiomata with a toybox in the waiting room and an equal profit-sharing arrangement with the other lawyer and the secretary. And part-time so she could pick up Rosa from school in the afternoons.

She did family stuff, mostly. Some conveyancing. Minor criminal work – shoplifting, car conversion, that kind of thing. The sort of thing city lawyers dismissed as social work. The major stuff went into town. She didn't mind. Even the minor stuff was interesting. Like she'd been involved with a guy who'd got into trouble during the Tour: a young Singaporean student who'd almost been deported.

Lyndsay was a marshal, arm in arm once more and leading the chant: 'One two three four, We don't want your racist tour!' Her long hair was tucked up under a motorcycle helmet.

Rua Squad had been stopped at the police blockade at the corner of Wallace Street and across the road a cop had this young Chinese guy, Peter Ho, in a stranglehold. 'Come on, Bruce,' he was saying. 'Let's see you kung fu your way out of that.'

Behind her Rua Squad pushed and shoved.

'Seven eight nine ten,' she called. 'Blazey's fucked it up again.'

Peter Ho's face was turning blue. He had got caught up in the crowd, he had not provoked attack, he was just trying to find his way home to his flat.

Lyndsay stopped chanting long enough to yell at the officer, to be certain of identification, to be able to represent Peter a few days later when he appeared in court and was threatened with the cancellation of his student visa and imminent deportation. She'd made bloody sure no such thing happened. She'd made bloody sure the cops hadn't got away with it. Some of them were all right, but some of them were racist bullies.

Even the minor stuff could throw up some interesting points of law. She'd had this case for example where a woman had come in, married twenty-five years and the husband had traded her in for a newer model. Marriage on the rocks, straightforward mat. prop. – except that they owned Samsung Imports, they were both fifty per cent shareholders, and he wanted to work through the Family Court.

'And he's such a bastard,' Lyndsay said. 'He's been planning it for ages, salting away money all over the place while he's been on business trips in Asia and it's going to be bloody impossible to trace it all and his wife's hopeless. Married straight out of school, never worked, contributed her inheritance to the firm and now she's on her own and she's terrified of everything: applying for a job, doing her own tax return, fixing the car. And she's broke. That's why she came to see me instead of someone more elegant.

'God, stop me,' said Lyndsay. 'I get so tied up in it all. That's the hardest part, don't you find? Keeping enough emotional distance to do the job properly. Tell me about your work instead. What have you been doing?'

Caroline had assisted with the purchase of a carpet cleaning company and a firm manufacturing plastic piping. She had also taken on Ron Brazier who had been one of Stanway's clients until Stanway had his stroke and a couple of months off recuperating. Ron had a kindly rumpled face which was probably why he was able to demolish List B buildings while retaining his place on the City Council.

He liked her way with an injunction against the Akarana Trust.

'Didn't know they were dead till they'd been gutted,' he said. 'Good girl.'

He liked the way she picked up a couple of loopholes in a finance document.

He leaned back, the Regal Theatre reduced to a pile of demolition timber and chunks of masonry and the site all set to go and said, 'And you're a bloody sight better-looking than Stanway, so let's keep it like this, eh?' She was not sure that Lyndsay would be impressed.

'I've brought in $60,000 this year,' she said. 'So it can't be too long till a partnership.'

And then, because Lyndsay asked direct questions, she had found herself saying it all: that David who had the office next door and who had arrived three months after her and had consistently brought in less in fees had become a partner, that Greg who had only recently arrived from Australia had already been offered a partnership. She hated hearing her voice sound peevish and irritable. She hated sounding like a child wailing, 'But that's not fair.' She hated hearing Lyndsay saying that it was bloody sexism no doubt of it and she should say so. Confront them with the facts. She was writing an article on women and the glass ceiling as it operated in the law for the *Journal* and this would be a perfect case to cite.

Caroline did not want to be one of Lyndsay's perfect cases.

'It's nothing to do with that,' she wanted to say. 'It was my own fault for not recognising the game plan. I thought so long as I worked hard and was nice to Morgan and Jeffries I'd be fine. After all, they're the founding partners, they're the ones who make a noise in meetings, they're the dominant presences around here. So I'd done all the right things – you know, talking endlessly about cricket or fishing, staying for a drink on a Friday – but I'd underestimated Stanway.'

Stanway. His grey little head popping round the door, one side of his face sagging to a floppy jowl. His, 'Ah Caroline, I wonder if I might have a word.' His smooth, 'We've given your application our most serious consideration but feel that it might be premature at this stage. The general feeling is however that you should most certainly re-apply for next year.'

She should not have poached Ron Brazier.

'I was careless. I stood on somebody's toes,' she said to Lyndsay, not wanting commiseration, not wanting advice, not wanting glib feminist analysis. 'That's all. It has been a worthwhile lesson.'

'You should leave,' said Lyndsay. 'Tons of places would snap you up and you're so lucky. You could go wherever you please.'

12. *Caroline Jane Carstairs learns from her mistakes.*

It was unwanted, but it was the right advice. Caroline did leave. Braithwaite Salmond had decided to open an office in Wellington and Caroline joined the firm on the promise, over beef miroton at the Chancery, of a partnership within eighteen months.

She moved south.

'Good,' said Lyndsay. 'We'll be able to meet for lunch sometimes. It'll be great to keep in touch.'

It was a good move. On the flight from Auckland she met Evan. Evan was an accountant. He was forty and divorced, he was tall and pleasant, he had thinning brown hair and three children, all grown, thank God.

They made a good team.

The second wedding was quiet, dark blue tailored linen and a little hat and dinner for twelve at Fino's, then back to the house in Karori with its villa windows overlooking the city. Caroline put the steeple clock on the mantel and her collection of art deco china on the dresser and settled in.

On Saturdays they played tennis, clad in snowy white, and in the winter they skied at Whakapapa and spent the occasional week mid-winter in Fiji. Caroline provided legal advice when Pallson and Co. took over Repton Engineering, and when Data International took over Acme Information Systems. She acted for some of the shareholders and prevented the takeover of Goldmann Holdings by Selbys. She met Lyndsay once a week at the ShapeUp gym where they exercycled and swam a few lengths then had a drink together overlooking the pool.

Lyndsay had moved into town. She and Lenny had separated and it was simpler to be in the city. Lenny had gone off to India to work at a people's clinic and Rosa was still at Girls' High so she had to earn enough to support them both so that meant a bigger firm though she still did family work, divorces, sexual abuse. Still did social work.

It's what she was good at, she said, but it was sometimes

pretty heavy going, explaining her rights in a marriage settlement over and over to a woman with an IQ of seventy. Dealing with all the emotion kicking round in custody cases and matrimonial property cases. She had been followed home more times than she could remember, had a guy sitting outside her gate all night, spent one whole Christmas wondering if another guy with a history of assault was going to kill her as he had threatened. She worried whenever Rosa was late home at times like that.

She lay back in the spa at the gym and looked up at the steam winding to the glass ceiling.

'It's so nice to relax for a bit,' she said. 'So nice to be able to talk about it all with someone like you, an old friend who understands. Because you can't dump it on your family and you've got to keep your guard up with colleagues, just a little. Just in case.'

Right now, she was dealing with Mrs Theobald. Mrs Theobald was one of those tough blondes, said Lyndsay. You'd think nothing could faze her. But she was married to this bastard who was some kind of builder. A developer.

Caroline stirred the water with her foot. 'I know,' she said. 'Theobald of Strada Inc. They're doing that subdivision up the Hapakaroana Valley. He's a client of Patrick O'Halloran who is a colleague of mine.'

'Dodgy as hell,' said Lyndsay. 'He's got connections with DiLonghi. Gus DiLonghi? You know: the one-legged guy with the artificial leg full of cocaine? The body on the beach at Muriwai? The one that had had its tongue cut out? That lot. Anyway, Mr Theobald has obviously been under a bit of strain lately, which is not surprising given what is likely to be revealed when that all hits the court in a month or so, and when he's upset about things he tends to beat up Mrs Theobald and Mrs Theobald's kids and a couple of weeks ago she decided she'd had enough of it all, so she's left and I'm acting for her against him and it's bloody scary let me tell you. I mean these guys are heavy. *Hawaii Five-O* types in white shoes and gold neck chains with big bumps in their trousers and even bigger bumps under their jackets.'

She reached over and flicked on the water jet.

'I envy you,' she said to Caroline. 'Dealing with nice quiet office blocks and tidy little warehouses.'

But it was not always quiet, or in the least bit tidy. One afternoon in 1988 she came back from lunch to find Sally chatting to Patrick from her desk among the aspidistras, ferns and rubber plants which lent the reception area at Braithwaite Salmond a faint air of the jungle. Sally turned as the lift doors opened.

'Ah,' she said. 'Here you are.'

As if Caroline had been caught out of bounds. As if she had been taking hours over smoked salmon salad and chilled white at some downtown eatery, when all she'd had time for was a ham sandwich at Danny's Diner and coffee to follow at her desk as she raced to finish a report before a two o'clock appointment and Danny's sandwiches were famed for wedging as a wad of bread and mustard midway down the gullet if swallowed hurriedly.

Sally leaned forward conspiratorially from among the ferns and said Lou would like a word if she could spare a moment.

Patrick had gone into his office but the door was open and she could see him taking a close interest in a file, a grey suit by an orderly desk, bookshelf in one corner, squash racket and sports bag in the other. *Mens* very *sana* in corporate suit *sano*.

'Can it wait an hour?' said Caroline. 'I've got Pallson coming in at two.'

There was something mildly irritating about the way Sally always addressed the side of Caroline's head, but then it was not to be unexpected. After all, Caroline had seen Sally hand in hand with Patrick in a restaurant in Brisbane.

Caroline had been visiting her parents who had retired to the Gold Coast and one Tuesday afternoon she had gone shopping and seen Patrick nuzzling Sally's neck while Sally read a menu and sipped one of those nasty drinks she enjoyed when she was in full party mood: something orange with a little umbrella on top and cherries and cream. At parties Sally began with just a small sherry, thank you, but as the evening progressed her tastes veered toward Tequila Sunrises and Malibu Dreams as her accent wavered uncertainly from Nga Tawa, which is what she hoped people would assume when she said she had 'gone to school in Marton', to a more plebeian district high.

Sally had looked up from the list of pasta and mezze and seen Caroline, a brief startled glance, and then her face had slammed shut.

Caroline had been just as startled. She had always thought that Patrick was the possessor of an ideal marriage, with an ideal wife and four ideal children, just as he was the possessor of an ideal Mercedes and several ideal clients. Strada Inc, for example.

It seemed that Patrick also had the ideal mistress. Sally was pretty and efficient and well informed, Secretary of the Year back at CIT and 'always prepared to go the extra mile', according to the citation which hung discreetly behind her desk. Caroline had not realised that she was prepared to wear out extra shoe leather in the pursuit of Patrick.

Neither had said a word about the chance encounter, but Sally had from then on refused to meet Caroline's eye. Today, the Nga Tawa accent was firmly between the teeth.

'He was most emphatic,' she fluted from the jungle. 'Just as soon as you came in, he said.'

Lou was on the telephone when she arrived. He cupped his hand over the receiver and said he wouldn't be a second, take a pew.

Years before, as a child, he had attended a minor British public school which was staffed almost entirely by ex-army men. By the age of twelve he understood intimately how to lay mines and defuse a grenade, a skill which had undoubtedly stood him in good stead in adult life. Under pressure he still tended to revert to a military vocabulary.

'My instinct is to simply send in the sappers,' he was saying. 'Take 'em out once and for all . . .'

Caroline felt irritated. She was busy, she had a lot to do that afternoon, and there was a choice in Lou's office between a hardback chair which made you feel as if you had arrived in the principal's office, and a sofa which was soft and difficult in a tight straight skirt so that you had to adopt the Lady Di position: legs at forty-five degrees, ankles demurely crossed. She decided instead to stand by the window looking down at the traffic on Willis Street as it clotted about the lights. By the window she occupied the high ground and Lou, when he was ready, would be forced to look up at her into the light.

'But we'll need to do a bit of a recce,' said Lou. 'We'll discuss strategies at four. Roger.'

He stretched.

'Glad you could pop in,' he said. Behind the black walnut barrier of his desk, with his little spotted bow tie and his domed bald head, he looked uncannily like Humpty Dumpty. He had fat white hands, the little finger on the right ringed with gold so tight that the flesh rode up in an uncomfortable ridge.

'Do take a seat,' he said. So Caroline chose the hard chair and Lou told her that in this day and age any company needed to travel light, to be a streamlined outfit able to move rapidly over rough terrain under fire.

Caroline watched his little pink mouth opening and shutting above the waggle of his bow tie.

Braithwaite Salmond had made that classical tactical error, Lou said, of attempting to open on two fronts and they had suffered the consequences. So there it was, and he hoped she realised what a very difficult decision faced the senior partners as they fell back, regrouped and tried to salvage what they could. Braithwaite Salmond was in trouble. Braithwaite Salmond was about to close its Wellington office. Forty-five people would have to be relocated or made redundant and some, including some of the partners, would have to move on.

'The best we can hope for at this stage,' said Lou, fat little hands clasped in prayer, 'is retreat with honour.'

And he was telling Caroline before it became public knowledge so that she would have time to look elsewhere.

'And what about the other partners?' said Caroline. 'Are they going to look elsewhere? What about Patrick, for example?'

Lou said that not all of them had quite her flexibility or employability.

God, it was almost a compliment to be selected, a mark of faith in her extraordinary abilities. Caroline straightened her skirt and walked over to the window and looked down at the street. A man had jumped from the parking building across the road only three months ago. His business had been in trouble, he'd had problems at home, a history of mild psychiatric disturbance. The road had been closed for twenty minutes in the rush hour while they hosed it down.

What an idiot.

'I have sensed a certain degree of tension at meetings lately,' she said. The traffic eased past the lights and down toward Manners Street. 'But I had no idea it was because of this. I must admit I had put it down to concern at our involvement with Strada Inc.'

Lou looked up, bow tie on the alert.

'Oh?' he said.

'Because of Theobald's links with Gus DiLonghi,' she said. 'And the possibility of accusations of laundering and so on with the Hapakaraona Development?'

Lou's tie was near-vertical.

'But now I know the real reason,' said Caroline. She walked over to the desk and shook Lou's little pink hand.

'Thank you,' she said. 'For warning me. I can see that we do indeed have our backs to the wall.'

Out in the office Sally looked up from the jungle. Caroline smiled at her and back in her room she heard the phone ringing next door in Patrick's office. She'd supplied the ammunition.

The squad was lining up.

Bang bang bang.

13. *Caroline Jane Carstairs knows when to consolidate her position.*

Caroline began to look elsewhere, and a couple of months later she had the office on the twelfth floor and the harbour view. She took her clients with her as Braithwaite Salmond retreated, trumpeting 'streamlined client services' and led by Lou the Little Corporal back along the road to Auckland.

She was busy re-establishing; Evan was busy hanging on as the tree was shaken at Marriot French & Co., Chartered Accountants, and the less determined apples fell off into voluntary redundancy or private practice. They were both a little distracted.

One night, Evan murmured, 'Oh Gilly, Gilly, Gilly,' into her hair as they slept after making love and that was the first she knew of it. Normally, she'd have had some warning. First, there would have been the sudden flurry of work necessitating nights back at the office or a receivership in Taupo or Nelson requiring trips away, annoying but necessary. Then it was only a matter of time till the dinner invitation.

'Why don't we have a few people over for a meal on Friday?' Evan would say, elaborately casual. 'We don't seem to have seen anyone for ages, since I've been so busy at work. I thought we could ask Nigel and Anne, say, and Tony and Fenella? We owe them an invitation. Oh, and there's this new consultant at work, Angela, who doesn't know many people here in Wellington yet. We could ask her.'

When Angela came he'd exchange only polite pleasantries with her, apparently preferring the conversation of other people, and when they had all left he'd say, 'Well, sorry about that. Angela's a bit dull really, not our sort at all. But at least we've done the decent thing.' And he'd stroke Caroline's back as they cleared away the plates and they'd make rough love all night. He adored having both the women he was fucking in the one room. Then there would be the gifts: bunches of tightly furled pink roses, like pursed lips. And gradually the excitement would fade and he'd revert to watching telly in the evenings or suggesting a stroll after dinner or a night at the opera. Caroline disliked Evan then: hated his droopy hangdog air and the way he placed his hand beneath her elbow as they crossed the street. She much preferred him devious and tricky and happy.

For her part, she tried to be discreet but no doubt he knew also. It was always the little things that gave you away. The name mentioned just once too often, the pointed avoidance in public, the chaste kiss at the door as the lover arrives with his wife for a party or dinner. And sometimes when it was all over they would confess to one another. Evan would lie beside her in the darkness and she'd tell him about Giorgio who was all talk and sexual innuendo in public but pretty hopeless really, a breast man who would lie there sucking away for hours if you let him.

'Not Giorgio,' says Evan, lying there in the dark. 'Not the Khandallah Stallion.'

'The same,' says Caroline. 'He can only get it up by asking you to climb out of bed and go and tidy the curtains or turn down the light or pick up his shoes off the floor: anything, so long as it means you bend over. And when you turn round he's lying there . . .'

'Like this?' says Evan.

'Yes,' says Caroline. 'And he's hard . . .'

'Like this?' says Evan.

'Almost,' says Caroline.

'And then,' says Caroline, 'he fucks you hard from behind. Twenty seconds of feverish pumping and that's it. I think our Giorgio probably prefers boys, in fact.'

'Twenty seconds,' says Evan, rolling over and reaching for her. 'I think we may be able to improve on his performance, don't you?'

'Oh yes,' says Caroline. 'Oh yes. Oh yes. Oh yes.'

But Gilly was a new development. She'd never been introduced to Gilly. Evan had never even mentioned her name until that night.

'I mean,' she said to Lyndsay at the gym, 'I hope this Gilly isn't some little bimbo who assumes marriage and babies are part of the deal. I hope she's not pressuring Evan to do something stupid. Divorces are so messy, and so expensive. And Evan and I have such a good relationship: I'd never worry about catching Aids or anything with Evan. He's always so careful. I mean we understand one another perfectly. We understand the terms of our contract.'

'Well, if you ever need a hand,' says Lyndsay, 'if Gilly doesn't understand the terms of the contract, you can count on me. If you ever need support, I'm here.'

A momentary image flashes across Caroline's inner eye: herself, Caroline, in an efficient yet comfortable single-woman's apartment, alone with her cat, eating alone in front of the television, ringing another single woman to go to the opera, or for a walk in the evening . . .

'I won't be needing support,' Caroline said. 'Evan knows when he's on to a good thing. One thing I know for certain is that he won't be wanting babies at his age. He's much too comfortable.'

'It's just that I've always been able to count on you,' said Lyndsay. 'And I want you to know that you can always count on me.'

Sometimes Lyndsay could be a real bore. Sometimes Caroline regretted suggesting that she join Tremayne Prentice. She had only done so in the first place because Forbes Mulgrew had been pressing for an old friend of his from Scots and the last thing Caroline wanted was another prop or lock for Forbes's team.

'What we need,' she had argued, 'is a specialist in family law. It would be a useful addition to our services.'

Expensive dissolutions, squabbles over property, claim and counterclaim – they could no longer be dismissed glibly as 'social work'. So Lyndsay came and most unexpectedly, she brought with her as a client Stanley Ho. Stanley Ho, who had bought the Clarendon Hotel, the West City and the Radcliffe Centre, who owned Motuareroiti Island and Windermere Run in Canterbury. Stanley Ho whose son Peter had been caught up in a demonstration and came within a whisker of being deported back in 1981.

Stanley remembered a good turn when he was looking for a company to represent his interests in New Zealand.

He was a most valued client. Tremayne Prentice were delighted.

14. *Caroline Jane Carstairs makes every minute a constructive minute.*

So on Friday 22 September, Caroline closes her office door and reviews her career. Not for long, because there's no point spending too long on the past. You must simply get on with preparing the future. She drafts and peruses and dictates the reports and letters which will keep her fees high and at five there are drinks in the boardroom and special congratulations for Lyndsay.

Caroline raises her glass with the others, and says well done and good luck.

Then she walks up Willis Street in a chill spring wind and into the warm steamy haven which is ShapeUp. She drags on her swimsuit and jumps into the blue water and begins her swim. One lap, two laps, three laps. The radio is playing and the music reaches her underwater through her thrashing arms. She is going to swim twenty laps faster than she has ever done it. She kicks hard and keeps her head down and, on the hour, the announcer rattles into the news. Through Bosnia and the World Court and activists and famine and protest – all that activity, all those human emotions, anger and greed and love and ambition, reduced to 30-second sound bites – she thinks she hears Margie's name.

Margie Miller.

The words drop bulbous and misshapen into the water.

Would that be Margie Miller from school?

HEATHER

'At the entry of Elizabeth Fry the prisoners
quietened . . .'

SHE MADE THEM LATE, WANTING TO VISIT ELIOT
on the way.

They were already pushed for time because the
McIlwraith family group conference had had to be postponed
to Friday morning so they didn't get away until close on
midday and Dorothy had arranged dinner.

'Just something very simple,' she had said. 'No fuss, you'll
have to take us as you find us I'm afraid,' but remembering
the no-fuss buffet for family and a few close friends which
had marked Matthew and Sarah's engagement, Heather
doubted simplicity.

'Just drop in,' said Dorothy. 'Any time. Say sevenish? For
seven-thirty?'

Trevor had the car packed when Heather got back from
two hours of the McIlwraiths locked in furious argument
and accusation, *fuck you, you can't make me, moll, slut, bitch,
bastard.*

'We'll be late,' he said.

'But it's Eliot's birthday,' Heather said. 'We can't just
drive past only a mile away and ignore him. It's bad enough
that he's missing his brother's wedding.'

'Hmmm,' said Trevor. Trevor had always been supportive.
He had never been judgemental about the way she parented
her older son, but, 'Hmmm,' he said, and he flicked his paper
in a way which stated as clearly as if he had stood on the

kitchen chair and yelled, eyes popping: well, Eliot should have thought about such things sooner. He's made his bed, now let him lie on it.

His narrow prison bed.

'If you're sure,' said Trevor. 'If it won't make you upset.'

'I won't get upset,' said Heather.

'Because it wouldn't be fair to Matthew,' said Trevor. 'After all, it's his big day.'

It was important to be fair. An equal share each of chocolate, a bike each, an exactly measured scoop of Neapolitan to each plate. An exactly equal fair share of love.

'I won't get upset,' said Heather. 'I'm getting used to it now.'

Flick went the *Waikato Times*.

'OK,' said Trevor. Studiedly neutral. Flick.

She had made Eliot a cake when she got in from work on Thursday, in a rush and late as usual because as soon as she had walked into the office that morning the phone was ringing and the Johanssen boy's placement had broken down and Mrs Rose was saying she'd had it up to here with him and last night had been the last straw and she wanted him out of here this minute, she had said she'd only take littlies, she didn't want older kids and you said a week and it's twelve weeks now and I don't get paid to be threatened in my own home. So Heather had soothed and said yes, she'd get onto it right away. But it took hours to find another placement, because who would take him? Who would take Daniel, with his eyes like twin bruises, plucked from a stinking cot when he was two and terrified of the dark and the bath for reasons nobody knew but anyone could guess at and tossed since then from home to home, always just a little too much for the caregiver to cope with, always just too much to handle. And the phone had rung incessantly and there were three new allocations to fit in next week and team meeting and supervision and Demelza Murphy had slashed her wrists again and Mrs Murphy had said she didn't know what had got into

Demelza she really didn't and Heather could have said, 'It's because you belted her with a jug cord for years and told her over and over again that she was dumb and useless,' but that wouldn't have helped, not now.

Besides, it might not even be true. Demelza may have slid into terminal despair with Mom Brady.

You couldn't always blame the parents for their children's behaviour. You truly couldn't.

So she had to stay late to write up a couple of reports for the morning and she finally got home at ten.

Trevor was sitting up in bed watching the news. She took off her coat and put on her jersey and slippers.

'Aren't you coming to bed?' he said, one eye on a school fire in Northland.

'I'm going to make Eliot a cake,' said Heather. 'There won't be time in the morning.'

'What are you going to put in it?' said Trevor. 'A file?' He flicked to Channel Two.

'That's not funny,' said Heather.

'Sorry,' said Trevor.

To Channel Three.

'I won't be long,' said Heather. 'I'll sleep in Matthew's room if you don't want to be disturbed.'

'That's OK,' said Trevor. 'You won't disturb me.'

Back to Channel One. There's a street protest somewhere, a forest of banners. 'If you're sure . . .' said Heather.

'Hmmm,' said Trevor.

She made Eliot a chocolate cake. With peppermint filling. He'd always liked peppermint filling. She measured and stirred and poured and thought about all the other cakes she had made for Eliot: the train cake she'd made when he was three and the Hickory Dickory Dock studded with Pebbles when he was four and the circus which was pink and yellow and decorated with a whole troupe of animal biscuits and the soccer pitch with green icing and birthday candle goalposts. His twenty-eighth cake was a more moderate affair altogether: plain chocolate with peppermint filling. She put it in a plastic container so it would not get squashed in the back of the car amongst their suitcases with Trevor's suit and her new dress and the wedding gifts which had arrived at their house for Matthew and Sarah: the duvet cover from the Van Fleets next door, the toaster from Matthew's Standard One teacher, who had a real soft spot for him, always said he had been a lovely kid, one of her favourites.

'I mean, Eliot was the bright one, wasn't he?' she had said, fluffy little Miss Rewi, twisting her spectacles on their blue ribbon, forty years of Cuisenaire rods and nature tables receding into the distance as she bustled into retirement. 'But Matthew was such a sweet, good-natured little boy. You couldn't help but love him.' The car would be crammed. Gifts and some pillows and a couple of casserole dishes and a heater they no longer needed because Matthew and Sarah were moving into a flat up in Brooklyn and those things might come in handy. And the dinner set she and Trevor had bought as their gift: a plain white German set which Sarah had picked out at Raneys. A sensible choice. Good china, and it wouldn't date. Sarah was a sensible young woman.

Heather put the cake carton amongst it all and went upstairs.

Trevor was asleep with his hand still on the remote and the TV flickered in a flurry of black and white in the corner by the dressing table. She took the remote from his hand and turned down the light.

'Hmmm,' said Trevor and turned in sleep, dragging the duvet into a tight cocoon so that a mean little draught slid in on her side. She lay as still as she could listening to Trevor's breathing as it steadied and found an even rhythm. She lay and looked up at the dark and thought: cake, done. Gifts, done.

Message left for Jenny asking her to look in on Demelza. Done.

Heather lay looking up into the dark. In the photograph

her sons are walking away from her, hand in hand. Matthew has his teddy in a blue bucket and Eliot carries a plastic laser sword. It glowed when you pressed a button and emitted a high-pitched beeping and Eliot loved it. More than the cowboy gun and holster, more than the bow and arrows and the machine gun with Authentic Firing Device As Used By The American Marines which Shona had sent from Sydney, year by year supplementing the plastic arsenal.

'We don't believe in giving them war toys,' Heather had said. 'There's good evidence that they encourage violent behaviour.'

'Don't be so prissy,' Shona said. 'Eliot likes them, doesn't he?'

Well, yes, Eliot did like them. He was in fact never without his sword. And his gun. And his helmet and plastic shield and bow and arrow set. At night when Heather went in to say goodnight she would find him tumbled on the bed, arms spread wide and the blankets in a wild tangle and by his head the laser sword beeping blue-white while across the room Matthew lay snug, cuddling his teddy.

She had tried throwing some of the weapons away, beginning with the machine gun with its infuriating Authentic Firing Device. Eliot was distraught.

'My dun,' he wailed, wandering disconsolately round the house. 'Where my dun?'

She tried distraction. 'Let's build some Lego,' she had said. 'Let's make an enormous castle.'

'My dun,' wailed Eliot. 'Where my DUN?'

And finally she had given in, dragged it from the bottom of the rubbish bin, taped up the broken trigger, restored it to its owner.

Tattatattatatta tat, went the Authentic Firing Device.

Eliot was happy.

In the photograph he carries the sword and he walks hand in hand with his brother towards the dark blur which is the rhododendron hedge Eliot calls the dungle where they have their hut. They walk away from her on sturdy legs, each in summer shorts, Eliot's slung low round narrow little-boy hips, Matthew's bulging over nappies. Sunlight spills over them so that their hair, one dark, one fair, shines and they are turned slightly toward one another talking seriously.

It was a good photograph, just a snap she had taken from the kitchen window one morning. But she had it enlarged and it hangs above the dressing table out there in the dark. She knows it is there, her two sons walking away and away from her towards the dungle.

Today he seemed thinner. His jeans were still slung low on narrow hips. She stood on tiptoe to give him a kiss.

'Happy Birthday,' she said. 'I brought you a cake. They've got it at the office.'

'Great,' he said. 'The food here's bloody terrible.'

'Are you eating?' she said, aware that she sounded like a mum, looked like a mum, sitting here in the visitors' room with its bored guard seated at one end of the huddle of grey plastic chairs and formica-top tables and the prison smell of cigarette smoke and stewed vegetables and confinement like mould on the air. The room is overheated, hot and stuffy. She can never think straight in a hot room. She can hardly breathe.

'Yeah,' said Eliot, but careless, as if it didn't matter whether he ate or not, as if all those years of making proper muesli on Saturday mornings and home-made bread and making sure he had a green leafy vegetable every day and fresh fruit and not too many lollies and chippies, as if none of that mattered.

His T-shirt hangs limp from the shoulders, plain black. His hair is short, clipped above the ears so that he looks absurdly young. She wants to reach out and cup the curve of his skull beneath her hand. When he was a baby his head fitted the palm of her hand exactly, firm and downy, like a peach. She feels a dull remembered aching in her breasts, as if her milk long dried were letting down.

'I hope you get some of the cake,' she said. 'It's not a very big one and the woman at the office said they share them out amongst the whole wing. I didn't know they did that. I thought you'd get it all.'

Eliot's leg jiggles beneath the table. There's a gap as wide as a jungle between them, as wide as a busy street. Even if she tried, she could never reach his head, never cradle it again in the palm of her hand. Not now. He looks out of the window to a lawn dead flat and ringed by straggling bushes which almost conceal the wire fence between them and the hills. A young man on a motor mower rides up and down, up and down, trailing a smooth grassy wake.

'It's chocolate,' she says. 'With peppermint filling.'

'Great,' says Eliot. 'Thanks.'

His fingers drum at the table top. His long white fingers. There's a yellow stain at the tip of the second and third.

'I didn't know you smoked,' she says.

Eliot looks down at his fingers. 'Oh yeah,' he says.

As if that didn't matter either. As if it didn't matter that he has had his measles vaccination at the proper time and his immunisation against polio and whooping cough and all the other terrors hovering in the air about him, as if it didn't matter that he has had swimming lessons and a Defensive Driving Course so that he would always be healthy and fit and safe.

'I could bring you some cigarettes next time,' she says. 'What kind do you smoke?'

Trevor will notice, of course. He'll not say anything but he will notice. She's indulging her son, encouraging bad habits, just as she always gave in when he wanted chippies smothered in artificial colourings and carcinogenic additives.

'One packet won't do any harm,' she had said.

Trevor had said, 'Hmmm,' and she had tossed Eliot his Cheesy Corn Pops and his Chitterlin' Snax and he had munched away happily. But now look where he is. Look what all that indulgence has led to.

227

The motor mower sweeps in a half-circle outside the window and her son's voice is lost in the roar. She thinks he says, 'Pall Mall.' But he adds, 'Don't bother. I can get them here. There's a kind of canteen.' His legs jiggle, ready to run.

When he was little he was always on the move, always restless.

'Hyperactive,' some of his teachers said. 'Can't sit still for ten seconds.'

'Is he destructive?' she had said. 'Is he aggressive?'

'No,' they had said. 'He's charming. But he's disruptive. He makes the other children restless.'

'How does he do that?' she had said.

He made them laugh.

'There are thirty-six kids in that room,' she said to Trevor, 'and it's designed for twenty-four. What do they expect? Plus the teacher's burnt out and just hanging in there for his super. Should I suggest they examine their classroom management techniques, try smaller groups? Or maybe just a tad more positive reinforcement?' Trevor said maybe, but other kids didn't seem to have a problem. Other parents were not being asked to exercise more control of their children.

'Could the problem be an allergy?' he said. There was good evidence that junk food caused hyperactivity. (So it was her fault: she was poisoning her child with Cheesy Corn Pops and Chitterlin' Snax.)

Or maybe the cause was too much television?

Trevor made a roster and pinned it by the set: each child to have exactly one programme per day and no more. That was fair. Matthew understood the need for moderation and order. He studied the programmes listed in the paper and made his choice, then copied the title and time down in the appropriate column. He was a natural for accountancy. Eliot argued that *Nice One Stu* counted as just one programme.

Trevor disallowed it. It was a catch-all title, he said, covering *The New Mickey Mouse Club*, *My Favourite Martian*, *Room 222* and *Daktari*, not to mention a couple of cartoons.

That's six separate programmes, and most of them American rubbish with that overgrown idiot in a school cap as an excuse for a frontman. 'But they're not separate in the paper,' said Eliot. 'Look. All it says is: "Nice One Stu! Stu's here, with his Special Blend of Fun!"'

He was right.

Trevor wanted to alter the wording on the selection list but Eliot said that wasn't fair: that was what Trevor always said you shouldn't do, alter the rules when you were losing. That's what he had said on Saturday when Matthew was being a pain and had all the hotels and he wanted to borrow just one and it wasn't fair. Trevor gave in. Eliot was pushing the limits as usual and refusing to enter into the true spirit of the thing, but . . . OK. Just this once.

Eliot was a natural for a lawyer.

His fingers drum at the table, the mower sweeps up and around and down, up and around and down. 'Did you get my books?' he says.

'They're in the bag with the cake,' she says. 'I couldn't get that business systems book at Dowlings. They'd run out of copies, but they've got it on order and I asked them to send it to you direct.'

'Great,' says Eliot, eyes following the mower over her shoulder. 'Thanks.'

As if that didn't matter either. As if exams didn't matter, as if the 90-plus average in School Cert. didn't matter, nor the A Bursary nor the easy admission to Law School. All so easy, despite her doubtful enquiries. Have you finished that essay? Have you done your science homework? ('Yep,' he said and off, scooting down the drive on his skateboard, wheels screaming into the curve.) Despite Trevor's regular lectures: you'll never get anywhere these days without decent qualifications, you won't get results if you don't put in the work. ('Yeah, yeah.') As if none of that mattered, nor all those years of preparation, catching him as he skidded past with some book carefully chosen to hold his fleeting attention.

'Sam I am, I am Sam. I do not like green eggs and ham . . .' He had liked that. Funny drawings. Funny rhymes.

'. . . and they went along and they went along until they met Goosey Loosey . . .'

He had liked that too. He liked action and plot and the trail of silly animals walking straight into Foxy Loxy's lair. Matthew had fretted, worrying for the little chicken.

'But what happened to him?' Matthew had said. 'What did the fox do?'

'He ate them, dumbie,' said Eliot. 'See: there's the bones in the picture.'

Matthew refused to eat chicken for weeks after.

'I hope Dowlings send you the book in time,' says Heather. 'When's the exam?'

Nyeroowmm, goes the mower. *Nyerowwwm*, and away towards the fence.

'Next week,' says Eliot.

'Next week!' says Heather. 'It won't arrive before next week.'

'Doesn't matter.'

'I could get a copy from the library instead,' says Heather. 'Or I could pick one up in Wellington and drop it off on the way home on Sunday.'

'Don't bother,' says Eliot.

'But you must have a copy,' says Heather. 'You must read it before the exam.'

Eliot frowns. That tiny cluster of wrinkles between the fine fair brows.

'Mum,' he says, 'it really doesn't matter.'

'But the exam . . .' says Heather.

'It's a Business Studies paper which will supposedly assist with my re-integration into society as part of the normalcy policy operating within this corrective institution, which I doubt, personally. In the meantime it gets me off three hours mopping corridors per week, it looks good on the file and I avoid yet another well-meant Intervention

Course. And I really don't give a toss about the exam.'

It doesn't matter. Nothing matters.

'It'll be incredibly boring anyway,' says Eliot.

Heather feels such a mixture of fury and grief at that, and such an overwhelming sense of helplessness, that she can hardly breathe. Trevor's right. Her oldest son is ungrateful and wilful, hell-bent on self-destruction.

He's made his bed, now let him lie on it. His narrow prison bed.

But he was so sweet, that little boy walking away from her in the picture to conquer the jungle with his sword in his hand. So passionate, the way he would settle on her lap for a minute and fling his arms round her neck and say *Mummy mummy mummy*, nuzzling into her neck and wanting to marry her when he grew up. She hugged him tightly in return and his hair was a soft fair whorl against her cheek, his body a thin bird body, whirring to run and impatient at confinement.

And anyway, what would Trevor know? Trevor was not after all Eliot's father.

Eliot was Wesley Rutter's son. Wesley was a poet. She heard him read one lunchtime back in 1968 in the university union, a skinny intense young man in a brown and yellow jersey with a stag knitted on the back, shiny houndstooth trousers, thick-rimmed glasses and acne.

'*The world is mad . . .*' he read in a high flat drawl which skidded at times into a guinea-pig squeak.

'*. . . caught in its nuclear nightmare the
politicians lie and kill
atomic destruction annihilation . . .*'

'Do you want my milkshake?' said Kathy Scott.

'*. . . blood slops on the streets of the ghetto
and everyone is mad mad mad . . .*'

'What flavour is it?' said Penny Tremewan. 'God, this guy's a dork.'

Wesley's glasses were slipping down his nose. His papers shook. His voice squeaked.

'. . . *the gunman takes aim and the people spill
their guts in stinking death . . .*'

'Banana,' said Kathy. 'It's revolting.'

'Do you think so?' said Penny. 'I quite like it.'

'. . . *maggots and flies crawl over the
bodies sucking the life from them all . . .*'

Penny sucks through the straw loudly. Slu-u-u-rp.

Two guys at the next table look over and laugh. Wesley
is scarlet and sweating.

'. . . *warplanes rain down terror on everyone . . .*'

His papers slide to the floor.

'. . . *when will we wake up from the nightmare?*' he says
lurching to retrieve them and bumping the microphone so
that it thuds at full amplification and teeters dangerously.

'. . . *when will this madness end?*

'Thank you.'

The guys thump their table ironically.

Yeah, they yell. They whistle. *Right on. More. More.* Penny
and Kathy laugh.

Heather saw Wesley later that afternoon sitting on his
own in the library reading room. He looked lonely.

'I liked your poem,' she said.

It took so little to cheer someone up.

Wesley looked up at her through thick pebble glasses
and his eyes were damp and surprised. He shoved the glasses
back onto the bridge of his nose.

'Thanks,' he said.

He smiled.

Two nights later she met him at an open party in Cum-
berland Street. She had gone with Kathy because the whole
hostel had been invited, but Kathy had hardly stepped in the
door to the flat before she had been met by Terry de Lacey
who was running for student president and now she was
leaning against the wall by the stairs and Terry was pouring
her screwdrivers from the bottle he'd brought and talking to
her quietly and earnestly. Kathy looked up at him from time

to time and laughed. Heather had a glass of punch and then another: someone had made it in the washing machine and it wasn't very nice, actually. It had orange slices floating in it and tasted of pineapple juice with just the faintest undertone of Rinso and it was making her feel a little dizzy. She'd have liked to sit down but they'd emptied the flat for the party and there was nowhere to sit so she pushed past Terry and Kathy who didn't notice and fought her way through the kitchen to the back step.

'Well, hi,' said a voice from the darkness by the clothesline. Wesley. In a check Viyella shirt and houndstooth trousers and socks and Roman sandals. His glasses shone in the light from the kitchen door.

'Hullo,' said Heather. The sudden shock of cold air was making her feel definitely sick. She sat down on the step. 'I'm sorry,' she said. 'But I don't feel very well.' Checks, tartan and houndstooth danced in front of her eyes. The clothesline tipped to an odd angle.

'It's the punch,' said Wesley. 'I know the guy who made it and he put absolute alcohol into it. You'll be lucky not to go blind.' Heather threw up into the hydrangeas while Wesley watched.

He said she would feel better after a strong cup of coffee and took her back to his flat and while she was sitting on his bed drinking it and waiting for the floor to steady he read her a poem.

Evil evil evil evil
World is evil
Life is evil
All is evil

It was by Ferlinghetti, he said, who was one of the greats, like Ezra the only begetter and old T.S. himself, and Ginsberg. And Buk.

Wesley's bed was saggy and soft. The coffee was hot and sour and there were little golden bubbles on top from the milk.

Come lie with me
read Wesley
and let my lizard speak to thee.

The coffee scalded her tongue. And then Wesley had put the Animals on the record player and he was sitting beside her and kissing her wetly. On her right ear. It was like being licked by a puppy. His tongue was warm and damp and he smelled of sweat and SpotBan and close up she noticed that every pustule had a dab of skintone cream on top like the icing on a tiny cake. Then he hugged her awkwardly and her coffee spilled over her dress. Well, to be exact, over Kathy's dress: the red woollen mini-dress Kathy has said looked miles better on Heather than it did on her though that was a lie of course, but it was a beautiful dress and far more partyish than the skirt and blouse Heather was planning to wear. And now it was covered in milky coffee and Wesley was saying sorry, sorry and dabbing at her with a rather grubby hanky and the warm damp had spread through the wool to her skin and was trickling down her stomach and through her knickers and Wesley was breathing rather heavily and the floor was rocking slightly like warm water.

Then Wesley was dabbing at her breasts and when she tried to stop him he withdrew his hand so quickly and looked so miserable behind the thick pebble glasses that she felt sorry for him and took his warm damp hand in her own and placed it back on her body. It felt rather nice to lie down even if it was on Wesley's unmade bed and before she knew it Wesley had taken off the glasses and without them he looked naked somehow and exposed, like a little boy, and then he was on top of her fully clothed and rubbing up and down and up and down and the static electricity between the houndstooth trousers and the woollen dress was crackling and shooting sparks into the dark room and every hair on her body was drawn bolt upright.

The next morning he came and sat beside her in the library.

'G'day, doll,' he murmured into her ear then opened his book. Heather was copying a translation of *The Nun's Priest's Tale* into her textbook. She had chosen English because she had got 69 in Schol. and English was just reading books anyway so it was easy, but she hadn't anticipated Chaucer.

A povre wydwe, somdeel stape in age
Was whilom dwellyng in a narwe cotage . . .

The library was quiet. She had half an hour before her tutorial. 'Whilom?' What did 'whilom' mean? She became aware suddenly of a pressure against her leg beneath the table. She moved slightly to the right.

This morning Wesley looked gawkier than ever and there was a patch of bloody toilet paper stuck beneath one ear where he must have nicked himself shaving. She moved aside, but the pressure followed her, a gently persistent rubbing, and a hand was touching her knee.

She moved once more, but carefully. She didn't want to hurt Wesley's feelings but people might notice. More especially Kathy Scott who was sitting only a few yards away, might notice. Heather tucked her legs firmly together but she was up against a bookshelf now and the hand was following, edging slowly, surreptitiously upward toward the top of her stocking.

Biside a grove, stonynge in a dale . . .

A finger flicked at her suspender. This was appalling. Kathy might notice, she might tell the others. Heather had intended simply to be friendly and cheer Wesley up when he had seemed a bit down, but this was going too far. Wesley was a drip. Wesley was a dork. The finger was creeping beneath the elastic on her knickers. And under, tangling in pubic hair.

A drip. A dork. Yet despite herself her body tightened into an excited knot. And when Wesley murmured quietly, 'Like another coffee, doll?' she put aside the Nun's Priest and the narrow cottage without a moment's hesitation and skipped the tutorial. This time they tumbled together onto the unmade bed and his wet lips were in her ear and over her face and he was fumbling at the catch of her bra saying, 'How do these things go?' and his hands were on her breasts and her body was arching under his touch and so long as she kept her eyes shut and didn't look up ever into his pimply face with the eyes rolled back so the whites showed and the mouth open saying over and over, Oh doll oh doll, it was thrilling.

Within a week he was out of the houndstooth trousers and she had shed the skirt and blouse. Within a fortnight they were naked and within three weeks she had lost her virginity.

They never went out together as the others did. She never walked hand in hand with him from lectures to the union or waited in the foyer at the hostel for him, sitting with the other girls to go to a movie or to a party. She'd simply look up from her place at the library and he'd be standing in the doorway. He'd catch her eye, flick his head. How about it? And she'd put aside her books and go.

At night she lay in bed at the hostel listening to the others drinking coffee next door in Kathy's room, feeling the new silky body with its tender places where Wesley had pressed or prodded and trying over the new words: penis, vagina, erection, condom, orgasm, semen, intercourse. Though Wesley had other words for them all, tough and unfamiliar male words: cock, twat, stiffie, Frenchie, come, spoof. Fucking.

She tried them over as she lay in her bed. I am having intercourse, she thought. Wesley's penis has been in my vagina. Or, translated into the new tongue: I am fucking. Wesley's cock has been in my twat.

She listened to the giggling from next door and it seemed to come from a great distance.

Within two months she was pregnant. For a month she pretended nothing was wrong. For another month she tried to get rid of it: she walked up and down York Place very fast and down all the steps in the Botanical Gardens, jumping hard and trying to shake herself loose. From some dim half-remembered novel she recalled gin. Gin and a warm bath. She put on some lipstick and eyeshadow and tried the Robbie Burns.

'Could I have some gin?' she said. The man behind the counter was reading the paper, ringing his bets for Trentham. He didn't even look up.

'Oh yes,' he said. 'And how much gin would you like?'

Heather thought for a minute. 'Just a bottle,' she said.

The man licked the tip of the pencil. 'Yes, but how big a bottle?'

'Um, a pint?'

The man laughed. He laughed and laughed but while he was laughing he reached up and took a bottle from the top shelf and said, 'Here you are, lassie. That's for trying. But just this once, mind.'

He was still laughing as she left.

That night after everyone had gone to sleep she poured a deep bath. Then she drank three cupfuls of gin mixed with Raro because it tasted horrible, worse even than Rinso punch, and then she lay back willing herself empty, empty, empty, watching the steam drift up and around the light bulb and looking down at the smooth pink curve of her belly where the tiny baby was curled up and the thought of it, trusting her and only the length of her little finger because she had looked it up in a book in the medical section at the library, made her cry. The steam rose and drifted and she had another cupful and then suddenly it was a sluggish grey morning and she was lying in an icy bath and shuddering. She had a headache and a streaming cold. And she was still pregnant.

Now sitting in the prison visiting room she wonders if that was what was wrong. Had she harmed her son before he had scarcely begun? Was the restlessness the result of foetal alcohol poisoning? Or had he sensed in some prebirth trauma that he was unwanted?

Finally she had told Wesley and Wesley had sighed and said, 'Penguin dust, bring me penguin dust.'

'What?' she had said.

'Gregory Corso,' he said. ' "Should I get married? Should I be good?" ' Gregory Corso was a friend of Ferlinghetti's. So they got engaged at Christmas and they married in January and she carried a large bunch of flowers to conceal the developing bulge which was Eliot.

She woke up on the morning after the wedding and lay trying out this new vocabulary: her husband lay beside her, her child kicked beneath her skin. She'd have to make them all happy.

It was a long birth: thirty hours during which she clenched against the rolling, bruising pain and the nurse said sternly she must relax, let the baby come. They had to use forceps in the end and there were two bruises on either side of his compressed gnome head.

Another injury she has inflicted on her son.

But she did her best after that: she made yellow curtains for the flat in North East Valley to cheer it since the sun reached it only for a couple of hours each day. The roof in the kitchen leaked, it was a long grey winter and Eliot's nappies dripped from the drying rack in front of the heater. Wesley said it was soul-destroying trying to work at one end of the table with damp spots falling on his poetry. He took over the front room and worked in there with the one-bar heater glowing and the curtains pulled against external distraction while Heather tried to keep the house quiet. She took Eliot out, not to cafés (he tipped over the chairs, he crawled behind the counter, he squealed, resisting arrest whenever she tried to hold him), not to shops or the library (he dragged the books from the shelves or tottered ominously between the racks of frail breakable objects). That left the Gardens and in the winter, the Tropical House where the fuschias dropped handfuls of scarlet and purple onto the concrete floor and Eliot could run up and down while she sat among the palm trees and the trickling of water and the heavy body scent of things growing and thrusting at the misted glass.

Wesley had a job at a bookshop to begin with but the pay was low and the guy who ran the place was a bastard and an idiot, had no respect for literature, just sold books as if he were selling butter or cheese. Wesley's bosses were always bastards or idiots, or nutcases or power maniacs, people who made his life miserable and eventually Wesley would have to leave and go somewhere else. It was either that or go completely round the twist. In the gaps while Wesley looked for something better and they scrambled for rent and power and food, Heather worked at a supermarket on the checkout because the hours suited and Eliot went to a succession of babysitters, chosen from among the cards in the dairy window.

Was that the problem? Did she deprive Eliot of quality care at a crucial formative period of his life? Did she not pay him enough attention, tired in the evenings and wanting only to make tea, watch TV, flop into bed?

Or were the minders negligent, or worse, surreptitiously cruel? Might Allie have pinched and slapped once Heather was out the door? Allie, in her floppy orange slippers and loose housecoat, making a few bob by taking in a kiddie or two? But the children seemed happy enough, tumbling about in Allie's chaotic backyard, and it was the best she could afford. Better than Mrs McClintock anyway, who ran a spotless place, ice-blue kitchen, ice-white toilet and four children sitting on potties on the immaculate lino with their clothes folded round their ankles. 'All my clients,' said Mrs McClintock, 'are potty trained within a month of arrival. Routine is vital for the small child.' She had had to choose and she had chosen Allie, because Wesley was a hopeless babysitter.

She had come home one afternoon to find the house silent. Wesley was writing in the front room and Eliot had gone. 'He was tired and scratchy,' said Wesley. 'He climbed on the kitchen table and tipped sugar over everything.' (He had indeed: there was a trail of it all over the floor, piled into a little castle with a daisy on top.) 'So I put him to bed.' But he had not shut the bedroom window. Eliot was at the corner of the street, walking along in just his singlet and holding his sword. 'Big dog,' said Eliot when Heather found him and scooped him up. He wound his arms round her neck. 'I saw big dog.'

Two days later she came home not to ominous quiet but to screaming. Wesley was sitting in the front room with the door shut and the Animals blaring and Eliot was in his room behind a shut door hammering. 'This is bloody impossible,' yelled Wesley over the racket. 'How the hell can I work here?' And he went out for a walk to clear his head, slamming the back door so hard that one of the panes of coloured glass shattered and indigo droplets glistened like water on the worn lino. Heather opened the door. Eliot lay on his bed, his bum in the air. A blue bruise was already spreading on his upturned buttock.

'Did you smack him?' she said the next morning when she found Wesley eating peanut butter from the jar for breakfast. Wesley licked the knife with his pointed tongue.

'Just a tap,' he said. 'The little bugger won't listen to reason.'

Heather hated him from then on. Eliot may have been a restless child, jumpy and uncoordinated, forever tumbling off steps or falling flat, but he was endlessly forgiving, and when he fell he did not cry. He simply climbed onto her lap, flung his arms round her neck and nuzzled at her and so long as she did not try to hold him there he was happy.

So when Wesley read Kerouac and decided to go off to see the country on a motorbike she didn't bother to try and stop him. Wesley wanted to gather material, you had to live before you could write, he needed to experience life in the raw, he needed to discover the real New Zealand.

'When will you be back?' she said, standing on the step to wave him goodbye. But Wesley would not say. What was the point of going off to live wild and free if you had a deadline?

He didn't come back and after a month Heather went on

the benefit and life became just her and Eliot and things could have been a lot worse. She could have been Karen for example. Karen lived in the adjoining flat. She had two kids under four, one of them scaly with eczema. His father had been an American GI in New Zealand for a spot of R&R en route for Vietnam. Gary had given Karen the best weekend of her life: a double room at the San Rafael, with an en suite and a balcony, and complimentary chocolates and a rose on the pillow and champagne in a silver bucket with the candle-lit dinner which they rang up and ordered on room service and he'd bought her a black negligée, which was like real silk, with a baby doll top and bikini knickers, and told her all about this place which sounded like Fuckit, but it was spelled differently, where you could stay in a hotel right on the beach and it was even nicer than the San Rafael and some day, he said, he'd come back and take her there to walk in the moonlight.

Karen had always liked a bit of luxury. She had had her chart done once by a lady up in Opoho who told her that Karen had been a lady-in-waiting to Marie Antoinette in a former life, so that probably accounted for it. And then Gary had left and Karen had written him a letter but it never got through or maybe he died or something because she never heard from him again.

So here she was with one son who had to be watched like a hawk or he would scratch himself raw.

Her other son was the son of the motor mechanic she'd met on the rebound from Gary, and got engaged to after only three weeks. A diamond cluster with marcasite shoulders and she had the dress all picked out and everything: guipure lace over an Empire line sheath with these little pearl buttons down the back and a fingertip veil, but two weeks before the wedding the mechanic rode his bike into a powerpole at 160 k's.

Karen was destined to suffer tragedy in this life. There was always a price to be paid for luxury.

Her current boyfriend was a fella called Mal who drove

a tour bus and came round once every two weeks on a Wednesday and when he came he brought her flowers and a bottle of wine and sometimes chocolates, the proceeds of the whipround for the driver who always had a birthday during the tour. Mal was all right, though he was married and had this kid up in Wellington. His wife sounded a real cow and Mal wanted to leave her but she kept threatening suicide and Karen didn't want that on her conscience.

Karen thought she was well-off. There was no one to boss her around and she got her little touch of luxury once a fortnight.

Heather looked after the kids every second Wednesday and on weekday mornings while Karen worked assembling lucky dips and Christmas tree stockings in a disused butcher's shop in Caversham. It was cold and it was boring but she got paid cash in hand, so it was pretty good really. She needed every penny, because Karen was saving up. Someday Karen was going to go to Fuckit.

Heather's mother wanted Heather and Eliot to move in with them. The unit was small but since Shona had gone off to Australia they would be able to manage somehow. Heather said thank you, but truly, they were fine. She found the unit depressing. Her father had emphysema. He sat in his chair by the heater wheezing and smoking roll-your-owns which her mother said was just the worst thing possible. Between breaths Dad told her not to be so bloody daft. He had few enough pleasures and his lungs were shot anyway, thanks to those buggers down at the foundry who never installed proper ventilation fans or issued them with masks, and for years they'd left him and his mates to work in dust and muck and a fat lot they cared, just so long as they got their pound of flesh and it was no go, was it? If you were at the bottom of the heap you bloody stayed there.

'You see?' said Heather's mother, wiping her hands on her apron and then pushing her hair back from her forehead. 'You see what I'm up against?'

Dad licked a cigarette paper. 'Make us a cup of tea and stop nagging,' he said. The heater was set to Cosy though the day was warm. The telly prattled away in the corner of the living room. Eliot was fractious and impatient to be outside, climbing and running, and there was no yard or garden in the little unit where he could play safely.

'We're very happy in our flat,' said Heather. 'Don't worry.'

'But I do worry,' said her mother. 'I worry about you and I worry about Shona. She seems to be all over the place and now you're on your own with a kiddie.'

'I'm fine,' said Heather. 'And Shona is too.'

Shona was fine. Living in Sydney with a guy called Mario who ran a nightclub and who was fifty-three but she said she was having a ball and there was no point in telling her mother everything.

'Stop fretting,' said Heather.

She painted daisies on Eliot's bedroom wall, she planted sunflowers in the little backyard, she took Eliot and Karen's kids for walks in the Gardens. She saw Kathy Scott in town one day in December and stopped to talk though Eliot was tugging at her hand and eager to be moving. Kathy was tall and beautiful and off on a tour with some drama group and she seemed to exist in another barely remembered universe.

Tug, tug, went Eliot. 'Come *on*.'

'Sorry,' said Heather. 'I promised I'd take him to Santa's Cave again. He likes those mechanical monkeys.'

'Oh,' said Kathy vaguely. 'Sounds like fun.' They looked at one another from across the abyss of motherhood.

'Well,' said Heather, 'nice seeing you. Enjoy the tour.'

'Thanks,' said Kathy. 'Enjoy the monkeys.'

She did. She enjoyed the monkeys. She enjoyed living in her little flat with Eliot. After three years of living with Wesley it was in fact extraordinarily simple, extraordinarily comfortable. And then one day Eliot disappeared. She was trying on a pair of slippers in Hallensteins. One minute he was there, sitting in his pushchair, the next he'd gone and she ran down

Princes Street, one foot in leather, the other in a woolly Sale Special. The lunchtime crowd parted for her, their faces floating strangely as she pushed through. There he was running fast and straight towards the intersection at the Octagon where the traffic was accelerating on the green. It was a strangely silent scene: just the child who was wearing a white T-shirt with Daffy Duck on the back and a pair of grey shorts she had made from one of her old skirts.

He lifts one foot and steps across the gutter and there is a truck turning. It has *Start the Day Right With Mega Vite!* and a sun rising above a curve of hills and trees. The wheels on the truck graze the kerb and the child walks out and she is in a cold silent world where her legs won't carry her fast enough and far enough. Then an arm reaches down from the unseen crowd and a voice says, 'I wouldn't do that if I were you, mate,' and her son is dragged back into life.

That was how she met Trevor. He gave her a lift home and it was only after she was drinking a cup of coffee with Karen and Eliot was asleep, arms and legs flung any which way on his sheepskin, that she realised she still had on one slipper and one shoe.

Trevor popped round next day to see how she was. She was fine, sitting at the kitchen table making playdough with the children. Mal was in town. Karen was out for drinks and dinner at Barringtons, in her little black dress and Heather's court shoes, and Mal had shouted Heather and the kids fish and chips for a treat: greasy paper and half-eaten chips littered the table and she tried to clear a space.

'Sorry about the mess,' she said. 'We do use plates here occasionally but it tastes better straight from the paper.'

Trevor said that was the whole point of fish and chips, wasn't it? No washing up. He was planning takeaways himself tonight and he'd certainly be eating them out of the paper.

'And how's my mate?' he said to Eliot. Eliot looked up at him briefly, lifted his fist and hammered his playdough cake dead flat.

'He's fine,' said Heather. 'I was the one that shook for an hour.'

She'd been too upset to notice what Trevor looked like the day before. He was just a hand under her elbow, a voice on a crowded street, a person driving her and her son carefully home. Today he was tall and balding and slightly rumpled. He was probably quite a bit older than her: mid-thirties she guessed. He was wearing a tweed jacket, one of those moorland blends, and grey trousers. Proper lace-up shoes. Conservative, she guessed. Some kind of professional.

And a ring on one finger.

But he seemed in no hurry to go home.

So she asked if he'd like a cup of coffee. Trevor sat down at the table on the wobbly chair and said that would be great. And then, because he still seemed unhurried, she asked if he would like something to eat. There were some eggs if he didn't fancy cold fish and chips. They could have an omelette. Trevor said he'd like that too and he had a bottle of wine in the car, would she fancy a glass of wine?

Karen got home at ten.

'Hullooo,' she called from the kitchen. And there they were, as she said, like some comfy old couple, sitting in the front room with the fire on. Heather never bothered to light a fire. On cold nights she simply got into bed with a hottie which was cheaper and having a fire just for herself seemed indulgent and unnecessary. She had had no firewood but Trevor had suggested they burn the wobbly chair: he had one practically identical which was in good condition and which he didn't need. So they snapped off legs and rungs and added the last shovelful of coal from the bottom of the bin and Heather had sat on the rug and sipped her wine, which was very nice and came from a bottle with a cork so it must have been expensive, and looked round at the little room. By firelight it seemed for the first time a cosy place. They had been talking about Eliot's eyes when Karen returned: Trevor had just asked her if she had ever had Eliot's eyes checked because he seemed to have a slight astigmatism, when Karen walked in.

'Sorry,' she said the next morning when she popped round to drop off the kids. 'Didn't mean to cut in on the action.'

'There wasn't any action,' said Heather. 'He was just checking that Eliot was OK. We were talking about Eliot's astigmatism. He's an optician.'

'Oh yeah?' said Karen.

'And besides, he's married,' said Heather.

'Not for long, he's not,' said Karen. She could be very annoying.

She could also be very right.

Eliot did need glasses. But there was nothing wrong with his sight the night he came into Heather's room and leaped on them out of the darkness, laser sword gleaming and beeping, yelling, 'Stop hurting her, stop hurting my mummy,' and she'd looked out from beneath Trevor's arm, both of them startled at the interruption, both of them elated still with the unexpectedness of one another's willing eager body, holding off the furious assault.

'Shh,' she'd said, cradling her weeping son. 'Shh. Mummy's all right.' Holding him against her warm naked breasts. 'Shh. I'm fine. Don't worry.'

'I'll go,' said Trevor.

'It might be better,' said Heather.

So Trevor had dressed and said he'd ring her in the morning and left, while they watched from the bed.

'Shh,' she said. 'Shh. It's all right.'

Maybe it wasn't. Maybe that was the moment of trauma which set Eliot on his way toward the bleak cavern of the visitor's room and the circling mower?

Nothing matters now. There's no point in endless recrimination, endless analysis. Eliot is here. A clever boy, all his teachers said so, but lacking in self-discipline. A child who flung himself from the garage roof when he was six to see if he could fly, who jammed a nail into an electric socket when he was seven because Mr Magoo had done it on TV. Who skated down the drive on screaming wheels and away from her, out into the traffic. Who ran and rode and drove too fast and smashed his friend Mo's Cortina but walked away with only a broken finger. Who passed exams easily, as if they didn't matter. Who could have become a businessman, a lawyer, a doctor, someone with a car and a suit and a house in the suburbs, but who chose instead to drop out in his third year and go off as a showie, operating the Shoot to Win with a range of bent slug guns. Who drank, as everyone does, and smoked dope, as everyone does, but who in that as in everything was incapable of moderation. Who drank more and smoked more and swallowed more and got caught.

Five hundred plants and an automatic watering system in a house out the back of Whitianga. Three years.

'And there's a man in there with him who beat his wife so badly she'll be blind in one eye for the rest of her life, and he only got two years,' said Heather.

'Eliot knew he was breaking the law,' said Trevor. 'And there's strong evidence that cannabis is harmful.'

'So is whisky,' said Heather. 'So are cigarettes.'

'I like Eliot,' said Trevor. 'You know that. But he has always pushed things to the limit. He has always tried to bend the rules. And possession is one of the rules.'

'Perhaps it's not a good rule,' said Heather.

'Hmmm,' said Trevor.

And now her second son, who has known always that there is a need for restraint and caution, who has the car and the suit and the flat in Brooklyn, is about to embark on the next orderly stage. Wife, home, children. 'Oh, what a pity,' she had said when Matthew said he was getting married, 'Eliot won't be there to be your best man.'

Matthew said that personally it wouldn't bother him at all and she had said, 'But he's your brother.' Forgetting for that moment that Matthew had denied him already, had told Sarah's parents when they asked, that his older brother was up at Linton, leaving them to assume the army. Sarah's mother had turned to her at the simple-buffet-reception-for-family-and-a-few-close-friends which had marked Sarah and Matthew's engagement, and said, 'And what rank does Eliot hold? Reg did his National Service in Britain after the war, and he's always saying – aren't you Reg? – that they were the best years of your life when you were young and fit. You still keep in touch with a couple of the others who were in your intake – don't you Reg? – after all these years.'

'Oh,' said Heather, balancing her sherry carefully as she negotiated a tiny canapé, 'Eliot doesn't hold rank. He's not in the army, he's in prison.'

It mattered that she did not deny this, that she said it straight and matter-of-fact. Lots of people had spent time in prison, naturally good and decent people could end up in prison through a combination of unfortunate circumstances. There was no need to feel shame.

But Matthew was ashamed. Matthew was more than ashamed. He was furious.

'What did you have to go and tell Dorothy that for?' he said when the two of them were alone for a moment by the picture window overlooking the rose garden. 'They're incredibly straight. Reg is the Executive Director at Powell International. They do not need to know about bloody Eliot.'

'Eliot's your brother,' Heather had said, startled at Matthew's fury. 'You don't deny him just because he's in trouble.'

'If he's in trouble it's his own bloody fault,' said Matthew. He was white, his hand trembled so that sherry was spilling on his shirt cuff. 'Why do you insist on playing Happy bloody Families all the time?'

'I don't,' said Heather. 'I just know from experience that full rehabilitation is impossible if there's no support and . . .'

Sarah was approaching, smiling, pausing to chat to this old family friend, to receive a kiss on both cheeks from an elderly aunt. Matthew leaned forward and hissed into Heather's hair, 'Mother, please do not social-work *me*.'

Then Sarah had her hand on his arm. She drew him away, and he was smooth once more and smiling and she knew him again for her Matthew, talking easily, happily to this roomful of strangers. Heather looked out at the roses arranged in neat rectangles around Sarah's parents' neat rectangular home. She hadn't been social-working her son. She didn't play Happy Families. Though Shona had said so too, back in January when she was visiting from Sydney.

Mario had left her. 'Traded me in for a racier model,' she said as she sat at the bench pouring herself another gin and tonic. A large one. A triple. Mario went for the Barbie-type, all legs and hair and big tits and for a while Shona had tried to keep up. She had done the workouts and the liposuction and the diet pills which left her speeding and half crazy, and she'd had a facelift.

She leaned forward. See? Two tiny scars like white insects perched on the pale skin behind each ear.

But he'd fucked off anyway and he was a slob and Tanya was welcome to him. She plopped an ice-cube into her drink. Gin slopped onto the bench.

'Whoops,' she had said. 'Man overboard.'

Heather fetched a handiwipe.

'So what are you going to do now? You can stay here if you like. There's tons of room now the kids have gone. You'd be very welcome.'

'In Hamilton!' said Shona. 'Hell, no! Thanks Heath, but I'm a city gal now. I'm going to go back to Sydney.' She paused, took a gulp, 'I am going to buy me a Porsche. A Carrera. You should see it, Heather. It's shiny black. All leather interior, sunroof, air conditioning, CD, the works.'

'Won't that be very expensive?' said Heather.

'Only $130,000,' said Shona. 'Only most of what I've been able to squeeze out of that cunning little tightarse, Mario. But it will be worth every penny just to see his face when I cruise by.'

'But that's ridiculous,' said Heather. 'What about clearing the mortgage? What about investing some in case you can't find a job, or in case you get ill, or for when you're old, or . . .'

'When the bomb drops or in case the world ends. Hell, Heath,' said Shona, 'lighten up a little. What's wrong with wanting to live a little now?'

'But I see women all the time in my job,' said Heather, 'who have made stupid choices, impulsive choices, and who never ever recover, when with a bit of careful planning they could have been comfortable for the rest of their lives.'

Shona looked mutinous – drunk and pink and mutinous. 'Well, I'm not going to be one of them. So just shut up and pour us another drink and stop bloody social-working me.'

Then she looked up, smiled suddenly.

'Poor old Heather. Always wanting to shuffle everyone into Happy Families, eh?'

Her mother had said it too, as they sat at the table in the unit addressing the cards.

'Thank you for your condolences in the loss of a dear husband and father. Your donation to St Christopher's Hospice is much appreciated,' above an embossed lily. Heather had licked an envelope.

'Were you and Dad happy?' she said. 'Did you ever regret coming back that time you went down to Dunedin?'

'What?' said her mother. 'No. Of course I didn't regret it.'

She had come back one night, quite suddenly. Just walked in the door and handed Dad her Post Office Savings Book. 'There,' she had said. 'You owe me ten quid.'

Dad was watching *Bonanza*. He left the book unopened. 'Bloody daft,' he had said.

Mum had tied on her apron. 'Now, I'll make apple duff for pudding.'

Shona punched out the cores and Heather peeled, careful not to break the long green ribbons and bring bad luck. 'Are they pirate apples?' she had said.

Her mother wiped floury hands on her pinny front. 'Och, no,' she said. 'I'm too old for that kind of carry-on.'

Her father had said nothing. He ate the apple duff in silence then went out to the shed. All evening they could hear him whistling 'Wooden Heart' as he worked on the model of the Hood.

Addressing cards with the taste of peppermint envelope gum cloying on her tongue, Heather needed to know that it was all right after all, that she had done the right thing in writing to her, pleading for her mother's return.

'You didn't come back just for us, did you?' she said. She needed to know that the quiet mother who no longer jumped fences and gathered what was free and hers by right had not been her responsibility. 'You and Dad did love each other, didn't you?'

Her mother thumped an envelope shut. 'We were married. We got along,' she said. 'Life isn't Happy Families.'

Every shelf in the unit was covered with daffodils. In jars and vases, on the TV and the mantelpiece above the heater, on the bench in the kitchen. Mum said there had been thousands growing wild in the cemetery and it was such a shame to waste them all on the dead.

So on the day before Matthew's wedding, Heather drives with her husband Trevor toward Otaki. Trevor is driving fast, too fast, 140 and he never normally goes over the speed limit. He says it is there for a purpose, but they are late now: very late and Dorothy runs a tight ship. He frowns in concentration as they sweep past an elderly Zephyr squirting smoke.

If they have an accident it would all be Heather's fault.

'Eliot liked his cake,' Heather says, by way of indirect apology, as a kind of propitiation.

'Hmmm,' says Trevor. Check rear mirror, flick on indicator, pull across allowing the proper defensive distance.

'He sends his love,' she says.

Eliot hadn't. He had said, 'Regards.' 'Give old Trev my regards.' They had stood awkwardly one on either side of that desert of tabletop, that endless icy formica. Then suddenly he had hugged her. 'Hey, Mum,' he had said. 'Oh, Mum.'

She put her arms round him then too, feeling his body against hers: flesh of her flesh, bone of her bone. She could not speak. They stood together until somewhere a bell rang and he disengaged, lightly, quickly. 'Give old Trev my regards,' he said. 'And tell Matthew to keep away from Rotary. They're a dangerously subversive organisation.' Then he was gone, away from her with that quick bouncy stride on the tips of his toes, for all the world as if he were about to break into flight.

So why did she say 'love'?

Trevor is drawing up fast on a sheep truck. It wheezes and squirts diesel, lumbering toward Wellington at a steady ninety. 'Bugger,' he says. This is just what they need.

Was inventing affection where it did not exist what Shona and her mother and Eliot meant when they said she insisted on Happy Families? Was it wrong to want the people she loved to be happy and to like one another?

The sheep's bodies press through the rails and a single anguished eye looks out at her. Poor old ewe, thinks Heather, her lambing done for ever, off to the works.

'It's horrible, isn't it?' she says. 'I think we should go vegetarian.'

Then suddenly her throat is clenching for that anguished round eye and the press of bodies and all those old ewes and old cows and wizened hens dangling upside down and jolting along toward extermination. Tears trickle onto her cheeks.

Trevor glances at her.

'I told you you'd get upset,' he says. But there is a gap in the traffic, a slight bend on the road ahead, it might be worth risking it. He'll give it a go.

He flicks on the indicator and accelerates out from behind the truck. As they draw alongside a rain of panic-stricken urine splatters over their car.

'You always get upset,' he says, as he switches on the windscreen washer.

The knot in her throat is too big for words. It's hot in the car and stuffy. She can hardly breathe. She sits there looking out as the Tararuas slide past on the blind side and the road ahead is a grey strip through a blur of soapy water, urine and tears, but silence is intolerable too.

She leans over and switches on the radio.

And that is how Heather hears about Margie Miller.

RAELEEN

'Alone and unafraid, Mary Kingsley set off
on foot to explore the jungle . . .'

RAELEEN HAS CHANGED HER NAME.

'Just Ra,' she said when asked.

It bothered the bureaucrats. 'Surname?' they asked, pens poised behind the counter, eager to fill in all the little boxes.

'No surname,' she said. 'Just Ra. No second name either.'

'Mrs, Miss or Ms?' they said.

'Just plain Ra.'

Ra fitted her properly.

Ra was enough to carry.

Ra lies in bed early on Friday morning. Outside in the half-world, half-darkness, half-light, a bird sings a single note to whistle up the spring.

Kuiii.

So you're back, thinks Ra. You've been off up north and now you're back to dump your kids on some poor dumb minder while you play around for another summer.

Welcome back.

Kuii, sings the careless, happy bird on the hillside.

Ra lies in the half-world and her stomach cramps. Once that would have signalled the blood: a mild cramping followed within the hour by bleeding, five days' bleeding with twenty-one days before the next. A rhythm as regular and predictable as breathing or heartbeat, a minute tidal ebb and flow within the dark, secret landscape of her body. But for some years now the rhythm has been lost. She has tossed about trying to catch the wave.

Once she had liked her body: it was easy. Her breasts were small so that she could run easily without bounce or jiggle. She liked her flat stomach and the curve of her buttocks and the black shock of her pubic hair and her long brown legs and her arms, finely muscled and able to do anything she asked of them, to stretch and lift and move free.

She was Raeleen Smiley, born lean and spare, like a greyhound or a thoroughbred for speed and vigour.

Raeleen, who lived in a little town in the South Island and had a mother named Marcia and a father named Ken and a brother who was eleven months younger than her and called Graham. Graham was brown-haired and lightly freckled like their parents while she was dark, a throwback, her mother said, to her great-great-great-great-grandmother who was a Maori princess from Stewart Island who had flung her cloak over a sealer to protect him from being killed and married him and had twelve sons. It was like a fairy-tale, though Mum said it just went to show how much women had to put up with in those days, what with no anaesthetics and no proper hygiene, and you'd have thought the princess would have put a stop to all that nonsense after three or four babies. You'd have thought the sealer would have had more consideration.

Raeleen Smiley was a runner. The fastest kid at South Primary, boys or girls, like her dad who had been a runner back before the war. With proper training there was no reason why she could not be up there with the best. She could be another Doreen. Raeleen's life was orderly: school during the week, athletics club in the evenings and at weekends, and in August a week in Dunedin when they went to Taiaroa and watched the albatrosses soar in from their long flight round the Pole, not touching land, the man said, for four years. They went to the museum where the canoe made from a single tree sailed straight up the main display hall, with its high carved prow. And at Christmas they always spent two weeks at a camping ground in Wanaka which Mum liked because it was so clean and had such good facilities. On the way they always stopped for lunch by the site of historic interest where the ancient Maori had paused on their journey to the coast in search of pounamu. Raeleen and Graham peered through the protective cage at the scribbles which were birds and people and fish.

'Did they walk?' she said.

'No,' said Graham. 'They took the bus.'

Dad said they made sandals out of flax.

'And they took slaves to carry the stone,' said Graham, 'and when they got hungry they ate them.'

Mum said, 'Please, Graham, not while we're having our lunch.'

Cicadas tapped away like a kind of static and behind them the river crisscrossed itself in sudden dashes of milky white between borders of willow. Away in the distance were the mountains walling off the head of the valley.

It would have been a long walk.

Raeleen went to school where she learned about New Zealand. She knew that first of all it was a woman lying on her back covered by the sky before it became a canoe and a fish. She knew that it had been found by Kupe accidentally and again by Tasman but was not really discovered properly until Captain Cook did a map. She knew about the Treaty of Waitangi and Hone Heke chopping down the flagpole, which was a pointless act of provocation, and then there were a few problems with people like the Hau Hau who believed you could stop real bullets by breathing, and then everything settled down and New Zealand became the social laboratory of the world and a model of peaceful co-operation between the British and the native people, who were of course protected by law instead of being colonised and exploited like the people of those less fortunate places colonised by the French and the Germans. Which was why

New Zealand would never become a mess like the Belgian Congo.

These were the facts which were scattered like bracken amongst the Latin roots and equations and chemical formulae which made up her education.

Raeleen was lucky to live in the social laboratory of the world because it gave her opportunities denied her mother and father by the Depression and the war. But one afternoon when Raeleen was sixteen she was sitting at a too-small desk in a too-small gym frock and what was the point of a new uniform with only a year to go? She was ticking off multiple choices: *The meaning of the underlined phrase is A/B/C/D. A synonym for . . . is A/B/C/D.* Beneath the grey serge her body prickled and her head ached and through the open doors she could see the blue wash of sky and the green expanse which was the back field and she was overcome suddenly by a boredom so absolute that the only solution was to tick off any old box and leave. Down between that row of mildly curious stares and out into the sun where she walked down to the beach, stopping only to buy a packet of matches at the school dairy, and out there on the shingle she burned her school hat. A flare and crackle of white straw. Then she dragged off her tie and her black stockings and ran home along the foreshore, barefoot.

Her mother was appalled. To fling away a good education just like that, to fling away her opportunities, but there was no fighting nature, was there? Dad said quickly that he was sure Raeleen would make a go of whatever she took on and did she have a job in mind?

She thought for a moment.

'Something with maths,' she said. It was her best subject in School C.

'I'll have a word with George Kalinsky,' said Dad. 'Over at the bank. He might have something suitable.'

So in the New Year Raeleen was standing behind the counter at the bank on Spenser Street.

'At least it's a job with prospects,' said her mother. 'At least it's not the kind of dead-end job so many girls like you end up in.'

At the bank, Raeleen made the tea and collected the post. Scale C. Junior Clerk. There were no exams, no assignments, no calculus, no multiple choice. And she took home £12 a week.

'A third to spend,' said her mother. 'A third to save and a third for your rent and keep here. You may as well learn good habits while you're young.'

February wore on. Outside the other girls biked past in their uniforms and panama hats but here she was in another uniform only this time it was a blue smock with a scratchy collar. Hair neatly cut or tied back as prescribed by management. Discreet street make-up. No bright nail polish or ostentatious jewellery. Receipts and bills, pens and stamps, neatly to hand, a poster above her head showing the outcomes of wise investment: young men and women waving from a new car or smiling in their graduate gowns or asking a London bobby for directions in front of Buckingham Palace. A fan high on the plaster ceiling stirred the warm soupy air faintly, sending little eddies across the room so that the poster bellied slightly like a sail and the notes and receipts rustled in their boxes.

It would have done no good to complain after she'd made so much fuss, but Raeleen's legs, aching slightly because of all the standing, jiggled with boredom.

Then Chris Lindstrom came in at five to three one Wednesday afternoon with the banking from Moose's Sporting Goods and as she tipped the coins and notes from canvas bags, trying to remember all the steps in the procedure (count, check, stamp, so that everything would balance), he leaned over and read the name tag pinned to her smock.

'Raeleen Smiley,' he said. 'New, eh?'

Raeleen said yes.

Ten, twenty, twenty-five, thirty . . .

Then Chris said would she like to come out to Camerons Bay on Saturday?

Raeleen tipped £5 worth of shillings onto the counter.

On Saturdays she usually went over to the park and the day disappeared into ten times 110 then a jog to recover or one of the ten-mile runs which her coach Rowley had decided would transform her from a sprinter to a distance runner. Girls weren't normally encouraged to consider 880 but Rowley thought that was a lot of hokum: she could do sixty-six seconds over 440 and he didn't see why she shouldn't have a go. Dad was keen too. He'd been a distance man himself and she was like him: strong at the finish. With training and motivation she could be there with the best. She could be another Marise.

The fan blew warm air overhead, ruffling Chris's blond hair. She made a little tower of shilling pieces.

'OK,' she said.

'You're a fast mover,' said Mary, who was her supervisor, after Chris had gone and the doors were locked and they were balancing up for the day. And she warned her that Chris had a bit of a reputation. 'Still,' she said, 'he's better than some. Better than Warwick Borlass, at any rate.' Warwick worked at Kamera Korner. He'd asked Mary out and she'd nearly frozen standing around for ages posing in Rumbles Park in her shorts and broderie anglaise top one Saturday afternoon and then he'd suggested glamour work, which seemed to involve taking off the shorts and top altogether. 'I'd rather take my chances with Chris Lindstrom any day,' said Mary.

Chris definitely sounded interesting.

So that Saturday Raeleen ran down the drive, her new two-piece concealed beneath a sloppy joe and shorts, and into a Holden stationwagon with two boards strapped to the roof and DON'T LAUGH MOTHER YOUR DAUGHTER'S INSIDE scrawled in pink paint on the rear window. Behind her, the living room venetians parted, then snapped shut. The Holden gunned blue smoke and they were away. Baz and Cooksie and Marilyn in the back seat, Chris skidding into every corner and a plume of white dust rising behind them on the beach road.

'She's pumpin' today,' said Chris. 'She's really pumpin'!'

'I do hope I can rely on you, Raeleen,' her mother said that evening. 'That boy looks a lot older than you.'

'Only two years,' said Raeleen from beneath the blankets. Her back throbbed still from where it had pressed against the gear stick when Chris had kissed her at the corner of Keats Street.

'Two years is a long time at your age,' said her mother. 'And boys have urges. You must remember that it is women who set the standard. He'll respect you for it.'

'Oh Mum,' said Raeleen, hot and squirming with embarrassment.

'I just don't want you to go getting yourself into trouble,' said Mum. 'And you could. I mean,' she said and Raeleen was puzzled by this, 'it runs in families.'

'What does?' said Raeleen. 'What do you mean?'

Her mother kissed her lightly on the cheek and folded her sloppy joe neatly across the chair.

'Never mind,' she said. 'You've been brought up to know what's right and that's the main thing.'

But it wasn't the main thing. The main thing was Chris's lean body easing into a sleek black springy. The main thing was lying in the sand by the car reading a magazine with the other girls while the boys bobbed about out the back beyond the breakers and the sun dazzled. The main thing was Chris's hand inching up beneath the sloppy joe. The main thing was his mouth covering hers.

She tried to set the standard but after a couple of weeks Chris said it wasn't fair of her to get around in that two-piece looking as if she was hanging out for it and didn't she know it was bad for a guy to dryf— to hold back all the time and he knew it meant a lot to a chick, the first time, but he'd be careful, he always used Frenchies.

She wished he hadn't said 'always' but his breath was warm on her neck, away down the beach the firelight flickered, his hands were beneath the sloppy joe, and she wanted him, she wanted him to touch this new quivering body.

The week shrank to a space between weekends. There was no time for training. Rowley sighed and said he'd seen it before: a promising girl getting to seventeen and losing motivation just as she was beginning to get somewhere.

Dad was disappointed. And Mum said she hoped Raeleen wasn't going to give them any trouble, not after they'd given her every opportunity.

The summer passed. A gritty wind skittered down the beach and the boys settled restlessly on grey waves like birds readying for flight. Raeleen sat by the Holden. She had finished her magazine and Marilyn who was training to be a beautician at Bowling's Pharmacy was telling her about this case of enlarged pores, just the worst she'd ever seen, and she'd recommended this amazing hydrogenating face mask and . . .

Raeleen's legs jiggled with boredom.

Baz was sitting on the tailgate eating a pie.

'Can I borrow your board?' said Raeleen.

'Go for it,' said Baz through a mouthful of steak and kidney.

She'd watched the boys surf often enough, and it couldn't be that much harder than roller skating. It couldn't be worse than listening for the second time that day to the story of hydrogenating face mask.

The board was astonishingly heavy and once in the surf it bucked like a wild thing, but she'd gone too far to turn back and she knew they'd be watching: the girls on shore, the boys out the back, so there was nothing for it but to hang on, paddle out and turn, facing the land which looked quite different viewed from the sea: a curve of hills rimmed by sand dunes and on the sand that row of curious people-dots. She tried not to think about sharks and in particular that big mother Baz was talking about this morning who'd ripped a guy's leg off down at St Clair.

The board juddered beneath her, lifted. She glanced over her shoulder and there it was: a wave bigger than any wave ever looked nearer shore, a wall of blue water with a foaming crest and then the board was caught in the trough and beginning to slide and she was hanging on and for just a second was kneeling upright before the wave was over her and she was flailing, mouth full, nose full and gripping the board though it slammed hard against her shoulder because it would be bad enough to make a fool of herself but worse to let the board loose in that surf.

The wave passed and she hoisted herself up gasping and hoping the top of the two-piece would be equal to the strain. She decided to have another go.

She came in only when her whole body was scraped and raw and trembling with effort.

'Hey,' said Baz. 'The surfer chick!'

Chris was standing by the car.

'Did you see?' she said. 'I stood up. Only for five seconds and I must have been hanging about twenty-five but I stood up.'

Chris turned away, inscrutable behind his sunnies. 'Marilyn,' he said, 'chuck us another beer will you?'

Marilyn picked up a can and chucked: a silly little underarm lob which landed short into the sand so that she had to scramble to retrieve it and her breasts, twin beachballs beneath straining lycra, quivered as she giggled. It was horrible. Chris watched Marilyn and talked short boards and long boards and twin fins all evening and as they were driving home he said, 'You looked bloody stupid.'

'It was my first time,' said Raeleen. 'Anyone would look stupid their first time.'

'Could be,' said Chris.

He stood in Mary's line at the bank from then on and in the autumn he stopped coming in altogether. She met Marilyn in Bowling's and Marilyn said Chris had gone over to Oz and Baz and Cooksie had gone up to Piha and she felt like a change too: she was going to bleach her hair totally blonde.

There was a restlessness in the air. Raeleen transferred to Wellington.

From her flat now she looked down on the harbour at the yachts skipping about on a stiff breeze, at the *Northern Star* and the *Corinthic* and the *Athenic* nosing away from the wharf and the restraining threads of paper streamers, and out between the heads to Tahiti and Curaçao and Las Palmas, tourist class and first class direct to the United Kingdom. And the planes surging up and away above the city. Everyone was on the move.

One of her flatmates was saving for her trip, another worked for GetAway Travel. Raeleen went out with Liam from Loans on Lambton Quay who sailed a ferrocement Hartley called *Runaway* and just as soon as he could afford an autohelm and maybe a GPS and some time off work Liam planned to sail up to the islands, to New Caledonia, then across to Fiji, Samoa, Tahiti. He had a map of Polynesia pinned in the galley with the route pencilled in red. In the meantime he sailed about the harbour issuing crisp nautical instructions from the stern, or attended to maintenance, dabbing for hours at the hull with blobs of epoxy resin and sanding and painting. In the summer he took *Runaway* to the Sounds where they moored in Punga Cove and Liam checked the split pins and lifted the boards to pump the bilge and fiddled with the stern gland while Raeleen held the torch. Around them hills and islands turned to dark whale humps in the twilight.

The land looked quite different viewed from the sea.

'Fuck,' said Liam from beneath the cockpit floor.

Raeleen thought of the canoe in the museum, dipping

and rising in the open sea following the red line between those tiny humps.

'How did they ever find these islands?' she said. 'Without radios or maps?'

'Stars,' said Liam, muffled beneath the deck. 'Bird flight and currents and stuff. Pass the grease gun.'

Back in Wellington you had a choice. You could:

a.   get engaged, arriving at work one Monday morning with a solitaire or cluster from the Ring Salon at Morecambes, or you could:

b.   take a ticket on the *Northern Star* or the *Corinthic* or one of those heavy north-bound planes.

Liam suggested the ring but Raeleen chose the ticket. She was going tourist class direct to ask a London bobby the way to Buckingham Palace.

The view from the flat now was a road in Brixton. Downstairs the landlord who owned the greengrocer's on the ground floor made wine in the bath tub. She passed him on the landing paddling about in his big bare feet with his trousers tucked to the knees while the radio blared.

'They seekeem air, they seekeem thair,' sang Angelo happily. 'Ee's a dedecated followerov fashion . . .'

Raeleen and her flatmate Bron bathed in the public baths over on Sealey Road. Bron was from Sydney. She and Raeleen found jobs at the Duke of Marlborough pulling pints and making the bright disinterested chat which kept the regulars happy. On their offdays they found the way to Buckingham Palace and the Kings Road and Westminster Abbey. They went to see Stonehenge and they went to see The Who. They tried vindaloo. They tried Guinness. They tried Moroccan brown and Afghani black and they dropped a tab of windowpane and went to see the lights on Regent Street. Huge golden bells and candles floated and drifted on the oily winter air and she might have been walking on water, the pavement glistening beneath her feet.

After Christmas the lights came down. The Duke of

Marlborough closed for a week and reopened as the Lincolnshire Poacher with smoke-blackened beams and leadlight windows and all the girls in tight frilly bodices and Sherwood green imitation leather microskirts. The regulars, gnarled hands cupping another bitter and one watery eye on the telly at the end of the bar were moved out, and a deer's head was hung above the fake fireplace looking as if he had just burst through the wall and was stunned at the sudden transformation.

The Lincolnshire Poacher was after the Americans.

'Hmmm,' said Eileen who was handling the decor when Raeleen tried on the new look. 'You're going to need a spot of uplift for that bodice to work.'

Raeleen and Bron huddled by the one-bar heater in their flat. They trailed to the baths through icy streets carrying their soap and facecloths. Raeleen stood in a concrete cubicle watching shampoo swirling away down the mould-rimmed drain and enough was enough.

'Let's split,' she said.

'OK,' said Bron from the next cubicle. 'Where?'

'I don't care,' said Racleen. 'Somewhere warm. Somewhere with a beach. Somewhere where I don't have to wear a double C Uplift Wonderbra.'

They left next payday. Clattered down the stairs, waved bye bye to Angelo who looked up from behind a heap of Brussel sprouts and ran like hell for the tube.

Raeleen sat in the cab of a lorry carrying yoghurt down the Route du Soleil to Nice, looking out at apple orchards in new blossom and fields covered already with misty green. Bron was spluttering on her first Gauloise and giggling with the driver, a madonna simpered from a wreath of plastic daisies on the dashboard and before their thundering progress the smaller traffic fled like shoals of shining fish. Raeleen looked out at it all and felt complete joy.

They found their beach eventually on Koriakos. Bare white rock, tiers of pastel houses intersected by chasms of black shade, olives gripping the hillsides with twisted knuckles and a sea as blue as Camerons Beach. She dropped a tab and later that night leapt from a rock into water which shattered into a hail of phosphorescent spindrift and when she surfaced there was Mike.

Sleek dark head like a seal and water glistening in an aura of gold and red and blue on his shoulders. What were the words? *Cherete? Kalos?*

'Gidday,' said the Greek god.

Mike had been born in Fitzroy. His dad came from Koriakos and the boiled-lolly houses round the bay were packed with his aunts and uncles and cousins.

'Like bloody rabbits,' he said. There were dozens more of them in Toronto and Chicago and London. There was nowhere in the world where you could get away from them. They'd come back here for holidays but most of the young ones left to find work. There was nothing much on the island unless you wanted to spend your life diving for bloody sponges.

'It's a pity,' said Raeleen. Stretching on sand, her body melted to warm milk. 'It's so beautiful.'

If you liked that kind of thing, said Mike. Personally he preferred St Kilda. Luna Park, the saltbaths, La Trobe Street on a Saturday night. Somewhere with a bit of life. 'This place is stuck in the Middle Ages,' he said. 'They still have arranged marriages. They've got no idea of privacy.'

He and Raeleen managed to avoid them, however, the omnipresent aunts and uncles and cousins, in the little cove behind the rock that night and in an olive grove the next evening and for two weeks after in a tiny hut high on the hill behind the town where they lay naked on a rug and drank the island wine amidst the clatter of sheep bells and cicadas.

'Christ,' said Mike as he stretched, then lit a cigarette, careful to cup the flame from any curious passers-by. 'This is more like it. I was going bloody mad. They've got me lined up with some chick from Brosta, but I've got my return fare all paid and in another couple of weeks I'm out of here. I like it like this. Casual. No hassle.'

They were discreet but one afternoon a woman spat in Raeleen's path as she passed the fountain in the square. Raeleen looked down at the gob of spittle as it oozed from her sandal.

'Poutana,' said the woman. Without particular emotion. 'Vroma.'

In the bakery she waited for five minutes as Georgios chatted to a friend and as the friend left he pinched her hard on the breast so that there was a bruise by evening. His face was completely blank. Georgios shrugged when she asked for bread though there were loaves behind him on the shelf, each marked with a neat cross.

And Mike seemed to have disappeared.

'I've got to get out of here,' she said to Bron. But Bron had met a Canadian called Cave-Bear Jim. She sprawled against his furry pelt and said, 'It's just the dope. It's stronger than you're used to. I feel like a dog this morning too.'

'It's not the dope,' Raeleen said. 'I mean, you've seen *Zorba the Greek*. They stone people in these places, you know.'

Bron reached for the suncream and Jim said if he was gettin' paranoid, he'd head on out to Ios, there was a whole buncha good vibes on Ios. So Raeleen went there, alone, Koriakos bobbing away from her through a diesel haze like a white shell. And on Ios someone said he was going to go up to Austria to work in the ski hotels for the winter, and someone else said she was going to pick oranges on this kibbutz near Tel Aviv and someone else said Afghanistan was outtasight, you could live for practically nothing in Kabul and there was this bakery off Chicken Street where they made the best hash brownies on this planet: straight from the oven and all the hash you could handle for less than a dollar. And Banyan: man, Banyan was like paradise. Beautiful and cheap.

The trails led away to islands and cities and mountains

and Raeleen followed, looping back and forth in loose, easy flight, sometimes alone, sometimes not. People asked her where she came from and viewed from Chicken Street it was from some tiny dots on a vast expanse of watery space. She might as well have come from a star. Everywhere she went she was a long long way from home.

Then the bleeding stopped. She was in Spain building a rock wall on a hillside terraced in a whole tumbling cataract of rock walls. Sven wanted to restore the terraces, Milo wanted to buy a milk goat and Camille wanted to lie in the shade of the fig tree by the house and smoke and write poetry. Raeleen was sorting through rubble, looking out the facing stones, the air was still, the heat cicada-stitched round her head like a heavy blanket. She knelt by the broken wall, queasy in the heat and realising that she had been waiting without realising it, with some part of her mind, for the blood to come and ease the heaviness. She sat back on her heels and did some rapid calculations. It had been ages since the blood. At least six or seven weeks. That night she lay on her bed and felt her body carefully beneath the quilt: the little breasts were swollen and tender to the touch, her stomach was firm and rounded. She seemed to be thickening all over, setting from air or water into solid clay. How could she not have noticed it sooner?

A couple of weeks later she was sitting solid and lumpy in a clinic in Kensington with twelve other women reading magazines. She read magazines for three hours. From time to time the receptionist would call a number and one of the women would stand and walk behind a thin partition erected across one end of the room from behind which their counselling was clearly audible. The other women kept their heads down and concentrated on the Queen and Elizabeth Taylor. On Thursdays and Fridays the clinic handled sexually transmitted diseases. Above the women's heads hung posters detailing the symptoms of pelvic inflammatory disease and gonorrhoea and syphilis and above Raeleen's head a little cartoon penis tugged on a condom like a ski hat: *Come Prepared For Anything!*

No one spoke.

'Number eleven,' called the receptionist. Like a caller at bingo. 'Number eleven?'

Legs eleven.

'Number eleven please?' said the receptionist, sounding irritable.

Raeleen walked on heavy legs behind the screen.

'You're sure?'

Talk with the counsellor.

'Yes, I'm sure.'

More magazines.

Blood pressure, pulse, surgery, feet up, legs spread, a tugging and pain beneath the green cloth.

And at last the blood.

She had never felt so tired in her life. She lay on the recovery bed feeling the last five years, the easy journeying, trickle away onto a thick pad. She felt light again but empty, like a shell. She flicked the pages of another magazine. There, in full colour, was a wide-open beach, a bright blue sky, a pohutukawa tree in full bloom. *New Zealand*, it said. *Land of Contrasts*.

The clinic was yellow and gherkin green, on the ground floor of Albert Wing. The window above her head looked out onto the brown bricks of Victoria Wing.

'Would you like a cup of tea?' said the nurse.

'No thanks,' said Raeleen. 'I think I'm ready to go home.'

She was ravenous suddenly. She went over to Sealey Street and ordered a whole cod dinner.

And two weeks later she flew home, eating breakfast then dinner then breakfast again and then her ears were popping and they were back, flying down through cloud to a country which looked quite different viewed from the air and bouncing across a paddock surrounded by sea and in a little tin shed a man in blue shorts rummaged through her single bag suspiciously and she stood there, loving his silly white socks and his sideburns and his toothbrush moustache and the way he waved the passengers through as if he were drafting sheep. And outside every hill, every tree, every ripple on the harbour was as shiny and precise as a fish's scale.

Her father said, 'Good to see you back, Rainbow.'

Her mother said she'd certainly taken her time, hadn't she? And what was she planning to do now?

Raeleen said she supposed she'd look for a job.

'What kind of job?' said her father.

Raeleen thought for a moment. 'Something out of doors,' she said. 'Somewhere near a decent beach. Somewhere up north.'

Her mother looked relieved.

She moved about for a time, to an apple orchard in Nelson, to a nursery in Gisborne, and one night in heavy rain her van broke down on a road near Oakura. She settled in her sleeping bag to wait for morning and when she woke there was Clarry peering in through the windscreen. Clarry had some leads up at his place. He gave her a jump and in return she gave him a hand with an unexpected order: one hundred proteas to pick, pack and dispatch and his lungs were playing him up these days, he wasn't as fast as he used to be. That was how she came to the hillside beneath the mountain which Clarry said was not extinct only dormant and which Mrs Kereopa next door always referred to as 'he'.

The old people would not live in his path, she said. In case he got wild. That pure white cone poised overhead.

And now Clarry is dead and gone, Werner is asleep on the sofa in the next room and Ra lies in the half-world feeling this body of hers beneath the quilt, caught between youth and age: the soft folds of skin beneath the arms, the crêpey skin at the neck, the wrinkles at eyes and mouth and her hair she knows is no longer black but speckled with grey. Her body has set off on its own again, charging through middle age. Her stomach cramps but it is unlikely to be the blood, after a whole year. She has looked it up in the medical dictionary at the library.

Menopause. In between *Mastitis* and *Menstrual Problems.* Standing there in the 618s she has ticked off the symptoms.

Disruption of menstrual cycle? Yes. Definitely. The sudden gush or flicker of pale blood, after years of dependability. The hesitation. The complete halt.

Irritability? Yes. But who wouldn't be irritable, with the Manions' bull in again across the weak place by the creek escaping overgrazed brown stubble for the lush growth between the irrigated rows of proteas and leucadendrons?

Your bloody bull's in my top paddock.

Half an acre of Rewa Gold trampled to twigs. And Ross Manion saying he'd get on to it. Right away.

Mr Mañana himself.

Who wouldn't be irritable with the Taylors spraying the boundary on a day with just enough of an easterly to drive Marzane all over a new planting of Harry Chittick so that the leaves twist and wither?

'You've wrecked six months' work,' she said.

And Rex said well, someone has to take care of the scrub and when was she going to clear her side? She said just as soon as she could get around to it but she was busy right now and Rex said it was a big place for one woman to manage on her own and he didn't know what Clarry had thought he was doing, leaving the whole shebang to her, she needed to get in some help and she said when she wanted advice she'd ask for it and what would help right now would be if he would trouble to wait for a dead-still day next time he felt like doing a spot of weed-killing.

Who wouldn't be irritable then?

Dryness of vagina? Not that she'd noticed. When she lay in bed in the mornings, her legs crossed and her fingers pressing and rubbing, her body still shuddered and her hand afterward was damp and salty.

Headaches? Depression? No.

Hot flushes? Not sure. It could have been sunburn after a day out on the hillside, picking.

Sleep problems? But who wouldn't be sleepless waking to heavy rain at 2 a.m. and an order to fill that morning? Who wouldn't be sleepless after a day tending flowers whose sole virtue was that they would last for months when cut, like embalmed bodies, all lipstick and manicure, and no life in them?

Marama down at the Health Centre dragged on a pair of rubber gloves like sloughed skins and said she was a bit early but if she hopped up on the table she'd just check everything over.

She sounded like a mechanic: check the brakes, check the lights, she'll be right for another twelve months.

Raeleen had lain there attempting to just relax against the tiny bite of the speculum but the only distraction was a poster of warts, moles and melanomas above the high bed.

Melanomas. Squamous Lumps. Solar Keratoses. She was regretting coming in. The minute you put your foot across the threshold at these places they had you on your back looking up your bum.

'Looks OK,' said Marama, a muffled voice from some-where down between Raeleen's spread knees. 'When did your mother go through menopause?'

Ah: that was the question.

'I don't know,' said Raeleen. How could she know? Two years ago her mother and father had crashed in the Cromwell Gorge on the way back from Wanaka, and at the afternoon tea after the funeral her cousin Laura had helped herself to just one more lamington and said she thought it was high time for a few home truths.

She was not Raeleen's cousin. Raeleen was not Marcia and Ken's daughter. Raeleen was adopted. Marcia had tried for years to have children and by the time she was thirty-five they had given up, but the moment they arrived home with

Raeleen, Marcia had conceived and that was Graham and wasn't that often the way?

Laura had wanted to say something for years. She had always felt it was wrong not to tell Raeleen since everyone knew: all the family and neighbours. You couldn't keep a thing like that quiet in a small town.

'It would have been just so easy,' said Laura, taking a wee bite, 'for some playmate to tell you. It didn't happen, by some miracle, though once when you were just a tot I remember you coming in one afternoon when I'd popped in for a cup of tea which I didn't do all that often even though Marcia was on my way back from town but you know how she was, always a bit stiff and starchy, a real Clitheroe, anyway you came in and stood in the door, such a serious little dot in one of those frilly dresses Marcia used to make for you and no doubt about it, she was a great sewer and you always looked a picture. Anyway you stood there and you said, "What's dopted?" Well, you could have cut the air with a knife and then Ken said and oh he was such a nice chap was Ken, much too nice for Marcia, I always felt she bossed him around, but he just picked you up and said it meant the best girl. And a minute or so later we could hear you outside the window telling Graham who was a bit inclined to hang around listening into adult conversations and hearing more than he should and you told him you liked being dopted, so there. So that was that and we never heard about it again. Well there you are. People made far too much fuss about that sort of thing in those days.'

'So,' Raeleen said, 'who are my parents?'

Laura brushed coconut from the bosom of her best jersey silk. Graham was leaning against the mantelpiece only a few feet away discussing the rise in mortgage rates with Raeleen's cousin Richard, and giving it as his opinion and he was in a position to know being in real estate that the government would never permit the rate to rise above seven and a half, not with MMP just around the corner . . .

Laura leaned forward and lowered her voice.

'That's the question,' she said. 'Marcia had never talked about it in any detail even to the family. But she'd flown up north to collect you: some Maori lass at one of those homes in Wellington, no doubt. Or maybe it was the father who was Maori.

'You can find out,' she said. 'I was reading about it in the *Woman's Weekly* just the other day when I was in getting my blood pressure done and there was an article about these twins who'd tracked one another down after forty years through one of these organisations and do you know when they met they were wearing exactly the same dresses and they'd both become librarians and they'd both married engineers? I mean talk about stranger than fiction!'

Graham bore down on them then, asking if Raeleen had a place now, or was she still playing at hippies in that van of hers?

Laura kissed Raeleen damply on both cheeks on leaving. Her breath smelt of coconut.

'Last week's *Woman's Weekly*,' she said. 'It's got a picture of Princess Anne on the front. You get in touch with that organisation and find out about your mum and dad. The truth never hurt anybody, did it?'

But what if your mother does not want to be found? What if she has other children, another family? What if she says no contact please? What then? You could understand it: something you thought long dead comes swimming up at you from deep water. Of course you would kick it aside. Of course you would want to kick clear.

You can do nothing except change your name. Just Ra, you say now when asked. No middle name, no surname. Just plain Ra. Ra fits better. Ra is enough to carry.

Kuiii, sings the bird in the half-world.

Raeleen's stomach cramps and if it is not the blood, for that is over now, it is most probably Flo.

Yesterday she killed Flo, the last remaining chook. All

the others had gone. Harley had got a couple back when he was a puppy and irresponsible and a ferret took four more before she'd been able to trap him and that had left Flo who had picked around the place all winter, until yesterday.

'What is this?' said Werner when he came in and found her chopping an onion for stuffing. 'Is this some kind of celebration? Is it your birthday?'

'No,' she'd said. Though it was a kind of celebration. Ra was making the place ready. She was removing all dependence. She was marking the moment with sacrifice.

But that was all far too complicated to explain to Werner.

They had eaten Flo with spuds and broccoli and the last of Clarry's plum wine and sat up late watching some updated western with real Indians and designer stubble.

It had been cosy.

And now her stomach cramped.

Flo was always a contrary bird, given to hiding her eggs in inaccessible places beneath the house where they smashed and stank out of arm's reach. She was exactly the kind of bird to get her own back.

Kuiii, sang the bird and the sun inched up and over and spilled light onto the trees.

Sigh, breathed Werner from the sofa in the room next door.

Beneath the quilt, Ra's legs jiggled. 'OK,' she said to Harley. 'Time to go.' She reached out for him on the mat where he slept each night, whimpering after the thousands of tantalising cats, the bobbing multitudes of rabbits who skittered through his sleep.

But Harley was not there.

She slid out of bed softly, careful not to hit the creaky board, and dragged some clothes from the pile on the chair: a teeshirt, shorts, a pair of knickers, socks. Black shirt, black shorts, black bra, black knickers.

'Why is all your clothes black?' Werner had said one night when they were sitting by the range toasting their stockinged feet in the open oven and having a smoke.

One hundred and fifty nerifolias tucked into their cartons and ready for the courier first thing in the morning. The rain gurgling in the pipe outside the window. Harley on the sofa and Ducati for once docile, curled on her knee.

Bliss.

'I like it,' Ra had said. 'It's deep, it's no-colour.'

Werner licked a paper. 'It is for sadness,' he said. 'It is for death.'

Ra exhaled on a long single breath. Smoke curled toward the ceiling.

'Yeah,' she said. 'Death. Grief. Night. But I like it.'

In the early morning, sunlight shimmering on ponga leaves outside her bedroom window and a bird piping in the day, Ra tugged on her black clothes, her shorts and T-shirt and knickers and socks which were black too with little yellow stars. She padded down the hall and where the sunlight caught the floor the boards were already warm.

The living-room door was open. From the hall she could see Werner lying on his back in a purple sleeping bag and by him, on the floor, lay Harley.

The night Werner had arrived Harley had barked and bared his teeth, furious at the intrusion, and she had had to hold him firmly as Werner unloaded his pack from the van and walked nervously up the steps.

'You keep a wolf?' he'd said.

'He's alright,' Ra had said, 'once he knows you.'

Harley growled.

'So he is a sheep in wolf's clothes?' Werner had said.

'Not entirely,' said Ra. 'But he's fine with my friends.'

Just in case. This young man she had picked up on the road near New Plymouth late one Sunday evening in the rain looked peaceable enough. Just another tourist intent on walking round the mountain, adding Taranaki to the Heaphy and the Tasman and the bungy jump and the white-water raft trip. Just another young German for whom her country existed as some vast confidence course. He was unlikely to transform into the Boston Strangler or the Yorkshire Ripper and anyway she was fit and almost as tall as him.

But it didn't pay to take chances.

Harley had tired quickly of aggression. He yawned and bowed to them both.

'He takes good care of me,' Ra said.

Harley licked Werner's hand and padded off to his place on the sofa by the door.

And now the defection was complete. He looked up at her guiltily from beneath Werner's hand.

'You trying to make it really hard for me, boy?' Ra whispered. Harley whimpered.

Werner stirred and flung one arm back exposing a tuft of fair hair in the pale cup of his armpit.

'Come on,' said Ra.

She didn't want another discussion. Last night Werner had lain beside her in the darkness and said, 'But why? This is a good place. Why do you want to go? And why do you want to go alone?'

It was too hard to explain. She had said nothing.

'Is it that you think I do this all the time? That I am the tourist, I go around the world, I screw whoever is there? I don't make love. I screw. I fuck. Is this what it is?' said Werner. 'Because I am not like that at all. I have slept with three women in my life. Only three. The first was my girlfriend when I was seventeen. The second I was in love with when I was working in Frankfurt. And I have told you about Monika – that I began to travel last year after we parted. I have been interested in some women on the way, it's true. I have talked to them in Bali, or Australia, and perhaps we have travelled for a while, gone to some beach to swim or dive – but I don't sleep with a woman just because she is nice or because we can talk or because it is a sunny afternoon and I have nothing better to do. I sleep with a woman because I love her. And I love you. And I think that you love me.'

It was the longest speech he had made yet in English. The words faltered, tiny, vulnerable, frail new things just broken from the shell. Ra felt them sucking at her, trying to get a grip.

Werner got out of bed, lit a cigarette. She watched the glow of it in the dark. When she was little and had woken from some childhood nightmare, her father (though he was not after all her father) used to soothe her with fireflies. He would light a cigarette and wave it about in the darkened room so that the tiny point of light swooped and flew, making patterns in the night.

Werner inhaled and she saw his face briefly, intense and young and unhappy.

'Do you not believe me?' he said.

Of course she believed him. She had watched him all winter, walking down the long rows of plants or standing at the bench in the shed, steady and earnest. She had eaten with him each night, the two of them cooking up some meal once it was dark, padding about the kitchen in their socks glad to be out of boots at last and in away from the cold, drinking a glass of wine or sharing a joint while they chopped onions, sliced potatoes, stirred the stew.

'And I am right?' he said in the poppyglow of his cigarette. 'You love me?'

Werner was very young. He believed you could say such things.

'Yes,' she said. 'But that's not the main thing any more.'

'So,' said Werner. 'What is the "main thing"? Why don't you tell me the truth? Is it because I am younger than you? Because that is nothing: just numbers. Is it because I am German? Something from your father?'

They had talked about that one night cooking a rabbit for her birthday. Werner had crushed some garlic and Ra had said her father hated garlic.

It was just something to say.

'He was on the run for three months in Italy during the war. They lived in some cave in the mountains and ate nothing but bread soaked in rainwater and garlic. He couldn't stand the stuff afterwards.'

Werner had said his father was too young for the war.

'So what happened?' he said. 'To your father?'

'He got shot,' said Ra. 'Oh, not badly,' she added when Werner looked startled. 'In the leg. And he spent the rest of the war in a POW camp. It wasn't for long because the war ended soon after. But he had a limp for the rest of his life and he'd been a good athlete too. He didn't like garlic and he wasn't too keen on Germans, either. He'd have a fit if he knew I had one living in my home.'

Werner took a potato and scraped it under cold water. Ra watched his hands working. Long slim hands with tapering tanned fingers. He had good hands, strong and dextrous. She had found an old guitar when she was clearing out Clarry's shed and Werner had tuned it, roughly he said, but it sounded fine.

'Blues always sounds off-key to me anyway,' said Ra.

At night he sat on the step playing, picking chords, easy and lazy and they were part of the night as his steady breathing was part of the morning.

Now he scrubbed the potato clean and nicked an eye from it neatly and said nothing and she wondered if she might have offended him. Perhaps she shouldn't have mentioned her father. The war was a long time ago, stuff for jokes on TV.

Don't mention the war.

'Bunch of bloody thugs,' Dad said of Germans. 'At your feet or at your throat. And don't think the '39–'45 show was the last. You can't trust the buggers.'

What are the shortest books in the world? British cookery. Italian war heroes. German humour.

Werner took another potato from the bag.

'I'm sorry for your father,' he said. 'We have a bad history.'

It had gone too quiet, too serious. She flicked his bare legs with the teatowel.

'Don't worry about it,' she said. 'It was years ago.'

Don't take it seriously. Please.

Because it was serious: her father (who was not her father) limping ahead of her through childhood, the way his leg made him groan on cold mornings, the way she ran as hard as she could in every race partly for herself because of the lightness and speed, but partly too for him. For the hug at the end and the, 'Well done, Rainbow,' and the way they could drive home, eating an ice-cream each and discussing strategy.

'You've got to run with the wind,' he'd say. 'You were so focused on cracking thirty-two seconds for the first 220 that you ignored the wind and ran straight into it and then you had nothing left for the home straight. The key is to use the wind where it is. Now, I remember once I was at this meet up in Napier and . . .' and so on to reminiscence, his face happy at the thought of her running as he had once done, up on his toes and ahead of the pack.

She had asked him once as they drove home, 'Do you wish you were still running?'

Dad had changed gear and said that was life, you took the knocks and got on with it and it could have been worse. His mate Murphy, for instance, had copped it in Crete.

He was silent for a while. She sat and watched the street signs flicker past. *Li Sing Takeaways. Felicity Florists. Risley's Music Shop. Radiogram Trade In! Save Save Save!*

'What a lot of bloody nonsense it all was, eh?' he said, his fingers drumming the wheel. 'What a bloody waste.'

The lights had gone green but they did not move. She had looked up then and seen that her father's eyes were full of tears.

He never cried, not even when Granna died. When Raeleen or Graham fell when they were little and grazed their knees or banged their noses, Dad had gathered them up fast and tossed them in the air and hugged them tight saying, 'No tears, no tears, who's the brave soldier?'

'And all for what?' he said to no one in particular. To Felicity Florists and Li Sing.

Raeleen reached her hand over and patted Dad's stiff knee and they swung round the corner on the yellow.

'Maleesh,' he had said.

The knee had killed him in the end, had killed them both, her mother and her father. A stupid irony. That was the coroner's opinion. Dad had not been able to move fast enough to brake at the corner in the gorge when he and her mother were driving back from Wanaka and that was what had caused the accident. A wet night, mud on the road from a slip, the car racing out into the dark across the shoulder and down to smash and flatten on rock and boulder.

There were no signs of struggle, the coroner said. But her father's foot was jammed beneath the clutch.

They had died on impact.

So her father had died because of the war after all: thirty years later in a river gorge thousands of miles from the Italian hilltop where the bullet had slammed into the cartilage and winged him on the run.

She had never talked about it to anyone. She had never cried.

Who's the brave soldier?

Werner put down the potato knife. He turned to her and placed his hands on her shoulders. Lightly, as she'd seen him handle the choicest flowers so that they did not bruise and the petals stayed closed over the soft cone at their centre.

'Mein Hase,' he said. My rabbit with long legs.

'Hare,' she had said when he had first touched her, first held her. 'And you'll soon learn the difference once you've shot a few. They're hell on the young plants.'

My hare who runs straight and true. His breath mingled with her breath and at her centre she felt a kind of wavering and against her will her body trembled.

'Hey,' she said. She pushed him away. *Flick* she went with the teatowel.

'Autch,' said Werner.

Flick, flick.

'It was all years ago,' she said. 'Years before you were born, like all the significant events of the twentieth century. You missed them all, didn't you? You missed the war . . .'

Flick.

'. . . and the assassination of Kennedy . . .'

'Hör auf,' said Werner.

'. . . and the Beatles . . .'

Flick.

'. . . and Vietnam and the first man on the moon . . .'

'Komm hör *AUF*,' said Werner.

'In fact, you're just . . .'

Flick.

'. . . a bloody . . .'

'Autch!'

Flick.

'Baby.'

Flick, flick.

And the moment had passed in squabbling, ice water splashed in her face from the sink, a towel flicking at bare tanned legs, and Harley yelping and barking and a chase from the house onto the lawn. The sort of yelling, pummelling fight she used to have with her brother, so that they had eaten the birthday rabbit late that evening, cheerful and pink-cheeked, and Werner had told her how he had been taking a piss behind the hedge in the bottom paddock because it was too bloody far to walk back up to the shed and just at that moment Lois Taylor had driven past in the Range Rover and, 'You know how she is,' said Werner, 'like the queen, waving to all the peasants.'

He mimicked her perfectly, her prissy little mouth pursed, her eyebrows arched in permanent disapproval.

'So I held on with one hand and carried on watering the hedge, and waved back with the other.'

They sat by the stove and laughed as she had not laughed in ages, that sudden slide from the serious to the silly. From darkness out into the light.

'No,' she said to Werner when he asked, 'Is it your father?'

'It has nothing to do with my father. It was something I heard this afternoon on the radio. Something on the News.'

The radio out in the shed, the buckets of leucadendrons, the tap dripping, the two of them standing either side of the table stapling cartons.

'The radio?' Werner said. The cigarette flared scarlet and she could hear it all in his voice: anger, hurt, disbelief.

Silence stretched between them. An empty road.

'OK,' said Werner. 'If that is how you want it. I shall go in the morning. And I shall not sleep here.'

He took his sleeping bag and she heard the rustling of it as he settled down on the sofa.

Kuiii, sang the bird.

'Shhh,' she said to Harley. 'Please don't disturb him.' Harley slid out from beneath Werner's hand and followed her down the hall. In the kitchen, she splashed her face at the sink in water ice-cold from some deep cavern beneath the mountain and smelling still of earth and darkness while Ducati slid in like a shadow through the gap in the window after a night out cruising the jungle and twisted round her bare legs begging and begging and wanting food now immediately please, please, please.

'Nice of you to drop by,' said Ra. 'But there's only rabbit so if you were planning on that tinned stuff you're out of luck.'

Ducati didn't mind. Rabbit would be fine, she just wanted something to eat, anything to eat, and she didn't care what though of course she'd have preferred that tinned pink fishy muck but if that was off the menu well, she'd settle for rabbit stew just so long as it was quick please, please.

Ra spooned some from the carton in the fridge. 'There you go,' she said. 'That's the last of it. You'll have to eat at Nanny's from now on.'

Gulp, gulp, gulp, went Ducati. And slid away, back through the window and into the jungle.

Ra went out to pee. The sunlight was full on the back porch and there were bees writhing about in the plum blossom by the dunny. She left the door open and sat on the warm wooden ring and the sun pressed tiny shining studs of light through young leaves onto her bare legs.

Then she dragged her hair into a ponytail and found her shoes in the pile by the door among the jumble of boots, cartons, beer crates and clippers, buckets and parkas. Werner's shoes were the same size as hers but they were easy to tell apart: his with the purple flashes and the worn left heel, hers plain with the little bump by the big toe.

Like their clothes which hung mingled on the line along the porch: a couple of pairs of black knickers, underpants, his T-shirt from Nepal with the big embroidered eye on the front and her jeans and his, all stretched and shaped by their absent bodies, faded where they had cupped buttocks, knees, cock, breasts, like flayed skins, like the shells left by cicadas when the summer's over and they take on new forms.

The lace broke, snapped in her hand. She knotted it roughly because she was irritable and not sure how it was supposed to go from here: the traveller comes, lean and tousled, to the farm gate and there's the lone woman who needs help. And sometime later, she draws off her doeskin jacket and her cotton blouse, her camisole and corset and *goldarn it* she's gorgeous, one mighty fine little lady, with a perfect body, big breasts, plumped up with silicone maybe, dusted with make-up for the cameras, but smooth and unblemished like sun-ripened peaches. And as the credits roll, the hired hand and the lady embrace before a searing sunset and everybody's happy.

Harley whines.

'You're right,' Ra says and stands up. 'That's enough of that bullshit.'

She finds her bag, packed and ready, and swings it over her shoulder. She shuts the door quietly, checks that the cartons are all ready for the courier in the corner of the shed, ready for Shuu-bun.

'It's some kind of ancestor festival round the Equinox,' Mark from MarkEx International had told her. 'The Japanese all go and put flowers on their ancestors' graves.'

She had laid the offerings carefully in the cartons last night, their heads resting on soft paper, doing it perfectly. Another last rite.

Harley leaps ahead, whining. Let's go, let's go.

'Right,' says Raeleen. 'I'm ready.'

And half way down the drive she begins to run, down between trees still damp with dew and a bird calling *kui-kui kui-kui* somewhere up on the hillside and Harley leaps ahead. At the gate he pauses. To the right? Towards the mountain? Or to the left? Towards the sea?

To the left, she says. To the left and at the corner Mrs Kereopa waves.

'Come *on*,' she says. 'Mereana's on the TV.'

So Ra goes in to watch Mereana sing good morning to the children.

'She's pretty, your mokopuna,' says Ra.

'Like me,' says Mrs Kereopa.

Like the young woman in the wedding portrait above the mantelpiece, the bride carrying a sheaf of white lilies, the groom serious in a lounge suit, standing on a studio terrace before a misty lake with white swans.

The tea is strong and sweet, two spoonfuls of sugar already stirred in, and there are scones straight from the oven and spread thick with butter. Mrs Kereopa thinks she's too skinny. All that running.

'Don't you get enough exercise up there, with those flowers?'

Mrs Kereopa does not like the proteas. In the old days they'd grown melons in that paddock, big juicy watermelons. Their shiny patent leather seeds tucked into succulent pink flesh, their mottled green rind like marble cool to the touch on a hot summer day. Birds rippling by the creek and a slice of watermelon stretching across your face like a smile.

'But the ground's gone cold,' Mrs Kereopa says. 'They took all the damn trees. Just cut them all down.'

The tiny shoots of titoki, mahoe and tawa, like the tiny upright feathers on a cloak, folded one across the other so that the water runs off from one pinion to the other and beneath the cloak the body is warm. Breast and belly and buttock and the muscled swellings on the upper arm, warm under the cloak. You take away the cloak and the body shrinks from the sky and clenches tight and nothing can grow.

'Now,' says Mrs Kereopa, 'just those hairy flowers. Like caterpillars, those flowers.'

'They're from South Africa,' says Ra.

'They should go back there,' says Mrs Kereopa.

Good morning, good morning, sings Mereana.

Ducati slips through the window. A lean grey shadow. She wraps herself around Mrs Kereopa's legs. Please, please, please.

'Ah,' says Mrs Kereopa. 'So you've come back, eh? You want your breakfast, eh?'

Yes please, yes please.

Ra picks her up. 'Con,' she says into her soft rumpled ear. 'You con artist.'

Ducati squirms, leaps to the floor and Mrs Kereopa spoons catfood onto a saucer. Gulp, goes Ducati. Gulp, gulp, gulp. She sits on the step to wash herself, delicately, paw by paw.

Mrs Kereopa watches Mereana, dabbing away the tears with her hanky. She's not sad. She weeps all the time these days. Once she had good eyes, could see her brothers coming in from the hill for their kai long before anyone else. But then she worked on the chicken farm. Dirt and dust and all the poor birds standing in their little cages. They got sick in there with no proper food and nowhere to move so they brought in sprays to make them strong. But the birds were still sick and her eyes began to cry.

All these tears.

Mereana sings the goodbye song. 'You want some veges?' says Mrs Kereopa.

She grows good veges. Potatoes in secret clusters, green flags of silverbeet, leeks with white smooth skin and a tassel of torn roots. In here between hedges of currants tangled with passionfruit she keeps the ground warm.

'Not today,' says Ra. 'I'm going for a long walk.'

Not today. On other mornings she has sat on the step while Mrs Kereopa sprinkles wheat for her chookies. She has talked then about her eyes, and how she came to live here, sent up from Wanganui to live with the old people, how they never went into town, refused it all. Even the pension. Nothing of the Pakeha. And how she lived with them till she was old enough to go nursing. One time she came home and there was a young man all lined up for her. It took a while to see what they were up to and when she did she said no way. She liked her life in Wellington. She had a perm, nice clothes, more shoes than she could wear in a week.

She spent all her money on shoes. She was a smart city girl, she wasn't going to get herself hitched to someone the old people had picked out.

But Turei was nice. Shy, you know. A country boy. Strong, good muscles. And she watched the way he was with her koro who was deaf and growled a lot. He didn't like it when people spoke too quiet. Made him wild. Turei was patient. And he made people laugh. So in the end she said yes.

Mrs Kereopa dabbed at her eyes with her hanky.

'And now the bed's cold,' she said. 'Just me and my little cat.'

Ra sits in the sun and eats a scone while Mrs Kereopa sprinkles wheat.

'Here, chookies,' she says. 'Here, girls.'

The hens mill about: Wyandottes and Leghorns and Anconas.

'So, where are you walking?' says Mrs Kereopa.

'I don't know yet,' says Ra and because Mrs Kereopa might understand she tries to explain it. 'I want to walk along the beach as far as I can to start with,' she says. 'Round to Opunake, right round the mountain. You see, I don't know anything about it or about me or about how I belong here. Do you know what I mean? I read things and I hear things on the radio and I don't understand them and I want to understand. So I'm going to go on a long walk. I want to walk for days and I want to walk on my own.'

'Ah,' says Mrs Kereopa. She puts four warm scones in a teatowel.

'There,' she says. 'You take that for your walk.' Breath and steam mingle in the cool morning air.

Mereana has gone and the News rattles out. Ra listens for Margie's name but she has disappeared already, displaced by a school fire in Northland, a ceasefire in Northern Ireland.

She puts a couple of scones in her bag and sets off down the road.

Kui-kui, sings the bird up on the hillside among the little shoots growing among the proteas: manuka, titoki, mahoe, tawa, all those seeds in their accustomed soil. All that scrub, but leave them alone a while and let's see what happens.

'*Kui-kui whiti-whiti-ora tio-o*,' Mrs Kereopa said, one morning on the back step in the sun. 'That's what that one says. Takes off up north for the winter. Then one day she's back. And when she's back it's time to get your veges in.'

Kui-kui whiti-whiti ora tio-o, sings the careless, happy bird on the hillside moving easily, lightly, between north and south.

SO HERE THEY ARE

'Joan led her army in triumph
toward Rheims . . .'

SO, HERE THEY ARE, ALL THE CLEVER GIRLS ON this day: the day they hear that Margie has fallen on Parbat.

Here is Kasia, who used to be Kathy and is no longer Kate, leaving Howard's hushed room for the last time. Here she is driving along Bealey Ave and here she is standing in the aisle of the Floraland Garden Centre. She is going to buy a fig tree. It will fill the gap where the weeping elm was felled by last winter's storms. Here she is deciding between a White Adriatic and a Brown Turkish. The plants are small yet, still contained in black plastic pots and years off maturity and it is quite likely that they will never bear any fruit. But what beautiful leaves they have, big and generous and each one shaped like an open hand.

They'll survive. Figs are astonishingly hardy.

'. . . *Songe*,' murmur the soft voices in Kasia's inner ear. '*Songe aux cris des vainqueurs, songe aux cris des mourants, Dans la flamme étouffés, sous le fer expirants . . .*'

And here is Heather, watching the Tararuas slide by on the blind side as she drives toward Wellington with her husband. She is crying: for her son, for her sister and her mother and father and for Margie, slipping to her death on the mountain, and for all the others she has wanted to save. The children with bruised faces and broken arms and welts where the jug cord has stung and the women slumped in empty houses watching the TV and waiting for the repo man and the men shovelling shit as hard as they can but never digging their way through. And beyond them the nameless millions, the ones she sees on television or reads about in the magazines and newspapers, the ones who stumble across an empty plain toward extinction or huddle captive in wire enclosures, who are shot and maimed or left in tiny cells where they can neither stand nor sit nor lie down. And the pathos of it all. The way the child skips on her bruised legs and the woman wonders if she could do her hair like that woman on the TV and the man sings 'Heartbreak Hotel' on his way home. All those frail shelters erected within the wire.

All carrying their own particular weapons and fighting their own way through their own patch of the dungle.

It's too much, too much to bear.

She weeps, without making a sound and with her head turned aside, but suddenly Trevor is pulling over, cutting straight in front of a truck, and stopping in a layby overlooking the sea. He takes her hand in his, he hugs her, warm and certain. Dub dub, goes his heart against her cheek. Dub dub.

'Darling Heather,' he says. 'Shhh. You fret too much.'

He holds her steady as the traffic rumbles past, cars and trucks racing up the straight to Pukerua. Sunlight slopes across Kapiti in brilliant golden bars. She takes a deep breath.

There's nothing for it is there, but to dab at red puffy eyes and straighten up? She'll have to look her best for Matthew and his new in-laws. And perhaps there'll be time to pop into Parsons for half an hour, to see if they have Eliot's book. And maybe she'll ring the office too, to check up on Demelza.

After all, somebody has to.

Here is Caroline swimming steadily up and down, up and down, in the pool at ShapeUp fitting in her twenty lengths before dinner. It's a good time to come to the pool as most people are in the bars or on their way home or preparing to go out for the evening and she has the lane to herself. But there's an irritating little piece of Elastoplast curled at the bottom of the pool like a tiny strip of pink skin, with a disgusting stained liner. Nothing is ever perfect. You can plan as much as you like but you can never count on other people not to mess things up.

She crosses the Elastoplast for the tenth, eleventh, twelfth time and the news of Margie's death has plopped into the water beside her. Caroline rolls over onto her back for a length to think.

She thinks about Margie climbing, all those years ago, hand over hand up the cliff and how that too could have been a mess had she, Caroline, not taken action to avert disaster. She thinks too about Lyndsay who started behind her at Tremayne Prentice but who has drawn even and now is passing her, climbing easily up the rock face. And there is the vision of poor Caroline, ordinary, unremarkable Caroline, working steadily but without due recognition, eating alone in some restaurant with a book for company, becoming besotted with her cat, drinking rather too much whisky before bed since only that and a Mogadon will ensure sleep.

It's a vision too pathetic to contemplate.

Only prompt action will avert it. Caroline rolls over and kicks out hard. She closes her eyes and finds a faster stroke. She breathes deep and steady. She has another eight lengths to go and as she swims, she begins work on a new Five Year Plan.

Here's Greer late on Friday afternoon, turning into Rangitikei Close, the spider poster on the back seat of her Honda City finished and ready for dispatch on time after all. There's a strange car outside her unit and the front door is open. Inside, Tom and Alice are watching television. Neither looks up when she comes in. Road-runner speeds across the screen *beepbeep beepbeep* only inches ahead of runaway train.

'Hullo, Greer,' says James from the bedroom door. Beyond him she can see Susan kneeling by the bed carefully folding her silk shirt and placing it in the overnight bag. 'I believe I've to thank you for taking care of my runaway family. And Tom for being sensible and phoning me.'

Susan takes a skirt from a hanger. She folds it along the pleat. She looks up just once at Greer and only for a second but it's enough. There is a flat red mark on her cheek.

'Get out of my house,' Greer says to James. And for once she is glad she is fat. She is huge. She is overwhelming. She expands to fill the whole hallway. She is solid with rage. She could easily pick him up between her huge fat fingers and squeeze him, just like that, on either side of the thorax. She could kill him and not even notice. James turns then and he sees it too. She's sure of it. He is frightened but he recovers quickly. He picks up a bag.

'Come on,' he says.

But he must pass her to escape and she is so big that she fills the whole hallway. He pauses.

'Do you want to go?' says Greer to Susan.

Susan stands by the bed holding her bag, her head bowed.

'Susan,' says Greer. 'You have got to say now: do you want to go or do you want to stay here?'

The silence is forever.

Booom goes the big black bomb on the TV, leaving a crater in the road and the baddie stripped and sooty black. *Cuckoo cuckoo cuckoo*.

'I want . . .' says Susan. And it's the smallest whisper. 'I want to stay here.'

James is still, his face is dead white. 'Ah,' he says. 'So that's how it is.'

But he sees Greer's huge neck-snapping fingers and he makes no move toward his wife.

'In that case,' he says, 'you'll excuse me. We've got to catch tonight's ferry.'

Greer stands aside then and lets him past. Tom switches off the TV and goes out to sit in the front seat of the car, staring straight ahead. Alice buries her face in her mother's side. The car draws away and Susan cries out as if she is being split in two.

Nothing's simple. But Greer lies that night curved around her friend Susan, who is curled at last in sleep around her daughter Alice, and in her fingers she feels the tingling which she knows will make her friend well again. She believes in that. It's a kind of faith she discovers she has been building for years, bit by bit, in behind the walls of her quiet everyday existence, and now it's in place it is strong. Properly aligned at last.

And here is Ra, walking along a black beach where the sea and the sky seem cut from a single sheet of shiny metal welded at the horizon with a strip of brilliant light. The tide is low and the sand is still wet, holding on its surface a perfect image of the sky so that when she looks down it is into clouds and she might be moving upside down suspended in clear air. With each step the image shatters and Harley runs ahead of her chasing gulls so that the sky mirror is broken over and over but constantly settles and is recreated.

So here she is between two worlds. The world that is wet, sticky and real, and the world that is its airy image. The world of those whose bodies do as they are told and those whose bodies slip out from under, bucking and tossing. The world of those who know who they are and those who don't. The world of those who are down in the dust of battle and those who watch from the hillside. The world of the old and the world of the young. The world of those who bleed and those who are dry. The world of those who sit quietly by a small fire and those who journey.

She settles the bag on her shoulder and finds her stride. A loose and easy flight.

And somewhere out there Margie falls and falls forever into that icy chasm and thinks, it's not the going up that's difficult.

It's the getting down.

That's what they always say and it's bloody well true,

she thinks, falling through a cavern white and blue arching up and away like a huge wave, falling in a twinkling hail of spindrift glittering around her like shattered glass.

She wonders if she should reach out to those icy walls, those curves and fissures, to seek a fingerhold. She still holds her hammer in one hand, her axe in the other but there seems little point now, so she opens her fingers and they fall away from her bounding on ledges sometimes above her, sometimes below and they all fall together glistening in the sunlight.

The sun is directly overhead. As she tumbles it swings into view like a golden eye, like the centre of a daisy, its rim blue sky and a white petalling of snow around the hole in the crevasse through which she has fallen after that lifetime sliding from the icy face of Parbat.

She twists her neck trying to get a fix on the sun. When she was little she read somewhere that you could see the stars at midday by looking up a chimney but Mum had had the fireplace taken out, nasty messy thing and too much of a bother to keep clean, and put a heater in the sitting room behind the shop instead. It was electric and could be switched on the minute you came in the door so that it glowed sending up regular spirals of smoky shadow from a pile of smouldering plastic coals.

Ah, thinks Margie, tumbling and twisting. Now I can find out about the stars.

There's a rattling behind her left shoulder and a black shadow like a bird, wings spread, falls toward her and passes, mouth open in a pink O, falling to her death. Margie feels unbearably sad for her. She tries to apologise, to say sorry, sorry. Such a stupid mistake. Such a tiny error. A minute shift of balance to the left, always her weak side, though she'd tried to build up equal strength. If she was going to fall she had always known it would be to the left.

She had climbed up carefully enough, with due respect, with absolute attention. A steady ascent, along ridges where the slopes dropped off on either side thousands of feet down to the glaciers, through loose snow and across walls of blue ice, pitch by pitch, inch by inch, kicking in hard, finding the places where she could take hold, fix the screw, the snow stake, breathe, concentrate.

Then the slog along the summit ridge, six breaths to each step up here in the thin air and the dub dub of the oxygen balloon and then the summit beneath a high pennant of wind-driven snow and the other mountains – peaks, seracs and glaciers – stretching away on all sides below them to India, to China, sea-wrack and billow.

She was being careful.

But midway down, a delicate traverse, heart pounding, lungs burning and their tents three tiny bright balloons only a few hundred metres below, she had reached to her left, and there was a butterfly.

A tiny blue butterfly, its wings trembling as it stood tiptoe on the ice and it was so astonishing, so beautiful, so unlikely at 7,800 metres, that she had paused, just for a second. Held her hand back just for a second and in that second she had slipped.

'I'm sorry,' she tries to say to the black bird flying with her, the two of them linked by a red rope which swings between them in loops and tangles.

Like skipping, she thinks. Like skipping at school when we were little. *All in together, girls. Never mind the weather, girls.* Jump and clap, jump and clap, plaits bobbing and the rope swinging over and under.

'Sorry,' she calls to the black bird but she has fallen away and the sun catches in Margie's eyes, a brilliant dazzle as she feels herself fall and rise into that golden eye. She flies up and up through that little round hole and looks down on it all: on the frozen press of mountains, at the tiny pinpricks of scarlet and yellow which are their tents where the others lie in soft downy bags, sip their sweet milky tea, read, eat mint cake and macaroni, chat, squabble, laugh, all funny lovely little humans with their warm skin and their framework of bone and their soft hair, doing funny little human things in this fearsome place where only a scattering of holy rice holds back the avalanche.

And she calls out to them too: 'Sorry, I'm sorry.'

But maybe it's pointless to apologise. Maybe it wasn't her fault entirely. Maybe Parbat simply shrugged her cold shoulder and flicked aside the mildly irritating little insect that was Margie. *Off you go*, she had said. *That's enough*.

People had said this was how she'd end.

'Aren't you frightened?' they had asked.

'Of course,' she had said. 'You'd have to be mad not to be frightened.'

'So why do you do it?' they had asked, over coffee in some sweet café, from the sofa by some comfy fire. Is it masochism? All this boiling snow for tea, all this cowering as avalanches pass by roaring in a hurricane wind. All that toiling to carry just the scraps necessary for human survival to some barely accessible point? Is it some kind of late twentieth-century thing: girls can do anything, where the boys are – that's where I want to be, that kind of thing?

'Not really,' she has said

'So, you do it because it's there?'

'Not really.'

'Then why?'

And Margie flying and falling forever says, 'It's because once, a long time ago, I discovered that the only way through is up.

'And I think you have to face what you're frightened of, you have to leap out into the sun before you can know you're truly alive.'

And I have lived, she thinks, as Parbat offers a cupped white hand to receive her.

And at least, she thinks, I've picked a big place to die.

And she falls up and out through the hole into the sun and do you know: when you look up you really can see the stars.

You can see the whole universe stretching forever and ever.

In the middle of a single day.